Praise for Dixie Browning:

"There is no one writing romance today
who touches the heart and tickles the ribs
like Dixie Browning. The people in her books
are as warm and as real as a sunbeam
and just as lovely."
—*New York Times* bestselling author Nora Roberts

"Dixie Browning has given the romance industry
years of love and laughter
in her wonderful books."
—*New York Times* bestselling author
Linda Howard

"Each of Dixie's books is a keeper guaranteed
to warm the heart and delight the senses."
—*New York Times* bestselling author
Jayne Ann Krentz

"Dixie's books never disappoint—
they always lift your spirit!"
—*USA TODAY* bestselling author
Mary Lynn Baxter

"A true pioneer in romantic fiction,
the delightful Dixie Browning is a reader's
most precious treasure, a constant source
of outstanding entertainment."
—*Romantic Times* magazine.

DIXIE BROWNING

A self-taught writer with a background in art and interests as varied as gemology, folk music, baseball and politics, Browning cobbled together a brand-new career in 1976, starting at ground zero. Now living with her retired husband on North Carolina's Outer Banks where she grew up, Browning uses the area she knows best as background for many of her stories. For a personal reply, fans may reach her at P.O. Box 1389, Buxton, NC 27920, or e-mail her at dixiebb@mindspring.com.

DIXIE
BROWNING

Undertow

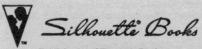

Silhouette Books

Published by Silhouette Books

America's Publisher of Contemporary Romance

SILHOUETTE BOOKS

UNDERTOW

ISBN 0-373-21831-1

Visit Silhouette at www.eHarlequin.com

Printed in U.S.A.

For Elizabeth Browning Fox,
daughter, best friend, invaluable critic. Liz,
this one has your fingerprints all over it.
Thanks for your invaluable input.

Prologue

July, 1976
Henry Island, North Carolina

"You do this one thing for me," she said, "and I'll make it right for the girls. I'll destroy George's will."

Not for the first time, he looked at the woman and wondered what it was about her that would allow him even to consider doing such dreadful a thing. "Maybe you won't," he suggested.

"I promise. You can watch me burn it." Her body slight, but arrow straight, she dared him to disbelieve her.

But he'd known her too long. He knew her promises. They eyed each other, a man and a woman, neither of them young, but neither of them old, either. Both knew that, in the end, she would have her way. She always had, ever since they'd been born three houses apart on a certain ridge in Buxton Woods, linked by a common name and by the kinship of their fathers.

Now they had a closer bond. And a darker secret.

"Burn it first," he said. "Then I'll do it."

"No, you have to do it first."

Where had trust gone? Her clear hazel eyes had always been able to see through his small failures to the great need inside him.

After a while, he nodded.

They didn't kiss to seal the bargain. Their time for kissing was long past. But each took the measure of the other, and in the end, family won out. He would do what he had to do to protect his own, just as her late husband had done.

But he couldn't escape the thought that she would have done it, anyway. The girls were hers, too, after all.

Chapter 1

May, 2003
Henry Island, North Carolina

It was stronger than Mariah had expected, whatever it was that drew her back to the island. Repelled her at the same time. Always had, ever since her comfortable childhood had been shattered in a single instant.

Sometimes she even dreamed about it. Not the nightmare—that was different—but the lazy days of pigging out on Krispy Kremes and big juicy sandwiches of homegrown tomatoes and mayo, impatiently waiting the requisite one hour before racing down to the water where her cousins were already swimming.

In her dreams the tide was always going out when she jumped off the pier. In her dreams she was always fighting a strong current that swept her relentlessly toward the inlet. She would almost rather have the nightmare. At least in the nightmare, there was nothing she could have done. What had happened, had…simply happened.

The rain started only minutes after the launch pulled away

from the dock. Her rain gear was in a trunk, left in storage to be shipped east once she decided on a location. Where had her brain been? Mariah wondered now, when she'd sorted through the remnants of the past seven years, leaving out just enough clothes for the next few weeks, packing away everything else to be sent on once she had an address.

As the kid at the helm of the stubby watercraft opened the throttle, spray from the rooster tail blew back on her, plastering her dark hair to her face, dripping down her neck. Shivering, she wondered how much trouble it was to crank up the heat pump. Her father had always been there to do that sort of thing. Throw the proper switches and all that. She seemed to remember something that had to be covered and uncovered each time, something to do with the deleterious effects of salt air.

There was salt air in San Francisco, too, but somehow, it wasn't the same. Nothing was the same. She felt as if she were suspended between two lives.

Tasting saltwater on her lips, she clutched the gunwale with one hand, her stomach with the other, and prayed not to be seasick. She'd never actually thrown up in a boat, but she could recall feeling queasy a time or two. This time, though, it wasn't being on the water that gave her this uneasy feeling, it was...

It was everything. Only everything.

"Sorry 'bout Miz Maud," the boy shouted. He'd said his name was Josh. He didn't look old enough to drive, but he handled the launch like an old hand. "She was your grammaw, weren't she?"

Swallowing her nausea, Mariah nodded.

Maud had been her grandmother, one of *the* Henrys of Henry Island, although she'd only married into the name. To hear her go on about it—one Henry had been a state congressman, another had been an ambassador to some tiny principality, two others had been wreck commissioners back in the nineteenth century—you'd think she'd carried the blood of generations of Henrys in her veins.

For that matter, she probably had. Most of the original banker families were kin, generations back. Nobody else to marry back then but each other, and whoever washed up on the beach from various shipwrecks. Maud had been hipped on genealogy, tracing back every old family on the Outer Banks to well before the days of Blackbeard and his ilk. If Blackbeard had been born a Henry instead of a Teach, she would somehow have managed to clean up his historical image, Mariah was sure.

"And now your dad, too," the boy yelled.

Mariah nodded. And now her father, too.

"Cormorant Shoal!" Josh indicated a long sandbar a few feet above the high-water mark.

Mariah knew it well, having visited the place with her mother several times to photograph the flocks of great white herons that congregated there during the day. She'd spent most of the time wading the shallows looking for clams and scallops, while her mother drank beer and laughed with the guide, only occasionally snapping a picture of a formation of birds, usually with her guide in the foreground, his white, strong teeth flashing in his dark, good-looking face.

Don't look back, Mariah warned herself sternly.

Don't look forward, either. Not yet. Not until you have some idea of what lies ahead.

The island drifted into view through a veil of rain, looking just the same as always. It had been years since she'd been here. She'd been prepared for a few changes, thinking only after she'd left Norfolk that morning that, with all the hurricanes that had swept up the coast during recent years, the cottages could all have washed out to sea. Would anyone have thought to tell her?

Oh, great. *Now* she thought of it.

Well, there was always Maud's house. With its wraparound porch and its fascinating nooks and crannies, it had been built long before the Second World War. It had stood up to Emily and whats-its-name, that other bad storm that had walloped the Banks a few years ago.

Surely her father would have told her if the cottage had been swept away. They hadn't kept in close contact these past few years—or ever, actually—but surely he would have warned her about something like that.

"Looks like your folks is visitin'," Josh informed her, throttling back to glide past two familiar boats belonging to her uncles. If she'd needed something to further depress her, that would do the trick.

On the bright side, the fact that some of her kinfolk were in residence proved that at least a few of the island's five houses were still standing. As they drew closer she could see that the old boathouse where she used to play as a child was still there.

"Want me to tote your stuff up to the house?" Josh asked. He lifted her two bags and set them on the pier. Since her last visit someone had bulkheaded the stretch of shore on both sides of the boathouse. Probably dredged the channel for back-fill. It had always had a tendency to shoal up.

"No, but thanks," Mariah said, handing over a folded twenty dollar bill. "I'll call it my weight-bearing exercise for the day."

She'd promised herself to start exercising—to run every single day. She'd been promising herself the same thing for too long, but this time she really, really meant it.

Busy taking in the changes since her last visit nearly eight years ago, Mariah scarcely heard the muffled roar of the powerful outboard as the boy reversed and eased past Uncle Nat's thirty-five foot *Island Belle*.

"Home again, home again, jiggedy-jig," she said, lifting her two bags and setting out across the sloping beach toward the path someone had dubbed Cottage Row, a narrow footpath that wound in front of the three cottages before cutting inland to Maud's house. Since last night Mariah had crossed three time zones, stopping off briefly to collect her father's ashes from the crematorium in Durham before catching another flight to Norfolk, and from there, an air-taxi to Frisco Airport.

She'd then hitched a ride to the marina and arranged to be ferried across the inlet.

Shifting her heavier suitcase to the other hand, she trudged on through the soft sand. The rain had wet only the surface. With each step, her heel broke through first, the rest of her foot following. If there was an art to walking in soft sand, she'd long since forgotten it.

She caught a glimpse of the roof, so at least the cottage was still here. It belonged to her now. She wished it didn't. Wished she could walk up onto the front deck and be greeted by one of her father's rare, awkward hugs.

And as long as she was wasting wishes, she might as well wish for one from her mother. Her mother's hugs had always been enthusiastic, usually accompanied by laughter and noisy air kisses. That was Roxie. As loud and spontaneous as Edgar Henry had been quiet and reserved. If nothing else, Mariah thought, her parents had proved the old adage about opposites attracting.

"C'mon, honey, dance with me! Liven up, you old stump—shake your tush for me!"

"I've got to finish these reports, Rox. Why not go take some more pictures? Take Mariah with you."

They were both gone now. And like it or not, there were more memories here on the island than anywhere else, which was one of the reasons she was here. To bring her father home again.

Aside from that, she was legally a Henry again, having gone back to her maiden name the minute the divorce was final. What was that old smiley-face slogan? Today is the first day of the rest of your life?

Darn right it was. Like her father, she had good Henry blood in her veins. And like Maud, she didn't need anyone else. Widowed and left with three children, a big, leaky old house, a skiff, a set of nets and a garden, her grandmother claimed to have spit in the eye of more than a few representatives of one government agency or another. Not to mention land developers, a breed she had heartily despised as she'd watched the rest of the Banks—at least the parts not taken over by the Park Service—being developed until they were scarcely recognizable. The year Hatteras had gotten its first set of stoplights by the ferry docks, she'd vowed never to cross the inlet again. So far as anyone knew, she hadn't.

Maud Henry, Mariah told herself as she headed up the conch-lined walk, was as good a role model as any battered, impoverished, unemployed and newly divorced woman could wish for. Maud had lived life on her own terms right up until the day a year and a half ago when, well into her eighties, she had dropped dead, reportedly while shucking oysters. The last time Mariah had seen her grandmother her long gray hair had hung down her back in a single braid, the bone structure underlying her lined and weathered face still flawless, her hazel eyes still so clear that it was impossible to think of her as an old woman. Rather, she'd been ageless. An icon. Someone to live up to, Mariah thought now, gazing toward the dense grove of live oaks and cedars, bay trees and yaupon, to the house where Maud had gone as a bride, lived out her life and died.

The three cottages—beach boxes, really; far too small by today's standards—had been built by each of the Henry offspring as they married and started their own families. Built facing Hatteras Inlet, they were perhaps a hundred feet from the new breakwater. Maud's house was located well back from the water's edge, built on the highest ridge of the island and sheltered by dense maritime forest.

"Indians knew where to build. Always set up their villages on the shore side," she used to claim, the shore side being the back of the island, facing Pamlico Sound, rather than the more exposed eastern side.

Thinking of her grandmother now as the light rain plastered her shirt to her body, Mariah wished she had seen her one last time before she died. Not that they'd ever been close. The painful truth was, Mariah had never particularly liked her grandmother. But as an adult she had come to admire those qualities that had defined her as a woman, strength and the courage of her convictions being foremost.

Maybe she should have come home more often, but she hadn't, and now it was too late. And if there was one thing she didn't need at this point, it was guilt. Her immediate family was gone; no amount of wishing would change that. Her marriage was over—there was nothing she even wanted to do about that. Acknowledging a gross lack of judgment was punishment enough without piling on guilt.

Behind a shaggy hedge that had more than doubled in size since the last time she'd been here, the familiar cedar-shingled cottage with the hot-pink shutters Roxie had insisted on, which no one had ever got around to repainting after she died, looked much the same…maybe smaller. The sign on the deck rail, faded now, said Layzy Dayz, the name Roxie had given the cottage before Mariah had even been born.

Lowering the suitcases to the bottom step, she frowned at the lighted window. Had anyone known she was coming? She'd tried to call when she'd stopped off in Durham, but there'd been no answer at either house. The last time she'd been in contact with any of her relatives was three weeks ago, when her father had died. Stunned at the news, she'd explained over the phone that she'd just been released from the hospital—nothing serious, she'd assured them, not that they'd asked—but she wouldn't be able to travel for at least a week.

She wasn't about to tell them she'd been hospitalized because of her ex-husband's post-divorce visit. "We all know what Daddy wanted, so I guess there's no time limit."

They'd argued, quite naturally, but Mariah had stood firm.

Edgar Henry, a methodical man who left little to chance, had left a living will and explicit instructions. When his time came, he preferred cremation and wanted his ashes taken back to Henry Island. As Mariah had told her aunt Tracy, spokeswoman for the family now that Maud was gone, there was no hurry. "I'll collect Daddy's ashes just as soon as I can get away, and take them out to the island. We can wait until later when you're all down there to decide what to do next."

And bless their hearts, they had come ahead to open up her

cottage and air it out. Good thinking, because she doubted if she could have found the strength to open a single window.

Even the steps were just the same. The third one still sagged in the middle, and there was an array of shells along the edges, mostly broken conchs, possibly leftover from her last visit.

Suddenly, she felt like weeping, which wasn't like her at all.

The feeling passed the moment she saw the pair of wet sneakers on the porch. Large ones. Setting the two suitcases down beside the door, she called through the screen door, which was hooked on the inside. "Hello? Anyone here? Uncle Linwood?"

Uh-uh. Wrong size. Both her uncles were small men.

"Aunt Tracy?" Her aunt Tracy was a Virgo. Cleaning was her thing—that and bossing the rest of the family, especially her husband, poor, sweet Uncle Linwood.

The silhouette that appeared in the doorway was far too tall to be either of her uncles. Peering uncertainly through the screen, Mariah stepped back. "Erik?" It had been years since she'd seen her cousin, Aunt Belle and Uncle Nat's son. Last she'd heard he was working in summer theater at Myrtle Beach. Hadn't he got into trouble over something or other? Was that Erik, or was it Tracy Anne, called TA by her friends?

No, it was Erik. Mariah had a lot of catching up to do once she'd caught up on her sleep.

"Hollowell," the man said.

The quiet voice should have been reassuring. It wasn't. And it certainly wasn't Erik.

"Can I help you?" he asked.

"You can tell me what you're doing here, for starters. No, don't bother. Just leave. Please," she added grudgingly. "Whatever you're doing, it can wait until tomorrow. Or next week."

He was probably a workman one of her uncles had hired to do repairs. Neither of them was handy with tools in spite of the fact that her uncle Linwood owned a small independent hardware and farm equipment store. Her father had been even more helpless. Besides, he'd rarely spent much time here, even before—

Even before.

"Sorry to disoblige you, but I've leased the cottage for the next six weeks. Maybe you were looking for one of the other places? This one's called Layzy Dayz, spelled cute and illiterate."

Deep breath. Hang on to your center, it's around here somewhere. "This is my fa—this is *my* house. I don't know who gave you the idea you could stay here, but you can't. You'll have to move. Maybe you can get one of my uncles to run you back across the inlet, or call for someone to come pick you up."

His hand moved to the light switch beside the door. It was a big hand, square palmed, long fingered—well-kept without being overly so. Mariah had good reason to notice a man's hands.

The sudden glare illuminated more than the stranger filling the doorway. Behind him she could see a whole new interior. New scatter rugs on the floor and even a few new pictures on the walls—beachy prints in cheap frames. Her mother would never have chosen those, and her father hadn't cared enough after she'd died to change anything.

"And you are…?" the man inquired.

"One of the Henrys," she snapped. Oh, God, now she sounded like her own grandmother. "The one who happens to own this cottage, so if you don't mind?" She pushed past him and stopped just inside the hall, wondering if this could be the start of yet another nightmare.

Yellow? Someone had painted the old cypress paneling *yellow?* That alone was a desecration. Roxie had wanted to paint the walls, but her husband had flatly refused. One of the few times he had refused her anything, so far as Mariah could recall.

She drew in a deep, steadying breath and said evenly, "How long will it take you to get your things together? One of my uncles will have a cell phone if you don't."

Without saying a word, he continued to stand there blocking the entrance. Her hands were trembling, her knees suddenly weak as water. *Move, you big jackass! If you don't get out of my way, I'm going to collapse on one of those tacky little carpet-sample rugs and sleep for the next three days!*

"If you'll wait a minute, I'll show you my lease."

"I don't care about your so-called lease, it's invalid. I told you, this is my house, and I did not rent it out. If someone else did, then you can take it up with them."

Quietly, in direct contrast to her own voice, which had grown increasingly strident, he said, "That won't be possible. Edgar Henry died three weeks ago."

Caught off guard, Mariah reached for support and her hand connected with one of the framed prints, causing it to swing wildly. She opened her mouth to argue, then shut it again, aware that the stranger was watching her as if she were some alien species.

Calm, she cautioned herself silently. *Hang on to that old center. You're in no condition to tackle an intruder, not without reinforcements.* "In that case, you can stay here tonight and we'll take it up tomorrow." Trying for dignity, missing it by a mile, she shoved past him, collected her luggage and left.

Maud would have been proud of her, though, she thought as she turned onto Cottage Row. She hadn't really lost the battle, she'd merely made a strategic and purely temporary retreat.

It wasn't really all that late, but with the overcast sky and the way things had grown up, nothing looked familiar. Through the blowing branches she caught a glimpse of light from Aunt Tracy and Uncle Linwood's cottage, called Boxer's Dream.

She passed by without stopping. She couldn't take Aunt Tracy, not tonight. Some four hundred feet farther on, lights shone from the windows of Belle's Acre, Aunt Belle and Uncle Nat's place. As children, they'd called it Belly Acre, thinking they were being so clever.

It would have to be Maud's house, then. Providing Mariah could make it another few hundred feet. Lord, she was tired! If the key wasn't in its old hiding place on the ledge over the third front window, she might just sleep on the porch, on the side away from the rain. There used to be an old wooden bench there, where Maud sat to shell beans from her garden.

So that was the daughter, Gray Hollowell mused, staring after the retreating figure. Not what he'd expected—especially not with those wet clothes plastered revealingly to her body. But then, he'd deliberately left his mind open. It was the only way he could work at this stage of any case, old or new.

"This is my daughter," Edgar Henry had said that day more than a month ago. "It was taken a few years after my wife died." There'd been an odd note in his voice as he'd handed over the photograph. Pride, Gray had first thought, but mixed with something more. Guilt?

No, something milder than that. Regret, perhaps.

He had studied the picture of a much younger Mariah standing slightly apart from a group of laughing teenagers. They were on a pier, with half a dozen king mackerel laid out before them. The skinny dark-haired girl was the only one not laughing. She was staring straight at the camera, scowling.

"I've got a more recent picture—her wedding picture—but she's turned away so that her face doesn't show. She hasn't changed all that much, though. About five-nine, too thin—always been thin. Same dark hair and dark eyes, sort of quiet. She's an artist. Got a diploma that says so, anyway. Painted me a picture once, but I never could figure it out. Abstract, I guess you'd call it."

A compact man in his mid-sixties, Edgar Henry had seemed oddly uncomfortable talking about his daughter, as though he found personal relationships somehow embarrassing. Hardly a demonstrative man, nor one to let his emotions off the leash, Gray had summed up at the time.

He'd asked about the daughter's husband, more from habit

than any real interest. The husband couldn't have been a factor in the case Gray had been asked to look into.

"They're getting divorced. Might've already gone through by now. About time, too, I gather."

He *gathered?* She was his daughter, his only child. Shouldn't he know if there was a problem with her marriage?

"I tried to call her a couple of times last week," Edgar Henry continued. "Kept getting her answering machine."

Gray had continued to leaf through the slim file. At that point he'd agreed to nothing. Still, this was the kind of case that not only paid the rent, it lit his fuse. He'd always been intrigued by cold cases. Cases that had gone unsolved for years, even generations. Cases everyone had given up on. A few, like this, that hadn't even been considered crimes at the time—rightly so, in all probability. But occasionally new evidence turned up that triggered a fresh investigation. A striking number of cold cases had been solved by simple word of mouth. These days, technology offered new approaches if anyone bothered to reopen a case. Sometimes—such as now—all it took was one single inquiry.

"It just never felt right, you know?" his client had said. "I mean I know it was an accident—at least, that's what everyone says—but lately, it's been on my mind a lot. It wasn't like the fellow she'd hired to take her out in his boat was an amateur. Jack was an experienced guide. He'd grown up around the water. I know accidents happen, but it was a new boat and a new outboard. It just doesn't make sense."

"No one questioned it at the time?" Gray was intrigued. A few weeks on a private island seemed tailor-made after what he'd been through, but even so, his conscience wouldn't let him accept the case if there was no case there.

"I was in Belgium when it happened. Mariah and Roxie— my daughter and my wife, that is—they were staying there together. My mother was there, of course, and one of my sisters and her family, but there weren't any strangers around, else they'd have been seen. It happened in broad daylight, middle of the morning."

Edgar Henry had been clearly uncomfortable talking about
the death of his wife and her guide in a refueling accident
nearly three decades ago. Odds were, that's all it had been—
an accident. Yet the man had been so determined, almost as
if he'd sensed that time was running out.

"Lately—I don't know," he'd said, looking uncomfortable,
"I've been feeling this…tension, I guess you'd call it."

In the end, Gray had agreed to take the case, but he'd refused to accept a retainer. "A few weeks free rental is more
than enough compensation, believe me. Any additional expenses I can bill you for. If there's something to learn, I'll dig
it out, and if not—well, I'll try not to ruffle any feathers."

Edgar Henry had insisted on an official lease. They'd both
signed. "I'd do it myself, but I'm in and out of the country—
you know how it is."

Gray didn't know. He'd been to England once, to Canada
once and to Mexico three times, each time following up leads.
But he'd nodded and promised to get on it as soon as he
wound up a course of physical therapy. He'd suffered some
damage a couple of months earlier when his shoulder had connected with a crowbar. Better his shoulder than his neck,
though, which was what the jerk had been aiming for when
Gray had caught him prying open the back door of a phar-
maceutical warehouse. A few inches higher and he might've
been paralyzed for life.

So that, he thought now, closing the door as the rain began
to blow in, was Mariah—Edgar and Roxie Henry's daughter
who, at age seven-going-on-eight, had witnessed the incident
that had taken her mother's life.

And now her father was dead, as well. Shortly before he'd
been scheduled to wind up his therapy sessions, Gray had read
an obituary in the *Raleigh News and Observer* for Edgar Wallis Henry, of Durham and Henry Island, North Carolina, son
of the late George Edgar and Maud Wallis Henry, predeceased
by a wife, the late Roxanne O'Brien Henry, survived by a
daughter, Mariah Carwile of San Francisco, and two sisters,
Tracy Boxer and Belle Detloff, of Durham, plus a laundry list

of nieces, nephews and in-laws. Gray had dismissed the extended family as irrelevant.

He'd been torn between following through on his promise and getting in touch with the family and returning the lease. Although in spite of—or perhaps because of—the lack of clues, he found the case particularly intriguing. If there'd been any question at all as to the cause of Edgar Henry's death, he'd have been on it like rain on a picnic, but the poor guy had died of a massive coronary. According to his family, he had no history of heart disease, but for a low-key fellow, he'd been in a high stress business. Maybe that explained the tension he claimed to have been feeling.

In the end, Gray had compromised. He'd called one of the sisters, Tracy Boxer, and explained that shortly before he'd died, Edgar Henry had leased a cottage on Henry Island to him for six weeks. He'd asked permission to stop by for a few minutes.

By the time he got there, Ms. Boxer had called in reinforcements. They hadn't liked it. Everyone had started talking even before the introductions were made. Detloff, husband of the younger sister, Belle, had taken charge. He'd flatly declared the lease invalid and offered to refund whatever Gray had paid.

It was because of their obvious hostility that he had dug in his heels. Stubbornness was one of his failings—had been ever since he'd taken on the class bully in second grade. Gray never pushed first, but when he was pushed, he sure as hell pushed back. He'd quickly developed a talent for it, but in later years he'd cultivated more subtle methods of accomplishing his ends.

The clincher had come when he'd reminded himself that Edgar Henry could have asked any member of his own family to look into the matter. He hadn't. Instead, he'd gone to one of the few private cold case specialists in the area.

About halfway through the conference—confrontation was more like it—a bleached-blond hottie with three rings in her navel, two ankle bracelets and a toe ring had wandered into the room, visually peeled him down to the buff, telegraphed her lack of interest with a shrug and walked away.

The whole thing had lasted less than twenty minutes. Through it all, Gray had never mentioned his real reason for leasing the cottage. Years of experience with such cases had taught him that more often than not, the family was involved. The fewer people who knew Edgar Henry had been about to open up an old can of worms, the better.

So he'd told them that he was recovering from shoulder surgery, and that Henry Island seemed the perfect place to do it. Small island, few residents, still fewer temptations. It was no less than the truth.

Then he'd gone back home, packed a selection of resort wear consisting of faded sweats and equally faded jeans, several T-shirts, his one pair of swim trunks—boxers, not briefs—his computer, his old freshwater spinning rod and a few books, and headed east, stopping on the way to buy supplies, as the closest grocery store was over on Hatteras Island.

Two days ago he had settled in. Both the Boxers and the Detloffs had been there to welcome him. The men had met him at the dock, telling him they had scheduled some repairs to be done on Henry's cottage, and offering to pay him a bonus if he'd change his mind.

He hadn't. He wouldn't. The repairs, he'd told them, would just have to wait, or if they'd rather, they could discuss it with his lawyer. Sheer bluff.

He'd located the cottage from Henry's description and settled in. The place suited him just fine. No fancy amenities—no hot tub, no swimming pool, plenty of cross ventilation and a view of the ocean out through the inlet, with Hatteras Island on one side, Ocracoke Island on the other and Portsmouth Island a hazy speck on the horizon.

For all its lack of frills, the cottage was a damned sight less depressing than the house on the Durham side of Raleigh where he'd lived with his wife, who had died three years ago of ovarian cancer.

Chapter 2

Even before she passed the dead live oak, Mariah could see the lights. Evidently her relatives had come en masse, over-flowing their two cottages and spilling over into Maud's house. How many cousins were there now? It was easy to lose track. Both Aunt Tracy's daughters, Lynette and TA, were married. Lynn had at least one child. Neither of Aunt Belle's two offspring was married, so far as Mariah knew.

They'd probably turned Maud's house over to the younger generation, and why not? There was plenty of room to spread out—only she did wish they hadn't spread quite so far. If there was a single unlit room in the old house, Mariah couldn't see it from the path. Maybe the upstairs bathroom, added only ten years or so earlier, along with the outdoor shower.

Spring cleaning. That had to be it, she thought, relieved to have found a logical reason for every house on the island to be lit up. Memorial Day was coming up shortly, and they were getting ready for the annual pilgrimage. Spring cleaning had been a ritual in Maud's day. They'd all been expected to par-ticipate in the grand turnout. All except Roxie. Either Maud had never asked, or Roxie had declined, but year after year, while the rest of them labored away at General Maud's command, Mariah's mother had either worked on her suntan—she'd had a fabulous tan for a redhead—or gone out on the boat with Jack, her favorite guide, to photograph whatever caught her fancy. As often as not, it was Jack himself, bare-chested, his khakis rolled up over dark, muscular calves, laughing for the camera.

Mariah set her suitcases down on the edge of the porch and flexed her hands. Darned if she was going to do any spring cleaning, not tonight. If she did any cleaning at all it would be at her father's cottage.

Even now, she couldn't think of him as dead. In her tapestry carry-on she had a plain, blue-glazed urn that contained the mortal remains of Edgar Wallis Henry, yet she still halfway expected to see him open the door of Maud's old house.

Instead, it was her uncle Nat. "Mariah? When did you get in? We weren't expecting you." His sickly smile said something else—she wasn't sure what.

"Hello, Uncle Nat. I don't know why not. I told Aunt Belle when she called about Daddy that I'd be here as soon as I could. I tried to call you all when I stopped off in Durham, but there was no answer at either house. I left a message."

"I'm sorry about your father."

Her gaze fell to the carry-on. Nat Detloff's worried look followed. "Is he...? Did you...?"

"I did and he is. Now, if you don't mind, I'm truly bushed. If there's a bed made up, I want it. If not, I'll bunk anywhere you point me. Evidently before he died, Daddy rented our place to some man named Hollowell. He refuses to leave and I'm too tired to throw him out tonight, but I'll do it tomorrow if I have to pry him out with a crowbar. What with missed connections, airport delays and stopovers, I feel like I've been traveling a solid week."

"Na-at? Who is it?" Her aunt Belle's shrill voice came from somewhere inside the house.

"It's Mariah," the slight, balding Nathaniel Detloff called over his shoulder. "She wants to know if she can stay here."

Belle Detloff came bustling down the front hall then, poking at her hair with one hand, tugging at the waistband of her flowered slacks with the other. Belle was a bustler by nature. Always busy, always slightly flustered, invariably kind. Of all Mariah's relatives, she was her favorite.

"Hi, Aunt Belle. Surprise?" She offered a tired smile, but it wasn't returned. No one offered her a hug. "I was just telling Uncle Nat that Daddy rented our place to some man, and—"

"Who is it, Belle? Don't leave the door open, the furnace will be running all night." That was Aunt Tracy. Her beloved family, thought Mariah, as a feeling of utter desolation swept over her. Whoever had said "You can't go home again," she was beginning to believe it. If home meant family—a sense of belonging, of uncritical acceptance—then she'd never had a home.

"Aunt Tracy, it's me, Mariah. Is there room at the inn for one more?"

Tracy Boxer, somewhere in her early sixties—short, blond and compact like her younger sister, but without Belle's ballooning bottom—appeared in the doorway. "Good lord, girl, shut the door! It costs money to heat this old place. Heat, in May—the weather's just crazy. I told Mama she needed to put in insulation, but you know her—if it was good enough for Daddy's folks, it was good enough for us."

"Sorry." Mariah heard herself apologizing and cursed silently. Unless she'd been misinformed, Maud's house, cranky furnace and all, belonged as much to her as it did to her two aunts. Except for the three cottages, which were individually owned, Maud had left the entire island and everything on it to her three children. Mariah had inherited her father's share.

"How'd you come out?" her uncle asked.

"Josh, from the marina. I paid him twenty dollars—is that enough?" Pay scales were wildly different in different parts of the country. She didn't want to have underpaid the boy, even though in his rush to get her here he'd managed to drench what little of her the rain hadn't already soaked.

"Is he still here? There's lots of places over on Hatteras. The season's barely got underway."

Mariah looked at first one, then another of her three relatives—one of them an in-law. "He's halfway back to the marina by now. Are you saying I can't stay here? I don't believe this."

"Mama, where's my shampoo?"

Mariah glanced at the staircase in time to see a pair of short, bright pink legs descend halfway. Two toe rings, a tattoo and an ankle bracelet. It had to be her cousin Victoria. "Vicki, is that you?" Her cousin was more than ten years her junior. Mariah barely knew the girl, but she remembered her love of bodily adornment, even as a child.

"Mariah?" Vicki, Belle's daughter, came on down the stairs, revealing what had to be a painful sunburn. Her hair, a flat shade of blond, was badly in need of conditioning. Her eyes were that distinctive shade of blue that nearly all her cousins had and Mariah had always envied.

"What are you doing here?" the younger woman asked. More like demanded.

"I—well, for one thing, I brought Daddy's ashes."

"Oh, gross!"

"Victoria!"

"Well, Mama, it is. I mean, Uncle Edgar's dead, for God's sake. Why couldn't we have just buried him in Durham in a regular cemetery like everybody else? Now we're going to have to be all gloomy and miserable during the holiday, and that's not fair."

Mariah edged past them and sank down onto the golden-oak bench seat where coats and hats had always been piled. Fortunately, it was empty. "Do you mind if we have this conversation later? I'm so tired I can't hold my eyes open." Not to mention hungry, her growling stomach reminded her. "There's a strange man in my house, and unless someone's over there cleaning, it looks like both your cottages are taken, too. May I please, please just go to bed?''

Another cousin appeared from the direction of the kitchen, a handsome young male this time. ''Who is it, Mama? Mariah? Where on earth did you come from? I thought you were out in California. I was fixing to join you out there in a week or so.''

''Hush up, Erik. Go let the cat in before he scratches a hole in the back door.''

The cat? Evidently the entire clan, pets and all, had taken over the island. ''Aren't you in school, Vicki?'' Mariah asked.

''I dropped out. I don't need any old degree to make money.''

''Oh.'' She waited for someone to point her to a bedroom. They didn't have to want her here, but they darned well had to let her stay. She had as much right as any of them.

No one spoke. Finally, she stood and looked at the stairs. If she remembered correctly, there were four bedrooms up there, although one of them was little more than a large closet. Maud had called it her box room. ''You're not all staying here, are you?'' Again no one spoke. ''Look, I don't care if I have to double up. Vicki? I don't snore—I probably won't even roll over for the next twenty-four hours. I just need a place to sleep.'' She was practically shouting. It was either that or burst into tears, and darned if she would cry. Never show weakness before an enemy.

Or was it never look a strange dog in the eye?

Oh, Lord, her mind was going. Going, going, gone.

''Don't look at me, I'm bunking with Lynette,'' said Vicki.

''Me, I got stuck with Mason,'' offered Erik. He sniffed as if he might be coming down with a cold.

Great. Just what she needed. ''Mason?''

''Lynn's kid, remember? A real pain in the ass—in the butt. Sorry, Aunt Trace, but he is.''

''Great. Do you mind telling me one thing?'' Mariah was shivering so hard, partly from being soaked to the skin, partly from anger, that she had trouble controlling her voice. ''Why can't you all stay in your own cottages? Don't tell me—you've invited a bunch of friends down for a two-week Memorial Day holiday, right? You knew I was coming to commit Daddy's ashes and you—you turned it into a damned circus!'' Her voice rose to a squeak she didn't even recognize as her own. She *never* cursed.

Aunt Belle gasped. "Mariah, hush up, honey. You're just tired, is all."

"No. Really?" Sarcasm dripped from the words. She was surrounded by relatives who were staring at her as if she were a two-headed Martian. "Darned right I'm tired," she snapped. And if she had to shoot her way to a bed, she would do it— that is, she would if she had a gun. Pointed fingers hadn't worked since she a child and had tried to force her older cousins, Lynette and TA, to take her over to Hatteras Island with them to see a Disney movie. TA had bent Mariah's finger backward until she'd screamed.

Belle turned to her older sister. "She can have the cook's bed, I guess. Faye's not due for another week."

"I'll take it," Mariah said before anyone could object. Grabbing her luggage, she was halfway down the hall to the kitchen when she thought to ask a question. "Who's staying in your cottages? Don't tell me TA's here with husband number—what is it now, number three?"

She left before anyone could answer. Right now, she didn't care if it was George and Martha Washington. She just wanted to lie down and forget this endless, miserable day.

So much for family. So much for returning to your roots.

Gray Hollowell ran, allowing his mind to range free as he jogged around the perimeter of the island. Catching sight of an old man struggling to lift a bundle of shingles, he slowed down. "Give you a hand with that?" he offered, not as winded as he'd expected to be.

"Much obliged if you can spare it." The old man looked him over, missing little, Gray suspected, despite his age. He had the leathery skin of someone who'd spent a lifetime on the water, but his eyes were clear and his smile, although somewhat guarded, seemed friendly enough.

Veering over to where he was standing, Gray hooked the heavy bundle with one hand. "You take the other side and we heave on my count. One—two—three!" Together they swung the bundle up onto a scaffold that ran along one side of a shack that looked at least as old as the man. Gray could have handled the thing easier alone, but he respected pride. Evidently the old guy was getting ready to make some repairs. You had to admire independence at any age, Gray thought. It was a rapidly disappearing quality.

Dusting off trembling hands, the old gentleman said, "Been rainin' in on me all winter. Thought I'd better see to fixin' 'er up 'fore another storm season."

They discussed the weather briefly, and the old man said his name was Orestes Wallis.

"Gray Hollowell." They shook hands. Orestes Wallis's grip was surprisingly strong for a man who couldn't weigh much more than a hundred ten or fifteen pounds.

"You renting one o' them cottages?"

"Layzy Dayz," Gray told him, ready to resume his run before he lost his momentum.

"Named 'em all." Orestes shook his head. "Never could see the sense in namin' houses. Boats, now, that's different." He glanced over his shoulder to where one of the old wooden, round-stern fishing boats was secured to a narrow plank wharf with a shed at one end.

"Nice looking boat. Anything else I can do?" Gray felt obliged to ask.

"You go 'long, son. I can get 'em up onto the roof a handful at a time now that I've got 'em that far."

By the time he'd circled the island, Gray had his breathing worked out so that he was barely winded. The dull ache in his shoulder could be accounted for by being on the water. Maybe he should have asked Orestes Wallis if living on the water aggravated aging joints. But then, how would he know the difference if, as Gray suspected, he'd spent his entire life here on Henry Island?

Gray was thirty-eight years old, no longer the ambitious State Bureau of Investigation rookie he'd been back when he'd considered thirty-eight to be middle-aged. Technically, it probably was, but he didn't feel old. At least nowhere near ready to hang up his gun and license.

"Hey, mister."

He turned toward the breakwater where a towheaded kid was dangling a line in the water. "Hey, yourself. Caught anything yet?"

"Naw, they're not biting. You the one staying in our cottage?"

"I don't know. Which one's yours?"

The boy pulled in his line. No rod, no cork, just a length of monofilament wrapped around a stick on one end with a hook and a nail for weight on the other end. "Boxer's Dream."

That would make him one of the older sister's grandkids, Gray thought, if he remembered the cast of characters from the file he'd been given. "I'm staying in Layzy Dayz."

"That's my uncle Edgar's cottage. He's dead now. I think my cousin's going to bring his ashes here and do something with them. How many ashes do you think he'll be? I mean, is it a big bunch, big as a man? I don't want to step in any people ashes. Yuck!"

Squatting beside him, Gray thought this was something the parents should have discussed with the boy. "It won't be much. Maybe about a pint. I think your cousin will either scatter them on the water or bury them somewhere on the island."

"Snails crawl on tombstones, did you know that?"

"Uh—no, I don't believe I did."

"Yep. They eat up moss or something and that's why you can't read the names on the old stones. My great-grandmamma told me that before she died. She was real old, maybe a hun'ert."

That would be Maud Henry. According to the file, she'd died fairly recently, more than a decade shy of the century mark. "How old are you?"

"Ten," the boy said proudly.

"No kidding? I was thinking you were at least twelve."

It brought the response Gray had hoped for, and he left the beaming kid securing a scrap of pork rind onto his hook. That would be Mason, son of Lynette, grandson of Tracy, great-grandson of Maud, according to the chart in his file. Gray always took his time getting a feel for the place and the people involved in a cold case before he started any real investigating. He wasn't into this spooky séance stuff. However, he did believe in going in with a completely open mind and all senses set on receive.

Mariah was waiting for him when he pounded up the path to the cottage. He was a little more winded than he'd expected, but then this was the longest run he'd done over rough terrain since his shoulder had been more or less reconstructed. He might've taken a few shortcuts today, but he didn't consider it cheating.

"Have you packed up everything?"

Full battle stations, he noted, amused. Arms crossed, dark eyes shooting sparks. Propping one foot on the third step, he leaned forward and bought time by pretending to tie his shoe-lace. She was wearing khaki shorts, midthigh length, with a yellow pullover sweater. His face was on a level with a pair of legs that could easily have graced a runway in one of those high-fashion shows he'd seen on TV, where the models walked like horses that had just been shod for the first time.

The rest of her, too, for that matter. Quality stuff. He'd noticed last night that her face hadn't changed all that much from the photo Henry had given him. Good bone structure. High forehead, high cheekbones, nose a tad too long, chin on the stubborn side. A pair of dark eyes that asked no quarter and offered none.

"No, I haven't," he said, straightening up again.

"Well…well, do it then, and hurry. I need to move in as soon as possible this morning."

Hands on his hips, he flexed his back, already anticipating a few stiff muscles. "Ma'am—Ms. Carwile—"

"That's Henry. Mariah Henry. My father—that is, when he leased this place to you, he had no idea—I mean, of course he couldn't know…"

Damn. Gray almost felt sorry for her. "Look, I need to explain something before this goes any further. You want to come inside, or do we have this conversation out here?"

He could see her wavering. Finally she said, "I don't see that any conversation is necessary. I'll refund your money, of course. And I can call a boy from over on Hatteras to come pick you up. I understand there are still vacancies over there, if you'd like to stay in the area."

Nicely done. He gave her credit for that. No yelling, no ranting, no threatening. According to her father, Mariah Henry Carwile, or whatever she was calling herself these days, was artistic and intelligent. She had at least one college degree and a résumé that included several years working with a well-known charitable foundation. What her father hadn't included, but Gray had already picked up on, was that underneath the polished veneer was a deep well of insecurity mixed with a healthy dose of belligerence. Surprising how often the two things went together. She stood there, all five foot nine elegant inches of her, seemingly relaxed except for the hands that were fisted at her sides.

No more sparks. There was a total lack of expression in those coffee-colored eyes now that told him something about her defenses. The fact that she even needed defenses, for one thing.

Gray had a knack for reading people. Sometimes what they didn't say was more important than what they did say.

"Yeah, well, I had this deal with your father, see?" You want to know what it is? Ask me. Go ahead—ask me, he goaded silently. "I'm working on a particular project, and this happens to be a great place to work from. So if you don't mind—and even if you do—I'll stay. You're welcome to join me, though. There's an extra room I'm not using.''

No response. He hadn't exactly expected her to take him up on the offer...although it might have been interesting.

Her jaw tightened. Barely unclenching her teeth, she said, ''If you change your mind, I'll be at the big house. I assume you know where that is.''

''Yes, ma'am, I'll just follow the yellow brick road.''

She lifted one eyebrow, reminding him of his high school days when he'd practiced the art of sneering and brow-lifting before a mirror, fancying himself another 007.

Oh, yeah—he'd been cool back before cool was really cool. Now he was middle-aged and lukewarm, at best.

''Well—thank you,'' she said grudgingly.

Gracious to the bitter end, he thought, watching her stalk off down the path. Vulnerable she might be—at least her father had seemed to think so, not that he'd put it in so many words. If Gray had to hazard a guess on no more evidence than he had now, he'd say she was the type to break before she bent.

Just before she was out of sight she waved to someone down near the breakwater. The kid, probably. Mason.

I might have had a son, Gray thought with a deep, dull ache that had dimmed over the past three years, but would never entirely leave.

Nor would he want it to. Sharon had been newly pregnant when she'd been diagnosed. Before they could decide whether to terminate the pregnancy before starting a course of treatment, she'd suffered a miscarriage. Things had gone rapidly downhill from there.

Over the years the anger, the bitterness—the need to strike out at fate—had faded. But not the emptiness. Not the loneliness. That would always be a part of him. A man needed something to focus his life around. Sharon's memory was his North Star.

Chapter 3

Three days later Mariah was still sleeping in the cook's room off the kitchen that had once been separated from the house by a raised wooden walkway. The walkway had been closed in after the wood-burning range had been replaced by a more modern propane model, the additional space turned into a pantry and laundry. Later, a small bedroom and bath had been added on.

She had seen Gray Hollowell only from a distance. He was still ensconced in her cottage, darn his stubborn hide. Short of hiring another lawyer, which she couldn't afford, there was no way to pry him out. With any luck he'd finish his project, whatever it was, and leave within a week or so. If he had a grant to study pelicans or hermit crabs or the sex life of the oyster toad, he could easily outlast her.

On the other hand, he was evidently paying rent, and she could definitely use the income. Unless he'd paid her father in advance, in which case she might get it eventually, once the will was probated—what taxes didn't confiscate and executor's fees didn't consume.

By that time she'd have either starved or found herself a job. Gone were the days when a woman could live off the land the way Maud had done. Or in this case, the sea.

As her father's sole heir, Mariah had received a copy of his will along with a summary of his estate. At the time, she'd still been stunned by his unexpected death, not to mention the effects of her ex-husband's last visit. She had simply scanned the documents and left everything in the hands of the bank officer her father had named as his executor.

Either of her uncles could have served in that capacity. Well, maybe not Uncle Linwood, but Aunt Tracy was the anal type—she'd have been a whiz. Mariah was glad her dad had named a stranger, though. It wasn't that she didn't trust her relatives, because she did. Of course she did. Still, this way just seemed more—well, more efficient.

"Mariah, you're not doing anything, are you? Could you hang these things out on the line for me? I've got to rinse this stuff out of my hair." Her cousin Lynette, who had once helped make her childhood miserable, stood in the doorway, a plastic bag over her hair and a bundle of dripping clothes in her hand. She'd always been pretty, even carrying a few extra pounds. But new lines of discontent were beginning to age her face. "You wouldn't believe all the goop it takes to look beachy. I got my hair streaked before I came down, but I still have to braid it while it's wet and then spray it with saltwater to make the strands stick together. Once it's dry, I've got this gunky stuff made with coconut oil and crushed bamboo I put on it, and then I twist it from the roots out, and then there's this oil—honest to God, if it didn't look so great I wouldn't bother, but I just love looking beachy in the summer, don't you?"

Mariah could only stare at her. "Couldn't you just, ah, go swimming and dry your hair outdoors in the sun?"

"Well, sure...I guess. But the water's too cold, and this other stuff smells better. Besides, sun and saltwater dries your hair out even worse than chlorine. Don't you—?" The older woman looked her over, from her unpolished toenails to her un-beachy hair. "I guess not," she said, and shrugged.

From upstairs came a loud protest. "*Ma*ma! Make Erik get out of my room! He's used up all my bronzer!"

"Jesus." Lynette rolled her eyes. "Aunt Belle! Your children are squabbling!" And to Mariah, she said, "Here, take this stuff before it drips all over the floor. Mama'll pitch a fit if you get one of her precious rugs wet."

The "precious rugs" were everywhere. Sand-catchers. Small enough to be taken outside and shaken, they were little more than colorful indoor doormats. Mariah missed Maud's lumpy old rag rugs, made from strips cut from cast-off clothing, faded slipcovers and old bedspreads. According to Aunt Tracy, they trapped sand and wore the varnish off the floor—which was probably true. All the same, the changes that had occurred since the last time Mariah had seen the place seemed all wrong. Anachronistic, if not downright tacky.

Maud would have hated it. Mariah thought, amused, that perhaps she'd inherited more from her grandmother than she'd realized. Not her looks, but at least her fierce streak of independence. Although Mariah's was still a work in progress.

From upstairs came the sound of dueling CDs. Punk rock opposed to some panting, gasping female whose voice originated somewhere north of her larynx. "Turn that thing down," Vicki yelled. "Mama, make him turn it down!"

Erik was twenty-six, going on fifteen. Vicki was trapped in an adolescent time warp. For once Mariah was almost glad she'd been an only child.

Dodging sandspurs, she hung out three towels, a two-piece thong bathing suit and a set of Lynette's underwear, making room among the wet bathing suits and sandy towels someone else had slung across the line without benefit of clothespins. Last night the jet stream had swerved again. The sun was out today with a vengeance. Of her four cousins—five, including Mason—three of them had spent the morning working on their tans, Lynn with her hair wrapped in a towel. Mariah had joined them briefly until TA, without opening her eyes, had started trying to find out how much alimony Mariah had been awarded.

"You didn't sign a prenup, did you? I'll never do that again. If I'd been smart, I'd have had a kid like Lynn did, then I'd be set for life, or at least until the kid was—what, Lynn? Eighteen? My God, you've got eight more years of child support coming in."

"Oh, yeah?" Lynette had said, without removing the cucumber slices from her eyes. "First you have to catch the lying bastard. Last I heard, he was lying low in one those little islands down south that's just far enough offshore so the court's not going to waste manpower chasing him down."

Mariah had stood, dusted the sand off her shorts and wandered away. She had her own financial problems to solve. So far she wasn't making much progress. She still had a few contacts in the Raleigh-Durham area, but for several reasons— most of them right here on the island with her at the moment— she didn't particularly want to start over within a half hour drive from where all her relatives lived.

Maybe she'd try fresh ground. Atlanta was big enough. Norfolk was close enough so that she could spend weekends here on Henry Island.

Seeing Mason playing near the old boathouse, she wandered over to watch him fish. "Aren't you supposed to be in school?"

"Mom sent a note. 'Sides, Granddad had these people he's supposed to meet here, so we came early. I'm trying to catch me some minnows. Fish don't like pork rind," he said gravely. "If I had me a spinning rod I could use artificial, but I broke the one I got for Christmas and Mom says I can't have another one till my birthday, only that's not till July. Do you have a spinning rod?"

What people? she wondered briefly. "No, but I bet I know where you can get a cane pole."

He'd been using a hand line, dropping it off the edge of the bulkhead where the water was deepest. She remembered when Lynn and TA, both more interested in boys, clothes and celebrities than in deep sea fishing, used to tease one of the men into taking them out in the boat just so they would have pictures to show off back at school. Boys were always impressed by the fish.

Mariah used to beg to be taken along, but as the boat was small and they could only fish two lines at a time off the stern, she had never caught anything during the few times she'd been allowed to go.

Why couldn't one of the men take the boy out fishing?

"Come on, let's go visit Orestes. You remember him, don't you?" Her father would have told her if the old caretaker-handyman had died since she'd last seen him.

"Sure I do…sort of. He's that old man who lives in that place Mama calls a bomination."

I'll just bet she did, Mariah thought.

So she took him to meet Orestes, who had to be close to ninety now, but had still been active and living alone on the far side of the island the last time she'd seen him.

"Is he kin to us?" Mason asked, skipping long the pine-straw covered woods path.

"He was a distant cousin of your great-grandmother Maud's, but not really close enough to count. I've known him since I was even younger than you are, though. He makes really neat boat models, or at least he used to. His eyes might not be good enough now."

She was relieved to find Orestes basically unchanged from the last time she'd seen him. Smaller, a little shakier—a lot shakier—but basically the same. He was out working on his boat, so they veered down to the wharf. The *Miss Maud* was still gleaming white, and Mariah vaguely remembered hearing that he still painted it in what he called the old way, thinning the paint with kerosene so that instead of sealing the surface, each time he swabbed it down with a mop dipped overboard, a little of the paint wore away, leaving the hull looking brighter than white.

The EPA would have been horrified, she thought, amused. She waved and he clambered out of the boat, taking an eternity to do it. "Sorry, we didn't meant to disturb you," she said.

"How do, young'un," Orestes said in greeting, his eyes skimming past her to dwell on the boy. At close range she could see the tremors that shook his shrunken frame.

She left the two males to talk fishing, while she leaned against a piling on the wharf, admiring the flawless lines of the forty-two-foot wooden fishing boat. Lacking the chopped-off stern and the flying bridge of more modern boats, she was as graceful as one of the great white herons that flew over the house every evening just before sunset.

There was a wooden skiff tied up nearby, much like the three old flat-bottomed ones that were turned upside down near the pier on the other side of the island, waiting for someone to scrape and repaint them and put them back in service.

They'd been waiting for more than a dozen years now. At least Orestes's skiff was in the water, with a small outboard canted up at the stern.

Gazing down at the mirrorlike reflections of both boats, Mariah felt the urge to paint for the first time in a long, long time. Before frustration could take hold—she hadn't painted in years, not since she'd married and moved to California—she wandered back to where the boy and the old man were engaged in conversation.

Mason turned to greet her. "Mariah, I am so old enough to remember my grandmom, aren't I? She was named Maud and she had long hair and walked funny, like she had a stick in her back. I 'member she told me about some soldiers and sailors and tankers blowing up and stuff like that."

"Maud was your great-grandma, son," Orestes said gently. "You got the look of her, all right—got that proud Wallis nose on you. Mind you don't get in too many fights and get it busted up, y'hear?"

Mariah tried and failed to remember what Maud's nose had looked like. Funny how details could slip away. She glanced up and met the twinkling eyes that had faded surprisingly little over the years. To Mason she said, "Remind me sometime and I'll show you a picture of her when she was younger."

Orestes cleared his throat. "Happens I got a few pictures, m'self. Got some canes all cut and cured, too, boy. You got time, I'll rig you up one."

Mason looked hopefully at Mariah, and Orestes said, "Go 'long, missy, I'll bring the boy home directly." He pronounced it "terrectly." It could mean anywhere from a few minutes to a few hours.

And so Mariah wandered back along the shore rather than cut through the woods the way they had come. The beach was passable all the way around at low tide, even though it narrowed in places. She could remember her mother calling the island Alcatraz East, but she'd laughed when she'd said it. Roxie Henry had laughed at everything. Big, gorgeous, loud and good-natured, she'd stuck out among the dour Henrys like a sunflower in a bed of chickweed. Looking back, Mariah had to wonder how two such different people had come together. Edgar Henry had been a quiet, average-looking businessman, more successful than either of his brothers-in-law, but hardly wealthy. He'd traveled extensively abroad, linking investors and businesses.

Mariah couldn't remember the first time her father had brought them here to meet his family, but she remembered spending summers and holidays here. First with both her parents, and then, after her mother's death, with only Maud and whatever aunts, uncles and cousins happened to be here. Her father had rarely spent more than a few days whenever he'd dropped her off.

Over the years Mariah had come to realize that Maud had never liked Roxie. But then, Maud had never liked a lot of people, her own granddaughter included. Mariah remembered thinking that when she got old she was never going to be mean to anyone, even if they were rude to her. Long years later, when she'd heard that men tended to choose wives who reminded them of their mothers, she'd laughed aloud.

Lord knows that hadn't been true in her parents' case. She

could remember seeing her parents all dressed up to go out, her mother smiling and teasing, her father looking glum and uncomfortable in his evening wear. She'd thought they were the handsomest couple in the world.

Not that they'd never argued, because they had. But never seriously. Certainly never violently. Mariah was an expert on domestic violence, both emotional and physical.

Roxie had simply liked the excitement of new houses, new places, new things. Edgar, a nester by nature, perhaps because he traveled so much and wanted a familiar place to come home to, usually gave in. They'd moved every few years, but he'd dug in his heels when it came to vacationing at Hilton Head or Figure Eight instead of Henry Island.

"But there's nothing there, for gawd's sake," Roxie had exclaimed more than once. "Your mother hates me, your sisters are both twits—what am I supposed to do, pick the worms off your mama's collards? Sit in the parlor and crochet doilies?"

Edgar would usually just smile and say, "Look after Riah, work on your suntan. Take pictures…"

If Mariah had any artistic talent, she had to have inherited it from her mother. Roxie had been an amateur photographer, a surprisingly good one considering the lackadaisical way she went about it. She used to tease Edgar, telling him he couldn't tell a Matthew Brady from an Ansel Adams, and no, Matthew was not one of the *Brady Bunch* and Ansel was not Eve's husband.

"I want Mariah to know her family, Rox. A kid growing up these days needs roots—someplace she can come home to lick her wounds when the going gets tough."

Looking back, Mariah thought it was an odd thing for her father to have said. Almost as if he could foresee the future. Not that any of them could have foreseen what actually happened.

"Yer mama is a redbird, yer daddy is a crow, jump in the water and go, girl, go!" She hadn't thought of that particular

childish taunt in years. If it had ever made any sense to her, she'd forgotten.

Oh, yes—Lynn and TA used to dare her to swim the inlet.

Maybe that was why she'd made her father teach her to swim all those years ago. She had kept it up since then, spending a few hours each week swimming laps, at either her father's club near Durham or later at her ex-husband's country club, a second-rate one, but with an excellent pool.

There was something about a maritime forest—the scrubby live oaks twisted by wind, hanging on against the bitter elements. Between visits she tended to forget, but after only a few days on the island, she felt it again—the old pull, as if she were somehow connected. As if her roots were as deeply planted in the fragile barrier island as these stunted, ancient oaks.

She rounded a big, uprooted cedar that had fallen victim to a recent storm, and came to a dead stop. Gray glanced up from the log where he was seated, gave her a measuring look and then smiled. "Those your best beach-walking shoes?"

She was barefoot. "I'm breaking them in."

"I'm taking a break. Join me?"

For reasons she couldn't have explained if she'd tried, she dropped down onto the other end of the log. It was a dead pine. There were a lot of them still standing on the island, their pale barkless trunks dramatic against the dark evergreens. "What kills them?" she asked. "The pines, I mean."

He shrugged. He had broad shoulders and a stubborn jaw. She instinctively sized up the physical strength and did her best to discern the temperament of any man she came into close contact with. She'd had counseling and taken a course in self-defense after the second time Bruce had attacked her. It had helped, but nothing could make her forget.

"Storms, initially," he said in answer to her question. "Once they've been damaged—ice storms or hurricanes— pines are prone to pine bark beetle infestation."

"Is that what you're studying?"

"Studying?"

"Your project. Lifestyles of the pine tree in a maritime forest?"

He grinned, and she had to admit that, for a man with a pugnacious jaw and fists that could probably crack black walnuts, he had an engaging smile. "I saw you earlier with the kid," he said, unapologetically changing the subject. "Boy needs a pal."

"I took him to visit Orestes. He's sort of a caretaker-handyman who's lived here for as long as I can remember. I left them rigging up a cane pole."

"Yeah, I met him earlier. Seems like an interesting fellow."

They fell into a surprisingly comfortable silence that lasted for several minutes. Half a dozen boats cruised near the inlet, some half a mile away. Closer in, two water-skiers crisscrossed the wake of a Hatteras-Ocracoke ferryboat.

Today, with the sun shining brightly, the water looked deceptively benign, but Mariah remembered too well from her youth how dangerous the currents could be. She wondered if anyone had thought to remind Mason not to go in the water alone.

Quietly, Gray said, "You probably remember a lot about the old days, this being a family place."

It was a leading question. For reasons she didn't even try to examine, she chose not to be led. "I know it gets hot as blazes. I know the mosquitoes can carry you off in the night. I know the bullfrogs croak loud enough to drown out the Marine Band."

"Is that what I heard last night? I thought the band was tuning up its bass fiddle division."

"I'm not sure a marching band has a bass fiddle division." Who was this man? she wondered. Why was he really here? Grants weren't that difficult to find if one knew where to look and how to go about applying. Had he said he was on a study grant? She couldn't recall.

"I brought along a freshwater spinning rod. You think Mason would like to borrow it?"

"He's expecting one for his birthday. Let him wait."

Gray nodded. Mariah felt oddly let down. She, who had never had a child of her own, had been all prepared to defend her position of teaching patience as opposed to instant gratification. Digging her feet into the sand, she leaned forward, resting her arms on her knees. She really should get up and go, but it was surprisingly peaceful here, with the sound of the water lapping against the shore and the sun bringing out the spicy, earthy scent of the forest. Nearby, the shrill sound of tree frogs, or maybe cicadas—she'd never been able to tell the difference—started and stopped abruptly. As a child, she used to wonder if there was a leader hidden in the woods, directing their chorus.

Matter of fact, she still wondered.

She really should go back, but once she returned to Maud's house it would be battle stations all over again. You'd think Erik and Vicki were no older than Mason instead of young adults. Actually, Mason was better behaved.

Gray's next question gave her the excuse she needed to linger. "Tell me about this family of yours. These days it's not often you come across a whole island that's owned by a single family."

She frowned, remembering the last time she'd talked to her father. He had called, they'd gone through the usual—his travels, the trouble she'd been having with her new car—and then he'd mentioned the island. "Hold on to it, Riah, no matter what, y'hear? Place like that, it's going to triple in value every year, what with the market going crazy the way it has. You might be tempted to sell out, but don't. When it's time to let go, you'll know it. Don't let anyone talk you into doing anything you don't feel right about, y'hear?"

At the time, she hadn't thought that much about it. She knew that, having to travel in his work so much, he valued the place where he'd grown up, but the more she thought about it now, the more it sounded like a warning.

"It goes back a long way," she said thoughtfully. "I don't even know how many generations, but I know Maud—that was my grandmother—she was responsible for hanging on to it back when the state and then the Park Service were acquiring property. I heard my mother say once that Maud knew every politician from Manteo to Raleigh—maybe even Washington—and probably had something on most of them.'' Mariah couldn't help but smile at the idea.

Gray chuckled, the sound trickling down her spine like electric fingers. ''Sounds like a formidable woman.''

''She was. For all I know it might even be true. How else would a place like this get basic utilities?''

''Same way outlying farms did back in the thirties and forties? Rural Electrification Act? I understand there's an underwater cable running across to Ocracoke Island to supply power. This wouldn't be much of a detour.''

''Maybe not.'' Mariah ran her fingers through her hair, lifting it off her neck. ''You know, I've never even wondered about it before. There might have been a Coast Guard station here once. I know there's one over on Portsmouth Island. There used to be one on the north end of Ocracoke Island, too, but it washed away. Henry Island might even have been part of one of the other islands. Hatteras and Ocracoke used to be connected back in the eighteen hundreds. Inlets are always opening and closing and moving. How long are you planning on staying?''

''Pow! Talk about coming out of left field,'' he drawled.

''Well, I asked you before and you didn't answer.''

''What if I said as long as it takes?''

''As long as what takes? No, don't bother to answer. What if I said no way?''

His eyes were either gray or green. She couldn't be certain, the way he was squinting against the sun. She had a feeling they were measuring eyes, the kind that could strip away defenses quicker than you could buckle them on again. Oddly enough, she didn't sense any real malice there, but then she'd been fooled before.

''I really do need my cottage,'' she said, trying not to sound quite as desperate as she felt. ''The other two are evidently rented out, so I'm currently bunking in the cook's room—

she's not here yet. It's hardly the most comfortable place I've ever slept. It used to be part of a boardwalk out to an old kitchen. They expanded it to make more room.''

Actually, it wasn't particularly uncomfortable, just incredibly noisy. The aunts were almost as bad as the cousins, yelling upstairs and down, banging pots and pans and tuning through static on the old kitchen radio, trying to catch a weather report. Aunt Tracy, the eldest by a year and a half, insisted on bossing everyone. Aunt Belle reacted by trying to defend her two spoiled, lazy brats. The uncles usually escaped, combining a run over to Hatteras for supplies with an excuse to go fishing.

Not that they ever caught anything. They could have taken Mason with them, though. Mariah's daddy had said once—oh, Lord, that was years ago—that some of the so-called sportsmen he knew went out in a boat, anchored and played poker and drank beer all day, then came in and said the fish weren't biting.

"Nice," Gray mused, bringing her back to the present. Lately her mind had had a worrisome tendency to wander. "Your folks bring their own cook? The thrill of the grill worn off already?"

"How'd you guess? Cooking is women's work, grilling is men's work, vacations are when someone else does everything. Mostly, we're living on sandwiches and dry cereal."

"Yeah, me, too. I'm planning on doing some fishing, though. If I catch anything, I'll share."

"Let's see, that would be…ten of us, and one of you. How about inviting Orestes? He looks like he doesn't get enough to eat."

"I, uh—I hadn't thought of including the whole clan. I'm not that good a fisherman. Not saltwater, anyway."

"Just teasing," she said, and for the first time since she'd arrived on the island some four days earlier, she felt some of the tension inside her unwind. She had yet to accomplish her mission, but it could wait another few days. Wait for a lull in the pitched battle that was life in Maud's old house. For something so final she really needed all her father's family around her.

"Who's staying in the other two cottages?" Gray asked.

"Birders in one, according to Uncle Nat. Lynn said a couple from somewhere in Virginia had rented the other one. According to Mason, Uncle Linwood was supposed to meet someone down here. Whoever it is, they'll be leaving in a few days."

"So maybe you could move in?" he suggested.

"Or you could." She picked up a stick and drew a circle in the sand beside her left foot. "Apparently the cottages are booked through the season. Uncle Nat handles the bookings, and he says—actually, he only implied—that Daddy really fouled him up by letting you have our place for—what was it, six weeks? Two months? Weekly rates are much higher."

She drew two dots and a down-curved line in the circle, then rubbed it all out with her foot. "Seriously, I'd really appreciate it if you could make other arrangements. Isn't there someplace on Hatteras or Ocracoke where you could do your studies? What about Portsmouth Island? Maybe you could arrange something with the Park Service."

When he didn't answer, she sighed.

He picked up the twig she'd dropped and drew a geometric design that reminded her of the schematic on the back of Maud's old washing machine, which was always giving trouble because no one ever thought to rinse the sand out of clothes before tossing them into the tub.

Mariah watched as he decorated the design with stick figures, then she stood and brushed the sand off the seat of her shorts. An artist he wasn't. If the stick figures were supposed to represent the human form, he could do with a few lessons in anatomy.

"Well, think about it, anyway," she said, moving down closer to the water's edge, where the walking was easier.

"Yeah, I'll do that."

Gray watched her walk away. It was a sight he was becoming familiar with—Mariah's backside. Long legs, straight back, dark hair dangling in a ponytail, with tendrils escaping to stick to her neck. She had the kind of skin that darkened gradually with exposure, never really tanning, but never quite fading, either.

He waited until she was out of sight, then got up and headed in the opposite direction. So far he wasn't making much progress with his investigation. Not that he'd expected to, not right away.

Funny thing about cold cases. Time was no longer that important. Some of the cases he'd tackled had happened before the age of computers, of DNA and all the other tools that could examine old evidence and come up with new answers. In the case of Roxie Henry's death, there was no evidence to reexamine and only a handful of people who might or might not have been present at the time.

He figured his best bet at this point was the old man. If he hadn't seen the actual explosion, he probably knew who had. After all this time, he might even have a few ideas about what had happened…maybe even why it had happened.

A powerboat cruised past, two men fishing off the stern. Yesterday Gray had watched a charter boat slowly circling the island. Three men had studied the shoreline with binoculars, while another one took pictures. No sign of any fishing gear.

Surveillance?

Interesting, he mused. Was it only a coincidence that it had happened so soon after he'd been commissioned to look into a decades-old accident that might not have been an accident?

Probably not. This was a prime vacation area, with the Memorial Day holiday only a week or so away. Some folks liked to get an early start.

"Edgar, my man, you left out a few crucial pieces of the puzzle."

Chapter 4

"Shut the door!" Tracy hissed. She was wearing her beach uniform of denim jumper, sneakers, panty hose and pearls.

"Mama, it's hot in here."

"Then turn on a damned fan!"

"Just do as your mama says, Lynn," Nat Detloff said quietly. He was a small man with a latent Napoleon complex. The only one of the family who stood up to him on a regular basis was his sister-in-law, Tracy Boxer. "All right, now, she's off somewhere on the other side. Tracy, did you find out where we stand legally?"

"Did it occur to you that if we start asking questions about what happens if a will turns up after all this time, it might cause those investors Merrick's got lined up to back off? They've already started the title search. If there's any question, the deal's off, because they're not going to settle for a non-warranty deed." Tracy fiddled with her pearls. "How do we know Mama didn't do something stupid, like giving that old man a clear title? Just because he never had it recorded doesn't necessarily mean anything, not if her signature was witnessed.'' Tracy paced a tight circle, casting worried looks toward the window that looked out over the bulkhead area.

"We don't," her husband replied. Linwood Boxer looked as if whatever he'd had for breakfast hadn't agreed with him. "I know she went and talked to him for a long time before she sent for that lawyer. Why'd she send for a lawyer if she wasn't going to write a will? Something was bugging her, but I'm damned if I know what. If I didn't know better, I'd have said she was scared of him or something.''

"Scared of the lawyer?" Vicki asked.

"Scared of Orestes, maggot brain. I say we get rid of him."

All eyes turned to the speaker. "Erik!" Belle said, shocked.

"I just meant we put him away somewhere. Hell, Mama, he's not able to take care of himself. I vote we do him a favor and have him put away in one of those places where he'll be looked after."

"You gonna pay for it?" his father asked. "Those places don't come cheap, boy."

"Besides, if he goes in on Medicaid, the state's going to come after everything he has—any property he might have an interest in. Are you willing to risk that?" Tracy asked the assembled group.

"Well, we're not even sure Mama gave him anything," Belle said. "It's just that I remembered hearing them talking a few months before she died—something about a will—and it got me to thinking the other day when that woman from Merrick's was talking about a title search. You all remember, you were there." Belle looked at her husband for corroboration. "So what if another deed or even another will does turn up after all this time? Mama said Daddy didn't leave a will, so naturally, everything went to her and now to all of us. But what if—"

"You don't even remember your father. Besides, even if he'd had a will, who else would he have left things to, the church? I doubt if he was even a member. Maud was his heir, and we were her heirs." That from Nat, who was ready to retire, and who had just seen his 401K go south in the latest market dive.

"Just because she didn't leave a legally witnessed will doesn't mean anything. We're all the immediate family she had, and you know how she felt about keeping things in the family." Linwood tugged nervously at a hangnail. His hardware and farm equipment business was suffering as one farm after another was sold off to create another housing development, but that was the least of his problems.

"That's right," interjected Belle. "You know how Mama was about the family name. She wouldn't have given Orestes a deed. But even if she did, he never had it recorded, so it won't count."

"Well, I mean, I just thought maybe..." Linwood again. He looked ten years older than his wife, when actually he was two years younger. "Look, all I know is they were arguing that day he came to see her before she died, and I'm pretty sure I heard her saying something about a will."

Nat had that praying-for-patience look. "Old fool could've been asking her to witness *his* will. You ever think of that?"

"Don't be silly," Tracy retorted. "Mama was too sick to witness anything, and besides, I'd be willing to swear Orestes doesn't own anything but that old boat. Who would he will that thing to? Who'd even want it?"

"I'll take it," Linwood Boxer said. "They've got one just like it on display over on Hatteras. Maybe it's worth something as an antique."

"I thought you wanted a bass boat, like the preacher has," said Belle, and everyone looked at her. "Well, I'm sorry, but you said—"

Nat took charge again. "Okay, so we'll go on looking, just in case. Orestes could've squirreled it away anywhere on the island—he's got the run of the place. If nothing turns up in the next day or so we'll just figure there's no deed, and if there was an old will, either Maud's or your father's, Maud destroyed it before she died."

Tracy spoke up again. "There's probably some kind of statute of limitations, anyway. I vote we move on. They're ready to get down to brass tacks. In a few days—''

"In a few more days Mariah will have buried Edgar's ashes and we can get her to sign a quitclaim deed for her share before she leaves,'' interrupted Linwood.

"Uncle Linwood, for gawd's sake!'' Vicki was painting her toenails a metallic teal-blue.

Nat looked at his daughter. Vicki had flunked out of college and now spent her days working on a tan—or in her case, a pink—until the season opened and she could land a job waiting tables up at Nags Head, where she hoped to attract the attention of either a scout from a modeling agency or a rich, brain-dead bachelor looking for a dumb bimbo to marry. Nat had given up hoping she would join him in the insurance business.

After some consideration, he had included her in the impromptu meeting, reasoning that the better she understood how much was at stake, the less likely she would be to let something slip that could cause problems. There was a reason why the state of North Carolina required a husband's signature before a wife could dispose of any real property.

"Well, I just wish you all wouldn't keep talking about dead people. It's depressing,'' Vicki said petulantly.

"People die, Vicki. Your father sells insurance, he ought to know.''

"We thank you for the support, Belle,'' Nat said, his voice laced with sarcasm.

Tracy attempted to smooth things over. "Look, Victoria, we're all mourning poor Edgar, but he obviously wasn't a well man. The way he raced around the world, eating all that foreign food, it's a wonder he didn't bring back some awful disease and infect us all.''

"Bottom line,'' Nat stated, "Edgar's dead. We're all just as sorry as we can be, but things are at a critical stage here and we don't need any more complications.'' He favored his son with a withering glance. "We're in this together, right? There's no room here for any sentimental claptrap.''

"In other words," said Linwood, "we forget about any glitch in the chain of ownership, get Mariah to sign over Edgar's share and then we sell to Merrick for enough money to pay everybody off. We'll still have enough left over to put us in hog heaven for the rest of our lives."

Lynette, filing her nails on the window seat, rolled her eyes. "Spoken like a true farm machinery salesman," she said, barely loudly enough to be heard.

It was Tracy, easily the strongest member of the family now that Maud was gone, who got on with the business at hand. "*If* Mama and that lawyer wrote a will, then a copy of it has to be on this island somewhere. At least we know it was never recorded."

"Aunt Tracy, I searched everywhere, including Uncle Edgar's cottage. There's nothing there. I even tried to check out that guy's computer. I mean, who knows who he is? Uncle Edgar's the one who sent him down here. What I want to know is why." Erik took out a handkerchief and blotted his nose. He felt so damned twitchy he could hardly stand still, but this was important. This was real money they were talking about, enough to get him off the hook. Once he was in the clear, he was going to clean up his act. Take his share of what was left and head on out to the West Coast, where the real action was.

But no more using and definitely no more dealing. He'd promised before, but this time he really meant it.

"She's down there looking at those old boats," said Lynette from her vantage point near the bay window.

Belle glanced around, blue eyes bright in her plump, pink face. "Why can't we just come right out and ask her if she'd like to sell? Her share would probably set her up for life."

Lynette said, "Why not?"

Nat shot his niece a sour look. "Right. And what if she says no, missy? What then? You gonna hold a shotgun on her and make her sign?"

No one spoke for a long moment. A plane flew over. Just outside the window, a mockingbird tuned up. "Or we could come right out and ask Orestes what they were talking about that day,'' Tracy said thoughtfully. ''If Mama wrote a will and asked him to witness it, she could have asked him to hide it in his house, knowing it's the last place anyone would look for it.''

As usual, Nat locked horns with his sister-in-law. ''For God's sake, Tracy, why would she hide the thing if she went to the trouble to write it? Chain of title, think chain of title. Your father died overseas, we all know that. Maud never mentioned any will, did she? There was never any problem with property rights, was there? She knew she was dying. If there was anything that needed straightening out, she'd have damned well done it before she died.'' He looked from one to the other, seeking agreement. ''One thing I'll say for her, Maud didn't fart around.''

Nat had reluctantly come to admire his mother-in-law, even though he'd never really liked her.

Belle looked troubled. ''Well, it seems to me we should just ask Mariah if she doesn't want to sell. I mean, it's an unbelievably good offer, and even if she doesn't need the money, she could always invest it.''

''Right. Why don't you just suggest a few good investments, Belle—she'll appreciate financial advice from someone who had no better sense than to borrow the max on five different credit cards.''

Belle crumpled. Nat turned to glare at his son as if to say, you're no better.

Tracy stepped into the fray. ''All right, what's done is done. All we can do about it now is get out the best way we can.''

Linwood said, ''Look on the bright side. There'll be enough left over, even after taxes, to buy us all a condominium in Florida. They don't have income tax there.''

''As if you had any income,'' his wife snorted.

Belle looked hopefully around the room. ''The sooner we ask her, the sooner we'll know.''

Ignoring his wife, Nat studied his nicotine-yellowed fingernails. ''Some ways, that girl's more like Maud than any of the rest of you. She takes a notion not to go along, we're all up shit creek.''

"You don't have to be so vulgar, Nathaniel."

Vicki said, "She's still down there looking at those old skiffs, Mama. Maybe if we put one overboard and she happens to take it offshore, it'll sink.''

"Victoria, hush your mouth! We love Mariah, even if she is inclined to be—well, difficult.''

"Huh! I'll say."

Erik moved over and gazed out at his tall, sophisticated cousin. He sort of liked her, actually. She was pretty cool. He'd lay odds she'd done a line or two, her and her fancy West Coast friends. To his sister, he said, "She's not difficult, she's just got better manners than you and Lynn, Miss Pimples.''

Vicki threw a cushion at him.

"I'll talk to her tonight." Tracy was back in her take-charge mode. They'd had this conversation too many times in the past, never getting anywhere, just going in the same old circles. "If we put it to her the right way, she has to see reason. It's not like she has any fond memories of this place. You kids made her life hell, as I recall.''

"And then there was her mama…" Belle looked as if she might burst into tears, something she'd been doing on a regular basis ever since menopause had overtaken her more than a decade ago. She was now in her early sixties, but some women, she liked to think, were more sensitive than others.

Nat Detloff stood and hitched up his Bermuda shorts. Even wearing his vacation clothes, he looked like the unsuccessful insurance salesman he was. "Look, this is no time to get soft. What it is is the chance of a lifetime. God knows, we all need it.'' His face looked old and bitter as he eyed his only son. "We know how Edgar would have voted. Like us, he'd have voted to sell out, right? I mean, his wife was killed right out there in front of his kid's eyes, for God's sake. I think he was starting to come around, don't you?'' He looked from one to the other, keeping the troops in line.

Belle said, "I don't know…Brother was more like Mama in some ways, and you know she'd have died before she sold off our heritage."

They all looked at her as if to say, *Well?*

Nat fought a battle with his patience and lost. "Dammit, we all know Maud never liked change, but change happens!"

"To quote a famous bumper sticker," Erik said under his breath, and Vicki snickered.

"I say we simply tell Mariah there's a party interested in buying us out. All she has to do is sign a quitclaim deed and we'll handle everything. Who's going to turn down a hundred grand just for signing an autograph?"

Belle's eyes widened. "But they offered us five mi—"

"Hey, there's four of us, not counting kids, remember? There's only one of her. 'Sides, Edgar probably left her plenty under the table, inheritance taxes being what they are." Nat glanced around as if for approval. "Okay, you with me? We'll just explain about the heavy land transfer taxes, the surveys and closing costs and God knows how many other expenses. What do you bet she'll take the money and hightail it out of here, no questions asked?"

He looked around, waiting for a rebuttal. Lynn went on filing her nails. Vicki was putting a second coat on hers. Erik, hands in the pockets of his cargo pants to keep them still, rocked back and forth in his Topsiders.

Actually, he'd done the whole family a big favor by getting caught short of funds when a certain business deal fell through. Now, instead of ending up as shark bait, he'd fixed it so his entire family was set for life.

Chapter 5

"What do you think? Are they worth scraping and patching up?" Mariah asked, resting her hand on the boy's shoulder. Mason had given up on fishing, laid his cane pole aside and come to stand beside her as she looked over the three old wooden skiffs.

"Do we have any outboards?" he asked.

"There used to be a small one in the boathouse. Some oars, too."

"Do you know how to oar?"

"It's called rowing, and yeah, I used to be pretty good at it." Mariah glanced at her tender palms. Ten minutes of rowing and she'd have blisters the size of biscuits. But, oh, it would feel good to get out in a boat and pit her strength against a clean, swift tide.

"I could help you push one overboard." Mason looked so hopeful she didn't have the heart to tell him these boats were probably too far gone, even if she had the time or the tools to restore them.

"Why don't you ask your mama if she'd mind, and if she

says it's all right, we can at least start scraping barnacles.'' It would be something to entertain the boy. Maybe she could convince one of her uncles to take him out fishing.

Meanwhile, she still had a committal service to plan. She could hardly just dig a hole and bury her father's ashes, or dump them overboard. None of her family had been the least bit dogmatic, but for that final act she needed something more formal. More ceremonial. At least she needed to be able to speak from her heart, and right now she didn't know what was in her heart, she truly didn't. Love, of course—but she needed more. Needed to feel her family was with her. What was left of her family.

So far, she'd felt just the opposite. They had all but invited her to leave.

A short while later, when she and Mason went up the hill for lunch, one of the two men staying in Belle's Acre stepped out onto the deck. The boy said, ''Hi, Mr. Shoemaker. We're going to scrape barnacles off a boat. If you want to help, you can.''

The middle-aged man smiled briefly and shook his head.

''Mom said they were prob'ly schoolteachers, but they're not in school,'' Mason said, glancing back at the cottage.

''Neither are you,'' Mariah reminded him.

''Yeah, but Mom got me an excuse. I'm supposed to write this paper about fish and stuff like that. For science class.'' When Mariah, momentarily lost in thought, failed to respond, he said, ''Man, I wouldn't want to teach school, would you? Why would anybody want to be stuck in a classroom all day?''

She wrenched her mind back to the present. ''It's a tough job, but somebody has to do it.''

The boy peered at her to see if she was serious. Deciding she was teasing, he grinned, showing front teeth that would have done credit to a beaver. ''Me, I'm going to be Harry Potter, or at least one of his helpers.''

''Go for it. First, though, you have to learn a lot of scientific stuff so you'll know how to be a proper helper. That's were school comes in.''

They stomped the sand off their feet and went inside. Meals were something of a problem, as Mariah had not thought to bring any supplies with her. She rationalized her position by reminding herself that not only had she been handed the chores no one else wanted, she'd been stuck in the least desirable room in a house that was one-third hers. Meanwhile the Boxers and the Detloffs, en masse, spread out over the rest of the house.

They ate sandwiches again. Today's version was salmon salad from a can. Tonight would probably be salmon patties, as there was half a case of cheap salmon left from a previous visit, and Belle claimed that fish didn't keep forever, even if it was canned. In the middle of seafood heaven, Mariah was getting a little tired of canned fish.

Twenty minutes later they were outside again, smelling of salmon, fresh sunscreen and insect repellent. Mariah never burned, but she wanted to set an example for Mason, who was fair-skinned like the rest of the family. And the mosquitoes really were out in force after the recent rain.

Gray was down by the bulkhead when they arrived. Mariah wondered idly how he occupied himself when he disappeared for hours on end. Something to do with his project, probably. Hands on his hips, he surveyed the three flat-bottomed boats. "Going to try and resurrect one of these relics?"

"*Try* is the operative word," she said dryly.

He nudged the middle skiff with his foot. It was the smallest of the three. "Starting with this one?"

His eyes were green today, not gray, with a dark ring around the irises. Mariah was struck all over again by what an attractive man he was once you got past that pugnacious jaw and the aggressive nose. Frowning, she considered the three boats resting keel-up on sun-warped timbers. "Actually, I thought the one on the left. It doesn't have as much paint on it as the others."

"That's a plus?" His smile was too guileless to be truly guileless.

Mason looked from one to the other, holding the chisel and

hammer gleaned from Maud's toolbox. "We could paint it, too," he said helpfully. "There's prob'ly paint in the boat-house."

"We certainly could if we wanted to," she replied. Then, turning back to the man, she said, "Correct me if I'm wrong, but won't wood swell faster if it's not painted? And don't we need to put it overboard and let it swell up so it won't leak? And if it doesn't leak, then where's the problem? We're not entering any beauty contest here, we just want a boat to use for fishing."

"Sounds reasonable enough to me. How about you, son?"

"Yep. Sounds reasonable to me, too." Hands on his hips, Mason mimicked the soft-spoken man.

Some forty-five minutes later Mariah sat back on the hot sand, knees drawn up before her. Laying aside her tools, she wiped away a film of dust and sweat from her face with a filthy forearm. "This is a job for early morning or late afternoon, not the middle of the day."

Mason was still chipping away. She figured he could do little damage with the dull chisel, and he was obviously intent on finishing the job today and getting the boat in the water before dark.

Gray worked slower, using an oyster knife and hammer from his own cottage. Or rather, from hers. He appeared to be favoring his left arm, and she asked him about it.

"Stiff shoulder. No big deal."

"Then I take it you're not a pitcher."

Without answering, he offered another of those too-good-to-be-true smiles. She wanted to ask him if he bleached his teeth, but thought the question might be too personal.

And asking about his injuries wasn't?

She'd do well not to get too chummy.

"You're a symphony conductor, then. You got carried away with your baton, right?" Go ahead, open wider—there's still room for another foot in there.

"Actually, I'm a detective. Ex-SBI, now self-employed."

She tilted her head and studied him openly this time. Everything about him, from the thick, streaky blond hair on his hatless head to the tantalizing pattern of wear on his ancient jeans. "A detective. Right. So why did you lead me to believe you were a scientist?"

"Did I do that?"

She nodded just as an errant breeze off the water sent a few strands of hair dancing across her cheek. With an impatient hand, she shoved it behind her ear. "You said you were here on a grant. That usually means studying something, and there's nothing here to study except…" With a wave of one hand, she indicated their surroundings.

Gray laid aside his tools and leaned back on his hands, long legs stretched out before him. "I don't recall mentioning a grant. I believe my actual words were that I was working on a project."

How much to tell her? he wondered. He'd made very little progress in the week since he'd arrived. Hadn't really expected to do more than get acclimatized. Sooner or later, he had to get to work, though, and the place to start was with the horse's mouth.

His gaze settled on her mouth. It was anything but equine.

"So? What is it, some big government secret? You dropped out of the SBI to hunt for a CIA mole inside the FBI? I understand there's a lot of competition among all the snoopy dogs."

"The snoopy dogs?" He tried not to laugh. There was something disarming about the lady, and he couldn't afford to be disarmed—not at this stage of the game.

"Well?"

He could have told her it was none of her business, but that would be a lie. It was very much her business, although he was damned if he could figure out how something that had happened twenty-seven years ago could threaten anyone now. Edgar had wanted justice, if justice had been denied, but he'd hinted at being worried about his daughter, too.

Or had Gray read too much into their two conversations?

"Ah ha! I was right, then. You're here on a secret mission

and if you told me, you'd have to kill me.'' Her reluctant smile widened into a gloating grin.

"Then I'd better not answer, had I? Being a local, you're probably familiar with a place called Harvey Point—a certain government establishment less than a hundred miles northwest of here that doesn't officially exist?''

Crossing her ankles, she scratched at a mosquito bite on her left knee. "Oh, and don't forget our local bombing range. That's even closer. I think.''

"I believe I can pretty well assure you that, unless the Park Service gets greedy, Henry Island is safe from government intrusion.''

She looked at him for a long time without responding. There were still questions in her eyes. She was fun to tease.

A little too much fun.

"Riah, if we leave the barnacles on, will the boat sink?'' Mason's voice broke the shimmering tension. He had picked up on her nickname, and coming from him, it had a nice, friendly sound.

It was Gray who replied. "If speed's not important, I don't think the barnacles would make that much difference, son. But on any project worth doing, it pays to do things properly from the start. It's a lot easier than going back and trying to redo something after the fact.''

"After what fact?''

Gray looked at Mariah as if to say *Over to you.* She grinned and shook her head.

Mason looked from one to the other. "You mean if we put it over and it sank, we'd have to go under the water to finish scraping it off? But if the barnacles don't matter, why can't we just leave 'em on? They wouldn't show.''

"Doing things right, whether or not it shows, is what matters,'' Mariah said. "It's a matter of principle.''

It occurred to Gray that even though his client had claimed not to be close to his daughter, someone had instilled in her a basic sense of responsibility. It could have been either of her parents—or both. Or it could have been the woman whose name was a byword in these parts. Maud Henry.

Gray would like to think he would have done the same for any child of his. He would never know.

"I'm for a shower and something cold to drink," Mariah said, uncrossing her legs and rising in one fluid motion.

From his vantage point on the ground, Gray admired the length of smooth, bare skin until it disappeared under the hem of her khaki shorts.

Classy. The lady was both sexy and classy. Hard to know how to handle a combination like that.

Not that he intended to. Handle it, that was.

"Yeah, me, too," he said belatedly. "How about you, son? Want to split a cold Pepsi with me?"

A dozen yards up from the shore, the two males took a left on Cottage Row. Mariah kept on going toward Maud's house. She hadn't been invited to join them.

Not that she would have, but it might have been nice to be asked. The more she saw of Gray, the more she liked what she saw. An intruder he might be, but he was good to Mason— good for him—and that meant a lot. In the short time she'd been here, Mariah had grown fond of her first cousin once removed. The last time she'd seen him he'd been little more than a baby. Evidently his father hadn't stayed around long enough to take an interest in him. His grandfather wouldn't even take him along on the supply runs, even though they often trolled across the inlet. And Erik, who could have acted as some kind of a male role model, lacked the patience.

Come to think of it, Erik, even though he was turning out to be the pick of the litter in Mariah's estimation, probably wasn't an ideal role model for a ten-year-old boy. Whether or not he was messing around with drugs, as she suspected. For one thing, he lacked the patience even to get a real tan, opting for a chemical tan, instead. Dealing with children required patience. It hadn't taken her long to realize that much.

Trudging through the hot, dry sand, Mariah amused herself

by wondering what Maud would have made of her handsome young grandson. Whatever her opinion, Erik would not have been left in the dark. Maud had never minced words. She'd considered her only daughter-in-law a tramp, and had said so more than once.

Roxie had only laughed. "What, because I touch up my hair? Maud, honey, you don't even know what color my hair really is. Even Edgar doesn't know, but he loves me, anyway."

Maud. Even now that she was gone, she was still a presence. Like the shadow of one of those huge birds that flew over the island—here, yet not here.

Mariah shivered, kicked the sand off her feet on the top step and opened the screen door.

Supper was the expected salmon patties. Belle fried the things, while Tracy sliced tomatoes and Mariah made potato salad. There was a perfectly good gas grill going to waste on the side porch. Nat claimed it was too rusty to use safely, and he was probably right. As an insurance salesman, he would know about hazards like that.

"Daddy, can I borrow the boat tomorrow?" Vicki wandered into the kitchen, her hair wrapped in a towel, her navel sporting an array of jewelry.

"No, you cannot. If you need something from across the inlet, put it on the list."

"How about a video? If we could borrow the video player from our cottage and hook it up, we might have something decent to watch for a change."

Television, like most things, was unreliable on the island, depending on the vagaries of the weather and whatever else affected the signal. They had a satellite dish, but the wind kept blowing it out of alignment and no one seemed able—or had the patience—to adjust it.

"Call over there and tell them what you want. I'll try to remember to pick it up."

"If I went with you, you wouldn't have to remember."

Nat, never the most patient of men, looked up from the spinning reel he was taking apart. "Just put what you want on the damned list, will you?" he snapped.

Vicki waved her hands. "Okay, okay. Let's see...Tampax and minipads. How about you, Lynn? TA? Y'all need anything?"

"Jesus, deliver me from women," Nat muttered. Raking back his chair, he stomped from the room.

Mariah grinned at her cousin and for once, Vicki grinned back. "Think I overdid it?"

"I think you did it just about right. We'll know tomorrow, won't we?"

Chopping celery for the salad, she thought, *I'm making progress. These gals aren't so bad, it's just that we never really got to know each other growing up.* Vicki and Erik were a decade or so younger, Lynn and TA just enough older to matter to a teenager.

Although they'd once all lived within forty miles of each other, Mariah had gone to a private school, while her cousins had attended public schools. The island had been a common denominator, but even then there'd been differences, and not just age differences. She'd been a swimmer; they'd been sunbathers. She had enjoyed wading the shallows, looking for shells and Indian artifacts from the early Algonquin residents, while they had tried on each other's clothes and makeup and whispered about boys.

As adults, the differences evened out. Mariah felt herself warming to the idea of family gatherings here on the island they all shared, carrying on a tradition Maud had started so long ago.

"My God, I'm going to kill that old man," Tracy Detloff announced, barging in through the back door after dumping the trash. The screen clattered against the wall. "On a day like today, with the woods dry as tinder and the wind picking up, that ignorant old pack rat is burning trash!"

"Didn't it rain just last week?" Belle, ever the peacemaker, queried.

"Not even enough to wet the sand." Tracy's voice was even more querulous than usual.

It had rained enough to soak her to the skin on her way across the inlet, Mariah recalled, but she wasn't about to get involved when her aunt Tracy was on a rampage. "Sweet pickles or dill?" she asked.

Tracy glared at her. Belle looked confused, as she often did. "Oh, dear—both?"

Mariah opened the jar of dill cubes.

"Smell that smoke? I just hope he's set fire to that old shack of his. God knows it'd be an improvement! While he's at it he might as well burn those two old eyesores out back."

The two stripped-down beach buggies parked in the woods behind the house had been ferried over here years ago. Mariah vaguely remembered seeing Orestes use one of the wheels as a winch to haul in his net, but so far as she knew, they hadn't been driven in years.

"If he burns down his house, where will he live? He certainly can't live here in Mama's house." Belle's color deepened. Mariah suspected it might be rosacea, as her aunt never went outside without a wide-brimmed hat.

"I'm sure he'll find someplace. God knows, he's sponged off us long enough."

"I think he was Mama's cousin or something, wasn't he?"

"Humph. If you ask me, he was hiding out from the draft board. Daddy went to war, along with every other able-bodied man on the banks. Not Orestes, though. Oh, no, he stayed right here, safe and sound, living on charity."

And working darned hard for whatever he got, Mariah imagined, taking care of Maud and three small children. She had never known her grandfather, but she did remember hearing her father say that George Edgar Henry had joined the merchant marine as soon as he was old enough, even though he'd been newly married at the time. Edgar had claimed the merchant mariners were like an unarmed navy, going in constant danger to get needed supplies to the troops. She'd thought at the time that it sounded heroic. She still did.

Mariah wished now she could have known her heroic ancestor, but he'd died long before she'd been born. She was ashamed to say that it had never occurred to her to ask about him, maybe because once Maud started in on the Henry family history, she went on and on and on. You'd think they were royalty or something. As a child, Mariah had found it boring. Now that she was older—now that it was too late—she found herself wanting to know more.

Orestes would probably be a wonderful source. She made a mental note to ask him about all the people he remembered living on the island back in the early days.

Tracy was still on a rant, slamming windows shut. "You wait, before the day's over, that old fool will come whining, wanting us to build him another house. Probably want us to buy him a double-wide and have it barged over here and set up. He might even want to move into one of the cottages—I wouldn't put it past him. Maud let him get away with murder, just because he claimed to be kin way back a hundred generations ago."

Belle's hands fluttered indecisively. "Oh, well—he'll have to move, anyway, won't he?"

Tracy glared at her younger sister—younger by a year and a half. Mariah was both fascinated and repelled by the interaction between the two women, one obviously dominant, the other submissive, but probably far more resilient.

Not until much later would she wonder what had been meant by Belle's last remark.

Chapter 6

With the acrid smell of smoke filling his lungs, Gray jogged along the pine-straw-littered woods path to be sure the old man was all right. Observant both by nature and by profession, he remembered seeing a section of stovepipe projecting through one of the windows that had been covered over by sheet metal. That usually meant a woodstove of some kind. Odds were there was no smoke detector in service, either.

Dammit, someone should be looking after the old guy. Sure, he valued his independence—he'd fight like hell if anyone tried to transfer him into something a little newer, a little safer. He wasn't ready yet for a nursing home, but what about a clean, modern mobile home?

On second thought, how many storms would that survive? Both the old shack and its owner were obviously made of durable stuff, a lot tougher than some of the modern-day counterparts.

Gray emerged from the woods to see Orestes shoveling sand over the ashes of what appeared to have been a fair-size bonfire. The old man glanced up, removed his baseball cap and wiped his brow with a grimy forearm. "What, you back again? Next thing, them girls is gonna start chargin' admission. Nickel a peep for a look at the old hermit."

Those girls? What girls? There was no real rancor in the observation, but little real humor, either. Evidently the old guy's grasp on reality had a tendency to slip.

"You claiming to be a genuine hermit?" Gray was more relieved than he cared to let on. He'd seen some grisly sights in his days with the Bureau. He didn't need to see the black-ened remains of an old man he'd been carrying on a friendly conversation with just a few hours ago.

"Nope. I let 'em think it, though. Don't hurt. Keeps 'em off my back."

"Wind's picking up. Good thing you got your trash burning done early."

"Stuff piles up. Don't do no good to save it—nobody left to save it for. Nobody that wants it, anyways." Orestes kicked sand over a small flare-up. "Good time to burn," he opined. "Fixin' to rain again."

Gray eyed the sky as if he knew what constituted a rain threat. A weather guru he wasn't, but some things he knew. He could usually tell when a man had something he wanted to say, but wasn't ready to say it.

This man was stalling. The question was why? Making up his mind who he could trust and who he couldn't? It paid to be cautious. Gray figured the old guy might have done a few things he shouldn't—most men made a mistake or two in the process of growing up. If he happened to have saved a few embarrassing souvenirs, that would explain the fire.

Whether or not he'd actually broken any laws was another matter. Apparently, the law on Henry Island was pretty sketchy. Whatever Orestes had or hadn't done as a young man, Gray had an idea the statute of limitations had long since run out, although he'd have been just about the right age at the right time for bootlegging.

As for the modern-day equivalent, Gray couldn't see him involved in a drug-manufacturing operation. Drug-running, maybe—with constant boat traffic, there was plenty of opportunity, but using what for transportation? An antique, five-horse outboard? An old 1940s-model fishing boat?

Besides, drug running was usually pretty lucrative. Right up to the moment when it turned lethal. If there were any ill-gotten gains around this side of the island they were either invested in the stock market or buried six feet under.

"You like wine?" the old man asked. He was still shoveling sand.

Whoa. Maybe he'd dismissed the bootlegging idea too quickly. "Sure. Don't know a whole lot about it, but I've enjoyed a glass or two in my time."

"Come in, I'll give you a bottle. Nobody to drink it with n'more. Keep makin' it, though—hate to see all them blackberries go to waste. Thinking 'bout makin' me some persimmon beer come winter."

The last of Gray's suspicions wisped away like fog on a sunny morning. He glanced at what appeared to be a two, maybe three room shack, and wondered if the floor would support his weight. Up on pilings, the place stood about five feet above mean high tide. Even so, it looked as if it might have been flooded a time or two.

The stench hit him before he ever reached the front door. There was no screen and the plank door was propped open by a gallon milk container filled with rusty water. "There's a nice breeze outside," he said hopefully.

"Yep. Blows right through. Poured off my mullet crock out back just before you come. Takes awhile for the smell to blow away."

Oh, yeah. Right. Poured off his mullet crock.

"I got glasses. Grab a seat and I'll fetch us a jug."

Trying to hide his reluctance, Gray followed him inside. In any sizable town, his host would have long since been corralled by some do-gooder and stashed in a shelter for his own protection. Here on the Outer Banks he was dirt poor, living in a shack that should have been condemned half a century ago, yet a damn sight more independent than most men, including Gray himself.

Social security?

Possibly. A small monthly check would probably cover his expenses with pocket change left over. There was a garden that appeared to be thriving. Plenty of fish in the water—clams, crabs, shrimp. Probably squirrels and rabbits in the woods, maybe even a few deer, although Gray hadn't seen any signs.

Except for a pronounced tremor and a tendency to shuffle when he walked, the old guy appeared healthy enough. He was planning to patch his roof, working off a scaffold. That alone would have intimidated most men half his age.

Aside from the smell, the inside of the shack wasn't quite as bad as Gray had feared. It was crammed with clutter, though. Stacks of yellowed newspapers, wooden cigar boxes stacked one on top of another. The place was a real firetrap, in fact, considering the only heat source appeared to be a small potbellied stove with its pipe poking out the window.

There was a faded calendar on the wall, dating from... *1946?*

Oh, come on! That alone was probably a collector's item.

A glass-fronted china cabinet painted battleship-gray held several mismatched dishes, none of which looked valuable, plus a few faded snapshots, a framed photograph of a strong-featured young woman, a few letters and a spool of white cotton thread. There was a humpback trunk shoved into one corner, and unless Gray was very much mistaken that was an old treadle sewing machine under a pile of rags.

"This here batch has got some age onto 'er," said Orestes, as he poured dark red wine from a half-gallon milk jug. "We had us some rain after that there early hurricane last year, made up a right good crop of berries."

Gray didn't keep track of hurricanes. He was also no wine connoisseur, but that did seem somewhat immature.

He sipped cautiously from a glass with faded decals on the sides, his expression carefully neutral. Maybe the jelly that had originally come in the glass had been allowed to ferment. It was sweet enough.

Stuff had a bite, though.

He sipped again. A *real* bite.

"Made me some blackberry brandy one year. Time you run it through a few times, ain't enough left to make it worth the trouble. Drink up, I got a closetful going to waste. I'll gi' ye a jug to take home with ye."

Gray tried to think of a way to steer the conversation in another direction. "Have you offered it to any of the, uh— Henrys?"

When a response wasn't immediately forthcoming, he took time to study his surroundings in more detail. The building itself appeared tighter on the inside than it did on the outside— an obvious impossibility. But then, Gray was no expert on construction. Under a scrap of worn linoleum, the floor felt solid enough. The interior walls were dark with age, showing watermarks at differing levels. An incongruous porcelain sink was attached to one wall of the room where they sat, its bright chrome drainpipe dangling uselessly underneath. There were no faucets.

Crude it might be, but the place was still standing after more than half a century of storms, which was more than could be said for any number of fancy beach castles farther up the banks.

Orestes sipped his wine, gazing out a window overlooking the sound. A good two minutes passed before he spoke. "She give me this piece of land to build on, y'know. Maud. Said she needed a hand after George Edgar shipped out. We'd knowed one another all our lives. Kin, way back, I reckon. She never done it legal-like, but then I never asked her to. Back then I was sleeping aboard my boat. She weren't called that at the time."

Maud wasn't called Maud?

"She used to be the *Seahag,* but I painted it out and called her after Maud when she give me this place. Christened her with a bottle of store-bought wine from up to Manteo."

He paused to finish off his wine and pour himself another half glass. Gray rocked and nodded, taking an occasional sip from his own glass, absorbing the ambience, while he filed away details. Later, he would sift through them, collate and file them into the proper slots. It was the way he worked.

"Maud, she was a right generous woman in most ways," Orestes said, his mind apparently focused on a time before Gray had even been born. "Hipped on family, though. His'n, not her'n." By that Gray concluded that Maud had considered her husband's family more important than her own. Nothing he hadn't already concluded.

"I built me this place, built it with me own hands 'bout the same time I built me that skiff out yonder." Orestes gestured toward the window. "Maud, she used to come set with me of a night back when they was a-blowing up tankers right off-shore. Whole house shook, dishes rattling on the shelves. Times we seen as many as three fires burning out there at the same time. Heard the explosions. Busted cisterns all up and down the Banks." He shook his head in remembrance. "Now'n again, I still wake up in the night, a-sweatin, thinking about them deep booms, them big fireballs. They was bad times back then, yessirree. We worried some about George, that we did."

He emptied his glass again and set it on the porcelain drain-board. Seated in an ornate and surprisingly delicate rocking chair made of varnished cane, Orestes fell silent, his eyes seemingly focused on a bittersweet past. "Yessir, she was a generous lady, was Maud. She was young back then. We both were. He hadn't have ort to gone off and left her by herself, but it was wartime. Buying bonds, saving tinfoil and tooth-paste tubes. Everything was rationed—gas, butter, meat. Dang near everything. I had me a sail and a centerboard on my skiff back then. Me and Maud, we used to sail over to Hatteras with our ration coupons for sugar and coffee and such."

All this was great background, Gray told himself. Now if he could only fast-forward a generation or so, he might learn more about the incident that had brought him here. "Good thing gas rationing ended, with the size of the engines you see these days," he commented.

"Wind's still free though. Still some fish out there, if these government fellers with their big guns and fancy trucks would 'low you to catch 'em. Folks could live real good out here on collards and croakers, same's they used to do, if they was to set their minds to it. Too soft, ever' dang one of 'em. Not a one of 'em's got Maud's grit."

And Maud was dead. Neither man mentioned that obvious fact.

Evidently lubricated by the blackberry wine, the old man continued on his rambling discourse. Gray took an occasional sip and nodded from time to time. He didn't push for dates or details. He could fill in any pertinent data later. All this was context as much as anything.

"George Henry's boy now—turned out he was the best of the lot. It sorrowed me some, him dying, it purely did."

That would be Edgar. He'd had two younger sisters, Belle and Tracy, but no brothers. There were undercurrents here that didn't appear to lead anywhere, but Gray tucked them away in his mental file.

"That wife of his, now—she was a real humdinger. Maud hated her. Told me so, more'n once. Never saw any woman set her off the way that 'un did, but then, that was Maud's way. She'd take a notion to do something and that was that. Once she took it in her head that you wasn't up to snuff, it didn't matter if you upped and walked across the inlet, she wouldn't change her mind. Nosirree, she never changed her mind about nothing. Many's the time I wish she had." There was a faraway look in his eyes, a wistful note in his voice. "Old enough to know better, we both were."

Gray started to take another sip of the sugary wine, but thought better of it. Instead, he stood. Orestes remained seated, rocking and gazing out at the ramshackle wharf where his fishing boat was tied up. "The boy—what's his name? Mason? He's got Maud's eyes, all right. If them women don't ruin him, he might turn out all right. If I write myself a will, you think you could witness it?''

"Oh, now wait a minute," Gray protested, setting his glass on the gleaming sink.

"Ain't about to ask one of them up there to do it. Can't trust a one of 'em with wills, nosirree. Maud knew what she was a-doing.''

She did? In what respect? Gray wondered, his mind scrambling to sort out the various bits and pieces he'd heard this past half hour.

"Something happens to me, I'd like for the boy to have my fishing boat. She's not fancy, but she'll not mommick you to death the way these fancy new speedboats will, a-smacking down onto every chop till they like to knock your teeth down your throat.''

It was a good opening, if not the one he'd been hoping for. "Next time you take her out, why not invite the boy to go along? If he's going to inherit your boat one of these days, who better to teach him how to operate it?''

"Way it is now, the gov'ment's got to give you a piece of paper fore they'll let you handle a boat. Back in my day, you didn't have to have no license for driving cars or fishing, nor running boats, neither. 'Course, there weren't no law to speak of back then, leastways not out here on the Banks.''

Not for those who chose to ignore the laws, Gray thought. In his specialized profession he'd had to become something of a historian. Could be the old man was right, though. About life on the Outer Banks, at least.

Clasping his knees, Orestes rose. He swayed once or twice, and a flicker of pain crossed his lined face. Gray chose not to insult his pride by reaching out to steady him. Independence was a rare quality these days, too rare to squander or to insult.

Both men walked out onto a porch that was in somewhat worse condition than the rest of the house, and Gray said, "Thanks for the wine and the company.''

Orestes nodded, but remained silent. He was eyeing the sky again, probably figuring the weather for the coming week.

Gray almost wished they would have a storm, just to verify the old guy's faith in himself.

With the tide now high, narrowing the beach to a few feet in some sections, Gray set off along the woods path again, eager to get away in order to mull over what had been said, as well as what had not. The last thing he heard before the dense thicket closed around him was something the old man was mumbling about stock going to seed.

Still talking about his garden?

Shaking his head, Gray only hoped he would be in as good shape, mentally and physically, when he was Orestes's age. At thirty-eight, he suddenly felt absurdly young.

As was his habit out of consideration for the satin finish on the pine floors, he toed off his worn running shoes, leaving them on the porch. It took a moment for his eyes to adjust to the dim interior lighting. It was in that brief moment that he felt it—a quickening of the senses that lifted the hairs on the back of his neck.

Someone had been inside.

Mariah? Lately she'd let up on her demands that he pack up, relinquish his lease and move out, but that didn't mean...

Not Mariah. She wouldn't have disturbed the atmosphere enough for him to feel.

Or rather, she would have disturbed it, only not in the same way.

After a moment he moved smoothly and quietly toward the kitchen, where he'd hidden his .45. He'd considered not even bringing it on this particular job, but having been caught unarmed a few times when being armed might have made a difference, he'd packed it at the last minute.

The kitchen looked the same as when he'd left it. Three cereal boxes backside on a counter, two of them opened, the third, behind the coffeemaker and a sugar jar, apparently still sealed. He pulled out the third box, opened it from the back and removed his gun, then turned and slowly surveyed the room. Peanut butter jar on the table, knife laid across the lid. Coffeemaker half-full but unplugged. A few crumbs beside the toaster and a few fruit flies circling two brown-speckled bananas.

Well, hell. Why would anyone be interested in his kitchen?

Or in anything else of his, for that matter? If they'd been looking for his lease in order to destroy it and declare it invalid, the kitchen was hardly the place to look. If they'd been looking for anything else...

But then, why would they?

All senses on standby, he checked out the rest of the house. His computer was right where he'd left it. Shut down, not left in sleep mode. Edgar had warned him about the frequent power glitches on the island. Told him they were at the end of the line as far as repairs were concerned, but they didn't dare complain too loudly as they were lucky to have power at all. The generators, he'd been informed, were for emergency use only, otherwise they'd likely turn up dry when they were really needed.

From what Gray had seen of the crew so far, he could buy into that.

Lowering himself onto the chair, he propped his elbows on the dressing table he was currently using as a desk and stared at the mute laptop. If a thief had come ashore looking for easy pickings, while the residents were out fishing or broiling their hides, they'd have snatched the computer and camera.

His camera was right where he'd left it, hanging on the bedpost. From habit, he kept his spare cash hidden in plain sight in a junk mail envelope mixed in with a stack of letters, none of them important or even recent. He was wearing his cell phone. His watch was a cheap one and there was nothing of interest in his medicine cabinet.

He turned his attention back to his laptop, called Gus because the five-year-old daughter of a friend had been "gusdusted" when he'd refused to allow her to play with it.

"What is it you're trying to tell me, old buddy? Somebody been tugging at your zipper?"

He punched the start-up button and waited.

And then it came to him. He was right-handed. His keyboard was always angled slightly to the right.

Gus was facing left. Not much, but enough to tell him that someone who was either left-handed or careless or both had been curious. The question was why? Gray wasn't worried about his files, even if whoever had been snooping around was a master hacker. He knew a few of those—even used them on occasion, but all of his recent cases had been successfully concluded.

As for the Henry files, all they contained at this point was pretty basic stuff. Nothing that couldn't be found in any newspaper account dated about the time of the accident. The thing had been written off as an accident, which it probably was. Most likely a discharge of static electricity.

All the same, some SOB had been fooling around with Gus. That in itself warranted his attention.

Mariah waited to catch her uncle in a good mood before confronting him about the cottage. Finally she decided there was no point in putting it off any longer. "Uncle Nat, was there a particular reason why you've been renting out Daddy's cottage when we weren't here?"

Her uncle carefully folded the three-day-old *Virginian Pilot* and then tossed it onto the floor. Looking as if he might be suffering from acute indigestion, he said, "Why not? Place needed maintenance. That cost money. Edgar never cared if the whole place washed away. Only time he even came here in the past five years was when Maud was buried. Paid his respects and left. Half Hatteras Island come over to bring food, and he didn't even stick around long enough to eat." Nat picked up the paper again, as if dismissing her.

Was that a dig at her for not holding a committal service for his brother-in-law's ashes? Uncle Nat could hardly accuse her of rushing things through just to get away.

She would do it as soon as she felt the time was right. So far, nothing had gone as she'd expected. How could she call everyone together for a solemn family service with half of them complaining about having to take time out from sunning and the others quarreling over whose turn it was to cook and whose to do laundry?

"What if I'd decided to come down for a visit and found the cottage rented out? Actually, that's what just happened."

"Edgar knew we were handling it. He paid his taxes on time," said Nat, clearly disgruntled. "About all he ever did, though. And what about the taxes on this place?" He waved his arm, indicating one of the few rooms in Maud's old-fashioned house that had not been recently redecorated. "Manteo hit us with another rate hike this year. I don't see why the rest of us should have to bear the entire burden."

"Uncle Nat, I'll be glad to pay my share of the taxes if you'll let me know how much."

"Just leave things the way they are for now. Your aunts have taken care of everything, seeing as how their precious big brother couldn't be bothered to keep the place up." Glancing up from the paper, Nat Detloff had the grace to look embarrassed. "Meaning no disrespect," he muttered, "but we all know Edgar was never interested in this place, at least not after Maud died."

"So the deal is that I let you go on renting out my cottage and my portion of this house whenever you're not using it yourselves, and with the proceeds you'll pay the taxes and keep up with the repairs?"

"Not to mention paying for cleaners to come out between renters, don't forget that. They don't come cheap, either, not even when we ferry 'em across ourselves."

In other words, don't expect much income, Mariah interpreted. "Who did the redecorating? Everything—well, except for this room—looks different. My cottage included, and I'm pretty sure Daddy didn't do it."

"Belle and Tracy. Waste of money, if you ask me. Your mama sure as hell wouldn't have bothered, even if she'd been alive. All due respect, but Roxie never cared a hoot for this place, or any of the people around here."

Deep breath, Mariah cautioned herself. *Remember that cen-*

ter, it's got to be around here somewhere. "Well…I suppose it's all right. I mean, I could have used the rental income, but if it takes it all just to maintain the cottage and pay the taxes and insurance, then I guess I owe you for managing it."

"Damned right you do, girl. Other places, they charge a flat percentage, and that doesn't even include extras, much less taxes and insurance. Flood insurance alone costs an arm and a leg."

She wondered how much commission he'd received for handling the policies. Naturally, he'd be the one to do it—he was in the business.

"Just don't go looking for any unearned income," he grumbled. "You need money, we can talk about ways and means. Think about it."

She didn't want to think about it. Mariah wasn't stupid—she knew what he wanted. What they all wanted. They wanted her to sign over her share of Maud's house so that they could sell it and let someone tear it down and put up one of those monstrous rental machines that were gradually ruining the old villages all up and down the banks.

So much for a quiet family retreat. As for what she stood to gain, the IRS would probably claim the lion's share—along with the taxes she'd have to pay after her father's will was probated. Maybe she should have majored in business instead of art. She was tempted to offer her share to one of the nature groups. Not that it would do any good, with the rest of the island in private hands.

More depressed than at any time since she'd arrived, she wandered back outside. The sky was clouding over. That meant that Vicki, TA and Lynette would be even more irritable than usual. Vicki was already the color of a boiled crab; she didn't need any more sun. Both TA and Lynette were rapidly reaching the stage where their tans took on ugly grayish tones in the creases, but they never seemed to get enough.

At least Erik knew better. She couldn't say much for his disposition, which seemed to be deteriorating daily. As much

as she hated to believe it, she was almost certain her cousin
was doing drugs.

But if that were the case, why was he wasting time here?
Wouldn't he be wherever the action was? That definitely
wasn't Henry Island.

Seeing movement in the distance, she looked up in time to
catch Gray Hollowell's wave. He was dressed in cut-off jeans
that had been worn to the texture of old velvet, an open-front
shirt that had been bleached colorless on the shoulders and
one of those Crocodile Dundee–style hats.

Stylish, he wasn't.

Welcome, he most certainly was. If she'd come here searching for a sense of belonging—for acceptance into the family
that had never shown any particular willingness to accept
her—then it was time she faced reality. Who better to help her
do that than a man who was totally unconnected to the precious Henry heritage?

Chapter 7

Gray was just setting out on a run when he saw her lope down toward the shore. He'd set out to run because he needed to think. Trouble was, he needed to be with this woman even more than he needed to think. Which said a lot, he thought wryly, about his objectivity. Evidently being down here in all this salt air had caused a few circuits to rust out.

"Want to join me?"

"Running? I'm not dressed for it," Mariah replied.

Without seeming to, he took in everything from her mid-thigh khaki shorts and her carelessly tied back hair, to the yellow baseball-style shirt with the bottom button missing. She wasn't wearing a hat. The faint flush on her cheeks could be sun, or it could be temper.

Hopefully, temper. She was a little too controlled, to his way of thinking. Emotional women were more...

Well, hell—born a chauvinist, die a chauvinist. They were just more feminine. There was nothing wrong with that, he thought defensively. Just because women were more emotional than men, that didn't mean they weren't every bit as strong. It was just that theirs was a different kind of strength. Sharon had proved that. In fact, he'd been the one to bawl his eyes out—she'd been the one to offer comfort, almost up to the end.

As for Mariah, he didn't really know her well enough to judge. He'd lay odds, though, that genuine bred-in-the-bone Henry or not, she wasn't quite as much at home on Henry Island as she would like him to believe.

Joining him at the water's edge, she said, "Sorry, I don't happen to have the proper gear."

"Me, either." His grin slipped out before he could snatch it back. One of his working rules had always been no personal involvement with any of the principals. Trouble was, this particular principal kept knocking his rules out of the ballpark without even swinging a bat. Just by standing there looking so damned…touchable. He could smell her skin, even underneath the faint chemical tang of insect repellent.

Granted, his social life was a big fat zilch. Not that he hadn't gone out with a few women in the past year or so— nice ones, and some not so nice. They'd left him cold. Including his doctor's receptionist, a Miss U.S.A. look-alike who'd turned up on his doorstep one evening bearing a home-made apple pie and wearing a smile that hinted at more ways than one of enjoying dessert.

Mariah probably couldn't boil water, much less bake apple pies. According to her father she was the "artistic type." If she happened to be hiding anything larger than an A-cup under those baggy shirts she favored, he'd be very much surprised. Voluptuous, the woman was not.

Intriguing, she definitely was.

And that was turning into a problem. Hollywood-type looks had never particularly appealed to him, at least not since he'd graduated from college.

There was nothing even remotely "Hollywood" about Ms. Henry.

Okay, so he would run with her and call it working, he rationalized as she fell into step beside him. He'd never been a dedicated runner, complete with spandex and name-brand gear, but he'd always done his best thinking when he was doing something physical. Running was usually the easiest option. Exercise opened his mind, allowed his subconscious to float to the surface. Sooner or later a pattern would begin to take shape, and once that happened he would pick out a few leads, then head for his computer and let his fingers do the walking.

She didn't talk, he'd hand her that. Shot the hell out of his concentration, or whatever the semitrancelike state was called, just by being there, but at least she didn't chatter.

They ran in silence for a while, taking a counter-clockwise route. He cut a glance at her after several minutes had passed unbroken by anything more than the sounds of birds, water lapping against the shore, a gazillion insects and a couple pairs of feet pounding the hard-packed sand.

Say something, dammit. How'm I going to find out anything if you clam up on me? The words drifted through his mind, triggering a rueful grin.

What, was he nuts? He was supposed to be an objective observer, not some hormone-driven jerk, looking to put the moves on the nearest woman. *Get a grip, Hollowell!*

Sighting a fallen log up ahead—another of what Orestes called the Emily pines, named after the destructive hurricane back in the eighties—Gray slowed his pace. "Break?" he suggested. They'd run little more than half a mile. He'd barely worked up a good sweat, but his subconscious hadn't kicked in. At least, not in a way that would do him any good.

"Sure. You didn't happen to bring a bottle of water with you, did you?"

"Sorry. If you can last until we get to Orestes's place, he has a groundwater pump and a barrel for catching rainwater. Or you might want to sample his blackberry wine?"

He made it a question, knowing the answer in advance. Her kind of wine would come with a cork, not a plastic cap—not even a metal screw-top.

She shook her head and dropped down onto the log. "Let

me catch my breath. Running through sand is different from running in a city park.''

"Tell me about it," he said. When she started massaging her calves, he considered offering to do it for her. Fortunately, common sense prevailed. Images, he reminded himself. Get her to talking about her childhood, like when she was about seven or eight years old—see what images take shape, how they fit into the rest of the picture. The players, the stress lines, the hot spots.

So he said, "This place must have changed a lot since you were a kid." It was an opening she could pick up and run with. Or not. He'd tried it before and failed.

"Mmm-hmm."

Not, then. After a while, he slanted her a curious look. "At a guess, I'd say the trees are taller—those that didn't get killed off by storms or bugs. Poison ivy's thicker. Nothing kills that off. The beach probably doesn't look near as wide as it used to when you were a pirate princess with a pail and shovel, digging for Blackbeard's treasure."

Her laugh was like music. Not the bluegrass kind he enjoyed, but the kind you heard and wondered what it was and why you'd never heard it before, and where you could buy the CD.

"Well?" he prompted when the laughter died and the silence turned into a vacuum. "You going to share the joke?"

She looked at him then, looked him square in the face, almost as if she were seeing him for the first time. "Sure, why not?" she said with a note that sounded almost like belligerence. Leaning over again, she sifted a trickle of sand through her fingers. "It's not a joke, not really, but I used to be convinced that the stuff that glittered in sand was diamonds until someone—I think it was Lynette—told me it was just plain old quartz. I chose not to believe her, so I went right on—you guessed it—digging for pirate treasure. I'd read stories about how pirates always used to come ashore on a deserted island to bury their plunder—probably to keep from having to declare it on their taxes,'' she added dryly, and he chuckled right on cue.

"I figured our island must surely qualify as deserted, with only Maud and Orestes and the other handyman who used to live here full-time. Back then, I wasn't particularly bothered by anachronisms.''

"Bet you couldn't even spell anachronism back then,'' he said, and she wrinkled her nose at him.

"Who says I can now?''

The other handyman, he mused. Probably too late, but it would bear checking out. "So what did you find? Spanish coins? Ruby necklaces? Pop-tops? A genuine Indian-head penny?''

"Whose dream is this, yours or mine?''

"Hey, don't look at me. I was strictly cops and robbers.''

"Oh? And which one were you?'' Her smile was teasing, her brown eyes sparkling. And he'd thought she wasn't pretty?

Try beautiful.

He steered her in a slightly different direction. "How old would you say Orestes is now?''

"Hardly old enough to remember Blackbeard,'' she said dryly. "Oh, I don't know—let's see, I seem to remember hearing that he and Maud were about the same age, and she was ninety-two when she died. I never realized she was that old until I read the obituary. To me, she seemed ageless. Or maybe she always seemed ancient, I don't know. The perspective of youth, I guess. She was in remarkably good health, though— at least she was the last time I saw her, which was a few years before she died.'' Mariah arched her back and then rolled her shoulders, and Gray couldn't help admiring her flexibility...not to mention a few other things. There was something to be said for understatement.

"She still lived alone except when family came for a visit. Still gardened and cooked, still looked after her chickens and walked across to Orestes's place to see if he'd caught anything in his nets,'' Mariah said thoughtfully. "Still went clamming and gathered her own oysters—I even remember seeing her out with a dip net once or twice when she got hungry for stewed hard crabs.''

"Stewed *hard* crabs?"

"Mmm-hmm. With potatoes and salt pork and pie bread and gravy. Messy as all get-out, but don't knock it until you've tried it."

"Right. That'll be about the same time I try headcheese."

They laughed together and it felt good. Like the sun beating down on his back felt good. Like the light southwest breeze stirring the hair on the back of his neck, reminding him that he was overdue for a trim. Felt good and right and healthy, like coming awake after a much-needed nap.

"Want to go back or keep on?" she said after a while. "If I sit here much longer I'll fall asleep."

"Your call. I don't have any pressing engagements that can't be postponed."

"What about your project?"

His project. Wasn't it about time to tell her? Something about the woman was definitely starting to slip under his guard. Maybe that streak of vulnerability that was so out of sync with her West Coast, big city polish. Which was really no polish at all, at least not the superficial kind of polish her female cousins worked so hard to achieve. Whatever it was, it was genuine. And damned appealing.

Trouble was, she was involved in what he was doing right up to the crown of her shiny black hair, and at some point he was going to have to tell her. With her father dead, Gray didn't even know whom he was supposed to report his findings to. Maybe he should just drop the whole thing. What difference could it possibly make after all these years?

Great. Now he was starting to feel guilty, and that made him mad because he had no reason to feel guilty. He could tell her and ask what she wanted him to do—go on with the investigation or consign it to history. Whatever role she'd once played, witness or victim, she definitely wasn't a suspect. She'd been a kid when it had happened.

"Well?" she prompted.

"Well, what? Oh, my project. Old history," he said, knowing it was both more and less than the truth. He wasn't going to tell her. Not yet. In some ways he was like a dog with a juicy bone—once he got his teeth around it, he didn't want to turn loose. "Places like this—the Outer Banks, Henry Island—they're gold mines for historians and genealogists," he said, digging himself in even deeper.

"Oh, Lord, don't tell me you're one of those."

"One of what?"

"You mean whom?" she countered.

"Whatever," he cracked, and they both grinned.

She said, "Sorry. I hate that, don't you? Go on—you were saying?"

"Actually, I believe it's your turn."

"And that's it? That's all you're going to tell me?" She poked him on the upper arm with the knuckles of her right hand.

"Ouch! You trying to raise a charley horse?"

"Did it work?" She leaned over as if to study his bicep, and underneath the pungent insect repellent he caught a whiff of something that smelled like fruit. Maybe peaches and coconut.

"Bony knuckles. I'd rather face you when you're wearing boxing gloves." He would rather face her wearing nothing at all, not that he was about to admit it. And if that didn't prove a few of his synapses were misfiring, then his name wasn't Grayson Elgin Hollowell, lover of bluegrass music, hot dogs, Braves baseball and unsolved mysteries. Any way you stacked it, it was no match for art, ballet and charity foundations.

Stewed *hard crabs?*

"Sorry," she said quietly. "I really am, you know. I guess it comes of being back here where I used to be the runt of the litter."

"Your cousins, you mean." She had no siblings. She'd spent most of her vacations here with assorted family members, both before and after her mother's death. The first time after it happened must have been a real killer.

She shrugged. "I was taller than they were, even then. I shot up like a beanpole when I was about twelve, but they were always stronger, not to mention sneakier. Besides, they ganged up."

Having met them, he could well imagine that her childhood hadn't been any bed of roses. No wonder she'd chosen to wander off alone and search for pirate treasure. He was on the point of questioning her aversion to historians and genealogists when a scream shattered the lazy stillness.

Mariah jumped up, looking around wildly. "Who—?"

"Mason!" they both said at once.

"Mason? Where are you?" Mariah shouted.

"That way," Gray said. The cry had come from a westerly direction. Which meant that either they cut through several hundred feet of dense, vine-shrouded forest or circle around and pick up the path behind Maud's house.

"Here I am! Hurry, I'm up a tree!" the boy yelled, his voice thin with terror. "I think he's rabbit!"

A rabbit? He'd been treed by a *rabbit?*

Gray dived into the thicket, with Mariah right on his heels. "Any poisonous snakes on the island?" He tossed out the question on the run.

"Not that I know of. Other snakes, though, so maybe," she panted. Jogging on a flat beach was one thing. Fighting through a dense jungle of scrubby vegetation that was knit together with vines of every description was another matter entirely. "Mason," she shouted. "Where are you? Keep calling so we can find you."

"I'm over here!" There was a pitiful waver in the voice that made her barge through a briar vine, oblivious to the thorns that dug into her legs and slapped at her arms.

Just before they reached "over here," Mariah caught sight of a strip of red tape tied around a tree. Farther along there was another marked tree. Without slowing up she wondered, marked by whom? For what reason? Had Mason stumbled on to something he wasn't supposed to find?

Gray stopped so suddenly that Mariah plowed into his back.

He was hot, damp and rock solid when she grabbed him to keep from falling. A dozen feet ahead, Mason was perched about ten feet off the ground in the crotch of a twisted scrub oak, his eyes wide as golf balls. All thought of red flags flew from her mind.

Gray said, "Jesus, son, you scared the—salt out of us."

"He's gone now, but I'm pretty sure he was rabbit."

Gray caught on first. While Mariah was still struggling to identify the enemy, he said, "What was it, a dog? Are there any wild dogs on the island, Mariah?"

Panting, she said, "Didn't used to be. Cats, though, so maybe."

"Mason, was it a dog? Was it acting funny? You know—staggering, or anything like that?"

"It wasn't a dog," the boy said. He'd loosened his hold on the tree trunk now and was eyeing the ground. "It was a raccoon, and he was coming right at me."

A raccoon. Not a cottonmouth or a rattlesnake. Not a feral dog. Rabid, not rabbit. Mariah moved forward to help him down, but Gray beat her to it. He reached up and the boy tumbled into his arms, hanging on with a panicky stranglehold.

Gray held him for a moment, then gently lowered him to the ground. "Did he act threatening in any way? It's important, son. If he was—sick, we need to know it."

Mason, still wide-eyed with fear, said, "No, but it's daytime, and this book we read in school said raccoons are noctitional creatures."

Gray took the boy's hand and started back the way they had come. "That's nocturnal. Smart fellow, though. It pays to look for anything out of the ordinary these days. Always be aware of anything or anyone who seems to be acting funny. Not ha-ha funny, just—different. Strange. Was your raccoon staggering? Foaming at the mouth? Moving in circles?"

Mason shook his head, his face solemn. "He just sat up and looked at me. When I hollered, he walked off, but he didn't stumble or anything like that."

It was hot and airless in the woods. Even with sweat stinging her new scratches, Mariah felt as if ticks were crawling all over her body. Gray broke through the bushes first, holding back limbs for Mason to follow. She hung back for another look at the row of flagged trees. Someone had cut a narrow line through the woods, marking it with strips of red tape. Who? Why? The few remaining maritime forests deserved to be protected, not sliced up like a sheet cake and parceled out in cottage-size squares.

A spiderweb brushed across her face. She was frantically finger-combing her hair just as Gray turned back. "You okay?" He looked her over and frowned.

"Let's just get out of here." She would deal with various stings, itches and livestock once she was in the clear.

Mason, his small face excited now that the immediate danger had passed, said, "But he was out during the day, and that's strange, 'cause they're only supposed to come out at night, at least that's what my teacher said."

"Generally speaking, your teacher is probably right, but I'm betting the raccoon was a lady, and that she has babies to feed. Did you happen to see her belly?"

"She was pretty hairy, but she had some pink things hanging down through her fur that weren't on the pictures I saw."

"New mama," said Gray. "She has to eat twice as much, probably twice as often to feed her babies."

"Could we go back and look for her babies? I've never even seen a baby raccoon."

"Not now, please," said Mariah, shuddering as she brushed at her arms and face.

"Talk to your mama about it," Gray said, knowing where that would probably lead. Maybe the folks up at Maud's house would stop throwing out scraps for the cats. So far he'd counted three cats, and none of them, he suspected, were household pets.

They made it back to the beach and Mariah walked right out into the water. Giggling, Mason followed her, and Gray said, "What the heck," and waded in, too, jeans and all.

The water was cold, but not icy. "Mama says it's too early to go swimming."

"Who's swimming?" Mariah retorted. "I'm drowning ticks, redbugs and spiders."

Grinning broadly, Mason shouted, "Me, too!" He belly flopped, thrashing his feet and arms, showing off, but mostly just being a little boy overboard for the first time since last summer.

She remembered the feeling from when she was a child. The innocent laughter, racing to be the first one into the water. By the time she'd reached Mason's age, the laughter hadn't been quite so spontaneous. By that time she'd been aware of the shadows, the undercurrents, the dangers that could lurk beneath the surface.

There were no shadows today, no current at all. Once past the initial shock, the water was refreshing. Gray moved to stand behind Mariah. "Drowning bugs, huh? Good idea. Want me to dunk you under and take care of all those critters crawling on your scalp?"

She bared her teeth in a wicked smile. "Not unless I get to dunk you, too."

"How about we join hands and submerge together on my count of three?" He reached for her hand, his watchful eyes still on the boy.

"Oh, goody! I've always wanted to try synchronized swimming." Her fingers meshed with his and she laughed.

Good thing he was standing in water up to his waist, because it wasn't exactly synchronized swimming he was thinking about.

Catching him off guard, she plunged, pulling him down with her. A moment later they both stood, gasping and shoving back wet hair, while a few feet away, Mason was still trying out his strokes. Fortunately, it was slack tide. There was no current to speak of and the water was shallow.

"He has a ways to go before he qualifies for the Olympic team," Mariah observed, laughing softly at Mason's antics.

"His mama should have seen to it that he had lessons long

before now. Did we drown any ticks?'' Gray waved Mason in toward the shore.

"Do you see any floating around?" she countered, wading beside him.

He wasn't looking for ticks, he was looking at the woman. She was well worth the effort, with her hair streaming down her back like wet black silk, her clothes plastered to her body and not a scrap of makeup in evidence. She shouldn't have looked sexy, but dammit, she did. The same cold water that should have shriveled his enthusiasm had tightened her nipples so that they stood out like acorns against her thin cotton shirt. That alone was more than enough to stoke his fires all over again.

"Come on, you two—race you to shore," he said, wishing he had a towel to drape around his waist. Better yet, a barrel.

Lynette was predictably angry, even after Mariah explained the circumstances. Mariah shrugged it off and headed for the outside shower to rinse off. After that, she dressed in her last clean pair of shorts, put a load of clothes in to wash and made herself a peanut butter and banana sandwich. Then she went outside to dry her hair in the late afternoon sun. Next time she came she'd bring twice as many clothes and a supply of groceries. Ice cream and Lean Cuisine. Balanced diet.

Dropping into one of the oily plastic lounge chairs her cousins used for sunning, she tried to organize her thoughts in order to get on with what had to be done. It was time she accomplished her mission and decided on a place to start over again. Clasping her hands on her stomach, she gazed up at the drifting clouds, allowing her imagination to float free.

She waited. Nothing came to mind. She tried closing her eyes. She tried focusing her mind. Nothing worked. If she'd expected some blazing revelation, it wasn't happening. No mysterious voice intoning, *You'll go to Richmond and become assistant curator at the Valentine Museum.* Or, *You'll move to Norfolk and go to work for the arts council, and in your spare time, make a name for yourself as a painter.*

Bah, humbug and other literary allusions. She hadn't painted in years. Her paint tubes were dried up, her genuine sable brushes probably long since digested by moths. She didn't even know for sure if they were among the things she'd packed and arranged to be shipped back east, she'd left in such a hurry. Grieving for the father she had never really known, her bruises still vivid and painful, she'd been intent only on getting away from her ex-husband. Bruce wasn't the type to allow a little thing like a divorce and a restraining order keep him from letting her know what a failure she'd been as a wife.

In the beginning he'd liked both her looks and his interpretation of her background—private schools, working for charity foundations, family-owned island. At least that's what he'd told her once when she'd demanded to know why he'd bothered to marry her. By then she'd seen through his incredibly good looks. He'd dropped all pretense of liking her—much less of loving her.

"Hey, why not? Your old man's a frigging aristocrat, and you've got the right look as long as you keep your mouth shut. I just took advantage of what you were offering."

She hadn't been offering anything, she'd simply been incredibly naive, but after a while she'd learned not to argue.

"Hey, my old man busted his ass working for people like your old man. Know what he got for it? A busted ass and twenty-years hard time, just for trying to help himself to a better life."

Bruce had told her he was an orphan when she'd asked how many of his friends and family he wanted to invite to the wedding. He had invited a number of business acquaintances who were also into what he called "investments."

Unlike her father, who had first introduced them, Bruce had been mostly into other people's investments, where he had no business being. How he'd escaped being put away for embezzlement or at least the misappropriation of funds was still a mystery. He'd been milking the trust fund her father had set up for her when she was born ever since he'd taken over its management, using the last of it to hire himself an unscrupulous divorce lawyer.

The first few months they were married he used to tease her about being his trophy wife. Like a fool, she'd thought he'd been trying to flatter her. She'd never been pretty enough to qualify as arm candy. Bruce had been in his mid-forties when they'd first met, but thanks to a personal trainer, a good hair stylist and the kind of clothes he enjoyed—and that she had unknowingly paid for after they were married—he looked at least ten years younger. He'd been incredibly handsome.

But the first time he'd struck her in the face, her rose-colored glasses had shattered. He'd claimed later that he'd been drinking because he'd just lost a big account.

The next time it happened, he hadn't bothered with excuses. He had simply belted her when she'd reminded him that they'd been supposed to go out to dinner with another couple, only he hadn't come home until after midnight. She'd made the mistake of asking where he'd been.

The third time he'd hit her, she'd moved out. He could have their upscale apartment. He could damn well pay the rent, too. She'd taken only what she could carry, driven over to Oakland and then headed south until she'd found a room she could afford that was reasonably safe, reasonably clean.

Her intention had been to file for divorce, but before she could find a job and an affordable place to stay, Bruce had instigated proceedings in one of those quicky divorces. He'd hired someone to find her and serve her with the papers. She hadn't been hard to find, as it hadn't occurred to her to cover her tracks. She had signed willingly. Anything to be rid of the leach.

By then she'd discovered that both her checking account and her trust fund had been raided. She'd sold her jewelry for only a fraction of its value, while she looked for work. The trouble was, she was either overqualified or underqualified for every position she'd applied for. In desperation she had taken an interim job at a small bookstore. Five days later, the regular clerk had come back to work after her maternity leave ended and Mariah had been let go. She'd returned to her room, opened a diet Pepsi and read over the help wanted ads, crying and cursing her useless fine arts degree. Not a single opening for an art teacher or administrator, much less for an artist.

Which she wasn't…not really. Not anymore.

And then, mere days after the divorce became final, Bruce had come to see her. Fool that she was, it had never occurred to her to move after the creep he'd hired had tracked her down. Thanks to a neighbor who had heard her screams and called the police, she'd ended up in a hospital instead of a morgue, with only two broken ribs, a dislocated collarbone, a concussion and several minor injuries.

Something else she hadn't known until it was too late: Bruce had a vicious streak a mile wide. He'd come after her when she'd reported him for fraud, even though the charge hadn't stuck.

She'd still been groggy from medications when Aunt Belle had called to tell her that her father had died suddenly of a heart condition no one had even known he had.

Now, drawing her knees up close to her chest, Mariah fought off tears. Sometimes even now it caught up with her. Grief mingled with anger, mixed with frustration. "Get over it," she whispered fiercely. That was what people said. They said it all the time, like it was easy to do.

So all right. She would get over it. First she would ask someone what those red flags were for. She had a feeling she hadn't been meant to see them, otherwise why were there no marks on the edge of the woods? If she hadn't plunged in after Mason, she would never have seen them until it was too late.

She would ask about that just to satisfy her curiosity. Then she'd ask the next person who went over to Hatteras to bring back all the newspapers they could find so she could study the classified ads, pick out a place that offered the most interesting assortment of jobs, get on with the memorial service for her father and leave.

Go now, and don't look back. Another melodramatic old

saying she'd heard a few times. Ingrid Bergman in *Casablanca?*

Even older than that, probably. Maud would have known. "Where the devil are you when I need you, Maud Henry?"

Chapter 8

By the time the sun had edged up over the watery horizon, Gray had done one complete lap around the island and was back at Layzy Dayz. Winded, he'd waved to Orestes in passing, but hadn't stopped. Patterns were starting to take shape in his mind and he needed to assimilate them before he added any additional parts of the puzzle. He'd been here long enough to catch glimpses of the larger picture; at least long enough to make an educated guess as to what parts were still missing.

What was missing was motive. When a wife died of unnatural causes, the husband was usually the first suspect. Edgar Henry had been out of the country, a fact Gray had checked out even though Henry had told him he'd been in Belgium at the time of his wife's death. Besides, it was Henry who'd asked him to look into the matter, saying that he wasn't entirely convinced it was an accident. A guilty man would have let sleeping dogs lie, wouldn't he?

"I don't know anything—I don't even suspect anything, not really, but it's been on my mind a lot lately," Henry had said. "I knew of another boat explosion where a man was killed.

It was before my time, but fumes can leak down into the bilge and it doesn't take much to set them off. Sometimes just a spark from metal striking metal. I don't think that's what happened in this particular case, though. The boat was too small.''

"So what are you looking for?" Gray had asked.

"The truth."

And with no more than that—a lease, a handshake and a file that laid out a cast of characters along with a rough timeline, Gray had taken on the job of discovering—or uncovering—the truth for a man who probably already had all the answers by now.

So far Gray had done little to earn his keep, other than collecting another layer of sunburn and a mild case of indigestion from living on dried apricots, cold cereal, peanut butter and hot dogs.

Item one: other than Mariah, that crew up at the old place they called Maud's house showed damned little interest in their so-called family heritage. Not a single pilgrimage to the graveyard that, according to the rough sketch he'd been given, lay somewhere in an oak grove over on the southeast side of the island.

Item two: the so-called birders staying in Boxer's Dream were no more interested in birds than he was. It didn't take a surveyor's transit to check out the avian population. Besides, he hadn't missed those survey marks. So far as he could tell, they bore no relation to any of the three cottages, or to Maud's house. And Orestes's place was at least a quarter of a mile away.

At any rate, that was happening now, and what he'd come here to investigate had happened in the past.

Item three: Orestes knew more than he was saying. Gray hadn't pressed for answers, knowing that would be the quickest way to cut off any flow of information.

Which brought him back to the few odd puzzle pieces that didn't seem to fit the picture: what, if anything, did the accidental death of two people nearly three decades ago have to do with present-day real estate? Were they connected at all?

Aside from the suspect birders, Gray had overheard a snatch of conversation shortly after he'd arrived that he was still trying to fit into context. He'd been looking around, getting the feel of the place, when he'd overheard the Detloffs and the Boxers behind one of the cottages discussing setbacks and property lines with one of the men who were supposed to be birders.

So the question remained: did the present interest in boundaries and setbacks have anything to do with an incident that happened twenty-seven years ago? Did it have anything to do with the reason Edgar Henry had seemed so concerned? Could the accidental death of his wife have been an excuse to get an investigator down here long enough to find out what was going on?

From what Gray had learned about Maud Henry, if any one of her offspring was even thinking of selling out, she'd rise up from the dead and take a horsewhip to them. Then, too, if that were the case, wouldn't Edgar have known? He'd been one of the beneficiaries.

There was also the small matter of Gray's prowler. Nothing, so far as he could tell, had been taken. Until he had more to go on, he'd put that one on a back burner. Some leases granted walk-through privileges to property owners, to check for damage or mistreatment. Might even include housecleaning services. His kitchen hadn't been noticeably cleaner, however, and his computer damned well hadn't needed dusting.

Absently, he took a sip of cold coffee and set the cup aside. Time to get down to work. First order of the day: hitch a ride across the inlet and track down the other handyman if he was still around. No one had mentioned whether he was older or younger than Orestes. Gray hadn't wanted to appear too interested, not until he'd had time to check out a few more things.

While he was over in Hatteras he could find out if any of the law officers or emergency personnel who'd been present back in the late seventies were still around. What kinds of records were kept in a case that had been ruled an accident?

If records were kept, the next question was where? That should be easy enough to find out.

While he showered, he thought about Mariah. Wondered what she was doing and whether or not she'd be interested in taking a day trip with him. He didn't want her around when he did any questioning, providing he found someone to question. All the same, he wouldn't mind spending some time with her. She could do some shopping while he prowled. She'd mentioned not having brought supplies over. They could get together again for lunch before returning to the island.

The fact that his interest might be a little too personal he rationalized easily enough. Edgar had been concerned about his daughter, probably more than he'd been willing to admit. To look after her interests properly, Gray needed to get to know her. Besides, he'd left his car parked in a lot near the marina. Might be a good idea to give it a little exercise, just to keep the battery up.

She was down by the waterfront when he emerged from the cottage, his hair still wet from the shower. A mug of fresh coffee in hand, he wandered down to where she and the kid were chipping away at barnacles. They had the hull pretty well cleaned off by now. Gray didn't know much about wooden boats, but he did know he wouldn't trust any boat with cracks he could poke his little finger through.

"You busy today?" he asked, close enough now that he could see the individual vertebrae where her shirt rode up as she leaned over the overturned hull.

She needed more meat on her bones. Nice bones—elegant bones—but they could easily carry an additional ten pounds or so. They might make a start on it today. Maybe a big barbecue sandwich and a double order of fries...

Mason looked up and flashed him a toothy grin. "We're going to get the key to the boathouse and see if there's some paint we can use," he confided. "I know how to paint. Riah said I could help her."

Riah. Ry-ah. Didn't there used to be a song about her name? "'They ca-all the wind Ma-riah...'" He sang the one line he remembered in an off-key baritone. Couldn't sing worth a damn, but he did it, anyway. It got a laugh, which was as good a way as any to start the day.

The air felt good. A few clouds—rain not imminent. Farther out, the water had that slick, muscular look indicating a strong tidal current. Oh, yeah, he was already starting to read the signs like a native. Amused by his own conceit, he squatted beside the sharp bow of the twelve-foot skiff and set his mug on the ground.

She said, "Ants."

He shook his head. "No sugar."

"Sugar on bread, but not in coffee?"

"Tomatoes, too," he admitted with an unabashed grin.

"You're strange."

Mason looked from one to the other, as if wondering what they were talking about. "Can I go ask Mr. Orestes for the key now?"

"There should be a key up at the house." Mariah stood, flexed her shoulders and worked the stiffness from her knees. Gray admired the effortless way she moved, even cramped from squatting too long. His shoulder was pretty much recovered from the crowbar collision, but he would never move as fluidly as she did.

"You happen to take ballet lessons when you were a kid?" he asked, half joking.

"What happens if I admit it? You're going to call me an elitist, aren't you?"

"Now, would I do that?"

"I don't know. Would you?" Mariah propped her fists on her hips and looked down at him.

"What's a leetist?" demanded Mason.

They both turned to the boy, who was poised to go find a key. Gray said, "You know what a snob is?"

"Yeah, it's kind of like a teacher's pet."

"Close enough," she said. "For your information, I took one summer of ballet lessons and I was awful."

"So there, too," he jeered softly, and they both laughed.

Her mother had looked like a dancer—whatever dancers looked like. Judging from the pictures he'd seen of her, she'd have been more at home in a Las Vegas chorus line than in a ballet troop.

By then Mason was halfway across the clearing. "I'll go ask Grandpop if he knows where the key is," he yelled over his shoulder.

Mariah said, "He was out here when I got up, chipping away."

"Nice kid. Strikes me he's left on his own a lot, considering all the family he has around."

"Too much. You'd think Uncle Linwood could at least take him fishing or toss a few balls with him occasionally. Erik, or somebody."

"Shouldn't he be in school?"

"He should be, but Lynn wrote him some kind of an excuse. I think she's planning on going home this coming weekend, though. Which means I might get to move into a real bedroom. I'll have to share with Vicki or TA, but at least I'll be upstairs where there's a breeze. The cook's room where I'm sleeping now has only the one window. No cross ventilation."

"I'm surprised the place isn't air-conditioned."

"I know, but Maud wouldn't hear of it. I notice two of the rooms upstairs have window units now. Trouble with air-conditioning is, once you get used to it, you really suffer when the power goes off."

Mariah perched on one of the other boats, having chosen a spot relatively free of barnacles. They were both facing toward the old boathouse, which had been built, according to Orestes, back in the late forties. Mariah said, "As far as I know it hasn't been unlocked in years. Both my uncles' boats stay over at the marina between visits, and I guess Orestes has whatever he needs in that little hut on his wharf."

Gray recalled seeing a shack no bigger than a telephone booth at one end of the three-plank wharf. He nodded and took advantage of Mason's absence to invite her to lunch over on Hatteras.

"Now? But it's—" She glanced at her bare wrist, then at the sun. "It's barely past breakfast time."

"I'm thinking about calling for a ride over to Hatteras—do some sightseeing, maybe some interviewing. For my project," he added when she shot him a questioning look.

"Ah, your mysterious project. You know, you never did get around to telling me what you're studying."

"Ride over with me and maybe I'll tell you. My car's over there. You're welcome to use it if you need wheels."

It was tempting. Mariah thought about it for all of thirty seconds. A few hours away from the island, away from bickering relatives and their dueling CDs. Away from the odd flashes of memory that still haunted her dreams, like those awful movie teasers that popped up on TV between programs—the ones that always seemed to involve an explosion with bodies flying in all directions.

Who in their right mind could consider that entertainment? To Mariah, it was the stuff of nightmares.

"Sure, why not?" she said. "Shall we invite Mason?"

Gray paused. "Do you mind if we don't? I'll take him fishing this evening after we get back. Orestes told me about a place where a plane went down out in the sound some years back. He said it's turned into a great place for fishing, sort of like a reef. He even offered the use of his skiff. He seems fond of the boy, don't you think?"

"What's not to like?" Mariah said, and then thought of the way the others, Lynette included, were forever telling him to go away, to play somewhere else, to do this and not to do that, and for God's sake, to stop asking so many questions, it drove a person crazy. "Okay," she said. "I need to pick up some newspapers, anyway."

"There you go," he said, grinning as if he'd just pulled off a major coup.

Mason was doubly disappointed. His grandpop didn't know where a key to the boathouse was, and he wasn't included on the trip across the inlet. He rallied when Gray promised him a boat trip that evening out to a place where, according to Orestes, sheepshead were just waiting to grab his bait.

As Gray told Mariah on their way across the inlet with young Josh at the helm, "I'd better bone up fast on saltwater fishing. I couldn't tell you the difference between a sheepshead and a pig's foot."

Once more he was treated to the tantalizing sound of her laughter, effective even over the roar of a sixty-horse outboard. "Should I volunteer my services, or is this strictly a male affair?" she teased.

"I don't know about Mason," Gray said wryly, "but, me, I need all the help I can get."

The weather couldn't have been more perfect, despite the few scattered clouds. A light breeze from the southwest balanced the warm late-May sunshine, producing temperatures in the high seventies. Mariah wore a pair of crisp white cargo pants with a yellow V-neck pullover. She looked casual, elegant and sexy as hell, and Gray told himself, not for the first time, to keep his mind on business. Even if it turned out that no crime had been committed—case closed—she was still a little too rich for his system.

But not for his tastes. God, would he evermore love to taste her.

He paid Josh and told him they'd be ready to leave by three-thirty. Gray and Mariah walked to the parking lot, discussing what they would have for lunch. Gray said he wanted fried chicken, mashed potatoes and string beans, with banana pudding for dessert.

"All that for *lunch?*" Mariah protested. "You're on the Outer Banks. This is seafood heaven, and you want all that heavy food?"

"Hey, can I help it if I'm just a simple country boy?"

"Simple, my left elbow," she scoffed.

"Besides that, I'm a widower. You wouldn't believe how long it's been since I've had a real home-cooked meal."

She stopped dead in her tracks and turned to him then, a

stricken look on her face. "I didn't know—you never said. Oh, Gray, I'm so sorry."

Damn. Why had he brought Sharon into this? His marital status had nothing to do with anything. Nothing at all. "No need for apologies," he said gruffly. "It's been three years, and I haven't exactly gone hungry." She could take that any way she wanted to.

Her hand was on his arm. It felt good there. She was touching him the way he'd seen her touching Mason, a comforting, I'm-here-for-you kind of touch, that's all it was.

He wanted more.

Embarrassed, he strode out across the shelled parking lot toward where he'd left his vehicle. "Jeez, what happened?" he protested, catching sight of the tan Tahoe. It was layered with dust and splotched with bird crap.

"Nothing a good hosing down won't cure," she said, laughing at his dismay. "Just be glad you didn't leave it parked on pavement. The gulls do a real number there, flying over and dropping scallops, leaving broken shells everywhere. After all this time, you'd probably need a new paint job."

Taking advantage of the bare-bones facilities, they hosed off the car, then opened the windows to allow it to air out. Then Gray handed over the keys and told her to meet him back here at half past noon. "If you're a little late, no problem." He reached out to tuck a strand of windblown hair behind her ear, using it as an excuse to touch her.

Only his hand never connected. Her eyes widened and she instinctively drew back. He swung his hand around and scratched his head, as though that's what he'd intended all along.

"See you later," he said casually, and watched her hurry around to the driver's side and climb in. Watched as she backed out of the parking slot and drove away. *Now what the hell,* he wondered, staring after her, *was that all about?*

But he was afraid he knew. Her father hadn't said anything about domestic violence, but then, she and her father hadn't exactly been close. The more Gray thought about it, the more convinced he was that Edgar Henry had been deeply concerned for his daughter's safety.

About what had happened before?

Or about what was happening now?

The thought of any man having hurt her in any way twisted painfully inside him. He continued to watch, even after she was out of sight. Standing there, his back to the busy marina, with the smell of diesel fuel and fish in his nostrils, the sun hot on his bare head, he allowed the sounds to fall away. Allowed his mind to float freely over nuggets of information, like a spent wave reaching the shore, arranging and rearranging seaweed, shells and various fragments into varying patterns, washing some back out to sea, leaving others behind.

A few pieces, caught in the undertow of time, might never resurface again.

He'd figured the docks were the most likely place to start. Luck was with him. He found the man Orestes had named within ten minutes. "Old man Harvey? That's him, right over yonder by that stack of fish baskets." The white-booted fisherman thumbed toward a bench several piers down, where an elderly man sat alone, watching the activity along the waterfront. "Comes here most every day it's not raining. Nowheres else to go, I reckon."

Gray sized him up without appearing to stare. He hadn't decided how to go about eliciting the information he was after. Direct was his preferred method, but direct didn't always work. From the looks of him, this old fellow might not remember what he'd had for breakfast that morning, much less something that had happened twenty-seven years ago. The one thing in Gray's favor was that old-timers usually liked talking about old times.

Stepping up onto the wharf, he watched a gleaming yellow cruiser idling alongside, then turned to nod to the man. "Mr. Harvey?"

Eyes clouded with visible cataracts turned his way. His vision might be impaired, but nothing in his demeanor indicated a lack of mental acuity. "Yessir?"

"Name's Hollowell. Orestes Wallis suggested I should look you up, since you used to work over on Henry Island." Okay, so he'd go for direct. Wilbur Harvey looked as if he might not be around long enough for indirect. "I've been checking into an accident that took place over there about twenty-seven years ago involving a boat explosion. Two people died. I understand you were there when it happened?"

Slowly, the man nodded his head, indicating either that he'd heard the question and understood it, or that he remembered the incident.

With the possibility of another live witness, Gray carefully considered his next question. Before he could frame it, Harvey said, "Well, I weren't right there when she blowed."

Gray's hopes plummeted. They rose again when the old man went on to say, "I was out a fishing my nets. I seed it. I heard it." He pronounced it "hyard." "It plumb near knocked me off my boat."

"You were that close?"

"Close enough."

"Tell me, do you recall—that is, was there anything else you remember?" Gray knew the dangers inherent in leading a witness.

"Well now, there was this gunshot. It come so close to the explosion, I thought for a spell I'd misheard."

Calmly, hardly daring to breath, Gray repeated, "Gunshot? I don't remember reading anything about a gunshot."

"Nope. Don't reckon you did."

"Did you, ah—mention it to any of the investigating officers?"

"Nobody never asked me. I weren't there on the island. Nobody got shot."

And as easy as that, the unexpected piece of evidence fell into his lap. Evidence that might even have led to a murder investigation had it been reported at the time. "Any ideas about who was shooting?"

"No, sir. I've not given it a whole lot of thought. Boys, I reckon it was. Back in them days seemed like there was a lot more shooting going on. Tin cans, mostly. Shoot 'em just below the waterline, see how many you can sink. It weren't huntin' season.'' He nodded, as if affirming his memory.

They talked some more, the conversation mostly general. Gray wasn't about to put the man on his guard, knowing he might need to come back for further questions at a later date. A few minutes later he left after buying the old man a cold drink and a pack of Nabs from a vending machine.

From a few hundred feet down the dock, he could see the island in the distance, shimmering above the water. No details, just the shape. It looked deceptively benign. He tried to put this latest piece of evidence into perspective, but was it evidence, or only coincidence? Even if the two things were related, all it revealed was possible method. He still had no hard leads—no leads at all. No crime scene folder to reexamine, because the incident hadn't been considered a crime at the time. No witness statements had been taken, so far as he'd been able to discover, just the usual gossip and speculation that had eventually died a natural death. A single question at the right time to the right man could have opened up an inquiry. That question had never been asked.

Gray still had nearly an hour to kill before Mariah was due back. Instead of nosing around, looking for someone else of the right age to remember the incident, or even what had been said about it at the time, he set out walking. Exploring. Picking the old from the new and trying to imagine the way the village might have looked twenty-seven years earlier, or even before that. In Maud's day, before Oregon Inlet had been bridged, before the highway. Before the tourists moved in with their big fiberglass sport fishing boats and their cozy twelve-bedroom cottages.

Money. It all came down to money. Which might or might not have any bearing on what had happened back when Roxanne Henry and her fishing guide had been killed. At a guess, he'd say not.

What about the fishing guide? Could someone have had a

grudge against him, and Roxie had just happened to be in the wrong place at the wrong time?

Gray slotted the question away as another area that might bear exploring. Henry hadn't mentioned the guide other than as being another casualty. His name had been Jack Gallins. What else had Jack Gallins been? Had he been involved in something more than guiding fishermen to where the fish were and lady photographers to picturesque sites?

From what Gray had learned about Roxie Henry, she didn't strike him as a serious photographer. The impression he'd gained of her so far was that she was a friendly type, good-natured and good-looking in a flamboyant style. Materialistic, artistic to the degree that she enjoyed nature photography, but not particularly ambitious. So far as he knew she'd never entered any shows, never had anything published or won any awards. Henry had mentioned a box of photographs. Gray would have to remember to ask Mariah about them, as they were probably in her possession now, not that he expected them to contain any valuable information.

What about incriminating information?

Something else that might bear checking out.

His thoughts returned to Mariah. If she'd inherited anything from her parents other than some old photographs and a valuable chunk of real estate, it was her mother's artistic streak and her father's attachment for the island—although from what little Gray had learned so far, he couldn't swear to the latter. His late client had admitted to having spent little time there once he'd left for college. He'd gone to Duke on an athletic scholarship, graduated and plunged directly into building a career. The impression Gray had gained in their two interviews was that most of his traveling had been done abroad, paving the way financially and otherwise for companies interested in overseas expansion.

But even after he'd grown too busy for frequent vacations, his wife and daughter had continued to spend time there. That was another piece of the puzzle that didn't quite fit. Roxie Henry, from all he'd learned about her, didn't seem the type to vegetate on an island full of in-laws, even if she had owned a cottage there. Granted, there was plenty of material for an amateur photographer, but how serious had her hobby been?

The only reason Gray could come up with was that she'd been guarding her daughter's inheritance. Probably knew to the penny how much a beachfront cottage, even a modest one, was worth. Back then, it would probably have been somewhere in the high five figures. Today, it would be well up into the six-figure range, the lack of accessibility adding to rather than detracting from the value.

On the other hand, she might simply have been trying to instill in her daughter a sense of family. Of a proud maritime heritage. Gray wouldn't judge the lady until he knew more about her—possibly not even then.

According to his map, there was a graveyard full of Henry ancestors somewhere in the deep, tick-filled woods, the late, great Maud included. Gray hadn't bothered to look for the site, seeing no real relevance. Maybe he should ask Mariah to introduce him, so to speak, to her ancestors. If she was ever going to open up, that might be the place for it. Whatever she'd tried to bury under that cool, casual facade, he suspected it might have something to do with her mother's death. She'd been a witness. That had to have had a profound affect on a child of seven-going-on-eight.

Under the dappled shade of a live oak tree at the edge of the parking lot, he leaned against a picket fence and waited for her to return. There was a graveyard just on the other side of the fence. He'd noticed several small graveyards scattered throughout the villages—family graves on family property, sometimes in front yards. So far as he could tell there were no Henrys among those interred near the marina, but that didn't mean there were no relatives there. He had a feeling he'd just latched on to one end of a long, tangled rope, one that was knotted and frayed, the unraveled strands leading to still more knots and tangles.

Chapter 9

They were late getting back to the island. Mason was waiting at the pier, his cane pole and a jar of worms in hand. His avid gaze moved back and forth between Josh and the big shiny outboard. Career plans in the making, thought Mariah.

Gray handed several parcels ashore and Mason set them aside. "Did you buy any ice cream? Mom said you should have taken a cooler."

"Sorry, son. How about the two of us going shopping next week? We can take a cooler and bring back some broccoli and spinach and a few heads of cabbage. How about carrots? You like those?"

Mason grimaced and then his face fell. "I gotta go back to school. It's not hardly worth it, 'cause it's almost summer already, but Mom says if I don't go I'll get put back."

Gray handed Mariah out of the boat, paid Josh and gathered up the largest bags. "Getting put back, man, now that's a drag. Half the time I catch a fish, it has to be put back because it's too small. You really think your mama would do that to you?"

Walking alongside the pair, Mariah saw the sparkle return to Mason's eyes. "You're joking me, aren't you?"

"Would I do that?" Gray replied innocently.

She wondered if anyone else ever bothered to joke with the child. Knowing him no longer than she had, she'd discovered a sense of humor that was purely delightful. It certainly hadn't come from Lynette.

"What do you say we try some artificial minnows and bait shrimp along with your worms?"

"You mean you're still going to take me fishing?" Mason was practically dancing by now. Ten years old, sunburned, sandy and freckled and already a heartbreaker, Mariah thought, watching the pair of them traipse up the five wooden steps leading to the front deck of the cottage.

To Mason's delight, Gray produced a carton of bait, bought at the marina just before they'd left. Mariah and Mason put the groceries away, while Gray disappeared to check his phone messages and e-mail. Mariah took the opportunity to look around the cottage that belonged to her, but was oddly unfamiliar. Some of the furniture was the same—a piece or two she seemed to remember from one of the other cottages; a side table from Maud's attic—but most of it was new and not particularly to her taste.

More Aunt Tracy than Aunt Belle, she decided. Belle favored fake antiques, while her older sister shopped mostly at big discount stores for whatever was on sale, determined to squeeze the last possible value from every penny. That came, Mariah suspected, from Uncle Linwood's lack of ambition. For as long as she could remember, his store had been on the verge of bankruptcy. She hadn't seen it in years, but she wouldn't have been surprised to find the same flyspecked calendar behind the cash register.

Mason was fidgeting in his eagerness to get started. He ran ahead on the path, and Gray and Mariah followed along, bringing a cooler of drinks, the bait, Gray's spinning rod, a cane pole and a tackle box.

Mariah had forgotten her hat again. Gray chided her for it

and she shrugged it off. "This late in the day, an hour of sun's not going to matter." She had planned to let the two guys go alone together, but Gray had insisted she come along.

"I'm not used to being around kids. I might need a hand if the fishing is as good as it probably won't be."

"Is that a conundrum, an oxymoron or one of those other thingees—I forget what you call it."

"A limerick?" He looked thoughtful, then grinned. "Probably not, it doesn't rhyme."

She shook her head. "He's going to want to adopt you, you know. I'd be on the lookout for signs of matchmaking if I were you. His mama's divorced and looking around."

"Lynette? I seriously doubt if I'm what she has in mind." Gray paused to untangle the cane pole from a wild grapevine tentacle. "I wouldn't mind having a son like that, though." His eyes followed the boy, who was almost out of sight in his eagerness to get started.

Mariah had never thought seriously about having children. At least, not since she'd realized that Bruce was too selfish ever to be a good father. That was even before she'd realized what an absolute loser he was.

But a son like Mason would have been a real joy, even if she had to raise him alone. Here on the island, with Maud's lingering influence as a guide...

By the time they reached the other side of the island, Mason and Orestes were bringing the skiff around. "She's all set," the old man said, holding the bowline in his gnarled hands.

As he scrambled aboard, Mason cast a longing look at the *Miss Maud* tied up at the other end of the wharf beside the net shed. "You could come with us, Mr. Orestes. There's plenty of room, isn't there, Riah?" The flat-bottom boat was barely twelve feet long, with three wooden seats, one forward, one aft and one in the middle. There was a bailing bucket, an oar, a homemade anchor and two ancient kapok cushions.

Orestes shook his head. Mariah thought his eyes were watering, but through her salt-clouded sunglasses, she couldn't be sure. "Not this time, son. I still got a few shingles to nail on 'fore the storm comes."

"Do I hafta wear this old thing?" Mason tugged at the orange vest that he'd obviously outgrown, that Mariah had insisted on bringing along. "You're not wearing one," he accused.

Lynn really should buy him a new one. "We have cushions," Mariah told him, eyeing the faded things dubiously. They looked as if they wouldn't even float, let alone hold someone up.

It took several tries to get the old outboard started. Once it caught, Gray throttled down and steered them out past the ramshackle wharf, then picked up speed to five knots, which was about all the antique five-horsepower motor would do.

Seated on the middle thwart, Mariah watched the diminishing island—the silhouette of Orestes's old shack, the graceful length of the *Miss Maud,* and in the distance, Maud's rooftop and the two chimneys. It occurred to her that, along with providing the old man with a home, her grandmother might even have given him the boat as a means of making a living. They were cousins, after all, or so Mariah had always heard. Second or third.

On his knees on the forward seat, Mason twisted around and shouted, "What storm was he talking about, Riah? Are we going to have a hurricane? 'Cause if we have one of those, I won't have to go back to school, will I?"

The old five-horse Johnson was nowhere near as noisy as the two-hundred-twenty-five-horsepower outboard on her uncle Linwood's Neptune, but it was noisy all the same. As soon as Gray idled down, she said, "I think it's probably way too early for a hurricane, but I haven't heard a weather report since I got here. Gray? Have you heard anything about a storm?"

"Orestes mentioned something yesterday, maybe the day before." He shut off the motor and dropped the anchor. "This look about right? I think I see the shadow of something over there." He pointed to a darker area in the clear green water.

Mason and Mariah peered at it, trying to visualize a sunken airplane.

"Looks like we're lined up about right," he said, sighting past a channel marker to the two chimneys. "Check out the markers?"

Mariah leaned closer and tried to follow his gaze. Her cheek brushed his shoulder and she moved back quickly, catching her breath. "Looks good to me. Even if it's only a deep hole or a patch of eel grass, there's probably a fish or two in the neighborhood."

He looked at her then, his face too close, his smile a little too knowing, as if he was perfectly well aware of how his touch had affected her. She wondered why she hadn't realized that first day what a remarkably handsome man he was. Handsome didn't necessarily call for flawless features, professionally groomed hair and clothes that cost more than the average family of four spent on food in a month.

Handsome is as handsome does. The phrase popped into her mind and she wondered, amused, how she'd managed to collect so many worn-out clichés.

Maud again, no doubt. Not that Mariah could recall hearing that particular one, but it was the sort of thing her grandmother would have said to a grandchild who could get into trouble without even trying.

The island was full of memories, a few of them painful at the time, but most of them sweeter in retrospect. Mariah had never gone out of her way to be obnoxious, she'd simply wanted to tag along with her older cousins, and they'd usually refused to include her. By that time she'd learned that grownups didn't want to be bothered with kids, but TA and Lynette were only a few years older than she was. It was a wonder they hadn't drowned her. She had truly been a pest.

"I think I might have forgot how to do it," she heard Mason say, his voice eager and serious at the same time.

Gray was kneeling behind the boy, cupping the small hand on the spinning reel with his own. "Keep your thumb here while you bring the rod back...like...this."

Mariah watched, feeling an emptiness that was almost like hunger growing inside her. Why couldn't she have met him first? Before she'd married Bruce—before he'd married his Sharon. Would he have liked her? She'd never been pretty, but she'd been passably attractive when she worked at it. Bruce had once called her looks patrician.

She almost wished he could see her now.

"This way?" Mason asked, his voice shrill with excitement.

The cast was made. The bait plopped into the water about three feet away from the boat. Gray congratulated the boy on not overcasting. "Next we'll work on placement," he said, and Mariah looked away. She stretched out her legs, lifted her face and closed her eyes, embarrassed to find herself envying a ten-year-old boy.

During the next hour or so, while the sun slowly settled into the sound, they wasted a lot of bait. Mariah didn't bother to bait a hook on the cane pole, leaving that for Gray. She was perfectly content to relax for perhaps the first time in weeks. In months.

In years?

That might be putting it a bit too strongly. Not all of those years had been bad. There had been good times, small triumphs and the satisfaction of being good at what she did, which was organizing and overseeing fund drives for the arts council and various charitable foundations.

All the same, she felt more at home here in a shabby old borrowed boat, with a man she hardly knew and a boy who was "blood of her blood"—another of Maud's sayings—than she did in the house where her father had been born, much less in any of the places she had lived during the course of some thirty-four years. Friends, a fishing pole, a boat...life was good.

Gray caught a small sheepshead on the cane pole. She remembered seeing her grandmother standing in the back door, telling Orestes she wanted two baking-size sheepshead, just as if she were ordering meat from a butcher.

A few hours later, the old man—not so old at the time,

although to a child he'd always seemed ancient—would come to the back door with two large, black-striped fish, already scaled, tailed, headed and gutted. Maud would score them, season them and bake them with salt pork on top and potatoes and onions along the sides of the pan, with flour and water to make gravy. She never once invited Orestes to have supper with them.

Now Mariah wondered why that was. Maud had been a fanatic about family and Orestes was supposed to be kin on her father's side.

But it was her husband's family that had always mattered, not her own family, the Wallises.

"Wake up," Gray said, so close to her ear she jumped. "Whoa, don't leap overboard." He laid a hand on her shoulder—a hand that smelled slightly of fish and motor oil and felt solid and comforting and welcome. "We're almost home."

Home? Confused, she looked around to see the island approaching through a sunset-gold salt haze. Mason was seated aft, his hand on the steering control, his small tense face filled with pride and excitement. He hadn't caught anything, but he'd hooked something really, really big, he bragged, over and over. Next time…

Island time, Mariah thought, knowing the boy would soon be back in school. The next time he came, Gray would probably be gone and so would she. Who would take him fishing then?

Orestes was waiting to catch the line and secure the boat. Gray handed out the fishing gear first, Mariah second and Mason last of all. The boy looked as if given half a chance, he would have slept beside the oily green outboard.

Mariah was half-asleep herself, although it was barely suppertime. She remembered feeling the same way after a day on the water with her mother and Jack.

Poor Jack, the forgotten victim.

"Mr. Orestes, I almost caught something really, really big— a shark, prob'ly. Mr. Gray caught a fish, but we threw him back so he could grow up. I'm going to come back after school's out and catch him again. You think he'll be big enough by then?''

Orestes smiled as he took in the boy's excitement. ''Let that 'un wait a spell, son. He's got a whole passel of big brothers. I'll take you out in the *Miss Maud* next time you come down and we'll set our hooks for one of them big boys, that suit ye?''

''Yes, sir! I'll write and tell you when we're coming so you can get ready and all, okay?''

Mariah saw a look pass between Gray and the old man that puzzled her, even half-asleep as she was.

On the way back to the other side of the island, Mason skipped on ahead to brag about the one they'd released, the one he had almost caught and the ones he was going to catch next time.

''Was that a man thing?'' she asked softly as they walked side by side along the narrow winding path. Feeling oddly as if her knees were made of rubber, she was carrying the cane pole and the empty cooler, while Gray carried the spinning rod and tackle box. ''That look you and Orestes traded. Like you both knew something you weren't willing to share.''

''Anybody ever tell you you've got a whale of an imagination?''

''Plenty of times. You like him, don't you?''

''Who, Orestes? Sure, I like him. You don't meet too many of that kind anymore. Lives life on his own terms, takes it as it comes and doesn't expect any favors.''

''Is he sick?''

They broke through into the clearing behind Maud's house. Clothesline, remnants of a garden, a couple of junked beach buggies. Mariah lingered, waiting. Eventually Gray said, ''Yeah, I think he might be.''

''Seriously?''

He nodded. He reached out to shoo away a mosquito that was hovering in front of her face, and this time she didn't even flinch. She was healing.

''Do you think he'd let me take him to see a doctor?'' she asked diffidently.

"I doubt it. Probably wouldn't even admit he needs one."

They were quiet for a few minutes, the only sounds being the hum of insects and the raucous screech of the seagulls. "I just thought... Never mind. I've got an overgrown imagination, but for a minute there I imagined he was thinking he might not be around the next time Mason came back." She paused as if waiting for a response. When none was forthcoming, she went on. "But that's crazy. He's still hauling out trash and burning it, climbing all over his house, nailing on shingles."

"For the coming storm. Right. You want to share peanut butter sandwiches with me, while we check on the weather report?"

"What, after that lunch we had today? I might not eat for the rest of the week. How anyone can eat such heavy food in the middle of the day, I'll never know."

"Hey, I come from country stock. You eat a big breakfast before daybreak, you work hard. You eat a big dinner at noon, you work hard. You eat a light supper, watch the weather news on TV and go to bed."

She yawned. When her eyes opened again, he was still there, looking big and solid against a pink, gray and gold marbleized sunset. She was tempted to take him up on his invitation, but she hated to fall asleep at the table, facedown in a peanut butter sandwich. She hadn't exactly been scintillating company today.

He did the last thing she expected. Leaning forward, he kissed her on the mouth. Lightly, lips closed, but a kiss all the same. Dazed, she watched him walk away as nonchalantly as if he hadn't just rocked her world on its axis.

She stared after him. So much for getting her act together. Next time she planned to be out in the sun all day, she would definitely wear a hat.

Mariah came awake abruptly. Staring at the ceiling, she wondered what had woken her. She yawned, scratched a bite and listened.

What *was* that awful noise? It sounded like a big lawn mower. All she could remember being used was a scythe to keep the weeds back, the only mower an old reel type that nobody ever used.

One of the old beach buggies? Did those things still run?

Wearing only her nightgown, she slipped outside just as one of the rusty old vehicles came barreling around the corner of the house at about eight miles an hour. Mason, perched on the edge of the seat with one foot stabbing the floorboards, shouted, "Help, somebody, I can't make it stop!"

She was off the back porch in a flying leap, running after the faded blue truck. "Hit the brakes! Mason, pull the emergency brakes!" She grabbed for the door as the truck passed by, but couldn't hold on. Instead, she made a dive for the homemade rear bumper, missed and fell flat on her face in a cloud of noxious exhaust fumes.

"Ma-son!" she screamed. "Jump clear!"

Struggling to get up, she stepped on the tail of her nightgown and fell again. Before she was even back on her feet the truck, driver and all, sailed over the edge of the bulkhead. Horrified, she took off at a run toward the place where the truck had gone over.

In mere seconds it submerged in a fury of bubbles, all except for one corner of the cab. With no back window and gaping holes in the floorboards, it had filled with water and sunk like a rock.

Without a moment's hesitation Mariah jumped in, feeling her way toward the driver's side door, which was tilted slightly downward. Had the window been half-open? She couldn't even remember if the thing had a window.

It did. It was closed. She dived, beat her fist impotently on the glass, then lifted her head to take another breath. By that time a few of the others were on the scene. Lynette was screaming, "Omigod, Mason! My baby!"

Tracy, her hair in pink curlers, was wringing her hands and

shouting orders. Someone—Gray, it turned out—splashed into the water beside her. He submerged and came back up again within seconds. "Through the back window!"

They both went under again, but it was Gray with his longer, stronger arms who reached through the glassless opening in the back of the cab and twisted a handful of shirt in his fist. Mariah, holding her breath, slid her arm past his and grabbed a skinny arm.

Together they managed to pull the boy through. The moment they surfaced, Mason wrapped himself around Mariah with a stranglehold, sobbing and coughing up water.

Bracing one foot on the sunken truck, Gray tried to loosen his grasp, seeing that Mariah was having trouble keeping her head above water. "Easy, son, you're all right now, we've got you."

But Mason only held on tighter, so Gray swam, towing them both in an unorthodox hold until they reached a place where Mariah could touch down.

"Here, let me take him now." Gray tried to pry him loose, but Mason refused to be pried. His weight hanging off her body threw her off balance and caused her to stagger. Gray supported them both.

By this time everyone was outside, arguing and shouting advice. Uncle Nat yelled, "Don't try to lift him up over the bulkhead, take him down to where it's shallower."

Mariah spared him a look over her shoulder as she felt solid bottom under her feet. What did he think they were doing?

Once ashore, Lynette and Aunt Tracy peeled the boy off her exhausted body with Gray's help. Aunt Tracy was scolding, Lynette wailing. Erik and her uncles were pointing to where the beach buggy had gone down, arguing over whether or not to get it up, and if so, how to go about it. Uncle Linwood said, "We'll have to hire a crane, barge it over here. You got any idea what that's gonna cost us?"

"What about oil leaks?" That from Erik, the neo-environmentalist.

"Shut up, boy!" snapped his uncle.

The women were—as Maud would have said—making over Mason, who was sobbing now, probably suspecting that this time he was in serious trouble.

Mariah stood and watched her relatives, unaware that her white lawn nightgown was all but transparent until Gray peeled off his wet shirt and draped it over her shoulders.

"Oh, my God," she said softly. "It's almost exactly the same place…"

"Don't," he said gruffly. He wrapped his arms around her from behind, just as he had done to Mason when he'd been teaching him how to cast.

He was hard and warm and she needed that—desperately needed something solid to lean on, because now that the adrenaline rush was over she wasn't sure she could support herself. Her thoughts flew back to another time—a time when she'd stood at practically the same spot and watched as her mother had died a horrible death.

"She never knew what happened," her father had said over and over. "Never felt a moment's pain." They had all tried to comfort Mariah, even her cousins, but it hadn't helped. Nothing had helped. She had seen it happen.

When she sighed, Gray dropped his arms and took her by the hand. "Come on, you need some dry clothes and then you need something to drink."

"What?"

"Never mind, just come on. I don't have any brandy, but I happen to have a jug of homemade blackberry wine." It served to break the spell so that she could move, at least.

The men were still arguing. "My God, this is just what we need with the Merrick people still here—a damned oil spill!"

"Shut up, dammit! There's probably no oil left in it."

"Who knew the thing would even start? The battery—"

"Where the devil did he find the keys? Did you give him the keys, Erik?"

"The keys were in the ignition, Uncle Linwood," said Erik. "At least they were back in February when we met those—"

He broke off, glancing around. "When Orestes borrowed it to collect firewood."

"Oh, shit—that old fool, he'll be the first one to go, believe me."

The women had all trooped up to the house, carrying Mason with them. Mariah wished she were the one to comfort him, to reassure him—to run him a hot bath and make him a breakfast of all the things little boys liked, whatever that was.

"I should go home and shower and get into something dry," she said.

"In that outdoor shower?"

"There's another one inside. How do you know about the outdoor shower?"

Gray did the Groucho Marx thing with his eyebrows, and she tried to laugh, but it sounded more like a broken sob. "Don't tell me you've been spying."

They'd reached the cottage by then and he led her up the steps. She didn't protest. Once inside he gave her a gentle shove in the direction of the only bath. Oh, well, she thought, why not? There was probably already a line outside the bathrooms over at Maud's.

She had no sooner peeled off his wet shirt and her own wet gown when he rapped on the door and said, "Are you decent?"

"Go away."

He laughed and said, "I've brought you something to put on. At this rate, I'm going to run out of clothes."

"You and me both," she muttered, adjusting the water until it ran hot enough to wash away the bone-deep chill. She couldn't seem to stop shivering, and the water really hadn't been all that cold for the end of May.

Twenty minutes later she was curled up in one corner of the couch, an old wicker affair with a new paint job and bright new cushions. She was wearing another pair of Gray's jeans—or maybe it was the same pair as last time—and another of his shirts that smelled disappointingly of laundry detergent, not the man himself. Her hands were wrapped around a steaming mug of hazelnut coffee.

"I'd have never figured you for a flavored-coffee guy," she said, mostly because she didn't want to say what she was thinking. She was still shaken by the feeling of desolation that had come over her for a moment out by the waterfront. In a rerun of all her worst nightmares, she'd seen a huge orange fireball that had been magnified in her mind over the years until it had taken on the shape of a Hollywood special-effects version of an atomic blast.

Children's minds were such creative things, capable of taking threads of reality and weaving them into larger-than-life nightmares. She only hoped Mason would remember the morning's events as an adventure and not the near tragedy they were. "I hope they go easy on him," she said quietly, and sipped her coffee.

"They'll counteract one another, I expect."

"Meaning?"

"Just that he'll get cried over, scolded and then someone— probably your aunt Belle—will insist on giving him something sweet to eat."

"The way you did me?" She held up her coffee mug.

"Hey, it's common knowledge—in cases of shock, you need sugar in your system."

"This is hazelnut preserves."

"So I hear the cook's due in soon," Gray said, unabashedly changing the subject.

"Tomorrow. Thanks for reminding me. You know what? This is starting out to be a really rotten day."

"I've got an idea."

She gave him a baleful look as if to say *What now?*

"Why not move in here? There's plenty of room. You know the place—it's yours, after all. I don't take up that much space."

"What about your project?"

He shrugged, and she said, "There's still the cot TA's been using." Better a little noise, she thought, than a lot of temptation.

A little? Try a king-size dose of temptation.

Chapter 10

The last thing Mariah remembered hearing before falling asleep was angry voices coming from the second floor. Someone was arguing. Lynette was saying, "I don't care, I can't just—"

Someone else—Aunt Tracy, she thought—said in a whisper that seemed to reverberate throughout the house, "Shut up! Now listen, we've come too far to—"

Don't wake Mason, Mariah wanted to say, but she was too far gone. She rolled over, covered her ear and slept.

Sometime in the night, the wind shifted. Blowing out of the northeast, it slammed shut a door that had been left open. The sound echoed along the passages of the old house, built of heart pine and cypress to last forever.

Mariah came awake suddenly and rolled over onto her back, staring at up into the darkness. Had that been a gunshot?

Door slam. Go back to sleep.

She turned over, jabbed her pillow a few times and tried not to think. Once she started thinking, she'd never get back to sleep. But it was chillier, and so she pulled the sheet up over her ear again. As long as her ear was covered she wouldn't be cold. Her mother had told her that as a child, and it always worked like a charm.

Sure it did.

Mariah huddled deeper under the single top sheet and wished she hadn't shoved the bedspread all the way down to the foot of the bed.

Stop thinking, she told herself. *And stop sniffing! Whatever that awful stench is, it's not a dead mouse the cat dragged in. Something outside…blowing in through the window…*

Rolling over again, she faced the wall, trying to convince herself that, because her eyes were still closed, she was still asleep. She should be exhausted, not edgy. After the early morning adventure she'd done nothing more exciting than chip barnacles, make sandwiches and wash another load of salty, sandy clothes.

And decline an invitation to move in with a man she was becoming dangerously attracted to.

What *was* that awful smell? Had Aunt Tracy set any mouse-traps? It was stronger now than ever. Inside the room—all around her, making her feel sick…sleepy….

Something bad. Really bad. She needed to get out—needed to call someone.

Breathing shallowly, she forced herself to move to the edge of the bed and slide off onto her hands and knees. Holding her breath now, she crawled toward where the door was supposed to be, telling herself she would *not* throw up.

Still on her hands and knees on the cool, gritty floor, she scrambled through the darkness until she bumped into a stool, veered left and managed to scrape through the doorway. The air near the laundry room was even worse. She had shuddering visions of putting her hand down on a dead rat.

Half crawling, half sliding on her stomach, she made it as far as the back door without breathing.

Mason—had to pull him out before he drowned!

No, no—they had already pulled him out of the water, hadn't they? Was he still down there?

Body parts floating—tiny bits and pieces—fish swarming closer, floating to the surface. *Mama, Mama!* A silent voice kept screaming at her. She tried to swim to the surface, but she was too heavy.

Floating…drifting…so heavy… Nausea and the urge to sleep faded slightly when a current of warm, humid air struck her face.

Gas?

Gas! She had to warn them before the boat exploded!

No, not the boat.

Paralyzed with fear, she opened her mouth to cry a warning, but no sound emerged. It was a dream, another nightmare—and horror of horrors, she knew how the nightmare ended. She had seen it a thousand times.

Move, dammit, move!

She shouted, but all that came out was a pitiful mewing sound. A thousand bright pinpricks of light danced in her head by the time she fell through the open back door. Gasping for breath, she gagged and sprawled on the ground, clutching fistfuls of wiry Bermuda grass.

Moments later—it felt like years—she flopped over onto her back and shouted up toward the open bedroom windows, "Wake up! Get out!"

The words came out not as a yell, but a whimper. Taking another deep breath of blessedly clean air, she struggled to sit up, and tried again. "*Help!* Wake up!" Oh, God, get them out—please get them out before someone or something strikes a spark. All those pilot lights. Uncle Nat's cigars…

She wondered if she was going to be sick to her stomach, decided she wasn't, and managed to pull herself to her feet. Swaying, she clung to the side of the house and tried to remember who was sleeping where, and who was more apt to hear her. At least it was quiet now—no TV, no weather radio, no more dueling CDs or loud whispered arguments.

"Aunt Tracy…wake up," she yelled as loudly as possible,

which wasn't very. She had no strength. What had happened to her strength?

The wind was blowing now, cooler, clean and salty. She sniffed, trying to remember all she knew about propane gas. Thank God the stuff had an odor, but was it lighter than air or heavier?

"Uncle Nat!"

And that was how Gray found her. She was clinging to the house, swaying, uttering pitiful little whimpers. At first he thought she was sleepwalking, but by the time he reached her, he knew better. She was buttermilk pale, her eyes like twin bruises.

He said, "Mariah," and reached her just as she collapsed.

"Gray, oh, thank God," she whispered. "You've got to get them out of there, there's a gas leak! Wake everybody, make them get out of the house!"

A light came on upstairs, silhouetting the figure of a man. "What the devil's going on out there? Folks are trying to sleep, goddamn it!"

Gray could smell it now, on her hair, her skin. "Gas leak," he called back. "Wake everyone and go out the front way. Don't turn on any more lights, just get out. Now!"

"Back stairs closer," Mariah said weakly.

"Closer to the leak," Gray said, knowing the appliances were located toward the back of the house, where she'd been sleeping. Stove, refrigerator and water heater—it had to be one of those.

He held her, unwilling to release her even long enough to see her face, to see if she was all right. She was plastered to him like paint, clinging with both arms, a single layer of thin cotton separating them. When the wind shifted, he'd waked up to close a few windows in case it rained. Too restless to go back to sleep, he'd wandered outside wearing only the boxers he slept in.

First the dune buggy, now this. The buggy hadn't been a

part of anything, only the misadventures of a neglected, curious ten-year-old. But this—!

The sweet scent of her body, overlaid with the distinctive odor of propane gas, eddied around them, enhanced by their combined heat. Leaving her arms in place around his neck, he managed to swing her up and carry her to the edge of the clearing, well away from the house. If it was going to blow, he didn't want her anywhere near.

Her face was still burrowed in his throat. "Did you— Are they…?"

"Shh, here they come now. It's all right, it's all right." Cupping the back of her head, he pushed it gently back where it belonged, in the curve of his shoulder.

Vicki emerged first, rubbing her eyes and whining. Then Tracy and Linwood and the boy. Mason—thank God. Next came Lynette, carrying a case of some sort—jewelry or cosmetics, at a guess. Finally the Detloffs emerged, Belle fussing, Nat still cramming papers into a briefcase. That left only Erik.

Gray started to call out when he heard someone moving behind him, on the cottage path. One of the so-called birders?

God knows, with all the shouting, it was a wonder Orestes hadn't come to see what was going on.

Belle looked around and said, "But where's Mariah? Erik, go wake Mariah. Erik? Linwood, Erik's not here!" she shrieked.

Sensing someone behind him, Gray said without turning, "Detloff?"

How the hell could anyone have gotten past without being seen? Could he have smelled the gas and run out the front door without warning any of the others?

"What's going down?" Erik asked nonchalantly. He carried a flashlight, but it wasn't switched on.

"How'd you get outside?"

"Out of the house? Back stairs. I thought I heard someone messing around the boats, thought I'd check up. Stray cats, I guess." He looked around and shook his head. "Man, this is the pits. Old place like this, it's a real hazard. How you feeling, Riah?''

She didn't bother to answer. Shrugging, Erik moved past to join the huddled family group. They were arguing about who was going to track down the leak and shut it off. By this time both pairs of renters had come to see what was happening.

Nat broke away to tell them, ''Nothing, everything's fine, go back to bed. Just a little family emergency.''

Right, Gray thought. *Like attempted murder.*

He wanted her out of there, now. Calling Belle over—he figured her for the lesser of several evils—he said, ''How about walking Mariah back to her cottage? She got a hefty dose of the stuff.'' Instinct told him the Detloff woman wasn't involved—not in this incident, at any rate.

''But where are the rest of us going to sleep? Oh, my Lord, what if the house blows up?''

''Hey, leaks happen, that's why they put a stink in the stuff. Safety measure.'' The word *safety* seemed to turn the tide, and the older woman urged a ghostlike Mariah along the cottage path. ''Come on, honey, you just need to lie down and forget about it. It's all right now.''

The hell it was.

Gray watched them out of sight, then strode across the lawn to join the men. The younger Detloff was standing off to one side, his glittering eyes darting from the men to the back door and beyond.

''Where's the cylinder?'' Gray asked.

''Around back. Thing's not going to blow, is it?'' Linwood led him halfway around the house and pointed to a pair of tanks half-hidden behind a huge fig tree. ''The grill has its own supply.''

''Where's the grill?''

''Side porch. Nobody ever uses it anymore. Tank's probably empty.''

It took less than two minutes to track down the leak. Less than that to cut off the supply. Someone had evidently turned off all the pilot lights. The equipment was too old for any of the modern safety devices. It occurred to Gray that both men could probably be charged with criminal negligence, at the very least.

He started to say something, but then Belle was back, full of hand-wringing lamentations. "I left her on the couch at your place—her place. She said she was feeling much better." Her eyes sought out her sister. "Tracy, where can we sleep? We can't go back inside—it might still blow up. Do you think we ought to go—"

"Shut up, Belle. Now listen, all of you." Nat attempted to take control, and Gray backed off, needing to hear what was said, but needing to get back to Mariah even more.

The women were all talking at once. No one was listening. Mason was wide-awake and full of questions. Lynette told him to shut up. So much for renewed maternal vows.

It was Tracy who called the chaos to order by issuing commands. "Erik, open all the windows in the attic. Lynn, you do the bedrooms and the bathroom. Turn on the ceiling fans to—"

Nat broke in, waving both hands in a slicing gesture. "Dammit, don't turn on anything, not even a light switch! Just feel your way inside. Erik, give Linwood your flashlight. Linwood, you two go in first and open all the windows, then come back out until the place has had time to air out."

"Mama, I'm thirsty," chattered Mason.

"Oh, hush up. I can't stand out here all night in these mosquitoes."

"How about candles?" asked Vicki. And when everyone turned to glare at her, she held up her hands and said, "All right, all right, I wasn't thinking."

"Now, why doesn't that surprise me?" Erik muttered.

"First thing in the morning I'll get a guy over from Hatteras to check things out," Nat announced. "Now get moving."

But when Erik started to pass him, he blocked him with his arms. "Not yet, boy. I've got a few questions for you."

Questions to which Gray would have liked to hear the answers, but he knew better than to expect any. None truthful, at any rate.

His first concern was Mariah. This hadn't been any accident. Criminal negligence be damned, someone had deliberately tampered with the system in order to asphyxiate her without necessarily damaging the house and the other occupants. Someone who was either extremely knowledgeable, extremely stupid or extremely desperate. To think one of those jerks had a hardware store and the other one sold insurance.

Once the gas cleared from the lower floor, everything would have been put back to normal, the tragic death written off as another accident. Or maybe suicide. They would all swear she'd been depressed, being back at the scene of her mother's death, bringing her father's ashes. A recent divorce…

Sure, why not suicide?

The one thing Gray was sure of was that Mariah was not suicidal. After tonight, he'd have to say she was a designated target. The question was why? A psychotic killer who crawled out of the woodwork every few decades to satisfy his blood lust?

Or something even more chilling, like cold-blooded murder for profit?

As he hurried along the crooked cottage path, oblivious to the cool night air on his bare skin, the thought of what might have happened—so nearly *had* happened—made him physically ill. Another few minutes and she would never have woken up. Her grieving family would have convinced each other that she'd been depressed. Poor Mariah—so young. So sad.

If there'd been an explosion, people would have talked for a while about the tragic coincidence—first the mother, then the daughter. Damned shame, but accidents happen, doncha know?

But if the place had blown, what about the others? It would take a real head case to blow up an entire family—and for what reason? Profit? Some imagined injustice?

All this and more ran through Gray's mind as he jogged

back toward the cottage. The birders, who were actually surveyors—he'd checked them out—were still outside on the deck when he passed by. They'd been joined by the pair from the other cottage. Gray hadn't got a line on them yet, but he was working on it.

All four stared at him. He ignored them.

Mariah. If he thought it would keep her safe, he'd get her the hell out of here, off this cursed island, if he had to steal a boat to do it. But he had a feeling trouble might follow her. Before he took her away from here, he had to know who, what and why.

Because he had a few dragons to slay.

Chapter 11

It had been close. Huddled on the wicker sofa with another of Gray's shirts wrapped around her for comfort as much as for warmth, Mariah thought about how close she had come to losing everything in the world that mattered to her. What little family she had, not to mention her own life.

She thought about the blue-glazed urn that was all she had left of her father except for the memories. She had even less than that of her mother. Because they had moved so often when she was a child, most of her deeply etched memories were of being here on the island, which remained the only constant in her life.

Never, before this trip, had she spent so many hours wrestling with the philosophical concept of death. It was strange in a way—or perhaps not so strange. Her father's death had come as a shock at the lowest point in her adult life. And then to come back to where her mother had died, to remember all over again...

Here on the island there was nothing to disguise the realities of life and death. Basic reality prevailed. Never again, Mariah vowed, would she be tempted to confuse a standard of living with the quality of life.

A calico cat wandered in, sat beside the door and licked her tail, then wandered out again. "Don't look so darned wise," she muttered. "What do you know about anything, just because you've got nine lives?"

If this was what was called a near-death experience, they could darn well have it. She wasn't into New Age stuff—wasn't even particularly religious, because she hadn't been raised that way. Neither of her parents had attended church, her father claiming he didn't have time, while her mother...

Looking back from an adult perspective, Mariah knew her mother had been the complete hedonist. Selfish, pleasure-loving, irresponsible. Yet there hadn't been an unkind bone in her body. That said something about her true worth as a person, didn't it? Mariah had loved both her parents unreservedly. She was certain that in their own way they had loved her.

This was all too heavy to get into now. Her head hurt. Her stomach still felt slightly queasy, and she stank. She wondered if Gray would mind if she invaded his bathroom and stole some aspirin. She might even steal a shower, if she could be sure she wouldn't slither down the drain. She still felt wobbly, weak as water. How long did it take to get the toxic stuff out of her system? she wondered.

Then it hit her all over again. If the wind hadn't shifted... If that door hadn't slammed...

She felt chilled to the bone, thinking of how close she had come to—to not being.

The aspirin bottle was in the kitchen. She tossed down two tablets and chased the dose with half a glass of flat-tasting groundwater.

The rest of the family drank bottled water, bringing it over to the island by the caseload. Mariah drank the homegrown variety out of sheer contrariness. No doubt it had something to do with memories of being called the little princess, as if attending a private school and studying art appreciation instead of something more practical somehow set her apart.

The truth was, she'd always envied Lynn and TA—and even Erik and Vicki. They'd had each other. Both families had lived within a few miles of each other, while hers had moved every few years, each time to a better part of town, to a bigger, showier house. Because her husband was gone so much, Roxie would quickly grow bored, and because he was gone so much, her father had felt increasingly guilty.

At least that was the way Mariah had always rationalized their gypsylike existence. They'd enrolled her in a private school just so she wouldn't have to be uprooted every time they moved.

"Well, heck," she whispered again, wandering back into the living room. She felt drowsy and keyed up at the same time. Should she go back? Was Gray expecting her to wait here or to go back to Maud's house?

Well, she had to go back. She'd left her father's ashes there, not to mention her clothes, her driver's license and social security card, along with every cent she had.

Sitting upright on the sofa in the dark predawn hours, she waited for Gray to come home. Waited for her headache to subside. While she waited, she made a mental list of all she needed to do before she could start putting her life back together.

First of all, she had to do something with her father's ashes. Either bury them or scatter them over the water—in a way, that seemed more appropriate. Then she had to order a monument.

Mariah had been waiting for a warm, fuzzy family feeling to come over her before she did the deed, whichever she decided on, but it wasn't going to happen.

The breeze blew in through the window, laden with the briny smell of seaweed. Was it only her imagination, or did it feel damper than usual? If it rained before morning, the windows would need closing. She'd asked her aunt to open them all before she left. Never again would she take fresh air for granted.

Gray came up onto the deck so quietly she wasn't even

aware that he'd returned until he appeared in the living room doorway. Even with her head pounding like a kettledrum and her stomach still undecided whether or not to turn on her, she couldn't help but stare. The man was quite simply gorgeous. The oddly shaped scar between his shoulder and neck did nothing to diminish his attractiveness. Unlike his hair, which was streaky blond and windblown at the moment, the stubble on his jaw and his body hair were dark. He was wearing only a pair of navy boxer shorts. Numbed and sickened by what had so nearly happened, she hadn't noticed either the scar or the potent appeal of the man earlier.

"Hi," he said softly. "You hanging in there?"

"Yep. Hanging in there," she said brightly. She swallowed hard and forced her eyes to lift to his face, which struck her all over again as being the epitome of male beauty, crooked nose, juggernaut jaw and bristles notwithstanding.

But it was his look of concern that did her in. That brought forth the tears she'd been holding back. Tears of sorrow, of fear—of regret for losing what she'd never really had.

Because she knew, of course. "Somebody did it deliberately, didn't they?"

"The leak?" He came into the room then, still naked, or the next thing to it.

When he glanced at his shirt, which she wore over her nightgown, Mariah sat up and arranged her feet neatly on the bright blue carpet sample under the coffee table. "I guess it could have been an accident. I mean, the stove's got to be at least twenty-five years old. I think the hot water heater might be newer—with everyone piling down there every few weeks, while they rented out the cottages, they probably needed a larger capacity."

Chatter, chatter, chatter. Sheer nerves, only why now, when the danger was past? She seemed to remember hearing that the threat of death was a powerful aphrodisiac—something about a reaffirmation of life in the face of death. Thank goodness Gray wasn't the type to take advantage of a momentary weakness.

"The valve was open, pilot lights turned off. No gas appliances in the rest of the house—I checked it out. The whole thing was rigged to fill the downstairs area—the area where you sleep—with only minimal risk of an explosion."

No more hiding behind a polite pretense, not with the ugly facts laid out in plain view. Mariah clasped her arms around her body. She was still cold, couldn't seem to get warm.

"Didn't you have a feeling something was going on?" Gray asked.

"You mean tonight or before?" The lift of her shoulders was so slight as to be hardly noticeable. She shivered, and he sat down beside her. It was close quarters, as she was seated in the middle of the sofa.

"I'm not talking specifics," he said, "just the general atmosphere. Think about it."

She thought about it. Atmosphere? The island was simply…the island. No matter how many times she'd moved, the island remained the one constant in her life. Always here, always waiting, never changing.

Waiting for what?

"Actually, the general atmosphere's not all that different from when we were children," she said thoughtfully. "I was a lot like Mason." She tried for a smile, but couldn't quite pull it off. The sound of the clock, a cheap new one designed to look old, was surprisingly loud in the predawn quiet.

Gray rested an arm over the back of the sofa and let his fingers brush her shoulder. "Yeah, I noticed the similarity. Neither one of you can stay out of trouble."

She rallied at that, and his arm came down around her shoulder. She pretended not to notice, but a smile tugged at the corner of her mouth. "Oh, sure, blame me. I unscrewed the whatchamacallit and tried to commit suicide. Why not just stick my head in the oven?"

"I didn't mean tonight, I just meant…well, generally."

"Right. Did you see me driving a beach buggy off the bulkhead?"

"Did you? Ever?"

That brought out a real smile. She couldn't help it, it was simply the effect this man had on her. Stimulating and reassuring at the same time. "No, but I did borrow Orestes's .22 rifle once to go goose hunting. Maud had been complaining because Daddy wouldn't go hunting—we'd come for Thanksgiving, and she claimed she'd much rather have stewed goose with rutabagas and dumplings than baked turkey."

"I'm not sure I want to hear how the story ends."

"Actually, there was no danger, either to me or any wildfowl. Orestes made me remove the bolt and carry it in my pocket for safety. If I saw a duck or a goose I was supposed to stop and reassemble the gun, load it and shoot the poor thing."

"Smart man."

"Dumb girl." She shook her head. "I was so determined to do something Lynn and TA couldn't do—and that Daddy wouldn't. He hated guns."

"Somehow, I doubt if your cousins would have been impressed."

"Just don't tell Mason, will you? I don't want to give him any ideas." Then she asked, "Do you have any cocoa?"

"You mean the bitter brown stuff or the packaged mix?"

"Either."

"Nope. Sorry. How about some hot milk to help you sleep again?"

"Fresh milk?"

"Canned or powdered. Sorry again."

Gray felt her shoulders droop. He hoped she was sleepy, although at the moment, sleep was the last thing on his mind. Not that she needed to know what he was feeling.

Yeah, right. Keep it a secret. It would have helped if he were wearing something a little less revealing than boxer shorts.

He rose and moved away, hoping she wouldn't notice the condition he was in. Spontaneous erections hadn't happened to him in years, and, while it wasn't entirely unwelcome—no male liked to think he was dead from the waist down—his timing could definitely have stood some improvement.

"Hey, brace up, lady. You're doing just fine," he said softly, encouragingly. It was a mystery how she'd managed to hang in there this long. Any of the others would have been having hysterics by now. Probably were, anyway.

"I'm fine," she agreed brightly, obviously nowhere near fine. Better, maybe, but she had a ways to go to reach fine.

"Look, you're going to sleep here tonight. I can lend you anything you need, and tomorrow you can move your things over here."

That got her attention. "Oh, now, wait a minute."

"Listen, Mariah, we both know something's going on around here. I seriously doubt if it involves any of the renters—" Or maybe it did, only he was pretty sure they hadn't been involved in tonight's attempted murder. "So until we know better, we have to consider your relatives, uh…"

"Suspects."

"That's one word for it."

She stood up and headed for the door, and suddenly they were too close. No longer touching her, he'd managed to subdue his enthusiasm. With the scent of her skin and the heat of her body bombarding his senses, he was once again inappropriately…enthusiastic.

He blocked the door. She didn't back down. Her eyes had an unfocused look, as though she were having trouble harnessing her thoughts.

"Whatever you think," she said, "I refuse to believe my own family would want to hurt me." She glared at his shoulder, the one with the irregular-shaped scar. Sounding drowsy, belligerent and somewhat confused, she said, "They—they might not particularly like me, but they're my relatives. We share common ancestors. My father—"

"I know, honey. Your father was their brother. Uncle, whatever." Denial, he told himself, was natural, only he wasn't as easily deceived. He'd seen things that would curl the hair on a billiard ball. "Look, why don't we sleep on it? Tomorrow we can lay everything out on the table and try to get a handle on what's going on, and why. Maybe it really was an accident,'' he said, knowing it was nothing of the kind. ''Maybe something rusted out—one of the fittings. Salt air can be pretty corrosive.''

He cupped her shoulders to steady her. Just to steady her, that's all, he told himself. The smell of propane had worn off, leaving the fruity scent of her soap, or maybe her shampoo. She went on looking up at him, staring into his eyes as if searching for…

For what? Answers? God knows, he needed a few of those himself. What was it with this woman? They were practically strangers. He'd promised her father to look after her, at least that had been the underlying message.

And now that the threat had been exposed, all he could think of was taking her to bed, making slow, mind-boggling love to every inch of her body and then, once he recovered, making fast, furious love to her until they were both too weak to worry about tomorrow.

''The other room's not made up. If you don't mind sleeping on my sheets, you can have my bed and I'll bunk here on the couch.''

She laughed then. Not her usual full-bodied laugh, but a break-your-heart chuckle that ended up smothered against his throat because he could no longer resist the temptation to hold her. ''What's so funny?'' he growled against her hair.

''You are.'' Her voice tickled his skin. ''The couch is five and a half feet long, at best. And you're what—six feet and then some?''

The way he was holding her, there was no way she could miss what was happening to him, yet she made no move to pull away. ''I could scrunch up,'' he said shakily. Or he could carry her to his bed and join her there, but it had to be her idea, because he was too much a gentleman to take advantage of her under the present circumstances.

Yeah, sure he was.

''One of us could sleep on the bed in the third bedroom,

for that matter,'' she offered. "It used to be the guest room, but it was rarely used.''

"Full of papers now.'' His lips found the pulse that was throbbing at her temple, brushed it lightly, then moved to her small, flat ear. "Been using it for an office.''

"Oh. Then I guess we could—um, bundle.''

Down, boy!

"Well, yeah—I guess we could do that. I could roll up in a blanket and give you the sheet and bedspread.''

"It's not really all that cold, it's just the wind shift. I think it might rain tomorrow.''

"Oh. Right. Then I guess a sheet and a bedspread would be enough.''

He was leading her to the bedroom, and to hell with his conscience. At a time like this, a woman deserved comfort. She needed to feel safe. If it killed him—and it probably would—she'd be safe in his arms until he could figure out what the devil was going on around here.

Mariah awoke the next morning—actually, only a few hours later—wondering if she could have added another chapter to her usual nightmare. Seconds later it all came back—the gas leak. Aunt Belle crying all over her and assuring her that nothing bad would happen to her.

Aunt Belle?

Oh, for heaven's sake, she was really getting paranoid if she could suspect Belle Detloff of any wickedness. Uncle Nat, now…that might be another matter. But not Aunt Belle. She wept over dead mice the cat dragged in.

A cat. Had she seen a cat in here last night, or had she only dreamed it? A calico cat that didn't look the least bit hungry?

So much for getting rid of feral animals. Gray might talk tough—although, actually, he didn't—but he was a lot softer than he wanted anyone to believe.

A lot harder, too, she remembered with a secret feeling of triumph. Oh, yes, she knew he'd been aroused last night when he'd put her to bed and climbed in beside her. He'd been careful to stay on his side of the queen-size bed, but even before then, when he'd held her in the living room, she'd felt his arousal. Felt it and ignored the almost irresistible temptation to take what he offered.

He would have made love to her, and it would have been good. Somehow, she was certain of that. For so long, when she'd thought of sex at all, it had been with revulsion. Over the past several years, sex had been unsatisfying, often painful and increasingly demeaning.

She could have let Gray know that she was willing—more than willing. She hadn't, only because she'd needed something else even more. Before she could afford to take the risk, she needed to feel secure, and right now that was the last thing she felt.

So she had selfishly allowed someone she trusted to watch over her through the night while she slept. When and if she ever went to bed with Gray Hollowell for any reason other than security, she would prefer to be clean, smooth, freshly shampooed and wearing something sexier than a rumpled cotton gown that reeked of propane.

All the same, the knowledge that she could have that effect on any man was sweet indeed. Bruce had often told her— among other, even less flattering things—that she had all the sex appeal of a wet sock. She had eventually come to believe him.

She yawned, stretched and yawned again. Gray was gone now. If the angle of the sun was anything to go by, it had to be nearly noon. The other pillow still bore the faint indentation of his head, and so she pulled it over and hugged it to her, thinking delicious, risqué thoughts. The kind of thoughts she'd never expected to think again.

Chapter 12

Breakfast was waiting in the kitchen. A cereal box, a can of dried apricots, a box of powdered milk and half a pot of coffee, staying warm on the heating element. Wearing her gown and Gray's shirt, Mariah poured a bowl of cereal, added a few apricot halves and ate it dry, washing it down with coffee that had to have been made weak, because it was just the right strength after heating all morning.

Her first thought was of what might have happened last night if she'd given Gray the slightest bit of encouragement. She felt her face growing warm.

Her next thought was of what actually had happened—or rather, what had so nearly happened. Last night she'd been bordering on paranoid. Hardly surprising under the circumstances. Gray hadn't helped matters by layering his suspicions on top of her own.

Things looked different in the bright light of day. It was usually during the hours between 2:00 a.m. and daybreak that her imagination tended to run amok. Four o'clock was her personal witching hour. If she woke up anywhere around that time she would lie awake for hours, scripting entire scenes in which she came off the heroine and Bruce offered tearful apologies for being such a total jerk.

Face-to-face she might be a bit wimpy, but alone in the middle of a wakeful night she was a formidable foe. Verbally, at least.

But Bruce was three thousand miles away. He could no longer hurt her. He'd never even been to Henry Island, although he used to mention it to anyone he wanted to impress. "My wife's family compound, you know." Bruce had been a big Kennedy fan. He would adopt an irritatingly off-hand manner and say something like, "They happen to own an island off the Carolina Coast—been in the family for how many generations, Mariah? Since Jamestown, at least. That was even before the Pilgrims, right, darling? We're thinking about building a place of our own there if we can ever agree on an architect."

The devil they were. Once she'd shown him pictures and described the amenities, or lack of them, he'd quickly lost interest in the island. Still bragged about it, though, to people he thought might be impressed.

But that was then and this was now. Almost the first thing she'd done on becoming a free woman was to promise herself that any decisions she made from now on would be made with her brain, and not her romantic imagination.

She was beginning to suspect that that might not be quite as easy to accomplish as she'd thought.

Even so, she was definitely going to move out of Maud's house. If the island's current inhabitants were going to choose up sides, she knew whose side she was on, and it wasn't her relatives'. Not until she'd found out more about what was going on. Because something definitely was, and she was right in the middle of it.

As for sharing a house with a man whose sexiness was all the more effective for being so understated, she was a big girl. She could handle it. No place was entirely without danger, but from now on she would choose her own dangers.

Or not.

There was no sign of the renters as she hurried along Cottage Row in her nightgown and Gray's shirt. After yesterday's excitement, everyone at Maud's house was evidently sleeping in; either that or they'd scattered in several directions. The windows were all open, but there were no CD wars and none of the usual bickering.

She went in the back way, quickly stripped her bed, dragged out her suitcase and began gathering her things. There would probably be a mountain of laundry waiting on top of the washer, as that duty, along with several others, had fallen to her.

Well, guess what. No more Cinderella, she thought with grim amusement. From now on, folks who wanted laundry done could darn well do it themselves.

The door to the laundry was open. Erik was leaning against the washer. Wearing only a pair of tennis shorts, he was going through pockets, muttering under his breath. He glanced up, a look of concern quickly replacing his scowl. "Hey, sport. You okay after last night's hairy adventure?"

"Some adventure. I can still smell the stuff. Are you sure it's safe in here?"

"Hey, would I be here if it weren't? No kidding, your boyfriend checked it out. I think he's some kind of government agent. You happen to know anything about that?"

He wasn't, not any longer, but Mariah saw no reason to enlighten Erik. Pretending a lack of interest, she searched the cabinet over the washer and reached for a jug of detergent. "Just so he knows plumbing, that's good enough for me. He's not my boyfriend, by the way."

"Whatever. You two sure looked chummy enough last night." Erik dumped a pair of cargo pants on the heap on top of the washer. "Anyhow, you're just in time. I've got everything ready." He nodded to the pile of chinos, cargos and sweaty briefs.

"Oh, goody. Here's my donation." With a saccharine

smile, she handed over her armload of shorts, shirts and miscellaneous linens.

Backing away, Erik favored her with a genuine, unrehearsed grin in lieu of the smile she happened to know he practiced in front of his mirror—the one that emphasized his dimples. "Hey, I'm not checked out on this model—sorry. Look, Rye, are you sure you're okay? I mean, that stuff last night—that could've been a real downer, you know?"

"I told you, I'm fine. Next time I'll be more careful." Let him take that any way he chose. She measured detergent, shoved aside the pile of laundry and opened the top of the washer, expecting him to leave. When there was work to be done, Erik was usually the first to disappear.

He obviously had something else on his mind. "You headed back to the West Coast anytime soon?"

"Not if I can help it," she said without even glancing up.

"Whoa, do I sense some deep, dark secret lurking behind those pretty brown eyes?"

"Stuff it, Erik. My head hurts, I've been gassed out of my room and I still have a funeral to plan. Besides, for your information, living's a whole lot cheaper here in North Carolina."

The grin faded. "Are you really that hard up? We…that is, I sort of thought Uncle Edgar left you pretty well fixed. Wasn't there a trust fund or something that didn't show up in the will?"

Having quickly sorted her laundry, she dumped in the first load and turned on the machine. "Not that it's any of your business, but Daddy's 401K ended up being a 101K, and anything else he left will probably end up in the pocket of the executors."

"What about alimony? Lynn says—"

Mariah knew what Lynn said. She didn't need to hear it rehashed. "Look, I walked out of my marriage, my husband filed for divorce and I didn't contest it because all I wanted was to be rid of the bastard." And because hiring a lawyer would've taken almost everything she'd had left after Bruce had finished draining her assets.

"Oh, wow, where'd all that come from?"

She shrugged. She thought she'd left all the anger back in California. "Anyhow, since you asked—my trust fund is gone and so are any expectations. In other words, I'm broke, or the next thing to it. I can't introduce you around Hollywood—sorry, but I've never been anywhere near the place. Don't know any show people, don't want to know any show people, so why don't you get over this dream of becoming an actor and help your father turn his business around? You might have the looks for Hollywood, but looks don't last forever, even with Rogaine and plastic surgery."

Erik let out a long, low whistle and said softly, "Wow. PMS?"

She had to laugh. "Don't push it, cousin. After last night, I'm not in a great mood."

"No kidding. Could've fooled me." His eyes glittered with hidden laughter. She didn't remember that look of secret amusement from the last time she'd seen him, but then, she didn't remember him with bleached hair and teeth, either.

She poked him in his washboard abs with a fistful of damp towels. "Seriously, Erik, you're smarter than that. Why not look around here on the Banks if you like it down here so much? See what's needed, then start your own business."

"I could say the same to you."

"Yeah, you could." The old washer finished filling and began sloshing through its cycles. With her luck, the sky would cloud over and she'd have to use the dryer, and Uncle Nat would be out squatting in the pittosporum, watching the meter spin round and counting the pennies. They used propane for almost everything because the power was so iffy, but like fuel for the generators, even that had to be boated out.

Life on a small island was not without its drawbacks.

Erik uncrossed and recrossed his ankles. With his fake tan, his blond hair and whiter-than-white smile, he really was strikingly good-looking. "Hey, I've got an idea for you," he said.

"What, you want me to open a laundry service?"

He chuckled. It didn't affect her nearly as much as it might have even yesterday. "How about an easy, painless way to make a whole bunch of money?"

"Sorry. I'd hate jail life, I just know I would. Want to stick around and help me hang the first load? I set it on short cycle."

He waved away the suggestion. "Nothing illegal, I promise. All it would take is signing your name and—"

"Don't tell me. It's like one of those e-mails from some foreigner claiming he needs to use your bank account to sneak his fortune out of some third-world country. All you have to do is give him the name of your bank and your account number, he'll deposit a fortune and you'll split it, right?"

"Man, you are one suspicious lady, you know that, cuz?"

She shot him a laden look. He could interpret it any way he wanted to. "I've earned the privilege. So what is it—you want me to cosign a loan so you can go to Hollywood and land a starring role opposite the bimbo of the moment?"

"Hey, look—I couldn't even land a role in the 'Lost Colony.' No kidding, this is something a lot easier than that. All you need to do is sign your name, and once the deal goes through, you'll be rich again."

So much for warm family fuzzies. "Your father already asked me. I said no."

"But why not? Don't tell me it's because you love this place—you haven't even been here in, what—seven or eight years? Your mother was—oops. Sorry, I didn't mean to remind you of that."

As if she needed reminding. "No way, forget it, and no. Erik, doesn't this island mean anything at all to you? Your grandparents, even your great-grandparents, are buried here."

"Sure it does. It's a great place. Kind of dull, but…"

"Tell me something—how much does one of the cottages rent for?"

He blinked at the switch of topic. "In season or out?"

GET 2 BOOKS FREE!

GET 2

HOW TO GET YOUR
2 FREE BOOKS AND FREE GIFT!

1. Peel off the MIRA® sticker on the front cover. Place it in the space provided at right. This automatically entitles you to receive two free books and an exciting surprise gift.

2. Send back this card and you'll get 2 "The Best of the Best™" books. These books have a combined cover price of $11.98 or more in the U.S. and $13.98 or more in Canada, but they are yours to keep absolutely FREE!

3. There's <u>no</u> catch. You're under <u>no</u> obligation to buy anything. We charge nothing – ZERO – for your first shipment. And you don't have to make any minimum number of purchases – not even one!

4. We call this line "The Best of the Best" because each month you'll receive the best books by some of today's most popular authors. These authors show up time and time again on all the major bestseller lists and their books sell out as soon as they hit the stores. You'll like the convenience of getting them delivered to your home at our special discount prices . . . and you'll love your *Heart to Heart* subscriber newsletter featuring author news, horoscopes, recipes, book reviews and much more!

5. We hope that after receiving your free books you'll want to remain a subscriber. But the choice is yours – to continue or cancel, anytime at all! So why not take us up on our invitation, with no risk of any kind. You'll be glad you did!

6. And remember...we'll send you a surprise gift ABSOLUTELY FREE just for giving THE BEST OF THE BEST a try.

"Average," she said grimly. Her headache was battling it out with the aspirin. The aspirin was losing.

"Average. Okay—twelve to fourteen hundred a week."

She translated the figure from West Coast to East Coast and her jaw fell. Erik hurried to say, "A little less in the off-season. A lot less if it's leased out for half the summer, like your dad let your place. I don't know what Hollowell's paying you, but I'm pretty sure it's not near what Dad gets renting it by the week. Man, was he evermore pissed."

Mariah did the math in her head. Math had never been her best subject, but any way you figured it, her uncle had been earning a small fortune renting out property that wasn't even his.

"Hey, there's a bunch of expenses, don't forget."

"I know. Uncle Nat told me about those."

"Well, that pretty much eats up any profit."

"Sure it does. So tell me—if there's no money to be made in rentals, why are the beaches all full of rental cottages?"

The air of subliminal excitement that reminded her of a kid on Christmas Eve drained away. "Erik?" she prompted. His given name was Charles. She happened to know he'd dropped the first part and insisted everyone call him by his middle name because he thought Erik Detloff would look better on a marquee.

Erik said, "Look, I don't know what Dad told you about these people, but you have to understand—"

"What people?"

"The, uh, the guys from Merrick Realty? Right now we're—that is, they're just working up a preliminary survey, then they'll do what they call another conceptual whatcha-macallit, and then we can get down to brass tacks."

Ah ha, she thought. So that's what the red flags were all about.

But they were nowhere near Maud's house. "Tell me this—why in the world would anyone be surveying the middle of the woods? Are you thinking of building your own cottage there?"

His smile was obviously forced. "Oh, well—yeah, maybe. That is, uh…"

Wet hands fisted on her hips, Mariah said, "Tell me something else then, *Charles.*" He winced, and she regretted the cheap shot, because whatever was going on here, it clearly wasn't Erik's idea. He was a follower, not a leader. Always had been. "Did the family put you up to this? Are you supposed to soften me up so I'll sign their damned quitclaim deed and give up my share of Maud's house and land? Is that what last night was all about—make me think the place is a hazard to scare me into signing?"

He looked sick. To Mariah's way of thinking, it was as good as an admission. "Don't bother to help me hang clothes, I can do it myself. *Cuz.*"

"Hey, look, last night—that was an accident. There was probably a leak and somebody—Uncle Linwood maybe—tried to fix it."

"Oh, sure. That's what must have happened." Smiling grimly but feeling sick inside, she shouldered her way out the door with the basket of wet clothes, letting it slam shut behind her.

Taking a moment to inhale the scent of laundry detergent, salt and the faintest hint of smoke, she told herself that she was being ridiculous. Paranoid. This was her family, for Pete's sake. So much had happened since she'd last seen them, she was simply behind the times. It took a while to catch up.

"Hey, Rye," Erik called after her. "Wanna go for a boat ride?"

She turned, puzzled. "With you? Why would I want to do that?"

"Look, it wasn't me, okay? I mean, like I said, it was an accident. Everybody knows these old gas appliances can be dangerous," he stated earnestly. "I keep telling Dad we ought to see about replacing everything in the house."

It was hardly a warm and fuzzy response, but it was probably the best she was going to get. Erik had always been able to turn on the charm, even as a mean little brat. He could also lie like a rug, she reminded herself.

On the other hand, maybe if she acted a little friendlier she could find out exactly what was going on, how far things had gone. Who was responsible and why. If she was going to get any answers, it made sense to tackle the weakest link. Time to come right out and ask questions.

"Okay. Maybe. Depends on where, when and in what."

"You ever seen this place from the backside?"

"Henry Island? Only a hundred or so times," she said dryly.

"Not since you were a kid, though, right?"

She nodded. There'd been a time when she'd been familiar with every shoal and channel between here and Hatteras Inlet, but shoals and even inlets could change, especially if there was a storm. There'd been several of those since she'd last been here.

"I'd really like to run something by you—these plans I've got, you know? Sort of get your take on it?"

Bingo. "Career plans or building plans?"

"Uh—both. What do you say? How about we pack a lunch and go out island-hopping? We could stop over on Portsmouth and Dredge Islands, look around and all. You wouldn't believe how much Dredge Island's grown up."

She really wasn't interested in how much Dredge Island had grown up. As for Portsmouth, it was a historic site that wasn't allowed to change, and besides, it wasn't that different from Henry Island. Larger, maybe, but that was about all.

"Is it a date?" he asked, favoring her with another glimpse of his forced dimples. "If it looks like rain we can try for tomorrow."

"Oh, all right—I guess so." She feigned reluctance. "Just let me go hang this first load out."

A few minutes later, pegging the laundry to the line, she thought maybe it really had been an accident. Gray said not, but he was no expert on gas appliances—even he admitted that much. Maybe she just needed to ease up and give them another chance. Cut them some slack, as Uncle Nat always said.

So they'd brought in a couple of surveyors. That didn't mean they were planning to replace Maud's house with one of those monstrous minihotels like the ones all up and down the banks; it only meant they were looking to the future. Maybe turning it into a bed-and-breakfast, or even a full service boardinghouse, since there were no restaurants handy. If her father had been in on it, he had never mentioned it to her, but then they'd lost touch these past few years. Mariah had cut him off deliberately, not wanting him to know what her life had turned into. Considering how often he was out of the country, it hadn't been hard to do.

But whether or not her father had agreed to a deal with a developer before he died, the family had her to contend with now, and she wasn't so eager to see the whole flavor of the island changed. Minor changes, maybe, she grudgingly conceded. Some things really did need to be updated. But the island had always been a family place, and as far as she was concerned it would stay that way, for Mason and any children the others might one day have.

Which reminded her of something else. The graveyard. Mason had mentioned it just the other day. Unless one of the others had shown it to him—and she seriously doubted that—he must have discovered it in his explorations. No wonder he was always full of ticks, chiggers and poison ivy. She hadn't been there in years. Not since her mother's memorial service, which she had deliberately blocked from her mind.

Her father had been like a stranger that day—that awful week. Years later she'd realized that severe jet lag might have been partly responsible, but he'd been devastated. Pale, trembling and red-eyed. Looking back now, she could never remember when they'd been really close—not huggy-kissy, bedtime-story close—but he'd loved his wife. He had cried openly all through the memorial service, and that had terrified Mariah, too, because fathers weren't supposed to cry. She remembered hearing him tell Aunt Tracy before they left that he wanted

Roxie to have a pink granite stone because pink had been her favorite color.

Or was it Maud he'd told? Oddly enough, Mariah couldn't remember seeing Maud that day, but then, she'd been too young and too distraught to do more than cling to her father's hand.

The next time she'd come to the island, Mariah had gone directly to the graveyard, expecting to see something that would remind her of her mother—which was totally absurd, but at the time she'd suffered from a wildly unrealistic imagination. She'd pictured a pink marble statue of an angel that would somehow have Roxie's features, her glorious red hair, maybe even one of the sarongs she'd liked to drape artfully around her voluptuous body.

Instead Mariah had found a small rectangle of pinkish-gray granite with the name Roxanne Henry and date of death. No mention that she'd been the spouse of Edgar Henry. Not even a date of birth, possibly because Roxie had kept her true age a secret, making a joke of it.

"Mommy, how come you're twenty-five years old now when Daddy said you were twenty-five when you got married and I'm seven years old?"

"It's the new math, darling. Didn't they teach you about it in school?"

And Roxie had laughed and blown out her candles, and Edgar had laughed, and then Mariah had laughed, too, even though she hadn't understood the joke.

Today, she decided, was the perfect day to visit the family graveyard. Lord knows, after last night things couldn't get much more depressing. It was going to rain. She had a clothesline full of clothes and the remnants of a headache. She was already depressed, and probably, as Erik had guessed, PMSing.

Thunder rumbled sullenly in the distance as she searched for the path. Maud had kept all the main paths cleared with a scythe and her old push mower, but evidently no one had been here on a regular enough basis since she'd died to tackle the ever-encroaching wild growth.

She came upon it suddenly—the fence made of PVC pipe. Hadn't her father mentioned something a few years ago about having a white picket fence erected? It was plain even at first glance that landscaping the family graveyard was a low priority. Vines of all kinds were running rampant. Grapevines, briars, Virginia creeper…

She waded in for a closer look, keeping a careful watch for snakes. There were more than a dozen older graves, including two with ancient cypress headboards, the carving barely visible now. Two small sunken places probably indicated unmarked graves. No one had ever said, and the few times she had been there, she hadn't thought to inquire.

The most prominent stone was a big double granite rectangle with the name Henry in foot-high letters. Her grandfather, George Edgar Henry, had been born December 5, 1921; he'd died December 9, 1949. More than fifty years later Maud had been buried beside him. Staring down at the weed-covered grave, Mariah thought of how young he'd been when he'd died—even younger than she was now.

Poor Maud. No wonder she'd often seemed so grim. She must have been terribly lonely all those years when he'd been away at sea. Had he come home at all during the war?

Well, of course he had. He'd had three children, after all. Still, it must have been heartbreaking to a young woman to have her husband—her babies' father—die in some foreign port. Had his body even been sent home for burial? Evidently so, if the marker could be believed.

To think Mariah had been feeling sorry for herself for her own wretched choice of a husband. She didn't know what true hardship was. A few bruises, the loss of material things…that was nothing compared to what Maud had lost through no fault of her own.

A brief flash of lightning was quickly followed by another rumble of thunder. Still lost in the past, she forgot to count off the seconds as, brushing away mosquitoes and briars, she made her way around the small plot in a clockwise circle, reading names on the stones that could still be read, touching others as if in silent communication. She would put up a monument for her father beside her mother's stone. Maybe a larger one that would include them both. A brighter shade of pink while she was at it. No angels, though.

She smiled at the thought, and then she came to her mother's stone. Her knees sagged and she caught her breath, staring down at the desecration. It looked as if someone had taken an ax to the name carved there. The real damage was negligible, but the intent—oh, God, that was truly sickening.

And then she realized what else she was seeing. The fence—that damned tacky PVC tubing, ran just to the right of Roxie's grave, leaving her outside the fence.

"Beyond the pale," Mariah whispered, dropping down onto her knees just as the first few drops of rain fell. "No, dammit, you're not going to leave her out, not my mother! She has as much right to be here as any of you. She's just as much a Henry as—as Maud was."

Through burning tears she caught sight of a flash of unnatural color trapped under the weeds. Using both hands, she swept away the pennyroyal and sandspurs.

A plastic rose. Someone had laid a cheap, faded-red plastic rose on her mother's grave. She didn't know whether to curse or to cry even harder. "Oh, God, this just gets— I can't— I'll be back tomorrow, Mama," she said, choking on tears and of all things, laughter. Here she was, on her knees, getting drenched, while she talked to a headstone. "I've got to go take in the damn-blasted clothes before they get any wetter, but tomorrow I'll come back and make your place nice again. Maybe I can find something pretty to transplant, and while I'm at it, I'll tear down that awful fence!"

Her throat ached. Her head ached. She was soaking wet and probably wallowing in poison ivy, but she didn't care enough to hurry. Twice she stumbled on one of the old footstones because she was crying too hard to see where she was going.

One more step and she would have run into him. "Oh, God," she blurted, "not again."

Gray opened his arms, and with one last sob, she walked into his embrace.

Chapter 13

"We really must stop meeting like this," she said, laughing, weeping, clinging. Gray remained silent. Nearby, lightning stabbed the water. A deafening clap of thunder shook the earth a moment later. Mariah gasped and tried unsuccessfully to swallow her sobs.

He didn't ask why she was crying, he simply held her, which was what she needed most in the world at that moment. The next thunderclap came hard on the heels of the last, and he said, "We'd better get out of here, away from these trees."

"This is so embarrassing," she said, rubbing her wet face against his shirt.

"Hey, my arms are your arms. Just say the word."

She managed a broken laugh, and then the rain came down in a solid deluge, blocking out everything beyond the arms that were holding her. Pulling away, she lifted her face to the rain and said, "Screw the clothes."

Gray raised both eyebrows and said, "Right. Screw the clothes." He hurried her toward the nearest shelter, which fortunately happened to be Layzy Dayz. If he'd taken her back to Maud's house Mariah might have said something she would later regret.

Once inside, she headed for the bedroom that had always been hers. The few times she'd been in the cottage before, she hadn't felt free to wander, not with Gray's belongings scattered throughout the house.

Now she opened the door on a room that had changed beyond recognition. Stunned, she could only stare. The old furniture had been an eclectic assortment of bits and pieces collected over some twenty-odd years, each one carefully chosen for reasons she'd long since forgotten. Her father had never questioned her various yard-sale treasures. Even as a child she'd been allowed to choose her own bedroom furniture, possibly as compensation for being uprooted so frequently. As much as they had loved her, and she had no reason to doubt that, her father had always been...*detached* was the word that came to mind. And Roxie had been, at best, a casual mother. That was probably why Mariah, needing a sense of security, had instinctively surrounded herself with things that had a history.

Now, instead of the old and familiar, she was surrounded by the new and tacky.

Gray hadn't lingered once she pushed him out and closed the door. Standing there, her arms clasped around her, she glared at the once lovely cypress-paneled walls that had been painted lime-green, her least favorite color. At the discount-store furniture, the red-and-green-plaid bedspread and matching curtains.

His computer and various file folders and clippings were there. He'd been using it as an office, she remembered now.

She wanted it back the way it was. The unfinished walls that had gradually darkened with age, the cast-off furniture, the rag rugs and limp white plissé curtains. This was her room, dammit! They had no right!

Someone rapped on the door and opened it. Gray handed her a towel, a soft, long-sleeved shirt and a pair of jeans. ''You know the drill by now,'' he told her, amusement coloring his voice. "I make the coffee, while you dry off and change clothes." He studied her as if looking for signs of imminent collapse, then began gathering up papers and stuffing them into folders.

"At this rate," she said dryly, "we're both going to be wearing sarongs."

"Hot damn. I get the bedspread. You can have the curtains."

She tried to laugh but couldn't quite pull it off. *Déjà vu,* she thought when he'd left taking the papers that had been spread over the bed with him. If fate was trying to send her a message, it had picked a lousy way to do it.

She purely hated it when she got like this. She almost never cried. When she did, her throat ached, her nose got all stopped up and she made these awful, embarrassing noises, mostly wails and squeaks. Quiet, ladylike weeping was not among her accomplishments.

Outside, rain continued to drum down, beating against the windows. In a veiled ballet, trees bent and swayed as the squall blew across the island and on out to sea. Lightning came less frequently now, the thunder slower to follow. One of the plastic porch chairs blew over—she knew the sound, having heard it often as a child.

"Eddie, why don't we get some of that wooden porch furniture from that place over in Frisco?"

"What's wrong with what we have? It's comfortable and it dries off easy."

"Yes, but we've had it for two years. Everybody has it. I want something new."

Her mother had always wanted something new. Looking back, Mariah marveled that she hadn't insisted on a new husband and a new daughter. The stoic Edgar had always pretended to brush off what he called Roxie's huggy-kissy attacks, but he hadn't tried too hard. He'd loved her. Who wouldn't? Not only had she been gorgeous, she'd never had an unkind word to say about anyone. Mariah had heard her father say that over and over, and as young as she'd been at the time of her mother's death, she knew it was true.

The thought of what someone had done to her grave—that pitiful grave with its scarred marker just outside the sagging length of white plastic pipe—brought forth a fresh outburst of sobs and squeaks. Then she thought about the plastic rose and let out a wail that had Gray hurrying to see if she'd hurt herself.

"This is just so stupid," she said, half sobbing, half laughing. "I hate it when I get started on one of these crying jags. I never cry—almost never."

He wisely said nothing, while she mopped her face with the shirt he'd given her. She sniffed and said, "I guess I've been saving up, but I'm done now, honestly. Got it all out of my system." Her voice took on a quasi-military decisiveness that lasted all of ten seconds. "I'm going to get on with what I came here to do and then—and then I'm going to—to g-go somewhere else. They can have their p-precious island if that's how they f-feel! Oh, shoot!" She swabbed at her eyes with her shirttail.

"You have my full support," he said gravely. "You're going to do something here and then you're going to go somewhere else and to hell with everyone, does that pretty much cover it?" He peeled off her wet shirt, took the dry one she still clutched in her hand and put it on, first one arm, then the other, over her damp bra, his touch as impersonal as if she were a department store mannequin.

Look at me, she shouted silently. *Touch me. Can't you see I need you? I'm falling apart!*

Methodically, he buttoned the shirt and then dropped the towel over her wet hair. A used towel, one that smelled of his shaving soap. "But in the meantime," he said, "you need to get warm inside and out. After what happened last night, and just now, you've got some rest to catch up on. Want me to go pack your things and bring them over here?"

"What? Oh. They're all on the clothesline," she said with a teary smile. "Most of them, anyway. I didn't bring all that much—I wasn't planning on staying this long.'' She gave a long, shuddering sigh. "You know what? This hasn't exactly been a banner day.''

"I can tell," he said gently, rubbing her hair with the towel.

"I'll have rats' nests, but don't stop, it feels too good.''

She stood head-down before him, while he towel-dried her hair. "Want to tell me what happened this time?" he asked.

"Not especially." Glumly, she stared down at her sandy feet and proceeded to pour it all out, in no particular sequence. The pink marble angel that had turned out to be a plain vertical marker, more gray than pink, with only a name and a single date. "The plastic flower, though—that was the final blow.'' She sniffed and said, "I need a tissue,'' and he held out a handkerchief, clean and smelling of detergent.

"The plastic flower?'' he prompted.

"And the fence.'' Resisting the urge to crawl into his arms for the comfort he offered—or worse, to shove him down onto the bed and give in to the irrational sexual attraction that seemed to flare up whenever he touched her—she managed to pull herself together. "They were going to put up a picket fence around the graveyard—that is, I guess Aunt Tracy was. She usually does stuff because Uncle Linwood gets everything wholesale.''

Gray nodded as if he knew exactly what she was talking about. He glanced at the room's only chair, and then at the bed. And then he led her back into the living room and sat her down on the wicker sofa with the bright, tropical print cushions, and she thought, Oh, God—he knows what I was thinking. How horribly embarrassing.

He chose the armchair farthest from the sofa and sat down. "Go on. Aunt Tracy puts up a fence because Uncle Linwood gets everything wholesale.''

Mariah hiccuped, sobbed and then laughed. "I hate making a spectacle of myself, it's so gauche. All right, what happened was that they—I guess it was Aunt Tracy, but I don't know for sure, it could even have been Maud. Anyway, someone must have paced off where the fence was supposed to go and then someone else—the men, I guess, or maybe she hired it done—they set up this cheap plastic pipe as a guideline to show where the real fence was supposed to go. There was some left over from when they plumbed in Maud's new washer. But the thing is, they—they left Mama outside.''

She fought back a fresh burst of tears. "Sorry," she muttered. "I don't cry like normal people, I save up just so I can make a fool of myself."

When Gray got up from his chair and settled beside her, pressing her wet head against his shoulder and stroking her back with one hand, she told herself that in the grand scheme of things, none of this really mattered. Not bawling her eyes out at the least provocation—not even this wildly inappropriate sexual thing that flared up whenever he touched her.

The fact that it wasn't entirely one-sided made it awkward, though, because she wasn't into casual sex. Wasn't into sex at all, yet all she had to do was look at him for her erogenous zones to come alive and her mind to take off on an X-rated tangent. The man was trouble waiting to happen. It was a good thing she'd soon be leaving.

Turning her face toward him, she blotted her eyes on his chest and said, "There goes your last clean shirt. Good thing we've got dryers all over the place. Does the one here still work?"

"It works. I seem to have used it a lot since you got here, matter of fact."

"Is that a sly dig?"

"You betcha. Sure you're not listed with the Coast Guard as an unmarked water hazard?"

She had to laugh. His arm tightened around her and she said, "Thanks for putting up with all the waterworks. Honestly, I'm normally about as emotional as a rock, just ask anyone. I don't know what's got into me lately."

He brushed his lips along her hairline and murmured something she couldn't quite make out, because of the suffocating rhythm of her heart. If he didn't stop stroking her shoulder with his thumb, she might just grab his hand and put it where she wanted it. Which wasn't on her shoulder.

"Mariah, maybe it's not such a good idea, after all—your moving in here."

"You're rescinding your invitation?" She pulled back to look at him. Those gray-green eyes were unusually dark, the lids lowered so that he looked half-asleep.

He wasn't asleep. "I don't think you're ready for—"

"For what? What do you think will happen if I move in?"

"Dammit, you know what I'm talking about. It's hardly something I can keep secret."

"What makes you think I'm not ready?"

He stiffened beside her, withdrawing his arm, but not moving away. She waited. "Well?"

"Riah, your father trusted me."

"So? I trust you. At least I don't think you had anything to do with all the junk that's been going on around here. You don't know me well enough to try to kill me."

With a muffled oath, he turned to her then, dragging her across his lap and pushing her back against the sofa pillows. "Don't say that. Nobody's going to kill you, if I have to take you back home with me to keep you safe."

"I'm safe right now. You're here. You want me—I can, um—sort of tell." The evidence was prodding her in the hip. "So why don't we—you know. Make love?" Darn it, she hadn't meant to say that, she'd meant to say *Why don't we have sex?* Mentioning love would only scare him away, and that was the last thing she wanted to do.

He closed his eyes, laughed, and then he swore softly under his breath. "Honey, to put it crudely, acute horniness is rarely fatal. I'll get over it. You don't have to—"

She shut him up, using the most direct method at her disposal. She kissed him.

It was almost like being gassed again, she decided, just before all rational thought blinked out. The same soaring, sinking feeling of being disconnected.

Fueled by mutual desire, the kiss exploded in a tantalizing

frenzy of hunger and need. Drunk on the taste of him, she thought with wonder that this was so right it was meant to be. That regardless of what else happened, this moment just might be the pivot point of her entire life.

Her breasts swelled to his touch as he unfastened her bra and pushed it away, fingering her thrusting nipples. She wanted to take off her shirt—everything—but she didn't want him to stop kissing her long enough to undress.

How could she get him out of his clothes? She was lying on his zipper and she didn't really want to move away. Eight years of marriage on top of a single brief relationship, and she had all the finesse of a fourteen-year-old in the back seat of a compact car.

"No, don't stop," she whispered as he began to pull away.

"Honey, this is a mistake." He smoothed her dangling bra down over her breasts.

"No, it's not. It doesn't have to mean anything, it's only—only—"

"Right. It's only. Riah, it wouldn't be fair to you—to either of us. Heightened emotions—this kind of thing happens a lot of times after…"

She sat up then, straightening her clothes, feeling mean and unwanted and unattractive. "Oh, for heaven's sake, don't start spouting pop psychology, I don't want to hear it." She managed to button her shirt all the way up to her chin, only to find an extra button left over.

He moved her hands away, unbuttoned and rebuttoned her shirt—his shirt—and all the while she stared disdainfully at a spot just above his left shoulder. "I think I'll go back to Maud's house now," she said with all the dignity she could muster.

"You're sure you want to do that?"

She leveled him with a look. Annihilated him with a flat stare, feeling ragged and unwanted and far out of her depth.

Since she had last stayed here, the living room walls, once raw paneling like the rest of the house, had been painted bright yellow, all the furniture either painted or replaced, the faded old denim cushions covered with a hot, tropical print. All that served as further justification for her anger.

Better that than being angry over the fact that she was half in love with a man she hardly knew—a man who wouldn't even take what she offered because it might complicate his life.

What about hers? What the bloody hell about her life?

Chapter 14

Mariah managed to avoid Gray as well as the others for the rest of the day. She hadn't seen Lynn at all since the truck episode. According to Aunt Tracy, she'd spent most of the day over on Hatteras shopping, and came back with a migraine. Mariah only hoped someone was keeping an eye on Mason.

Feeling dull and muddled, she dumped into the dryer the basket of wet laundry that someone had brought in off the line. While she waited for the machine to do its thing, she climbed up onto the stepstool and cleaned out the cluttered shelves. It obviously hadn't been done in a zillion years.

That task finished, she set up the ironing board and pressed her uncles' shirts, even though they didn't really need it. Busy work. Recognizing it for what it was, she did it nevertheless. By the time she unplugged the heavy steam iron and plopped it on the washer to cool, she had almost convinced herself that the Boxers and the Detloffs weren't really guilty of anything other than wanting to move forward with the times. She'd been under a lot of stress lately—for the past five years, at least. It was no wonder she was jumping at shadows. Throw in the hairy adventures of a ten-year-old Superman, a highly questionable "accident," plus an unexpected attack of lust, and…

Well, it was no wonder, that's all.

Maybe it was a Southern thing—this obsession with family. She hadn't even realized she was Southern—at least, she hadn't considered what it meant—until she'd moved to the West Coast. Everything there was…different.

Around the Raleigh-Durham area, a fund-raiser was apt to be barbecue and all the trimmings, with a choice of beer or soft drinks. In San Francisco, it usually meant big white plates on which was centered a three-ounce arrangement of some ambiguous food decorated with flowers, accompanied by whatever wine had been donated by the caseload for the occasion as a tax write-off.

After several years of trying to fit in, she still preferred the homegrown style to the trendy, pseudo-sophisticated West Coast version, which was usually filled with people from other parts of the country trying desperately not to let their roots show.

She needed her roots, dammit. Needed the anchor, the stability, not only of her Carolina roots, but her Henry Island roots. She used to joke about "the importance of being Henry" when Maud got started on one of her tirades.

Leaning against the dryer as it finished the last load of towels, Mariah felt a vague ache in some unspecified area of her psyche. If she didn't know better, she might even believe she'd imagined this whole melodramatic mess.

Trouble was, she did know better. She just didn't know what to do about it. Lynn and TA were easier to get along with as adults. She might try harder to build a relationship. Even Erik and Vicki had grown up—marginally. Mariah didn't remember her aunts and uncles being quite so stressed, but then she might not have noticed before.

She had a feeling the stress was money-related. Should she ask them outright if they were in financial trouble and risk being told it was none of her business?

If they wanted to sell Maud's house to someone who would tear it down and replace it with one of those huge rental machines complete with hot tubs, sunroofs and swimming pool, and all they needed was her signature, then that was definitely her business.

Inevitably, the island would change. Nothing on a barrier island was immune to change, even when an attempt was made, as on Portsmouth Island, to keep everything the way it had been in the past.

But she didn't have to help it along.

She put away the towels and left the rest stacked on the dryer, then wandered into the kitchen to search for a certain mug she remembered from years ago, one she'd always loved.

Her aunts were there, arguing about what to fix for supper. Tracy looked up and announced, "Faye's not coming."

Belle said, "She called while you were out to say her mother was having gall bladder surgery."

"Oh. I'm sorry. Did Uncle Linwood get any fresh bread last time he went over? We're down to one loaf in the freezer."

Belle said, "Put it on the list. I see the iron's out. Riah, did you happen to press my Appleseed slacks? I declare, with all the rain and humidity, I have to change three times a day."

"Tell me about it," Mariah said dryly, and started seeing what she could help put together for the evening meal.

After supper, she went outside with no real purpose in mind. Certainly no destination. She had a few fences to mend. One big fence, but she didn't know how she could ever face Gray again.

The sun was still a finger's length above the sound, casting the sky and water in brilliant shades of rose and orange and gold, with deep lavender streaks. As a painter, if she'd tried to duplicate it, she'd have been accused of committing "tourist art."

And badly, at that.

"I wonder if anyone ever painted a black-and-white sunset."

At the sound of his voice, her knees threatened to buckle under her. "I was just thinking," he said, "that no matter how many colors you used, it still wouldn't be enough. How does an artist paint light?"

"Contrast," she said. Keep it cool and impersonal. "By painting everything else in shadow. It's never enough. The gimmicks show. Vermeer came close—maybe Turner."

"I don't know this guy Vermeer, but if Ted Turner ever painted anything like this, I must have missed it." Gray gestured to the western sky. If his comment was meant to break the tension, it served the purpose as well as anything could.

Mariah blurted out the first thing that came to mind. "The cook's not coming. Something about her mother's gall bladder."

"Oh, good. Or bad. Depends on your point of view, I guess."

"Look, about what happened earlier," she said, "I'm really—"

He cut her off. "Nothing happened, Riah. Well, yeah—it did, but I think we handled it pretty well. As long as we're going to be working together, we might as well get it out into the open."

Get what out in the open? "Are we? Going to be working together, I mean?"

He rubbed the back of his neck, studying the pattern of footprints in the sand. "Yeah...I'd say we need to. I don't like what's been going on around here lately. Your father wouldn't, either. He's not here to keep an eye on you, but I am." He looked at her then. "You said you trust me. Is that still true?"

The warm glow cast his features in bronze. His hair, overdue for a trim, had that windblown look that was typical of island hairstyles, male and female. He was quite simply the most gorgeous man she'd ever seen. And yes—she trusted him.

"Speaking of what's going on, I didn't tell you everything about what got me so upset earlier. The thing is, I hadn't been back in years. To the graveyard, I mean."

He moved to stand beside her, but made no attempt to touch her. She didn't know what she would have done if he'd taken her in his arms again. Climbed all over him, probably. "Honestly, I don't usually make a fool of myself over a plastic rose and a bunch of plumbing material," Mariah added. "Mama's monument—it's such a tiny little thing, too—she'd have hated it, and it's not even really pink."

He nodded as if he knew exactly what the problem was. That was just one of the things that was so seductive about the man—he listened and tried to understand, even though Mariah was sure that half the time she didn't make much sense.

So she said, "It was bad enough that when they put up that blasted pipe they left her outside. I don't know which was worse—that or the fact that someone had chopped at Mama's stone, chipping where her name was."

She took a deep, shuddering breath and intoned silently, *I will not cry, I will not cry, I will not!*

"Vandals?" Gray stiffened beside her. She sensed it more than saw it. There was a different note in his voice.

She shrugged. "Who else? Off the beaten track the way we are here, there's always summer people out in boats, water-skiing, wind-surfing, fishing. Sometimes kids come ashore just to look around. I mean, they're here on the Banks for a vacation—they pay for room and board and they think that entitles them to go wherever they please, so they go out in these high-powered boats with ice chests full of beer and they race around, scaring serious fishermen and throwing up these enormous wakes."

She glanced sideways to see if Gray was paying any attention. She never talked this much, not ever. What was it about this one particular man that drew her into telling him things she'd never told another soul? Spoken aloud, most of it sounded so petty. Disgruntled, at the very least.

"Yeah, I noticed the activity's picked up just since I've been here. The upcoming holiday probably accounts for some of it."

"It's a great area if you're a surfer or sunbather, but there's not much manufactured entertainment here if you're easily bored. Some people cruise around and come ashore just for the heck of it, looking for…whatever. They probably don't set out to steal or vandalize, but sometimes one thing leads to another. We used to see piles of beer cans on the beach. Firewood. Sometimes other things, too."

He didn't ask what the other things were. She thought he could probably guess. Condoms, mostly. Once she'd found a rusted hunting knife and occasionally she'd find duckbill caps that had blown overboard.

The last hint of breeze died away. She could hear the whine of mosquitoes, and started itching in advance of their attack.

He said, "We'd better get inside, else they'll be sucking our bones dry."

"All this rain—they'll be worse than ever."

Talk about the weather. Talk about the mosquitoes. Talk about anything but what's really on your mind. "I ran out of repellant. I think someone borrowed my supply."

"You're welcome to mine."

He waved away the drift of insects hovering near the screen door and hurried her inside before she could change her mind. Back to the scene of the crime, she thought, embarrassed and amused at the same time.

"At least the rain's over," he said. "Have you thought any more about moving over here?"

"Oh, I don't think that's a good idea." She thought it was a terrific idea. That was part of the problem. She'd rather sleep in a bed where she'd nearly died than risk opening herself up to a trauma of a different kind.

"I promise not to jump your bones if you won't jump mine." He turned it onto a joke, but it wasn't one. They both knew it.

"I worry about you, Riah," he said, his expression suddenly

serious. "Why not get your things and bring them over here? I'll open some windows and air out your bedroom while you're gone."

The fact that she actually considered it told her just how dangerous it would be. "Thanks, but I think I'll stay put. Now that the cook's not coming, there's no reason to move out."

He didn't argue. Had she hoped he would?

Probably. Being thirty-four years old, with a bad marriage behind her, didn't necessarily make her wise. She had pretty well proved that. Something was definitely going on here— something bad. She didn't want to believe anyone in her family was behind it, but all the same, from now on she would definitely keep her eyes open.

"See you tomorrow," she said after he'd brought her a can of insect repellant. "Thanks for this." She held up the can and hurried away, wondering how other women handled unwise attractions.

Almost before she could close the screen door back at Maud's house, Lynette flew at her, nearly knocking her off her feet in a tearful embrace. Mariah hadn't seen her to speak to since the beach buggy episode, which seemed like ancient history by now.

"Oh, my *gawd,* what if you hadn't *been* there? My baby would have *drowned!*"

"Um—how's your headache?" This was a Lynette Mariah didn't know and didn't particularly care to know—not now, at least.

"Better, but, oh, Riah—thank you, thank you, thank you! I'm going to be a much better mother from now on, I promise!"

Sure you are. So why did you disappear all day, leaving your son to entertain himself?

Mariah edged toward the door. "That's all right, Lynn. He'd have managed to get out. The water wasn't all that deep, really."

Well, it was. Kids drowned in bathtubs, and Mason could

have been knocked out or injured, but there was no point in bringing that up.

"Oh, honey, I just want you to know I'm sorry."

She was sorry Mariah had been there? Or she was sorry about something else? "Sure, well—all's well that ends well, as they say. You might want to buy him a new life vest before you come down again. In fact, if I were you, I'd see that he had swimming lessons."

Fat chance, she thought, unless the swimming instructor was rich and good-looking.

Lynn promised, and Mariah considered asking her about what was going on with the island. The mysterious renters who didn't seem interested in any of the usual beach pursuits. This thing about Maud's house...

"Lynn, could we talk?"

"Oh—yeah, but first, we're leaving tomorrow and I have to round up Mason's stuff. He's scattered his clothes all over the place. I can't even find his good shoes. If I bundle it up, will you get it started washing?"

She'd had all day long, Mariah thought, but that was Lynn. Never do today what you can put off until tomorrow. Mariah had been unofficially nominated as laundress, but that didn't mean everyone else was helpless. She made up her mind on the spot. No more. Being a doormat wasn't going to get her anywhere.

"Sorry, I won't have time. I'm moving into our—my cottage." That is, she was as soon as she could muster up the nerve to go back after having just declined the offer. If she was trying to prove just how steady and centered she was, that was hardly the way to do it.

Lynette backed off, her eyes wide. "Has he left yet? I didn't hear him go."

"Gray? He's still here, but there's plenty of room."

"Well...I don't know."

Impatient, Mariah stepped back. "You don't know what? Look, I need to borrow some sheets. I don't know what's over there anymore, everything's so different."

"Well, sure...I mean, help yourself. Does Mama know you're moving over there?"

Thoroughly irritated by now, Mariah said, "Do I need Aunt Tracy's permission? You've all done everything possible to make me feel like an outsider here, so don't go crying any crocodile tears just because of Mason and the truck and that gas leak." And with that she turned and stalked off, leaving the other woman staring after her.

Lynn hadn't been the one to tamper with the gas fittings. Nor had she been the one to batter Roxie's gravestone. She was too lazy, for one thing. Besides, if the gas thing had been deliberate—and Mariah was inclined to think it had—then she wanted to believe it had been done by an in-law, not a blood relative.

Had things changed all that much? Or had it always been this way, only she'd been too stupid to see it?

Well, no more Ms. Nice Gal. She might be slow to catch on, but she was neither blind nor stupid. Right now she was in what her mother used to call a "go-to-hell mood."

Edgar, don't start with me, I'll bite your head off. I'm in one of my go-to-hell moods this morning.

And then Edgar would show up after work with a big bouquet of pink flowers, or if it were a really serious go-to-hell mood, he'd probably bring jewelry. It didn't have to be expensive, as long as it was showy. In that, Mariah thought with reluctant amusement, her cousin Vicki and her mama were a lot alike. Vicki would have loved Roxie if she'd been old enough to get to know her, but Roxie had died before Vicki was born.

We're going to talk, ladies, Mariah thought. We're going to have us a heart-to-heart real soon. If there's any hanky-panky going on around here, I need to be in on it.

It was almost completely dark by the time she stamped the sand off her feet on the deck at Layzy Dayz. Gray met her at the door. He didn't say a word about her sudden about-face. "Want to divide up the chores?" He reached for her two bags, leaving her to carry the stack of linens back to her bedroom. Neither of them acknowledged the tension that practically shimmered in the air. Mariah wondered if he was even aware of it.

All right, so she needed him, dammit. But she didn't want to need him. Didn't want to need anyone, but especially not Gray Hollowell. Because aside from his comforting and protective capabilities, the man was a stealth hunk, and she was feeling just raw and insecure enough to be affected.

What was that phrase the old cartographers used to describe unexplored territory? "Here they be dragons."

She didn't want to believe there were dragons on Henry Island. She had returned to the island hoping to heal, but that hadn't happened. Bruce had come close to destroying her self-confidence, telling her she was letting her looks slide, that she needed to see a plastic surgeon about getting her nose fixed and her boobs inflated. He'd told her she was boring as hell and lousy in bed, and for the life of him, he couldn't figure out why he'd married her.

For the life of her, neither could she. Her only excuse was that they'd both seen what they'd wanted to see instead of what was really there.

No more rose-colored glasses. From now on, she would look long and hard before she leaped—that is, if she leaped at all. What was it one of the recent presidents had said? "Trust, but verify"?

That sounded like a good idea. A fine idea, in fact.

Chapter 15

Tipping back the chair in the room he was using as an office, Gray stared out the window the next morning. Little had been said the night before, which was probably for the best. Now, listening to the small sounds coming from the room just down the hall, he found it impossible to concentrate.

Doors opening and closing. The rattle of coat hangers. A dresser drawer being forced open, followed by a soft-voiced oath. The damp air down here did a real number on doors and drawers. He could vouch for that. Hearing her sneeze, he grinned and murmured, "Bless you."

Unwanted images kept interfering with his concentration. Mariah in a wet cotton nightgown, her dark, hard nipples and the shadowy triangle below her flat belly clearly visible, the way she'd looked after they'd carried the boy ashore.

And wearing the same gown, her face the color of wet plaster, after narrowly escaping asphyxiation.

Mariah, wearing his shirt or her own baggy shorts and shirts, still managing to look like a fashion model. The best he could figure was that she had an innate quality that had less to do with the way she looked than the way she carried herself—the woman she was inside.

"You need something?" he asked when she appeared in the doorway. He casually slid a week-old newspaper over the notes he'd been making, the list of questions still to be answered and the diagram he'd drawn. When visuals formed in his mind he often put them on paper, the better to analyze them. His father used to worry about what he'd thought of as his son's ambition to play professional sports when Gray would diagram football plays or baseball strategies. Sports were fine, but he'd counted on Gray's becoming a third-generation tobacco farmer.

By the time Gray had entered high school, both had known that wasn't going to happen. Times had changed.

"I just saw Mason go by, headed down the woods path. Do you think someone should go after him?" She scratched her arm. Innate quality or not, she was something of a mess, with several visible scratches, plus a few bites and a rash on her left ankle that was starting to look like poison ivy.

"In case he gets treed by another rabbit, you mean?" Gray stood and flexed his shoulders.

"Just a thought. I mean, he'll be going home soon, and I'd hate to see him get in any more trouble before he leaves."

Gray said, "In case you wondered, Mason couldn't have done it. It took a wrench and a pair of pliers, and I can't see a kid like Mason—especially so soon after the beach buggy thing—tinkering with something else he didn't understand."

She nodded. "It never occurred to me. Anyway, I'm sure he doesn't deliberately try to get into trouble, it just sort of…happens."

But not that kind of trouble, Gray told himself. That had been the work of someone who knew precisely what he was doing. "He needs other kids to play with. Maybe next time they come out to the island he can bring a friend."

She shrugged as if to say she doubted it. Having met the boy's mother, so did Gray. Lynette Boxer, or whatever her married name was—they'd never been formally introduced—

didn't strike him as being particularly maternal. "He's probably just going to tell Orestes goodbye," he said. "He seemed taken with the old guy."

Mariah nodded. Even tousled from bed—maybe especially then—her hair looked thick and cloud-soft. He happened to know it smelled of peaches and coconut.

He cleared his throat and rearranged several items on the table that now served as a desk. "You got a problem with that? You want to go after him?"

"Do you mind?"

"What, me going, you going or both of us going?"

She relaxed visibly. "Both of us. It's silly, I know, but we both know there's something going on around here that's...not right."

"Give me a couple of minutes."

She edged toward the door. "Sure, take your time, I'll be out on the deck."

If she was worried, she covered it well. He backed out of his program, shut Gus down and scanned the room, making certain there was nothing in evidence that he wouldn't want seen by other eyes. His notes were written in his own form of shorthand, which was good as any encryption. The list was getting longer, the questions piling up, but a few things were starting to take shape.

He stepped into a pair of shoes and grabbed a hat before joining her outside. "In case you were worried, I checked the condition of the other beach buggy. Two flat tires and a missing battery. It's not going anywhere."

"I just hope it doesn't occur to him to try and launch one of those old boats before he leaves, he's so eager."

"Wouldn't surprise me, if he could figure out a way to do it. He's a smart kid. A little too much energy."

"And too little supervision," she said, hurrying along beside Gray. "He seems awfully young in some ways, but then, I'm no expert on children."

"Might stave off another adventure if you promise him that the next time he comes down there'll be a boat available."

She shot him a curious look. "Will there be?"

"Could happen, if I help you get one ready."

She seemed to be considering his suggestion. "You know, Erik offered to take me out in his father's boat. Maybe he'll extend the invitation to include Mason."

The morning air was like a steam bath, rich with the scent of cedar, seaweed and honeysuckle. "You turned him down, right?"

"Who, Erik? Well…not exactly. That is, I didn't make it definite."

"Don't go."

It was the wrong tactic. Mariah was done with taking orders, but she knew better than to make an issue of it.

"Listen, somebody rigged that gas leak deliberately. That means—"

"You don't know that, not for sure." So much for not making an issue of it. "Maybe there was a leak and somebody tried to fix it. You said yourself the stuff's all old and corroded and needs replacing." She refused to think anyone in her own family wanted her dead. In the middle of the night she might have a few misgivings, but in the bright morning sunlight, the whole idea seemed absurd.

"Who, your aunt Belle? She doesn't strike me as the mechanical type. The other one, maybe, but I think Ms. Boxer's too smart to try anything that dangerous."

"Well, TA's gone, and Lynn and Vicki wouldn't risk their manicures. Uncle Linwood would probably know how, but he's too soft. He won't even kill a snake. Uncle Nat's tough, but I'm sure it's mostly bluster. He's no murderer. Trust me, I've known him all my life. His bark's a lot worse than his bite. Well…maybe not a whole lot worse, but he wouldn't do it."

They weren't running, but they were walking fast. As walkers they were pretty evenly matched. Gray couldn't help but wonder if they'd be as well matched in another respect.

At the moment, though, he had other things on his mind. Sex would just have to wait. He couldn't risk the distraction.

But the thought of what she had felt like in his arms—what she'd tasted like—was enough to turn his powers of concentration into so much confetti.

Stick to business, man. Think of her as just another client. Yeah, right. Easy for you to say.

A low-angled morning sun slanted through the trees, sending down shafts of dusty gold light through the darker green, picking out red-and-gold blossoms of some wild, tree-climbing vine. The whole place was alive with the sound of birds—mostly fledglings, all squawking for attention. Gray wasn't artistic, but even he could appreciate the natural beauty.

He cut a sidelong glance at the long-legged woman keeping pace with him on the narrow path. Her father had said she was intelligent. Artistic and intelligent. He'd forgotten to mention sexy and a shade too idealistic for her own good, but then, a father might not notice those things about his daughter.

"You left out a couple of relatives," he reminded her. Back to business.

"I know, I'm thinking. We agree Mason wouldn't. As for Aunt Tracy, I'm pretty sure she wouldn't, either. She's bossy and she'll walk all over you if you let her, but she loved Daddy. He was her big brother. Deep down, I'm pretty sure she probably loves me, too."

Deep down, they were all pretty shallow, if he was any judge. "What about poster boy?"

"Erik?" They were approaching Orestes's side of the island. "Not counting Mason, I guess he's my favorite. No mental giant, but good-natured and fun." She frowned. "But they're all worried about something. Sometimes I hear them arguing after I've gone to bed. The other day both uncles jumped all over poor Erik. It sounded pretty rough. I couldn't tell who was angry with whom about what, but…" She sighed. "I think Erik uses drugs. I wish he wouldn't, because—well, just because."

"You trust him?"

"Erik? I guess I don't really trust anyone," she said. "I hate not being able to trust my own family, but until I know what they're really after—well, let's just say I'm not about to sign anything.''

For an idealist, she showed a surprising streak of common sense. "What do you think they're after?"

"My share of Maud's house and the land it's on, for starters. A lot of land, probably. I don't think it's ever been surveyed—at least, not until now. Everybody just picked a location and built—no permits, no red tape, no nothing, which is really wild. I guess the bureaucracy doesn't have arms long enough to reach this far, or maybe it's because the whole place is privately owned.''

"Count your blessings."

Somewhat breathless now, Mariah said thoughtfully, "Maud's is clearly the choice spot on the island, though. High ground, well protected... Look how many hurricanes it's endured, and it's still standing.''

"You think that's all?'' Gray asked.

"All of what?"

He shrugged. "All they're after."

"Maybe. Probably. Oh, I don't know.''

He said, "You'll be leaving pretty soon, right?"

"What gave you that idea?'' Without slowing her pace, she pointed out a baby blue jay that was fluffed out bigger than the mama that was busy poking food into its open beak.

"You mentioned having to go somewhere. I just thought...''

He needed her here. Dammit, he wanted her safe, but he didn't want her to leave. He needed her here where he could watch over her. If that gang up at Maud's place were all in this together, they could easily split up to cover her when she left. Hell, they were already splitting up. He needed to stay here, and he needed her to stick with him, because he was starting to have a bad feeling about what went down all those years ago. It might or might not have anything to do with what was going on now, but what was happening now definitely involved Mariah. And, while Henry hadn't mentioned anything specific, he'd been concerned enough to reopen a twenty-seven-year-old case.

"Oh, look!" Mariah stopped suddenly and pointed. "Here, kitty, kitty," she crooned.

Gray followed her direction and saw a skinny gray cat a dozen yards off the path. Seeing them, the cat took off.

Mariah said, "She looks hungry. Didn't she look hungry to you?"

"Riah, it doesn't pay to feed feral cats. They just multiply and there goes your bird population. I doubt if even half of the little guys we've seen fluttering around and squawking this morning will make it through the summer."

"Fine. So you starve the cats so they're forced to kill the birds. Makes perfect sense to me," she said, obviously meaning just the opposite.

"Feral cats also spread rabies and other diseases."

"Oh, and you're some kind of an expert, right?" she snapped.

"I grew up on a farm. I guess the perfect balance of nature depends on where you happen to be standing when the question comes up. In a barn where there's plenty of feed, you get mice. You bring in cats to eat the mice that eat the grain. Cats are cute, mice aren't. Cute rules."

"That's awful! What about birds?"

"Oh, now you had to go and complicate things. Honey, we're not going to do much to change Mama Nature's pecking order. It's still a work in progress."

"Right," she said softly, a sly grin setting her eyes to sparkling. "And that wasn't a calico cat I saw in your house the other day?"

Ignoring the question, he said, "Come on, Mason's probably pestering Orestes to let him take the *Miss Maud* out for a run."

They hurried on, not speaking again until he said, "It always causes problems, but I guess that's human nature."

"What's human nature?" She was panting slightly now. "Causing problems?"

"Feeding strays. Thank God— I guess. Screws up old Darwin's theory about the survival of the fittest, but all the same…"

They broke into the clearing, loped past the pit toilet and the collard patch and looked down toward the wharf. No sign of either Mason or Orestes. "At least the boat's still tied up," Mariah said, scratching a bite on her neck and raking the rash on her ankle with the side of her foot.

"Purely as a matter of curiosity, who feeds the animals here when the family leaves? The renters? I doubt if Orestes does."

With a reluctant grin, she shook her head. "Not him, for sure. I think he must be a lot like Maud in that respect. Maud was strictly a survivalist. I used to think she was hard, but now I'm not so sure she wasn't right—about some things, at least." Looking up, Mariah waved. "Oh, there they are."

And there they were. The boy and the old man stepped out onto the narrow strip of sagging porch that wrapped around two sides of the shack. They waited until Gray and Mariah came closer and then Mason piped up. "I came to say good-bye, but I guess I forgot to ask Mama. Is she mad at me?"

"I don't think so, honey." That from Mariah. Gray had a feeling Lynette hadn't even noticed the boy was gone.

"Mr. Orestes is showing me his boat models and his files."

"His files?" Gray looked from the boy to the old man. He'd spent a smelly, memorable half hour inside the old man's house drinking syrupy homemade wine. If there were any files in there—or any boat models, for that matter—he'd missed them. Which wasn't too surprising, given the amount of clutter.

By that time they'd reached the steps. Gray hadn't intended to stay and visit, but he followed Mariah's lead. "If you haven't been inside before," he warned softly, "you're in for a treat."

"Oh, I have, lots of times." She smiled up at the weathered, white-haired man, who was holding on to the railing with both hands. "Orestes used to let me smoke, didn't you?" At the old man's nod, she went on to say, "Back when I thought smoking was cool because Lynn and TA both smoked, Orestes used to let me roll up newspaper into a long tube and light one end from the stove. It tasted awful and went out almost immediately, but you wouldn't believe how grown-up I felt.''

Mason was staring at her. She grabbed him gently by the shoulders, leaned down and said with mock sternness, ''Don't you dare do anything stupid like that, you hear? Your mama would ground you for a year, and I'd back her up.''

''Hey, okay, okay,'' Mason said, laughing. ''C'mon, Mr. Orestes, show 'em your boat models and all.''

Gray was more interested in the ''and all,'' but that could wait.

The next few minutes were spent inside the dim, sweltering cabin admiring the crude replicas of various fishing boats. The scale wasn't perfect and the workmanship lacked finesse, but they were clearly done by a man who knew and appreciated boats.

Evidently they were kept in the bedroom, which was why Gray had missed them earlier. Now they were displayed on the sink, the sewing machine and the ledge of the battleship-gray china cabinet.

Orestes reached for a stubby carved boat. He'd sat down as soon as they'd come inside. His hands trembled so that he might have dropped the small model if Gray hadn't gently taken it from him and set it on a chair.

''Thankee, son. Now that there, she's what you call a Core Sounder, like my *Miss Maud*. Built down to Harker's Island on the Core Sound. That there one over on the sink, she's a pogy boat. Trawls for menhaden—see that there big net reel? The one over there by the door—'' he indicated a stubby white model with a garish orange superstructure ''—she's a shrimper like one I used to work on out of Oriental before I come back up the Banks. I weren't but about fourteen, fifteen back then.''

Gray listened with one ear as he quietly scanned the room for something resembling a file. There was a drawer in the china cabinet with a cupboard underneath, either of which could hold files.

Or maybe it wasn't that kind of file. Maybe the old man had been showing off the tools he used in building the boat models. Mason was enthralled, and it occurred to Gray that as role models went, the kid could do worse.

"I'll just set these out of the way," Orestes said. He reached for the trawler and nearly knocked it to the floor. "Dad-gum hands," he grumbled. "Some days they shake worser'n a halyard in a hurricane."

Both Gray and Mason lunged for the model. Mason caught it before it struck the floor, and Gray said, "Let me put these things away. They're far too valuable to risk an accident."

Thus he got to see another room. Evidently the shack consisted of a bedroom, a sitting room which he'd seen before and a narrow kitchen. The kitchen held only an old-fashioned kerosene stove, a small table, an iron-stained sink with a pitcher pump and a shelf holding two cans of Campbell's tomato soup, a box of salt that was beaded with moisture, a jar of sugar, a bottle of Texas Pete hot sauce and three prescription medicine bottles.

Without examining them more closely, Gray couldn't tell what they were. Something to control those tremors, hopefully. There was an empty plate and a fork in the basin. A small assortment of pans hung from nails on the wall.

Dammit, someone needed to look after the old guy. He was thin as a rail, his color wasn't good, and today he looked as if he could barely stand unaided.

The bedroom was crowded with stacked boxes and an iron bed frame that held either the world's lumpiest mattress or a genuine old-fashioned feather tick. There was nothing so far as Gray could see resembling a file folder, much less a filing cabinet. More cigar boxes were stacked in one corner, and behind the door was a rifle, an old bolt-action .22. Probably the same one Mariah had borrowed as a child.

His father had used just such a gun for hunting squirrels and rabbits. A little fried squirrel might make a nice change from salt mullet and tomato soup, but Gray figured Orestes's hunting days were long past.

"Come set a spell," the old man said when they returned to the living room.

"I guess we'd better get on back before somebody starts to worry about Mason," Mariah said. "Right, Mason?"

The boy nodded, but it was obvious that he was dying to stay. Amused, Gray thought he'd found the perfect playmate. One who wouldn't be apt to lead him into any more trouble than he could find on his own.

"Let me give you another jug of blackberry wine," the old fisherman said when Gray edged toward the door. "I reckon ye done drunk up the last one I give ye."

Gray hadn't, but he didn't see any need to say so. One thing he did need was to breathe some fresh air. The stench of fish, cabbage and something else—probably dust and mildew—was overpowering. Was he the only one who noticed?

Evidently not, as Mariah said, "Whew!" once they set off across the clearing.

"Boy, that place sure doesn't smell very good, does it?" That from Mason. Orestes had given him an envelope filled with old photographs, and he was carrying it as if it contained the crown jewels.

"Drained his mullet crock the other day," Gray said solemnly. "Takes awhile for the smell to go away."

"What's a mullet crock?" Mason looked from one to the other of the adults.

"Beats me," Gray said. "You know what a mullet crock is, Riah?"

"It just so happens that I do," she said, pausing to scratch her ankle again. And she went on to explain the process of salting down the fatty fish to cook or to use as bait, draining and adding more salt from time to time.

"Fascinating, the things these West Coast socialites know about, isn't it?" Gray teased, and she took a swipe at him.

He had to stop teasing her; he was starting to enjoy it a little too much.

They came to the place where the path split, one branch leading to Maud's old house, the other to Cottage Row. Mason said, "Are you going to bury your daddy before we leave, Riah? Could I come? Mr. Orestes said he's coming when you do it. He said I could come if I wanted to, but I didn't have to. He said it was going to be a mem—a memory service. What's that?"

With a stricken look at Gray, Mariah dropped to her knees and took one of the boy's thin brown hands in her own. "A memorial service, Mason. It's when a group of friends and family come together to say goodbye and to talk about—well, in this case, my daddy."

"Is it like Memorial Day? That's a holiday, 'cause we talked about it in school."

"Well…sort of, I suppose." She looked up at Gray as if to say, *Help me out here, you jerk! Can't you see I'm in over my head?*

"Tell you what," Gray said. "How about we set a time and I'll ask your mama if you can stay over another day? Hey, you're a Henry, too. This is a family affair. Mariah needs all her friends there, because…" This time he looked to her for help.

She rolled her eyes, but rose to the occasion. "Because it's sad for me. You know how it is when you lose your—" She could have kicked herself. Any memories Mason might have about his own father probably weren't all that great. "That is, when you have to say goodbye to a close friend?"

"Like you and Mr. Gray and Mr. Orestes. I'm s'posed to say goodbye, so maybe if you ask her, Mom'll let me stay to help you say goodbye to your daddy, too. I don't hafta be back in school till Tuesday, 'cause this is a holiday."

Mariah hugged him, and received a tight hug in return. Gray nodded and said, "Go for it, guy. I'll speak to your mama."

Mason ran toward Maud's house and the two of them turned toward Layzy Dayz, Gray carrying the jug of wine. He said, "What's that old saying about being hoist with one's own petard?"

"I'm not sure what it means, but I think we probably both have been. I never knew it was so rough, dealing with kids."

"They ask the impossible and you end up promising things you can't easily deliver. Any problem with having the service tomorrow? Emotional or otherwise?" He held the door for her. It wasn't locked. No one ever locked anything on the island.

"I promised, didn't I? So I'll do it. It's probably best, anyway. I can't keep putting it off, waiting for the—" she made quotation marks in the air with her fingers "—right time."

"I'll help any way I can, but right now you're going to promise me to stop scratching those bites before you get an infection."

That night the boathouse burned to the ground. Gray was awake when he noticed the glow reflected through the window of the room he used as his office. Unable to sleep, knowing Mariah was right down the hall, he'd been going over his notes and diagrams and coming up with possibilities and probabilities. So far, no plausible motive had presented itself, much less any tangible evidence. It had been his experience that in a small family place like Henry Island, there was almost never a crime without motive.

He went to the front door to see what was causing the glow, and then he yelled for Mariah. "Call Maud's house! Bring buckets! The boathouse is on fire!"

It was too late for buckets. They stood and watched, the Boxers, the Detloffs, Gray and Mariah, in an assortment of sleepwear, curlers, slippers and bare feet. Only Gray was fully dressed, although he hadn't taken time to put on shoes.

His arm went around Mariah, who was shivering even though the night temperature hadn't dropped more than a few degrees. Heat from the fire could be felt all the way across the clearing. There was a small explosion, followed by another one and then two more in rapid succession. Mariah flinched and buried her face against his chest.

"Paint, probably," he said softly. "The cans expand…"

Mason, wearing Spider-Man pajamas, had edged closer and was pressed against Gray's other side. He said, "I guess now we'll have to buy more paint for when I come back next time.

I asked Mr. Orestes if there was some boat paint left over in there, and he said he thought so. He said he'd look for the key and get it out.''

Ka-chink. Another piece of the puzzle fell into Gray's hands. Only where, he wondered, did this particular piece fit? Into today's puzzle or yesterday's?

Or were they the same puzzle?

Chapter 16

Nat Detloff placed a call to the fire department at Hatteras, assuring them that everything was under control, that no help was needed. Lynette took a sleepy Mason back to the house, while the others stood and watched the fire burn itself out. It took a surprisingly short time. By the time the old cypress building was reduced to a few blackened rafters and joists standing guard over a pile of glowing rubble, Mariah knew she would never be able to sleep.

What next? She had deliberately returned to the island, a bittersweet journey at best, to say goodbye to her father. She had allowed herself two weeks to put the past behind her and reconnect with her roots before picking a location and establishing herself somewhere in the area. Now it seemed as if everything on both coasts had fallen apart. Maybe she should relocate to Arkansas or Oklahoma.

Huddled slightly apart from the family, the four residents of the other two cottages, the rentals, stared at the dying embers and whispered among themselves. All men, all nondescript; one youngish, the other three middle-aged. No one bothered with introductions. At this point Mariah didn't much care if they'd come to carve the island up into bite-size pieces and auction it off to the highest bidder. Tomorrow she wouldn't feel that way, but for tonight, she'd had enough of Henry Island and everything connected to it.

Thank God Gray wasn't connected. She gripped his hand just as a blackened timber supporting the last section of roof collapsed, sending up a shower of sparks. Staring as if mesmerized, she forgot to breathe until her lungs suddenly demanded sustenance. Was this what drowning felt like? She inhaled sharply.

"Stop it," Gray murmured.

She sucked in another gulp of air. "Stop breathing?"

"Hyperventilating."

She suspected he'd meant more than that. He saw through her too easily. Shivering, she said, "It was probably spontaneous combustion. That's what usually starts fires in a case like this. Paint—probably paint thinner, too, and motor oil. Old rags. I don't think anyone's even been inside in years. There were some oars and life jackets, but Uncle Nat and Uncle Linwood keep their boats across the inlet when they're not here, so any servicing that needed doing probably got done over at the marina. They'd rather pay than do it themselves— or maybe it's a package deal. Rent space, get service thrown in for free." She took a deep breath and said, "I don't know, though, parking garages don't work that way."

She was chattering like a monkey. She never chattered.

Oh, sure, like she never cried.

They both continued to watch the occasional sparks. Small, earthbound fireworks. She tried to identify several visible lumps. Paint cans? Old engine parts? There used to be at least one outboard in there, probably the same one they'd used when they'd gone out fishing. Orestes must have taken it home with him. She was pretty sure neither of her uncles, and certainly not Erik, wanted a dinky little five-horse outboard.

Fortunately, the three old skiffs were far enough away so that the fire hadn't touched them. She'd have to see about buying another pair of oars before Mason came back, though. "Is this still Saturday?" she asked suddenly.

"Sunday morning, just barely." Gray slipped off his shirt and draped it around her shoulders. She thought of several wisecracks she might have made about the shirt off his back, but none seemed appropriate. Or even worth the effort.

Huddling into the welcome warmth, she tried to recall what the inside of the boathouse had looked like the last time she'd seen it. She'd wanted to go in after something or other—a crab net, probably, but Orestes had stopped her. He'd told her he'd locked it up because it was a mess inside and he didn't want anyone tripping over something and getting hurt.

Orestes had spent far more time on this end of the island back in those days. In fact, he used to fish a net right out in front of the pier, once it had been rebuilt after the explosion. As young as she'd been at the time, she remembered watching him drag his net slowly back and forth, making pass after pass. He always pulled it up on the far side of the boat, though, so she never knew if he caught any fish or not. It seemed an odd place for fish to hang out, but maybe they were attracted to the seaweed that grew on the old pilings.

After a while the summers and the holiday visits had melded together in her mind. The first few times her father had wanted to bring her here after her mother died, she'd cried and refused. Pitched a real tantrum, which wasn't like her at all. Her father had insisted she needed to go back, that they both did. He'd compared it to getting back on a horse after being thrown. Ponies had been new in her life at the time. She'd just started having riding lessons with a private teacher, as if learning to stay on a pony could help make up for her loss.

Coming back the first time had been a whole lot worse than getting back on a horse, even though by then the pier had been rebuilt and the waterfront on either side was in the process of being bulkheaded. By the next trip the bulkhead was finished and the harbor dredged, the spoils used as backfill. Everything on the waterfront had looked different.

Still the old image had lingered. It lay waiting in ambush

even now, daring her to forget. If only she could learn to block out the worst memories and hang on to the best, she might not feel this miserable ambivalence.

Maybe it was time to give in and sign over her third of Maud's house, which obviously didn't include a bedroom. She might even let them have her cottage to rent or sell if they wanted it and could afford to buy it. She could certainly use the money.

But if she did that, she'd feel like a traitor. Her parents had built the cottage, arguing over styles, room sizes and colors. Never angrily—she couldn't remember any real anger between them, but some of their discussions had been…lively.

Her dad's sisters had complained that being the favorite, he'd had the first choice of building sites, and naturally, he'd chosen the best. They'd squabbled about it for years.

Edgar Henry had been born right here on the island. Her mother had died here and what was left of her—*Oh, God, don't go there!*—had been buried here. Mariah herself might have been born in a hospital in Durham, but whatever roots she possessed had to be here. How could she bring herself to cut the last tie?

Gray tucked her arm though his, covering her hand with his own. He didn't look at her. Didn't speak. She wondered if he even realized what he'd done. It was something a caring stranger might have done under the circumstances.

Whatever else he was, he was far more than a stranger.

She edged closer. Now that the fire had died down, the night noises had resumed—the shrill sound of insects and tree frogs, the deeper croak of a bullfrog and the occasional squawk of a night heron.

The whispers. The others were still standing in a knot some distance away. The four renters had joined the Boxers and Detloffs now. From time to time, one of them would glance her way. Curiosity, probably. Mariah didn't bother to smile.

Suddenly the insect chorus cut off as if directed by an unseen hand. Into the silence she heard Erik say, "Listen, y'all, I've got a plan."

Someone else—with whispers, it was hard to recognize voices—hissed, "Forget it, dammit. Haven't you done enough?"

That was followed by some mumbling, then Lynette said, "Dammit, Daddy, why don't we just tell her?"

Tell who? Mariah wondered. Me? Tell me what? She wanted to march over and shake them all. That's what she'd been wanting—all she'd asked. To be told what, if anything, they wanted from her, and just what the devil was going on.

"Now, let's not quarrel. Why not go inside and have some nice hot chocolate?" Aunt Belle, the peacemaker in action. Despite their differences, Mariah thought, she really did love her family. Didn't always like them, but she had to love them. They were all she had left.

Linwood wandered over to where Gray and Mariah stood. "You think it's safe to leave, Hollowell? Not much wind— we had rain recently."

"I'll keep watch," Gray replied. "I'm closer."

"'Preciate it. I'm bushed." His yawn seemed oddly exaggerated to Mariah, but then, this whole night was starting to feel like an out-of-body experience.

"Come on, we can watch from the house," Gray said after the others had gone. Still holding her arm, he steered her back toward the cottage.

She waded, head down, through the soft sand. It could rain half a day and still be bone dry just beneath the surface. Obviously the boathouse had been dry enough to burn.

"Mama wanted us to build a boardwalk up from the waterfront, but Daddy said it wouldn't do any good. The first time we had a good nor'easter, it would be covered in sand again."

"You notice anything odd?" Gray paused and peered at the shaggy hedgerow of pittosporum, oleander and Russian olive. They had nearly reached the cottage by now. The others were already out of sight.

"Odd like what?"

"The renters didn't turn off at the cottages."

She stared at him. "So?"

"So if your aunt Belle's going to be making hot chocolate for the whole gang, why weren't we invited, hmm?"

"Maybe because she doesn't have enough? How do I know? It's too hot for it, anyway." And then she thought of what he'd said. "Besides, you're probably mistaken. Staring at a fire for so long does things to your night vision."

There were no security lights, only the pale luminescence from a cloud-veiled moon. Gray kicked the sand off his bare feet going up the steps, reminding her to do the same. She said, "We need a footbath, but standing water breeds mosquitoes. I remember Maud telling Mama that when Mama wanted to buy this fancy birdbath with a spouting dolphin she saw advertised in a flier. 'No standing water,' she said."

"And what Maud said was law, right?"

"You know what?" Mariah looked up, feeling oddly reassured by his solid presence. "I wish she were here right now. Maud. I might not have always gotten along with her, but whatever was going on, she'd have sorted it out in short order. One thing she was good at was maintaining order among the natives." Mariah laughed a little, surprised that she even could.

"Something's definitely going on, all right," he said almost absently. Then, more decisively, he added, "Listen, Riah, why don't you go back to bed, try to catch a few hours of sleep. I'll stay up and watch to see that the fire doesn't flare up again." By that time they were inside, and he hooked the screen door behind them.

"Forget it. I'd never be able to sleep." She looked down at her feet and grimaced. They'd have to be washed again. She felt grimy all over, in fact. "What time is it?"

He glanced at his wrist. She'd removed her watch when she'd gone to bed. "Two-seventeen. You want to talk?"

"Talk?"

"You know—you tell me yours and I'll tell you mine?"

"Haven't we had this conversation before?"

"Several times. We were just getting to the good parts."

Intrigued, but wary, she nodded. "Let me wash off first—I feel sooty. And I want something to drink, too, but not hot chocolate. Why on earth would anyone drink hot chocolate in this kind of weather?"

"Comfort food," he said. "Go on, wash whatever needs washing. I'll meet you back in the living room."

Gray opened the refrigerator, then closed it. Her diet cola wasn't going to do it, not tonight. The last thing she needed was caffeine, so coffee was out.

The wine. That godawful blackberry wine. With her background, she was bound to have a discriminating palate, but tonight called for something a little out of the ordinary. Whatever else it was or wasn't, Orestes's homemade blackberry wine was definitely that.

She'd put on a loose cotton thing shaped like a folded bedspread. On her it looked good. Her face was too pale, her eyes shadowed from lack of sleep—or from too many memories. What with one thing and another, she'd had a hell of a week.

Sinking onto the sofa, her legs—scratches, mosquito bites, poison ivy and all—gracefully crossed at the ankles, she said, "I've got to plan Daddy's service. I want to do it before Mason goes home. I don't know why, I just think he needs it. Daddy was his great-uncle and he barely even remembers him, but still…"

"Right. But still. Here, try this." He handed over a wineglass half filled with deep-red liquid. "I'm not sure about the vintage—tastes like last Thursday, but it's probably last summer." His low chuckle raised a faint answering smile. "Go ahead, it'll boost your blood sugar and relax you so you won't feel so shaky."

"I don't feel shaky," she said, but she took it and sipped, made a face, then sipped again. "This is awful."

"Yeah, ain't it just?" He took a swallow and shuddered. He didn't want to do this, but it had to be done. The first time he'd seen her in person, just over a week ago, she'd looked as if a loud noise would cause her to shatter. In some ways she looked stronger now, in other ways, even more vulnerable. "You want to talk about it?"

"Talk about what?" She knew damned well what he meant, but she was going to be stubborn.

Fine. He could match her stubborn and raise her one. "What's bothering you. Let's start with the fact that your mother died right out front when the boat she was on blew up." He watched closely for a reaction. Mariah flinched, but quickly recovered. "It's common knowledge, Riah. Besides that, your father told me about it when he leased me this cottage. It's the reason he let me have the place." He waited for that to sink in.

She took two more swallows of the wine, set the glass down, then picked it up again, all without taking her eyes off his face. Dammit, she had to have suspected. He hated feeling as if he'd done something underhanded, but that was the nature of his work. He was a private investigator. Maybe he should have leveled with her before this, but that would have muddied the waters. They were muddy enough, churned up with the way he was coming to feel about her. Personal relationships had no business in any investigation, but try telling that to his libido.

Gently, he said, "Why do you think he let me have the place for half the summer when he could have rented it out for a lot more by the week?"

She refused to meet his eyes. "How do I know? Vicki said you probably blackmailed him into giving it to you practically for free."

He leaned back in his chair, legs crossed at the ankles, hand loosely holding his glass. "Blackmail, huh? Now what could I possibly have had on your father? I saw him exactly twice. He struck me as a solid citizen—moral, law-abiding. Uptight and a bit worried, in fact. But not over anything I might find out about him personally."

"He was. I mean, all of the first part. I don't know if he was worried or not. I hadn't seen him in a few years. He traveled mostly in Europe, flying out of Raleigh-Durham. Besides…'' She pinch-pleated her nightgown. By now he figured he'd seen all the nightgowns she'd brought with her, all two of them. Both were plain cotton, round necked, sleeveless and unfitted. On her they looked sexy as skimpy black lace.

"Besides?" he prompted. Come on—we're getting there. How can I help if you won't let me in?

He could have run a profile on her, but he'd chosen not to. As a private operator he no longer had direct access to some sources, but he had friends who did. In the beginning, it hadn't seemed relevant. Now, it would be taking unfair advantage. A personal intrusion.

"This project of yours," she said. "Is it something my father would have been interested in? You said history—or was it genealogy? Does it have anything to do with medical research? He died of a heart condition he didn't even know he had. As far as I know, it doesn't run in the family."

She still didn't get it.

Cards-on-the-table time. "Sorry, I'm not on the trail of some medical miracle. I don't have the background for it. You know I was once with the SBI—I told you that. I'm in private practice now, specializing in cases that were never solved. What's called cold cases." He waited for that much to sink in, and then said, "Mariah, your father came to me and asked me to look into your mother's death."

He was prepared for anger or flat-out disbelief. Instead of either reaction she continued to stare at him. Wondering which rock he'd crawled out from under?

Dammit, he felt low enough. Maybe he should have leveled with her from the first. "Mariah? Did you hear what I said?"

"I heard you."

One thing he'd have to say for her—the lady didn't shock easily. Evidently she'd rolled with a few punches. Literally, if the clues he'd picked up from her body language were anything to go by. It would explain some of her defensiveness. The piranhas she called her family would explain the rest.

He gave her enough time to respond. When she didn't, he

said, "Occasionally, years after the fact, certain evidence comes to light and an old case is reopened."

She looked at him then, those dark eyes puzzled in her too-pale face. "What case? My mother's death was an accident. I was there— I saw it."

"You saw an explosion."

"They were…Jack was refueling the engine. I went back to get Mama's sunglasses."

"Sweetie, run back and get Mama's good sunglasses, will you? They're on the kitchen windowsill."

"Wait for me! I'll be right back!"

She'd been halfway to the cottage when her mother had called out to tell her to get herself a hat. Mariah had turned around, which was how she'd seen it happen.

"What happened to the, uh—wreckage?" Gray asked now.

"How do I know? It sank, I guess." She lifted her hands in a gesture of exasperation. Or of helplessness. "Ask Orestes. Now, are we done with this topic? Because I can tell you, I don't want to talk about it anymore."

"Just one more question."

"No more questions. There was an explosion and my mother died, and that's the end of it."

"What caused the explosion?"

The quieter his voice, the more belligerent her answers. "I don't know what caused it! Obviously there was a spark and the fumes just exploded." She gestured wildly with her arm, sloshing wine dangerously close to the top of her refilled glass.

"What caused the spark?" Gray had his own ideas about that, based on what Wilbur Harvey had told him. It was far-fetched, but then, so was murder in a place like this. Thank God he'd had the forethought to check out the boathouse before it burned. It hadn't taken a forensics lab to see what had, in all likelihood, caused the gas tank to blow.

"Whatever usually causes sparks. Someone lit up a cigarette?"

"Did either your mother or the guide smoke?" Irrelevant, but he needed to draw her out, to bleed off some of the pressure that had built up inside her over the years. She was already starting to calm down. Evidently the wine, as bad as it was, was doing the trick. That, or being able to let some daylight into what had to have been an ongoing nightmare.

Finally she said, "I'm pretty sure Mama didn't, not then. I remember hearing Daddy say she'd quit again, so she wouldn't have had her cigarettes with her."

"Gallins was an experienced waterman. He'd have known better."

"So what are you saying? Someone planted a bomb onboard the boat?" Looking belligerent and vulnerable at the same time, Mariah reached for her glass again and drained it. "Is that what my father thought? Did he ask you to look for—what, bomb fragments?" She snorted in disbelief, then got up to pour herself another glassful.

It occurred to him that she might need to slow down…or maybe not. A few hours of alcohol-induced sleep might be worth the price she'd likely pay tomorrow.

Sitting down again, she drew her feet up onto the cushion. "I can't believe this. It's just too weird, after all this time. I mean, it's not as if the place was crawling with strangers. Not back then, at least. There was nobody around but family. I know— I was here. I wasn't even eight years old but I can remember it as clearly as if it happened yesterday."

"A child's memory might distort certain images and leave out others altogether," Gray suggested, watching for a reaction. He was feeling his way here. He didn't want to lead her, he only wanted to help.

That, and to find out anything she could remember that might help him sign off on one element of the case, at least. "Can you think of anyone who—sorry, but there's no easy way to put this—who might have wanted to see your mother dead?"

Mariah shot to her feet, swaying and glaring down at him. "Absolutely not! They might not have liked her—well, not everybody did, at least not the family—but I don't think they'd kill her! I think some of it was jealousy, because we lived in bigger houses and better neighborhoods and I went to a private school." She sat down, staring moodily at the wall. "I guess I didn't realize it then—the way they felt and why—but I've thought about it since I grew up."

He nodded. Over a period of nine years with the State Bureau of Investigation and five more in private practice, he'd seen family dynamics at their best and at their worst. Not much surprised him anymore. "It happens," he said simply, wanting to haul her down onto his lap and stroke away the tension until she was soft and drowsy. Then he would lift her up, carry her to bed and—

No, dammit, he would cover her up and shut the door.

"Mama used to make fun of them," she mused, calmer now and seated again. On the couch, not his lap. "Oh, not seriously, because Mama was never mean, but you know—like when Maud would say something like 'The Henrys don't dye their hair, they make do with what the good Lord gave them,' Mama would laugh and say, 'Well, honey, this one does, and your little boy just *loves* it.' I used to think it was so funny, because Mama had wonderful hair and Maud's hair was the same color as dead grass." Mariah bit her lip, faintly stained now by the dark wine. "Daddy used to shake his head and say, 'Women,' the way Uncle Nat does now. Then he'd go off somewhere, but he wasn't really mad. At least I don't think he was." Her eyes went wide. "You don't seriously think... But Daddy was in Europe when it happened." She shook her head, rejecting the possibility that her father could have somehow been involved.

Gray hastened to reassure her. "Don't even think that, Mariah. If that had been the case, your father would never have brought me in on it."

She appeared to relax a bit at that. "I know, but what exactly did he tell you? Why did he go to you in the first place? I mean, why even bring it up after all this time?"

Gray glanced at his own empty glass. He'd give ten bucks for a beer, but he'd already finished off the Corona Lights he'd brought with him. During the brief period he'd been on painkillers after the last operation, he'd tapered off alcohol. Not that it had ever been a real problem, but a man living alone could slip into some bad habits without even realizing it. Once he'd gone off all medication, he'd decided to cut down, but not out.

"It wasn't so much what your father said as what he didn't say. My guess, based purely on instinct and observation, is that he knew, or at least suspected, that his heart was about to blow. I'm no expert on medical matters, but your father struck me as a man who wanted to put his affairs in order. It never occurred to me at the time, but looking back on a few things he said…"

"What things?"

Gray shrugged. "Maybe not the words so much as the way he said them. He talked a lot about you. He gave me a picture of you and your cousins and a bunch of fish. They were all laughing. You weren't."

She frowned, as if trying to remember the occasion. "Was I wearing a sailor hat?"

He nodded, and she said, "Oh, Lord, I remember that picture. I'd just turned thirteen and they took me out on the water but they wouldn't let me fish because they said there weren't enough rods, and then I got sick, but they still wouldn't take me back in. They were mad with me because Daddy and Aunt Belle made them take me along. These two boys from Hatteras had come over for the day in a boat to take Lynn and TA out. I remember they wanted to water-ski, but the boat wasn't fast enough, so they settled for fishing."

Some things, he thought now, hadn't changed all that much. They were a peculiar bunch, all right, the proud Henrys of Henry Island. If what he suspected turned out to be true, the old woman was due to start rotating in her grave most any time now.

And if it turned out there was any basis for his most farfetched suspicions, a few seismographs were about to start spiking.

"So, have you learned anything yet? It was an accident,

right? 'Cause it had to have been an accident unless it was a bomb, and nobody 'round here would do something like that. Like I told you, there was nobody here but family.'' She frowned. The lady was getting ever-so-slightly smashed. ''Well, Orestes, o' course. And Jack, but he was killed, too. 'Sides, our family's known his family f'rever. I think I remember hearing Daddy say they were in school together over on Hat'ras, only Jack was a few years younger.''

And maybe into a few things he shouldn't have been, Gray added silently. He wasn't ready to go there. Not yet. Where boats and a transient population were found—and there'd been plenty of both even twenty-odd years ago—then drugs were not only a possibility, but a probability. Conclusive evidence on that point would be hard to come by after all these years without access to police records.

What he couldn't figure out was what, if anything, Roxie Henry's death had to do with the fact that all but one of the Henrys seemed eager to sell. Money easily explained the latter. A whole lot of money, as it turned out. He had checked out real estate prices in the area.

But the price of land didn't explain what had happened twenty-seven years ago. He had most of the puzzle parts before him now, but the picture stubbornly refused to materialize. He had a feeling that no matter how things turned out, Mariah was going to be badly hurt.

''I believe I'll go to bed now.'' She enunciated carefully, setting her glass aside. ''Got to go over things in my head. Best time for thinking. I'll do Daddy tomorrow, then Mason can go and I can…whatever.''

Chapter 17

Her head spinning, Mariah lay awake, while Gray stayed up to keep watch on the fire. Typical of the man, she told herself. Thought he had to look after everyone. Mason—even Orestes.

She wanted Gray here with her. In bed. Doing wonderful things to her body, making that warm glow burst into flames, even though she would probably remember only half of it, if that much, tomorrow. She'd had too much of that awful wine. She never overindulged, never. She'd seen too many people come totally unglued and make fools of themselves ever to risk having it happen to her.

She had nearly begged him to come to bed with her. Thank God he hadn't kissed her good-night. One of them needed to stay sane, and obviously she wasn't up to the task.

Blurred images tumbled through her mind and she struggled to concentrate. Orestes was ill. He hadn't showed up at the fire tonight, but then, from his side of the island, he might not even have seen it.

Could've seen the glow, though—like the tankers offshore during the war that he and Maud used to talk about.

Mason was expecting something profound tomorrow. A memorial service on Memorial Day weekend. The fitness of the timing suddenly struck her, and she thought, *I can do this, I can!* She would think about Daddy's generation and then think of Mason's, and say something about passing the torch.

Or maybe not. Under the circumstances, that might not be the best analogy.

Oh, Lord, she was drunk on awful wine and she still couldn't sleep.

Hours later she awoke with a blinding headache and an unfocused sense of urgency. She had something important to do today. "Daddy…"

Oh, please, not today. She had no idea how to go about arranging a funeral, much less what to say. She could plan a fund-drive with one hand tied behind her. Plan an art exhibit from securing gallery space to lining up judges, hangers and awards—from getting out the invitations to arranging for the refreshments. Piece of cake.

Planning a funeral took an entirely different set of muscles.

The sun was pouring in through the east window, which meant it was still morning. Last night the boathouse had burned; she did remember that much. She'd still been awake, trying to compose a suitable epitaph, when Gray had shouted to tell her.

That poor old boathouse. Nobody ever used it anymore, but still, it was almost like losing another member of the family. Snatches of last night's conversation began filtering through her throbbing brain and she closed her eyes again.

Gray wasn't a simple overaged grad student with a grant to study the genealogy of the horseshoe crab. She'd already known that much. What she hadn't known was that he was here on the island in an official capacity that had to do with her. Or at least, her family.

Was that what all the tea and sympathy had been about? Or rather, the wine and sympathy? He hadn't got her drunk in order to seduce her; he'd wanted to interrogate her. If she could've drummed up the energy, she'd have been furious.

Why on earth had her father hired him to investigate what had obviously been an accident? What, all these years later, had either of them hoped to discover? He could investigate all he wanted to, but it wouldn't change the facts. Roxie Henry had died an accidental death and been buried here on Henry Island. There was a gravestone to mark the event. Not much of one, true, but Mariah could definitely do something about that.

Her father had died of natural causes in Durham. He would be memorialized today here on the island where he'd been born. Mariah would think of something beautiful and meaningful to say. And for an encore, she would tear down that damned PVC fence.

Why would a detective be interested in her mother's death? It wasn't as if she'd been shot or stabbed or poisoned. She'd been down at the pier, standing in the stern of the boat, laughing and waving away a swarm of greenheads, while Mariah struggled to untie the lines, and then Roxie had taken off her old sunglasses with the crooked earpiece and said, "Sweetie, run up to the house…"

No matter how many times Mariah relived that moment, nothing ever changed. Instead of looking back, she'd do better to look ahead.

Look ahead to what? A warm, weepy wake, followed by a promise of future family reunions complete with croquet on the lawn and covered-dish suppers?

Fat chance. All her family wanted from her was her share of Maud's house so that they could tear it down and build one of those monstrous rental machines. Maybe even divide up the island and sell off lots. Another few years, if they had their way, and Henry Island would be wall-to-wall cottages.

"No way," she muttered, shielding her eyes from the glaring light as she prepared to get out of bed. "Not on my island." It might not have any hot tubs—didn't even have a dependable water heater, for that matter, but Maud's house had been good enough for at least three generations of Henrys. It was good enough for Mason, and maybe even Mason's children in another ten or twenty years. Children needed a sense of heritage far more than they needed expensive toys. Roots could lend stability in a wildly unstable world.

Oh, yeah, she thought, wincing at her own pomposity. She was full of theories about how other people should raise their children. The one thing she had to be grateful for now was that Bruce hadn't wanted children. That would have been disastrous.

Mason was leaving today. That meant she needed to get up, first making sure her head was firmly attached to her shoulders. Then she'd shower and get dressed in time to tell everybody where and when the ceremony would be held. If she'd made up her mind by then. Scatter the ashes on the water or bury them in the graveyard?

Not the damned graveyard—not until she'd had time to do something about it. It would have to be the water's edge.

There, one decision had been made for her. She would scatter the ashes on the water, knowing the tide would ultimately carry them back to all the places her father had played as a child. She might even think of something to tell Mason about his great-uncle Edgar, such as the way he used to pitch a softball to her, throwing it arrow straight, but flinching whenever she threw the ball back because she couldn't throw straight if her life depended on it. Mason played Little League. He'd appreciate that, and it would be a link between her father's generation and Mason's. Continuity was important.

Next she needed a Bible.

First, though, she needed coffee. She should have known better. She never got drunk. A glass of white wine with dinner, and tonic with a twist for other occasions. Okay, so she had a headache and her stomach was none too secure. She deserved it. She had no one to blame but herself.

Tough, but them's the breaks, kiddo.

Who used to say that—Erik? Lord, no. Too retro for Erik. It came to her then. Jack Gallins, that's who. A long, long time ago. Amazing that she even remembered, but she did. The time she'd grazed her shin trying to be the first one out of the boat. He'd picked her up and swung her over the side, saying, "Tough, but them's the breaks, kiddo. Next time, don't be so impatient, let somebody help you out."

And the time she'd been trying to find clams with her big toe the way he'd showed her, and been bitten by a hard crab. She couldn't have been more than five or six, but she remembered it so clearly—a tiny fragment of time.

Poor Jack. He'd probably been buried over on Hatteras— what was left of him. On her way back up the beach she might try to find out where his family graveyard was. She could afford the time to stop and pay her belated respects. Actually, Jack had shown far more patience with a pesky, tagalong kid than any of her family members ever had, and she'd scarcely given him a thought since the accident. She wondered now about his family. Had he left a wife and children behind? Grieving parents? She'd been too young and too overwhelmed to ask at first, and then she'd simply forgotten.

She yawned, winced and wished her head and her bladder weren't both demanding attention so that she could steal another half hour of sleep. Bless his heart, Orestes meant well and she wouldn't hurt his feelings for the world, but she'd sooner drink pure grain alcohol than touch another drop of his blackberry wine.

Bracing herself, she sat up, swung her legs over the side of the bed and nearly fell into the chair that was supposed to be over in the corner. She couldn't remember sitting in it last night, much less moving it across the room, but she must have done it. Who else?

"Gray," she whispered. It hadn't been a dream then. He must have put her to bed and left the chair there so she wouldn't fall out.

Oh, please—don't let her have been sick all over him.

By the time she left the bathroom and went in search of coffee, she felt marginally better. Looked like death warmed over, but at least she felt clean after a brief cool shower.

At the kitchen door, she halted. "What is that awful odor?"

"Ready for lunch? Or in your case, we'll call it breakfast."

"Don't talk dirty."

"Hey, it's fish. Orestes came by earlier and brought us some salt mullet, already soaked out. He told me how to cook the little devils, and I've got a plateful all ready. How do you like your egg?"

"Raw. Massaged into your face. Do you have to be so darned cheerful this early in the morning?"

"You looked at a clock yet?"

"My eyes are crossed. I can't see straight."

He moved to her side, spatula in hand, and tipped her face up to the light. "Poor baby, you had a snootful last night, didn't you?"

She closed her eyes. "I don't want to think about last night. Last night never happened. Did you put me to bed?"

There was a long pause, and then he said, "Yep."

"I was afraid of that. I don't remember going to bed, but I do remember you telling me my mother was probably murdered."

"Whoa," he said softly. Placing the spatula on the counter, he took her by both shoulders and said, "Listen, Riah, neither of us knows exactly what happened when your mother was killed. A few things have come to light lately, though, that indicate—"

"Foul play? What are you doing, trying to justify the money my father paid you to investigate?" She regretted it the moment the words left her lips, but she felt mean and miserable and she needed someone to take it out on.

Besides, he was just too damned chipper—not to mention too damned attractive in his last clean pair of jeans, which happened to be the ones that were worn and faded in strategic places, that had drawn her attention in the first place to just how...manly he was.

And that was even before she'd had any firsthand evidence.

His lips thinned. He was still holding her shoulders as if he'd forgotten where his hands were. Finally, grudgingly, she apologized. "I'm sorry. Honestly. That was a rotten thing to say. Whatever Daddy paid you, I guess he thought it was worth it."

"If it makes you feel any better, he paid me by letting me have this place for six weeks. Like I told you, he wanted someone to look into things down here and I needed to get away for some R and R. Since then a few things have come to light that I doubt even your father suspected. But even if they hadn't, I never go back on my word, Mariah. Never."

Great. Guilt-laced embarrassment heaped on top of a hangover. What a way to start the day. A day that was supposed to be special. She didn't even want to know what had come to light. Not now. One crisis at a time was all she could handle.

"I've got to plan Daddy's thing. I have to do it today—I promised Mason."

"I know. I'll help any way I can. I've already spoken to Lynette. She's agreed to wait to leave until later today." His voice rumbled deep inside his chest, like distant thunder. How had she come to be leaning on him? She wasn't a leaner. Never had been. She'd always prided herself on her independence. She was like her grandmother in that respect.

"How about I make you some toast," he said, his voice gruff and sexy and incredibly gentle. "We can start with that and hot tea."

"And aspirin. Please. My head's splitting." She was going to have to restock his medicine chest at this rate. His closet, too.

"Figured it was something like that. Let's settle your stomach first, then we'll see about your other complaints. I'm pretty good with my hands."

Eyes widening, she pulled away. He said, "Massage can help in cases of tension headaches. I'm not sure if that includes hangovers or not, but we could give it a try."

"Thanks, but I don't really have time for a massage, I've got to get this memorial service organized. Lynn's not going to hang around much later than midafternoon. Holiday traffic shouldn't be all that bad today—not as bad as tomorrow, anyway, but if I know Lynn, she'll be itching to go. Probably has a date tonight back in Durham, and that's a good five hour drive from Hatteras.''

''Okay, let's get organized, then.'' He reached for the kettle and poured steaming water over a tea bag, then removed a couple of slices of bread from the freezer and popped them into the toaster.

She sat because she didn't know what else to do. The thought of organizing anything at the moment was a joke. She couldn't even organize her own emotions, much less a semi-public ceremony.

Holding the tea bag aside with her finger, she dutifully sipped tea and nibbled on dry toast. Gray got out a pencil and paper. ''Now…you planning on, uh—burying or scattering? I can dig if you want to bury—in fact, I'll go ahead and clear out a place. I guess that's needed first, right? I take it we're clear on any necessary permitting.''

Crunch time. ''I've decided to scatter his ashes on the water. He grew up playing in it. Boating, swimming—whatever you can do on water, Daddy did. Besides, Mama…''

Reaching across the table, Gray covered her hand with his, squeezing as if to cut off her thoughts. ''It's fitting. I think he'd have liked it. You have any particular place in mind?''

''Not really. Maybe over to the right of the bulkhead. The beach there's wide enough for everyone to stand.''

He jotted down a note and muttered, ''Beach, standing—no chairs.'' Looking up, he asked, ''Have you thought about what you're going to say, or are you going to let everyone speak in turn, pay their last respects and all that? How about getting a preacher over from Hatteras or Ocracoke? Although scheduling on such short notice might be a problem.''

''No preacher. Daddy wasn't churchy. He was a good man, but you know—not organized, religiously speaking. Do you know how many funerals I've ever attended?'' She shoved aside her unfinished toast. ''One. My mama's. It was—well, from my point of view at least—it was awful. I was crying,

Daddy was crying—I don't know about the others, but it seemed to go on and on and on.'' She frowned. ''Did somebody play the harmonica or did I just imagine that? Maybe Orestes—no, he wasn't there.'' After a bite of toast she said thoughtfully, ''I wonder why.''

Gray cupped her face in his hands. She swallowed hard, forgetting all about her headache and her queasy stomach. He was right—he did have good hands.

''Listen, your father belonged to you more than he did to any of the others. Do it any way you want to do it—you have the right and I'm sure he'd have approved. He was proud of you, Riah. He told me that.''

''Oh, Lord, now I am scared. When it comes to something really personal…'' She shook her head. ''Don't ask.''

Stroking her cheeks with his thumbs, he said, ''Hey, don't sweat it, you'll do just fine. Don't think about anyone else, they don't matter. Just think about your father. Say what you think he'd like to hear.''

She pulled away. Broke contact, because it was either that or curl up in his arms, where she felt safe. Where the rest of the world seemed to disappear until only the two of them existed.

He cleared his throat and picked up his pencil again. ''Okay, where were we? No preachers, no music. How about a Bible verse or two?''

''The valley of the shadow? Now I lay me down to sleep? My brain's not working yet. Can you think of something appropriate?''

''This is your deal. Like I said, you're the one who needs to feel right about it.''

She heaved a sigh and thought about it. Raking back her chair, she said decisively, ''You're absolutely right. I'm going to go outside and stand by the water and open my mind until something drifts in.''

Gray switched off the stove, grabbed the canvas outback hat she'd seen him wear several times and plopped it on her head.

It slipped down over her forehead. "Sunglasses?" he suggested.

"Please. I'm wearing my eyes wrong-side out today." She crammed her hair up under the hat, resettled it, and this time it stayed in place. Wobbly, but worth it for the shade. And then she jammed her sunglasses on her face, wishing they covered more of it, and left.

Somehow, she wasn't too surprised when he followed her. They strolled down to the water's edge, over a bit to the right, where the beach was widest. "What do you think? This looks like a good spot to me," he said.

"I think so, too."

"Now stand here a few minutes, open your senses and see what comes through."

She shot him a quizzical look. "I wouldn't have taken you for one of those *X-Files* types."

"You never know, do you?" His grin went a long way toward cutting the last shreds of tension.

Tension of one sort, at least. Thank goodness he didn't offer his special de-stressing massage. Next time, she might not have sense enough to refuse.

Chapter 18

The service was held at one forty-five that afternoon, under a rapidly graying sky. Those in attendance appeared to pay more attention to the sky than to the solemnity of the occasion. It was definitely a come-as-you-are affair. No one brought what Maud used to call Sunday-go-to-meeting clothes to the island with them.

Mariah certainly hadn't.

"My friends—my family." She cleared her throat and tried to think of how to say what was in her heart without sounding pompous. "Daddy and I weren't as close as we should have been. You knew him longer than I did, so if any of you want to speak—I mean, to say something about him...to him..."

Oh, God, she was no good at this! She should have found a preacher and turned it over to him. At least then the occasion might have had a little dignity.

Lynette glanced at her watch. Mason looked far too solemn for a little boy of ten. Orestes hadn't showed up, after all. Mariah wasn't even certain anyone had told him when or where once they'd decided.

Uncle Linwood kept checking the sky as if expecting the worst, and no one volunteered to speak. She wished she had asked Gray to bring Orestes here, if he had to carry him bodily. He was using a cane now. Only a week ago he hadn't needed one.

Things were changing too rapidly. The very atmosphere was unsettling. She needed to get through this and leave—go somewhere and collect herself before she came back and dealt with whatever else was going on.

I'm sorry, Daddy—where was I?

Gray stepped forward and handed her a bouquet of red honeysuckle and some white fuzzy wildflowers. He said, "Do it. I'm with you."

She did it. Waded out thigh deep and opened the top of the urn, which Gray had already loosened. She threw urn, ashes and lid as far as she could. The urn flew sharply to the left, scattering a veil of gray until it splashed into the water.

Finally pitched me a curve, didn't I, Daddy?

And then she said the first thing that popped into her head. "'Full fathom five thy father lies, of his bones are coral made. Those are pearls that were his eyes. Nothing of him doth fade, but doth suffer a sea change, into something new and strange.'"

After a moment of stunned silence, she backed ashore, murmured, "Amen," and burst into tears.

Gray waved the others aside, not that anyone rushed to comfort her. "Edgar would have liked that. I don't know where you found it, but it suited the occasion perfectly."

The others left. Mariah squeaked and wailed, and Gray shoved a handkerchief into her hand. "W-were you a Boy Scout, by any chance?" She managed to smile through her tears.

"Yeah—once upon a time. Why?"

She pulled herself together then. With all the practice she'd had lately, she was getting good at quick recoveries. "Always prepared."

"I think that's the Coast Guard's motto, but close enough.

Now, want to go see Mason off? I don't think Lynette's planning to hang around much longer."

With a shuddering sigh, Mariah nodded. "It's from Shakespeare's *Tempest*. Probably not verbatim. Daddy used to read it aloud to me after Mama…you know. The pearls and coral sounded so much better than any pictures my imagination conjured up." Then she said briskly, "Come on, we'd better hurry."

Gray hung back as she marched toward the pier, her wet shorts flapping against her thighs. Then he sauntered along after her, his eyes narrowed as he watched the others. Neither he nor Mariah glanced at the blackened ruins of the boathouse as they passed.

Gray knew that Orestes had been there earlier that morning before anyone else was awake. Seeing the distinctive tracks of a man and a cane, another piece of the puzzle had fallen into place. Gray didn't look forward to having to tell her, but maybe together they could decide what to do.

First they needed to see the kid off. Then she needed to eat something and settle down with a book or maybe some music. Something soothing to help get her through the next few hours until she felt ready to move on to the next step. As it happened, he'd brought along a CD player and a handful of his favorites. Bluegrass wasn't exactly restful, but he had some good classic country.

Linwood was already untying the lines, ready to cast off. Lynn lingered on the pier, talking to her mother. Mason was in the boat, looking speculatively at the powerful outboard. Seeing their approach, he climbed out onto the pier and ran to meet them.

"Hey, I thought you weren't coming to say goodbye, Riah. Mama said you were prob'ly too sad."

Gray swooped down and picked him up. There were times when a kid of ten was too big for such public displays—and times when he wasn't.

"Would we miss saying goodbye? Heck no," Gray told him. "Right, Riah?"

"I'll be back in two weeks," the boy said excitedly. He looked from Gray to Mariah, who was composed now, if still somewhat red-eyed. More from last night's overindulgence, Gray suspected, than from the emotional overload. "Mom said I could get my birthday present early, and this time I'll take better care of it, so will you wait for me? Can we go fishing again? Mr. Orestes said he knows a real good fishing hole nobody else knows about, and he promised to show me. You can come, too—both of you, 'cause there'll be plenty of room. He said we could go out in the *Miss Maud,* only she's really noisy 'cause she'd got a—a dry something. I forgot what, but anyway, can you—"

"Mason, come on, we don't have all day."

"Yes, ma'am." Heaving his small shoulders in a huge sigh, the boy slithered down from Gray's arms and turned to go.

"Hold on there, partner, haven't you forgotten something?" Gray leaned over and held out his hand, palm outward.

Beaming, Mason slapped it and the two of them went through an impromptu multipart handshake. Then Mariah held out her arms and he flew into them, squeezing her around the hips.

"Oh, for gawd's sake, come *on!*" With an apologetic look at Mariah, Lynette added, "Sorry, hon—sorry about Uncle Edgar, too, but traffic's going to be bumper-to-bumper going up the beach. What do you bet more than half of them will be drunk?"

Tracy snorted. "Fools. You drive real careful, now—and call when you get home. Linwood, don't forget to pick up some milk while you're over there. Get one from the back—they put the oldest ones up front."

Once the passengers were settled, Linwood backed out, opened the throttle and headed out into the channel. The Detloffs had already gone up to the house. Now Tracy, looking neat and unflustered in her funeral garb of a denim jumper, pearl earrings and canvas sneakers, her gray-blond hair lacquered into a short pageboy that defied both wind and humidity, turned to follow.

Gray and Mariah lingered on the pier, watching as the boat grew smaller. They waved at Mason until Lynette made him sit down and face forward. Then Gray moved behind Mariah and placed both his hands on her temples. "No discernible tremors from this side. How's it feel from the inside?"

Mariah managed a chuckle, which had been his aim all along. Or maybe his aim had been simply to touch her. "Better," she said. "A whole lot better. He'll probably be a smart-alecky teenager next time I see him."

"Maybe not. Couple of weeks won't make that much difference."

They turned and headed back to the cottage. She got as far as, "I won't be here in—" but broke off when they spotted Erik coming out onto the front porch of Layzy Dayz. "Was Erik with the others at the...Daddy's commitment?"

"Standing a few feet behind his folks. He left just before they did."

"All I remember is wading out and pitching the urn as hard as I could, and seeing the flowers you tossed drift apart and float away. They were lovely. Thank you."

"You're welcome," Gray said gravely, taking her arm as they approached the cottage.

"A little dignity would have been nice, but then, Daddy would have understood. He knew me long enough to know that if there was an inappropriate way to go about things, I'd be the one to find it."

They were both smiling over that when they reached the steps. Mariah glanced up and said, "Hi, you looking for me?"

And then she remembered the darned boat ride. She really, really didn't want to go, especially not now. Not today. After these horrendous past few days she wasn't sure she could deal with one more event.

On the other hand, if she wanted to find out exactly what was going on, Erik was probably her best bet. Vicki, even if she knew anything, wouldn't be able to tell her without getting it all mixed up.

Ignoring Gray, Erik said, "How about that boat ride, Riah?"

"Now? It's clouding up."

Gray moved ahead and opened the door. "Come in, Mariah. I'll put the kettle on."

"How about you, Erik? Hot tea and salt mullet? If you're hungry you can have my share of the fish."

"Yuck! I'm not that hard up," he said, but followed them inside.

They migrated to the kitchen. Gray put the kettle on, then leaned his hips against a counter, watching as Erik moved restlessly around the room, touching things, opening and closing drawers. "Checking for roaches or just taking inventory?" he asked finally.

"Sorry." Erik seemed even jumpier than usual.

Mariah's suspicions solidified. She wanted some answers and she wanted them now. The trouble was, if she asked point-blank what was going on, she got either lies or evasiveness.

Two could play that game. "How about a nice cup of hot tea?"

"Hot *tea?* I thought you were kidding."

"It's hardly an exotic poison," she said dryly. "I don't know about you, but aside from everything else, I've got a hangover. My first, in case anyone's interested."

"No stuff—your first? What'd you get into last night? I could sure a little pick-me-up," he said hopefully. "And I don't mean tea."

"Gray, get him whatever's left in the jug." To Erik she said, "Orestes was in a generous mood. Not only did he give us some salt mullet, he gave us some of his homemade blackberry wine."

"No way. That is, no thanks." He eyed her oddly, as if he wanted to say something more. "Later," he said abruptly, and left.

Mariah turned to Gray with raised eyebrows. "Was it something I said?"

He poured boiling water over a tea bag. "Something you didn't say. I think he was hoping we had a hidden stash."

"Well, yes, I figured that much, but first he asked me about the boat ride."

"And you told him no thanks, right?"

"Actually, I didn't tell him anything, not about that. First I need something to eat, but not mullet. Maybe some more toast. I'm feeling a lot better, but sort of empty."

"Yeah, funerals can be draining. That's probably one reason all the neighbors bring food. I didn't notice anyone trotting over here with cakes and casseroles."

She busied herself getting out the canned milk and a container of pimento cheese that was only a week or so past its sell-by date. "I hardly gave them time. Anyway, this is sort of different."

"Different how?"

"It's usually friends and neighbors who bring food, not immediate family. Daddy was their brother. I'm sure Aunt Tracy and Aunt Belle are grieving as much as I am."

"Sure they are," Gray said, his voice laced with skepticism.

"Look, I'd rather not talk about it, okay? It's done, and now I have to start thinking about what comes next."

He pressed her into a chair and handed her the cup, then got out a fresh tube of saltines and a knife. "Okay, but first let's talk about this boat trip you're not going to take with cousin Erik."

She scowled at her tea. It was too hot to drink. "Let's don't."

"Then let's talk about something else. In case you hadn't noticed, Erik's a big boy now. He's not into fishing or any other water sport so far as I can tell. So why the boat trip? And why is he satisfied to hang around with a bunch of relatives in a place where the hottest action is seeing how many ornaments his sister can latch on to various parts of her body?"

Mariah glared at him. "Vicki is Erik's sister."

"Exactly. Like I said, there's no action here. Detloff strikes me as the type with a short attention span. In other words, he bores easily.'' Gray pulled out a chair and straddled it, resting his elbows on the table. Over on the counter a plate of fried corned mullet slowly congealed in its juices.

Mariah sipped her tea, ignored the crackers, which were stale, anyway, and scooped out a spoonful of pimento cheese.

Gray picked up a half-eaten slice of cold toast, sprinkled sugar on it and bit off a corner. For a while neither of them spoke. Then he said, ''Want to go with me to pay another visit to Orestes?''

''Not particularly. Why? That's disgusting,'' she said, indicating the sugary toast. ''Don't we have any jelly?''

''I like sugar on my toast. Why? Because the boathouse burned, and there's no reason for it to have caught fire.''

''Spontaneous combustion.''

''After all this time? I doubt it. And because Orestes has been doing a lot of burning lately. And because I've got this prickly feeling between my shoulder blades, and I need a few more answers.'' And because, while the old man hadn't shown up for the commitment service, there'd been that distinctive trail along the woods path early this morning, leading directly to the ruins of the boathouse.

''Try calamine lotion for your itch. As for answers, I doubt if Orestes knows anything about anything, and even if he does, can you trust his memory?''

''Can you trust yours? Granted, he's old, but you were, what—seven years old when your mother died?''

''Going on eight.''

''Right. But chances are, you and Orestes remember different things about that day. Like who was where and what they were doing.''

''What did he know and when did he know it?'' She repeated the familiar lines thoughtfully. ''I never thought about it before—I mean, who was where. I think Maud was somewhere—I can't remember seeing her that day, but what difference does it make now?''

"Probably none at all. Sometimes, though, just asking a question can trigger a chain of events."

"I've had about all the events I can handle, thanks." Mariah shoved the cup away. "This stuff is tasteless. Don't we have any Earl Grey?"

"Sorry. Gray Elgin's the best I can do." His smile invited her to forget her doubts, worries and fears and think about things neither of them had any business thinking about. "My middle name. Now you know everything about me, and I don't know anything at all about you except that you swim like a fish, you kiss like a dream, you're allergic to poison ivy and you don't particularly care for sweet wines."

He thought she looked flushed, and was delighted. For a sophisticated San Franciscan, the lady was full of surprises.

"Roxanne," she said. "My middle name. I was named after my mother."

Gray nodded thoughtfully. He'd known it, of course. That kind of basic information was in the file her father had given him. "One of the things I asked him the other day—Orestes, I mean—was if anyone had brought up the wreckage, and if so, where it was stored."

"What are you saying—that Orestes has something to hide? That he burned down the boathouse? That's crazy."

Gray scraped back his chair and stood. "Probably." He chose not to mention the gas can nozzle with a single bullet hole he'd found hidden under a heap of old net in the boathouse. "Why don't you stay here and take a nap? I'll be back in an hour or so."

"Maybe I will. Not that I can sleep, but at least I can start making lists."

"Right. Lists are a good way to focus the mind."

Gray hadn't been gone more than ten minutes before Erik let himself inside again. "Riah? I just checked the weather. We're okay for now, but it's starting to look iffy for later in the week. So how about it?"

Chapter 19

"Oh, shoot," she muttered. "Sure, why not?" If Gray were here he'd just try to talk her out of it. She had her own agenda, and this didn't have anything to do with his mission. Erik hadn't even been born when her mother was killed.

"Get a hat," he said. "You got any sunglasses?"

She had sunglasses, but not a hat. She borrowed Gray's canvas safari hat again and crammed her hair up underneath to make it fit. The last thing she needed was a blistered nose. It hadn't happened before, but that wasn't to say it couldn't, gray sky or not. Her whole life had turned into one of those Murphy's Law things.

"I'm ready."

"You're wet." He glanced at her shorts, which were mostly dry now, but still damp around the seams.

"I'm not wasting any dry clothes on a boat ride. Do you want to go or not? Because I need to be back in—in an hour."

He led her down to where Orestes's old skiff was tied up. She said, "I thought we were going out on your father's boat."

"Too noisy. I hate trying to talk over a noisy outboard."

She interpreted it as meaning his father had refused to lend him the keys. "Just so we get back in time." Actually, she preferred the small skiff. How much trouble could you get into in one hour with a five-horsepower outboard? Besides, the old skiff had sentimental value to her after yesterday's fishing trip.

The very fact that Orestes had lent him the boat counted for something, too. While she might not trust the old man's judgment where wine was concerned, she trusted him implicitly when it came to character. And Erik, no matter how messed up he might be at the moment, was Maud's grandson. How far from the oak could an acorn fall?

All right, so he was a druggie. She couldn't swear to it, but all the signs were there. On the other hand, the fact that he was here with his family, in a place where there was no chance of scoring a hit or whatever the proper parlance was, said something about his character, didn't it?

Family feeling. Maud had instilled it in all her offspring. Mariah would like to think they had passed it on, but only time would tell. It was the kind of thing that rarely showed up in the early years.

Once they were out on the water, away from other influences, she was pretty sure she could bring Erik around to telling her just what was going on. It was worth a try, at any rate. If he lied, then she would know definitely that something was going on, because he'd never been able to lie convincingly. Even as a kid, he'd always worked too hard at it. His eyes had always given him away, not by being too evasive, but by being unnaturally direct.

She leaned back on one of the faded kapok cushions, letting the hazy sun and the sound of the outboard lull her senses. Light splintered off the surface in the distance, but up close the water was clear bottle-green. She'd always loved the color, pictured it that way whenever she thought about the island. She'd learned to swim in these same dark waters.

Random thoughts filtered through her mind. Through sun-shaded eyes she studied her cousin, wondering what his real purpose was in taking her out. Oh, sure, he wanted to mine what he thought of as her "connections," no matter that she'd told him she didn't have any, but was there another reason? Were the aunts and uncles up to some financial skullduggery that Erik thought she should be warned about? If it involved her, then she needed to know.

And if it involved Henry Island, it definitely involved her.

"Remember Dredge Island? Can you believe how much it's grown up just since we were kids? Wonder if anyone owns it...."

"State, probably," she murmured without opening her eyes. The drone of the outboard and the motion of the boat combined to make her feel drowsy. Now that her father had been laid to rest—in a manner of speaking—it was as if an enormous weight had been lifted from her shoulders. She was in no hurry to take on another load, but she had a feeling this couldn't wait much longer.

"Riah, about the other night—the gas leak and all," Erik said, and reluctantly, she opened her eyes and sat up. "I mean, no kidding, if anyone wanted to blow you up, they wouldn't have turned off all the pilot lights. Gas plus fire equals boom, right?" And then he winced. "Ah, jeez—I'm sorry, I shouldn't have reminded you."

As if she needed reminding. "Funny thing," she mused. "It occurred to me that if anyone wanted to get rid of me without hurting anyone else, that's exactly what they'd have done. What do you think, Erik—is someone trying to get rid of me?"

He looked horrified. "Jesus, Rye, no way! I mean, why would anyone want to do that?" He was staring at her. He always made eye contact when he was lying, as if to disprove the common theory.

Trouble was, he did it when he wasn't lying, too.

The wind whipped her hat loose and she caught it just in time and tucked it under the seat. "Oh, I don't know. Just this crazy idea I had. I mean, if it's all about getting my signature

on a quitclaim deed, then I might be persuaded to sign if—
if—someone else promised to do something for me in return."

He gave her a wary look. "Like what? I'm not saying that's
what it's about—not that anything's going on, but you know—
if you thought something was, that wouldn't be it." And then
he grimaced and said, "Ah, shit."

She had to laugh. "Three guesses why you didn't land that
role in the 'Lost Colony.' You can't act worth a toot. Erik,
you are so transparent."

"Hey, I'm not acting."

"Then you really are that stupid? Oh, come on—you
thought I didn't know you all were planning to sell Maud's
high ground the minute you could get a clear title, so that
some developer could come in and build one of those Mc-
Mansions on it? Give me a little credit. You've got surveyors
crawling all over the place with their little red flags, and it's
supposed to be a big secret?"

Instead of answering he pretended to fiddle with the throttle.
The engine took on a different note as they neared the inlet.
With the outgoing tide running strong, most of the fishing
boats were either trolling outside or on the far side of Dredge
Island near the ferry channel.

She'd been facing aft, watching Henry Island fall behind—
watching Erik try unsuccessfully to sell her a bill of goods.
Glancing over her shoulder, she said, "Don't you think we're
getting too close to the inlet? I'm not sure that old outboard's
rated for this much current."

"Hey, it's cool, I've got everything under control." Right
on cue, the thing started running smoothly again. Flashing his
dimples, Erik said, "Tell me something, cuz. Why'd you come
out with me if you thought—you know, about the gas stuff
and all?"

Crunch time. She sat up and leaned forward, bracing her
arms across her thighs. "Why? Because I want to know exactly what's going on and who's behind it." And because
aside from Vicki, she added silently, you're the weakest link.
"I'm willing to make you a deal if you'll call off the dogs."

"Ouch. What'll you give me not to tell Mama and Aunt Tracy you called 'em dogs? But go on—I'm listening." They were moving slower now, the engine sounding smooth, but increasingly labored.

But that was all wrong, Mariah thought abstractedly. With the current sweeping them along, it shouldn't have to work so hard. She glanced over her shoulder toward the turbulent waters of the inlet. Suddenly uneasy, she said, "No kidding, Erik, I think we should turn back now."

"Chicken. Okay, okay, I'm getting ready to come about. So what's this deal you're talking about?"

Abstract thoughts tracked quickly through her mind. Thoughts about heirs and wills and deeds. Maud had left everything equally to her three children...hadn't she? Even if she'd died intestate, the direct line of descent was clear. When Edgar had died, the same thing held true. Edgar's share went to Mariah; everything else stayed the same.

"Deal?" she said, "Oh—the cemetery. Have you seen it lately?"

"Seen what?"

"The graveyard. It's a real mess. Nobody's been there in ages, and it's all grown up, and that's not even the worst of it."

"The worst of what? What the devil are you accusing me of now?"

"Well, for starters, I think you're into something you wouldn't want the folks to know about. Erik, I know where that sort of thing leads, and believe me, you don't want to go there. Look, I'll make you a deal. You clean off the graveyard, mow the weeds and grub out all the vines, and for Pete's sake, take down that hideous pipe fence someone put up. That's the first thing." She raked her blowing hair from her eyes. "Next, promise me you'll lay off drugs. Get help, if you need it. I'll do everything I can to get you on the waiting list at a rehab facility, but in the meantime you've got to promise me to keep Henry Island chemical free. You do those two things and tell me what's got everybody around here so antsy, and I won't tell Uncle Nat about your little problem." She waited for a reaction. It was the only card she had to play, and it wasn't even a face card. "Uncle Nat would skin you alive, you know that."

"I'm not admitting anything, but what if I do all that? Will you promise to sign over your interests free and clear?"

"To Maud's house? Sure, for a third of whatever it brings. I don't look forward to sharing the island with a lot of strangers, but it's still better than anyplace else I can think of." She looked nervously over her shoulder again. "Erik, turn back, I don't like this."

"Maud's house," he repeated thoughtfully. "What about the cottage?"

"Layzy Dayz? No way, that's mine free and clear. They can't think I'd sell that, not unless I was dead broke and deep in debt."

A funny look crossed his face, but he said nothing.

"Well, do we have a deal or not?" Actually, she thought it was an extremely generous offer, all things considered. A few hour's work on his part, plus doing something he needed to do for his own sake. In exchange, she'd do something she really didn't want to do, but probably would have done in the end, anyway. Otherwise, knowing Uncle Nat, he'd start soaking her for maintenance and other expenses. At the moment, she couldn't even support herself, much less support an old eight-room house on a storm-prone island.

Just then the engine sputtered and died completely. In the sudden silence, Erik swore and Mariah lunged for the oar. Before she could work it out from under the seats, he stood and jerked it from her hands. "I'll get it, I'll get it," he snapped.

"Just do something with the outboard, we're drifting too fast!" The boat rocked dangerously. She grabbed the gunwale and leaned over to see how deep the water was and how close the nearest shoal was, just in case.

Not a glimmer of a shoal, just deep, bottle-green water, the slick surface turgid with undercurrents. "Dammit, Erik, give me that thing if you're not going to—"

She never got to finish. Something struck her a hard blow on the back of the head. Blinded by pain, she lurched headfirst over the side.

The tide caught her immediately, sweeping her toward the inlet. Numb with pain and shock, she surfaced and reached out to where the boat was supposed to be.

Only it wasn't. "Erik!" she screamed. Disoriented, she pedaled her feet and moved her arms, propelling herself in a circle. "Er-ik! Help me!"

The boat was rapidly falling behind. She felt the first hint of an undertow and tried to conquer panic with reason. Her shoes—that's what was pulling her down. She tried to toe one off and when that failed she doubled over and tugged them off, one after the other. The water was cold, but not icy, deceptively calm on the surface as the muscular tide raced to meet the sea.

She swallowed a mouthful of saltwater and gagged. "Er-ik! Throw me a cushion!"

"Hang on," he shouted. The boat had turned sideways, but was still drifting toward her. He appeared to be trying to paddle with the single narrow-bladed oar, only from her perspective—he was standing and she was low in the water—it looked almost as if he were sculling against the current instead of with it. But that was crazy.

She yelled again, tried to wave and went under. She knew better than to try to swim against the tide. She was good, but not that good. Her clothes weren't helping, but she couldn't waste time undressing.

"Erik! Throw the cushion!" she screamed, stunned to see how far apart they were now.

And then, even above the increasing roar of the clashing surf, she heard it. The low throb of the outboard as it caught up again. The skiff was moving away, slowly but relentlessly heading back toward the island.

Fear momentarily eclipsing the pain in her head, she knew

then that she was never intended to survive. This was the reason Erik had been so friendly.

And she'd thought he wasn't an actor?

All right then, it's up to me, an inner voice whispered calmly. Treading water, she scanned the horizon, looking for anyone who might have seen what happened. Anyone in a boat who was close enough to help her.

How had he dared, with at least half a dozen fishermen in plain view?

No one was even looking. They were all moving toward a slick where gulls were diving and squawking. Don't let it be bluefish, she thought frantically. Bluefish had teeth like razors. In a feeding frenzy, they would strike at anything. She should have kept her shoes on; they'd have provided some protection…if they hadn't pulled her under.

Oh, dammit—Oh, God—somebody, help me! "Help me!" she screamed.

If she could just make it to shore, or even to a shoal where she could touch down, she could flag down a boat and—

She swallowed another mouthful of water. Chop from the inlet was slapping her in the face now. Frantically, she managed to work her pullover off over her head, the wet cotton knit clinging like seaweed, dragging her under several times before she could free herself.

Cold. She was freezing cold. The shore was getting farther and farther away as she was carried relentlessly toward the middle of Hatteras Inlet. Toward the breakers that lifted, crested and crashed down on hidden sandbars, creating dangerous rips and undertows.

"Help!" she yelled weakly, sighting a small fishing boat in the inlet. The boat disappeared in a trough. Save your strength, the rational portion of her brain instructed. The calm voice of reason was small and growing weaker. Time to stop trying to fight. If she could just go with the tide and manage to avoid the undertow, once she made it through the inlet the current would ease off, and she could swim to shore.

Something brushed past her leg, something hard and long and slick. *No, please—! Oh, God, not that!*

She froze, struggling to control her breathing—knowing that once she succumbed to panic, she was doomed. *You can do this.* The voice of reason spoke again, only it seemed to come from a greater distance now. *Keep your head, tuck your feet up close to your body and don't move. Whatever it is, it'll soon lose interest and go away. Head up, use your arms for balance. Slowly, slowly, that's right—that's the way.*

It's not really cold, it only feels that way.

Great piece of reasoning. *Daddy, you always said I was smart.*

She turned onto her back to float over an oncoming wave, only to have it crash down on her face. Someone whispered, "Save your strength, don't fight it." She was too waterlogged to float, anyway. Easier to sink, shark or no shark.

Allowing her feet to dangle again, she used her arms in a lazy lateral movement and bicycled her legs slowly, holding her breath each time a wave slapped her in the face. Blinking through the stinging salt, she thought she saw a fishing boat in the distance, moving toward the inlet.

A mirage? "Look at me! See? I'm right here!" She tried to wave, but another wave slapped her in the back of the head. Pain momentarily blinded her. When she looked again, the boat was still there...nearer?

Nearer. Now, if only it was moving slowly enough to see her, but fast enough to reach her in time.

Her head was pounding. She didn't know it if it was bleeding, but Erik had whacked her good with that oar. And blood attracted sharks. She vowed to kill him if she lived, because he'd done it deliberately, just as he had deliberately rigged that gas leak.

She knew that now. Her dear, sweet cousin, the weakest link. Good thing she hadn't confronted the strongest link.

God, please don't let me drown. I'll do whatever I have to do—I'll do good deeds every day and go to church—but first I'm going to kill that lying little bastard.

Hypothermia. It was affecting her brain. Either that or the knock on her head had smashed half her gray cells.

Dammit, she was *not* going to die. She had too much to do!

Was that a bell, or were her ears ringing? There was a bell buoy outside Hatteras Inlet; she could hear it from the island when the wind was right. That meant she was almost through the worst, didn't it?

Where was that boat?

Another wave slapped her in the face. When her eyes cleared, she heard someone shouting behind her. "Ri-ah! Hang on, young'un, we're a-comin'!"

Instead of heading around to the back of the island, Gray set a straight course toward the new pier, throttling back only at the last moment to ease past the Detloffs' cabin cruiser. Hulls thumped, scraped, then thumped again. He was no expert at handling anything larger than a twelve-foot bass boat, but he'd been driving since he was twelve and he was a quick learner. Orestes could never have managed alone. By the time Gray had reached him little more than an hour ago, the old guy had been struggling to get himself down to the wharf.

"She's out there with that devil," he'd shouted as soon as Gray emerged from the woods path. "Hurry, boy! No time to waste!"

Gray hadn't stopped to ask questions. He'd come on another mission, following the distinctive trail through the woods. Not that he claimed to be a tracker, but those cane marks were unmistakable.

"I'll need your help," he'd said, catching up with the old man just as his knees buckled.

"He's got Edgar's girl. He come after my boat—didn't even ask me, just took off with her. I watched from the house, seen 'em round the point and head down toward the inlet."

Gray didn't have to ask who had taken the skiff. Linwood wasn't back from Hatteras yet, and Detloff the elder was holed up with the real estate people. "You want to show me how to operate this thing? What about fuel?"

"I keep her filled up. Keeps my tank from rusting out. Hurry, son, set me aboard. I ain't walking too good n'more."

He hadn't been walking at all. Gray had picked him up as if he weighed no more than Mason, which wasn't far from the truth. Under the baggy old overalls and loose shirt, there was little but skin and hollow old bones.

Gray knew the signs. He'd pretty well made the diagnosis after a closer look at the medication, but respecting the old man's dignity, he had hesitated to bring it up.

With Orestes giving instructions from a kitchen chair that had been bolted to the deck, and Gray at the controls, they'd managed to get the *Miss Maud* out into the channel. Orestes had manned the binoculars. They'd been running for perhaps ten minutes when he said, "There, he's a-comin' back in. Dad-burn devil's by hisself, too! Open 'er up, son."

Gray was rusty, but he still remembered how to pray. *Please help me find her before it's too late—and God, don't let it already be too late!*

The tricky part had been maneuvering into position to pick her up without running over her, especially as she was already in the inlet. Once Orestes had spotted her, he'd started shouting instructions. Gray had done the rest.

"Easy there, son—don't let one of them things broadside you, they're a-runnin' strong today."

A few yards away from the dark bobbing head, Gray had throttled back, maintaining steerage, reacting automatically to the old seaman's commands. "Bring 'er bow around—steady now, steady on, throw 'er into Reverse."

Gray had shouted her name. For one timeless moment she'd seemed to be floating facedown, her hair like dark seaweed on the surface, but then her head had lifted and she'd waved. Barely raised a hand, but at least she'd still been able to do that much.

Thank you, God— I owe you one.

Back at the island, Gray left Orestes in the boat. He couldn't carry them both, and the old man wasn't going anywhere. It was a miracle he'd been able to do this much.

"You want me to get Belle over here to help you?" he asked, carrying Mariah up to the cottage. She was awake now. She'd slept all the way in. After hauling her aboard, using strength he hadn't known he possessed to keep from bruising her on the gunwale, he'd laid her out inside the cabin. The twin engines were enclosed, so even if the boat hit a chop and rolled, Mariah wouldn't be in any real danger. At least it was warm in there. Hot as an oven from running flat out all the way to the inlet.

"How'd you know?" she asked now, her voice weak and hoarse. It was the first time she'd spoken since they'd taken her aboard. Gray felt like bawling.

"Orestes. He saw Detloff take the skiff. It spooked him enough so he was trying to go after you himself when I got there." Fuller explanations could come later.

"Orestes," she said with a sigh, and closed her eyes again.

Inside the house, he peeled off the few clothes she still wore—her khaki shorts, her cotton underwear—and miracle of miracles, the only thing he felt was overwhelming tenderness and thankfulness.

Well…almost the only thing.

She needed warmth. He thought of lowering her into a tub of hot water, but until he could climb in with her and keep her from going under, he wasn't about to take the risk. So he pulled back the thin covers on his bed and laid her there, drawing the sheet up under her chin.

"Ear," she said. "Cover it, too."

He covered her ear. He'd have stood on his head and wiggled his own ears if that's what she'd asked him to do. He moved away from the bed, waited until he was sure she was asleep—a matter of seconds—and then he turned and headed back out to the *Miss Maud.*

He hadn't decided what he was going to do about Orestes. Even if what he suspected was true, this shifted the balance. Maybe more than it should, all things considered, but—

''Well, hell,'' he muttered softly, watching the old wooden boat round the channel marker and head back around the island. Somehow the old guy had found the strength to reach the controls. God help him if he lost his grip and collapsed with the throttle open. There was more than one hazard out there.

Justice would have to wait. It had waited twenty-seven years. Another day wouldn't matter. As for young Detloff, that could wait, too. After seeing that lump on the back of Mariah's head, Gray had a pretty good idea what had happened—and why. A few phone calls would take care of things until he had time to deal with it personally.

And then he hurried back inside and hooked the door behind him.

Chapter 20

Gray dragged a chair over beside the bed and sat, watching carefully for any sign of trouble. He had no way of knowing how much water she'd swallowed or inhaled. Not too much, else it would have come back up by now. She was going to have a few bruises, though. He'd been as gentle as possible, but she'd been a dead weight when he'd hauled her in over the side. Orestes had managed to hold the boat steady just long enough, supporting himself by hanging on to the wheel, a heroic effort that had used up more strength than he had to spare.

But then, the old guy owed her far more than he could ever repay. Gray would have to deal with him. He wasn't looking forward to it.

Now he reached for the fingers that were curved around the hem of the cotton thermal blanket he'd pulled up over the bedspread. They were too pale, too cold, the skin pitifully shriveled. If he had any lotion, he'd have used it. Maybe a heating pad...

He didn't have a heating pad, but after only a moment's

hesitation he did the next best thing. He peeled down to his boxers and climbed into bed beside her, close enough to give her the benefit of his body heat, but not close enough to disturb her.

As for disturbing himself, that was another matter. They both knew they were headed toward something, but this wasn't the time.

With the possibility of a concussion, she shouldn't be sleeping. Exhausted, she needed rest. Catch 22. Most of all, she needed warming, and that he could do. At regular intervals he'd have to rouse her and check her pupils, but ten minutes one way or another wasn't going to make that much difference. He wasn't about to hijack another boat and rush her over to the medical center on Hatteras, and he doubted seriously if any of the medics over there made island calls.

Her skin was still cold, but gradually she responded to his body heat. She murmured in her sleep and wriggled closer, her back against his chest, her butt against his groin.

One hundred. Ninety-nine. Ninety-eight. Ninety-seven...

"Ah, jeez, sweetheart, don't do that," he whispered. He chaffed her shoulder gently. She roused just enough to capture his hand and draw his arm around her waist, holding it against her middle.

Her skin felt like velvet—cool, soft velvet. He held his breath, trying to detect her heartbeat, resisting the temptation to move his hand higher.

He'd come so damned close to losing her, he felt sick.

Her ear was uncovered again, and he used his chin to work the blanket up over it again. Without dislodging his arm from her waist, he drew back to examine the lump on the back of her head. "Time to wake up, sweetheart," he said softly. "Don't go too deep now, come on back and let me check your pupils." She stirred, but didn't wake up. "Open your eyes, Riah." When she didn't respond, he repeated the command. "Come on now, sweetheart, let me see those big brown eyes of yours, hmm?"

"Horrible bedfellow," she murmured.

"Bedfellow? I thought I was a heating pad."

"Turn down the heat, I'm burning up."

So was he. If she didn't realize it, then she was worse off than he'd thought. Her bottom wriggled closer. His groin swelled in response. He groaned and tried to ease away.

"Bastard—I'm going to kill him," she muttered.

Fortunately, Gray knew who she was talking about. Sliding his hand from under hers, he pulled away and sat up. "You'll have to stand in line. Honey, if you're warm enough now, we really do need to check you out. First your knot, then your eyes. If your skull's cracked, you're not going to be killing anyone anytime soon."

She obliged by rolling over onto her face so that the back of her head was fully exposed. Carefully, he fingered her matted hair aside and winced. "Jesus," he whispered. "What'd he hit you with, the anchor?"

"Oar. Am I bleeding?"

"Lucky you didn't bleed out."

"'Fraid of that. Felt a shark…bump my leg."

"Probably a dolphin." Hell, it could've been Jaws and his brother-in-law, but she didn't need to hear that, not now. "Hey, you're home safe. You might as well know now, I'm not letting you out of my sight for the foreseeable future."

"Good. Back to bed, hmm?"

Was she rational? Was she even fully awake?

"In a minute. Honey, I hate to do this, but you need to roll over onto your back now. I'm going to look at your eyes, then I'll make you an ice pack for your head, and then we're going to sit you up awhile, okay?"

She turned her head enough to stare up at him. Brown eyes, the color of weak coffee, red-rimmed from saltwater, but the pupils were even.

He leaned over and kissed her then, just a small kiss—not carnal, only caring. They'd deal with the other when she was back up to speed again. "Stay here—don't run off now, I'll be right back."

Once out in the hall, he braced his hands against the wall

and gently thumped his forehead three times. How could he have allowed this to happen to her? He was supposed to be taking care of her, dammit—he'd promised. That's what Edgar had sent him down here for; he was convinced of it now.

"Gray?" Her voice sounded hoarse, probably from all the saltwater she'd swallowed. Maybe from yelling for help.

"Yeah, honey, right here."

"Bathroom."

"Maybe later. Right now you need rest more than you need a hot bath."

"Gotta pee."

Oh. "Well, sure, I'll just come help you up and wait for you and—and then we'll see about that ice bag."

Shut up, you jerk, just do it.

He waited outside the bathroom door until he heard her flush, then he waited another minute and called out. "Need any help? If you're serious about a hot soak, I guess we can borrow a life jacket." Ha ha. Big joke.

The door opened and he nearly fell inside. She jumped back and nearly lost her balance. "Just stop hovering," she snapped. "I'm all right. I'm fine now, really, so stop treating me as if I were suffering from some horrible disease."

He held out his hands, palm outward. "Hey, I come in peace, okay? You took a pretty hard whack on the noggin— probably swallowed a few gallons of seawater, too. It just occurred to me that you might need to take it easy for a few minutes before you go marching off to battle again."

Something in her too-pale face seemed to soften. "I know— I probably do, but indulge me, will you? What was that old line? 'I'm mad as hell and I'm not going to take it anymore'?"

"That from the *Tempest,* too?" He knew better. He remembered the movie.

"Strictly from temper," she said with a rueful smile. "Sorry. I need to get the bitchiness out of my system before I take on the clan."

"Be my guest. You can take a few practice pokes at me if it'll help."

Several emotions flickered over her face, like cloud shadows racing across a dune. "Make you a deal—you fix me something to eat and I just might spare you my left hook."

"Hey, if it's anything like your curve ball, you got yourself a deal." It occurred to him that it was already too late. He was down for the count and he hadn't even seen the punch that floored him. "Soup and toast?"

"No sugar," she cautioned.

"Yes, sugar," he said with a grin that part relief, part sheer admiration for her spunk.

Over tomato soup and peanut butter toast, Mariah described the situation as she saw it. She was wearing his old gray sweats. Miles too large, they felt marvelously soft and warm. "It's all about money, isn't it?" Without waiting for his comment, she said, "I'm going to pretend for right now that they're not my kin—that I never met any of them before. Maybe then I can be more objective." He nodded. She spooned up more of the soup. Suddenly, she was ravenous. "Being on the water always makes me hungry."

"In that case, you're definitely entitled. Pig out."

After finishing the last of her peanut butter toast, she continued. "Anyway, it's pretty obvious what's going on. Now that Maud's gone, they're planning to divide up not just her house, but the entire island." She shot him a look, as if expecting him to disagree. When he didn't, she turned her attention to spooning up the last of her soup. "Why couldn't they have simply told me that in the beginning?"

"Would you have agreed?"

"Absolutely not! I'd have been horrified."

"Right. And if you'd refused to sell, then what?"

"So instead they try to trick me? They wanted me to sign a quitclaim deed, supposedly for my share of Maud's house. What do you bet it was for the entire island?" Her chin threatened to crumple, but she squared it and went on. "That's an awful way for family to treat family."

"Agreed. But for the time being they're strangers, remember? We're being objective here."

Mariah didn't want them to be strangers, she wanted them to be family. She *needed* for them to be family, but it was looking less and less likely. "They're planning to sell off everything they don't actually need, just like all the other beach developments, aren't they? Before you know it, there won't be a tree left standing. Cottages as far as the eye can see. Great big, showy houses on teensy little lots."

"Close, but no cigar."

Ignoring him, she continued. "We always considered Maud's house sort of the hub. It's the highest ground, which ought to make it the choice site, but the beach lots will be probably be even more valuable." Another thought suddenly struck her. "What about Orestes's place? Do you think he has a deed? Because they're probably going to want that, too. That's what Aunt Belle meant when she said he'd have to go, but I doubt if he'd even consider it, not for any amount of money."

Gray nodded, but didn't comment. Mariah wished he would, because she desperately wanted to be proved wrong. Shoving aside her empty bowl, she said, "The catch is that they can't do anything without my cooperation because all they own outright is the land their cottages are on. And until Daddy's will can be probated..." A look of comprehension dawned. "My God. You don't suppose—"

"They wanted to get rid of you so the entire island would revert to the other two heirs and their spouses? I doubt it. I haven't seen a copy of your father's will, but—"

"He left everything to me," she said thoughtfully. "I don't even have a will, which means..."

"Riah, I think your father might have suspected what was in the works. If they approached him and he refused, their reaction might have been what triggered his uneasiness. He didn't say anything to me about a plan to sell out, but—" Gray raked back his chair and left the kitchen, returning moments later with a thin roll of paper. "Found this down behind the dresser the other day. I didn't mention it at the time, but someone came inside when I wasn't here and went over things pretty thoroughly. Nothing was taken. Logical conclusion—they were looking for something specific."

"Who? What?"

"At a guess, the who is probably your boating companion."

She closed her eyes. "I hate this, I really do. I sort of liked Erik—I mean, he's totally materialistic and pretty messed up, but at his age, a lot of boys tend to be—"

"Tend to be what, Riah? Misguided? Call it like it is. If what I suspect turns out to be true, then…"

"Then what?"

"Later. Right now, I want you to see this. It'll give you some idea of what the stakes really are."

He unrolled the tube, anchoring the curling ends with the sugar bowl and a coffee mug. She studied it, turned it around and studied it some more. "But this is—right there, see?" She stabbed with her finger. "That's the little creek that starts just this side of Orestes's garden and cuts into that marshy area. And here, right here—"

Mariah picked out one familiar area after another, including a cross representing the cemetery. She lifted a stricken face. "How could they possibly even think of carving all this up and selling off slices? If this is what they're planning to do, there won't even be a Henry Island anymore."

"Look at the next drawing," he said, sounding both grim and sympathetic.

Mariah hadn't realized there were two sheets rolled together until she released the top chart to reveal what was underneath. "Oh. My. God," she whispered reverently. "*Swimming pools? A golf course?*"

"And two tennis courts. Obviously, someone's dreaming big."

"You found these here? In our cottage? But that means—"

"Not what you're thinking. Edgar would have said something if he thought things had progressed to this stage. All three cottages have been rented out, remember? I understand

Detloff usually did the booking. Detloff could have brought anyone in here before that, though. Developers, investors— any one of them could have left this behind. It's what's called a conceptual drawing, something a developer would use to interest potential backers.''

Slowly, she shook her head. First attempted murder and now this? "I'm starting to think we need our own sheriff over here.''

"Happy to volunteer my services, ma'am, until we can hold a proper election.'' Gray offered a fleeting smile, little more than a warming of the eyes, but she accepted it gratefully. Right now she needed all the reassurance she could find.

Shoving the rolled-up plat aside, she fingered a curling corner of the wildly enhanced drawing of what Henry Island Resort would look like. The legend at the bottom identified the property. Even without it, the distinctive shape of the island would have been unmistakable.

But nothing else was familiar. A marina where the bulkhead was now, with three long piers instead of a single short one. A glass-fronted club house with colorful umbrellas on an outside deck instead of the old boathouse. And that was only the beginning.

"Has anyone mentioned anything to you about a will?''

She looked up. "Daddy's will? I'm pretty sure they all saw copies, even though they weren't beneficiaries.''

"What about your grandmother's will?''

"Maud's? I don't know. I never asked, I just assumed...''

"Your father included a copy of his mother's will in the file he gave me. It was handwritten, witnessed by Orestes Wallis. It left everything she owned in equal shares to her three children.''

Mariah looked at Gray, waiting. It was only what she'd expected, not that she'd given it a lot of thought.

"It was dated July 1, 1976.''

Silently, she repeated the date. And then a slow sense of horror crept over her. "But it couldn't have— I mean, it's only coincidence." The same week her mother had died? "It has to be a coincidence."

"Does it?" He stood and rolled the two drawings together, shoving them into a drawer holding plastic placemats and spare stove-burner liners.

"Look, I need to make a couple of calls and check out something online. Will you be all right for a few minutes?"

"What about Erik?"

"That's one of the calls I'm making. Do you know what he drives?"

She shook her head. "Other than here, I haven't seen him in years."

"Okay, so we'll get him some other way. You got any idea where he's staying? Does he live in this area, or in Durham?"

"Sort of…all over. I mean, it depends on whether or not he can pick up a job. He works as a waiter sometimes. Summer theater, bartending. Vicki mentioned that he'd spent a lot of time recently down in Myrtle Beach."

"I'll put out a BOLO—a Be On Lookout. Attempted murder is a pretty serious crime."

Attempted murder. She'd once baby-sat Erik and Vicki, while the others went over to Hatteras to a movie. She'd been fourteen, Erik had been about five, Vicki just a toddler.

"Tell me about it." Mariah gingerly touched the back of her head, where a knot the size of half a tennis ball throbbed and stung. The skin had definitely been broken, but evidently she was tougher than her beloved cousin thought.

She doubted if there was any aspirin left in the bottle. This whole trip had turned into one big headache. In the normal course of events—whatever normal was—she had headaches so rarely she'd forgotten how miserable they could be.

Hearing Gray's voice coming from the next room, she got up and emptied the last of the soup from the pan into her bowl. Should she go over to Maud's house and confront them with the evidence? Somebody owed her some answers. Dammit. And yes, from now on she would curse as the occasion demanded. It was either that or punch holes in a few walls.

She was so *hurt.*

And so damn-blasted *furious!*

"Let me check your pupils," Gray said when he returned a few minutes later.

"I'm fine," she said grimly. "Go do whatever you have to do."

"Mariah, let me see your eyes," he ordered gently.

"Oh, all right." She shoved her face toward his and opened her eyes wide. "There, you see? There's nothing wrong with me other than an overload of righteous indignation. At least nothing an ice bag won't cure."

She continued to glare at him, seeing his gray-green eyes darken, his pupils grow larger. "Whose examination is this, anyway?" she murmured just as his face blurred. Not smart, she remembered thinking just before his lips touched hers.

That was her last rational thought before the world eclipsed. She didn't recall standing, but she was leaning against him, his arms wrapped tightly around her. The heat of his body, the scent and the taste of him, swamped her senses like a warm, erotic fog.

He twisted his mouth over hers, parting her lips, exploring gently at first, then giving in to the fierce hunger they both felt, which had been lurking under the surface for days. Just as she was about to beg him to come back to bed with her, he drew away.

"Lady, you're pure quicksand," he said with that wonderful whimsical smile that was so at odds with his rough-hewn features.

She took a deep, steadying breath and murmured, "You're no Rock of Gibraltar, yourself." She wasn't about to call him irresistible, but he was. There was nothing she could do about it but go with the flow and hope for the best.

They clung together, waiting for the fires to burn down to a manageable level. This was not the time. When it happened, she didn't want any distractions.

"Time for you to go back to bed," he said. "Alone."

"Killjoy." As aroused as she was—as he obviously was—

she could still tease. A whole new world of possibilities was opening up, a world she could hardly wait to explore.

"I need to go check on Orestes—he's in pretty bad shape. I need to be sure he made it back, but I don't want you here alone."

"Take me with you."

He shook his head and then kissed her on the tip of her nose. "Not this time. Who do you trust most? Vicki?"

Mariah grimaced. "I trusted Erik, remember? If Lynn were still here, or TA…" God, her family! Who did she trust not to try to kill her? Again. "Aunt Belle, I guess. I can get her started about her garden club, and she'll go on for ages."

"Erik's mother? You sure?"

She nodded, and he said, "Mrs. Detloff it is, then. I'm leaving my gun here, just in case, but I seriously doubt if you'll need it."

"I don't want a gun, I just want things to be the way they always were," she said plaintively.

Had they ever been the way she'd imagined them? How many generations deep did family ties go? Evidently, the ties had frayed.

Reluctantly, Mariah disengaged herself, wrapping her arms around her chest to make up for the loss of warmth. "I thought Erik was the weakest link. That's why I went out with him— I thought if I could persuade anyone to tell me what was going on, he'd be the one. Shows what great people instincts I have, right?"

"Honey, in a case like this where this much money is involved—we're talking tens of millions here—all bets are off. I'm pretty sure they know I'm onto their game now. Your aunt Belle's not going to make things worse than they already are. Boxer's not back yet and Detloff's holed up with the surveyors. I'm taking the other aunt with me to check on Orestes. At this point, I'd rather keep her in sight."

Gray waited for a response, and finally, Mariah nodded. It wasn't as if they could call 911 and wait for reinforcements.

"Just don't let anyone inside until I get back with Belle. I'm locking the doors."

"Why? You just said—"

"Indulge me, okay? I tend to be overprotective."

"Then go take care of Orestes. And thank him for me, will you? Just as soon as I'm out and about, I'll go thank him in person. If he hadn't—"

"Shh, go lie down on the sofa. Stay awake, though. You'll have to get up and let us in."

So it had come to that, Mariah thought, hearing him lock the door before he left. Locked doors here on Henry Island, the safest place on the Outer Banks where everyone knew everyone else and most were kin, to some degree or another. At least among the old families.

They both tended to trust Belle more than any of the rest of the family, even though she was Erik's mother. At this point, Mariah found it hard to trust anyone. She reminded herself that this was the woman who, against all advice, fed every stray animal that showed up. The woman who sent money to every cause, legitimate or not. According to Vicki, she had a whole desk drawer full of those little address stickers so many charities mailed out, and she paid for every batch, even though she never used them.

But then, Vicki was her own favorite charity and probably resented the competition.

All right, so Mariah would trust her aunt, but that didn't mean she would turn her back on her. Better Belle than Aunt Tracy, who could lead a battalion into war without turning a hair.

On the way to Maud's house, Gray glanced toward the pier. Boxer still hadn't returned from taking Lynn and Mason across to Hatteras. He might have had other business over there, business he wasn't particularly eager to disclose.

Gray would like to believe he was at the sheriff's office, giving them a line on his nephew. Going on offense before he was forced into defense. It would have been a smart move for all of them, but it wasn't going to happen. They were in way over their heads, and desperation made them doubly dangerous.

On his way down the first day, Gray had stopped by the sheriff's offices both in Manteo and Hatteras as a common courtesy, to show his credentials and give them some idea of his mission. No one had taken him seriously.

"Come on, are you kidding me? Hey, I wasn't even out of diapers when that one happened," one young deputy had said. "Heard about it, though. They say you could hear it all the way over here."

"Yeah, time to time you get stuff like that," another man had commented. "Bunch of jerks don't know a dick from a dipstick. You wouldn't believe how many dumb asses the local sea rescue squad has to go out and haul in."

"I understand the guide was a local," Gray had prompted.

"Oh, yeah—that was Jack Gallins, wasn't it, Royce? He was a cousin on my mother's side. Third, or something."

When Gray left, they'd still been arguing family relationships, but at least he'd established his credentials and laid the groundwork. When he'd called over just now to report an attempted murder and describe the perp, they'd been all-business.

"License plate?"

"I don't even know what he drives, but I'll let you know within the hour if I learn anything. Can you run the name?"

"Will do. You say he tried to kill somebody?"

"Took a woman out in a stolen boat, got her near the mouth of the inlet, knocked her in the head with an oar, threw her overboard and took off."

"Jesus H. Christ," the deputy muttered. "Attempted, you say. Somebody bring her in?"

"Right. Orestes Wallis."

"Old Orestes? You gotta be kidding! He's a hundred and ten years old."

"I'll get back to you as soon as I know more." Gray had given them his cell phone number.

"I'll put the word out. We'll let you know."

With any luck, Gray thought as he loped up to Maud's front porch, the creep would flip his car and end up in traction, minimum. It was going to be ugly, any way it went down. Family affairs like this always were.

He didn't bother to knock. "You." He pointed at the small woman in the pink flowered slacks. "I need you to stay with Mariah."

Belle's eyes went round as blue marbles. "Is she—?"

"She's fine for the moment, considering she was knocked in the head and dumped out just this side of Hatteras Inlet."

The other sister came in, rolling down her sleeves. "Belle? You!" She glared at Gray. "What are you doing here? What's this about Mariah? What was all that ruckus down at the landing earlier today?"

"Nice of you to inquire. Mariah's fine, considering your son tried to kill her for the second time." The gasps from both women were gratifying, but he didn't have time for that now. "Ms. Boxer, take whatever you need. The door's locked—I'll go with you and unlock it, but then your sister and I are going on a rescue mission." He turned to the older woman. "Be ready five minutes from now. If you've got any first aid equipment, bring it along."

Talking while running wasn't easy. Gray could manage well enough, but the woman beside him was old enough to be his mother. Thank God she wasn't. He didn't want to be here, he wanted—needed—to be back with Mariah. But resources on this damned island were entirely too limited. He was forced to make do with what was available.

"Tell me—what this is all about. Erik's...lazy and not very bright. Belle spoils him. I know—he's impulsive, but he's really not a bad boy."

Impulsive. It fit the profile. "How well do you know your nephew?"

"Known him—all my—life. Has anything—happened to—Orestes?" She was winded, but she managed to keep up. He'd give her credit.

"We'll see."

Chapter 21

Belle Detloff usually bustled, Mariah thought with a mixture of sadness and nostalgia. Like a woman who knew she had a lot to do, but couldn't quite remember what it was. Now the two of them sat, tense and self-conscious, in the lemon-colored room, looking everywhere but at each other. Whatever good times they had once enjoyed on the island—and in retrospect, Mariah had to admit there'd been more good times than bad— had come to an end.

"Would you like me to plump up your pillows?"

"No, thank you, Aunt Belle." There was a pistol under the orange one. Gray had insisted, and Mariah had been too tired to argue, knowing she would never use it, no matter what.

"Well then, how about a nice cup of tea?"

"If I drink any more tea I'll float out of here. I've done all the floating I want to do for the foreseeable future."

That brought on the threat of tears. Belle's, not Mariah's. Mariah had shed all the tears she intended to shed over this damned island and its inhabitants, past, present and future.

All but Orestes. "I hope he made it back all right," she said, thinking aloud.

"Who, Nat? He's not back yet. He was over at the—" Her aunt broke off, her plump cheeks flushing. "And then he left right after Linwood did to mail some letters Linwood forgot to take."

So both her uncles were gone now. Linwood had left to take Lynn and Mason across the inlet right after the memorial service...such as it was. All that seemed as if it had happened days ago, yet only a few hours had passed since she'd waved goodbye to Mason from the pier moments after saying a final goodbye to her father.

No wonder she was so exhausted. If it weren't so tragic, it would be funny.

"I just want you to know that none of this was my idea, Mariah," Belle Detloff said earnestly. "I mean, Nat—well, we all need money. Children are expensive."

Children? Erik and Vicki hardly qualified as children.

"The store's been losing money, and I borrowed some on my credit card."

"Borrowed money on your—? Good Lord, Aunt Belle, that's awful!"

"That's what Nat said. I didn't want to tell him—Nat, that is. Erik promised he'd pay it right back, but..." Her voice trailed off. Her eyes, bluer than ever in her flushed face, threatened to overflow. "Anyway, Nat thought—that is, we all thought..."

"Thought what? That it might be a good idea to knock me off so you could inherit my share of the island and sell everything to the highest bidder?"

Belle gasped, one plump hand fluttering over her bosom. "Oh, my mercy, no! We would never do anything to hurt you. I hope you know that."

It occurred to Mariah that her aunt might honestly believe it. "So the gas leak was an accident? The couplings just happened to unscrew themselves?" She didn't know exactly how it had happened. She wasn't that mechanical, but then, neither was Belle. "And what about the fact that Erik knocked me in the head and left me to drown? Was that an accident, too?" She tilted her head to one side. "You know what? As a holiday retreat, this place leaves a lot to be desired."

All right, so she sounded bitter. She was entitled.

Belle looked ready to sink through the floor.

"Aunt Belle, did you ever stop to wonder how I could sign away my property rights if I were dead? None of you even knows whether or not I have a will. I could have left my share of the island to a sanctuary for feral cats, and there'd be nothing you could do about it. Even if I didn't leave a will, if there was the slightest suspicion of foul play it would be years before any of you could get a clear title." She didn't know this for a fact, but it seemed logical. She'd once heard her father talking about property disputes on the Banks, where the same dozen or so families intermarried generation after generation, where property descriptions often used an eroding sound or oceanfront as a boundary, running so many feet or yards to some ephemeral swamp or ridge.

"Well, Erik said—"

"Yes, Aunt Belle? What did Erik say? By the way, has he called you yet to say when he was coming back?" Mariah had never realized how good she was at sarcasm. "Because if he calls, please tell him for me that he's a far better actor than I thought. Academy Award material, in fact."

Belle groaned. She said something about hot chocolate and bolted from the room, only to poke her head back through the doorway. "It's just that—well, he has these debts and—"

"Debts?"

"These awful people—Erik said they were—well, he said they were upset with him, and he had to find a lot of money somewhere. We borrowed as much as we could from Linwood and Tracy, but with the store going under and all, it just wasn't enough. And then we got a letter from these Merrick people, and it was like the answer to all our problems," she said breathlessly. "But honestly, none of us ever dreamed..."

Erik had obviously dreamed. Dreamed that once the last

obstacle was cleared away, millions would flow like manna from heaven and he'd be out of whatever trouble he was in, all set for a life of fun and fame. He'd have gone through his share in no time at all, Mariah thought sadly. He wouldn't have been the first heir apparent to ruin his life waiting for the promised riches, so sure all his problems would disappear like magic.

"I understand, Aunt Belle." Unfortunately, she was coming to understand all too well. "Why don't you go make us some hot chocolate?" No matter how apologetic she might sound now, her aunt was one of them, Mariah reminded herself, both saddened and amused at how quickly she had come to divide the players into two groups. She and Gray were *us*. Everyone else was *them*.

Too restless to sit still any longer, she followed her aunt to the kitchen. Only the kitchen was empty, the back door still closed. Gray had locked it before he'd left. Curious, she continued down the hallway past the two front bedrooms and the bath, glancing into each room they passed, to the room beyond. Her bedroom. "Aunt Belle?"

Startled, the older woman grabbed the top of the dresser for balance, leaving the bottom drawer partially open. "Oh—you scared me."

"I don't keep cocoa mix in my bedroom. We probably don't have any, anyway." Aunt Belle as a burglar? Had the whole world gone crazy?

"Clothes—that is, I thought you might want to get dressed." Her aunt's nose turned red. Her eyes had a glassy look, as if they were about to overflow.

"I'm perfectly comfortable the way I am."

"I was, um—looking for clean sheets. I thought I'd make up your bed nice and fresh, and then you could—that is, we could…"

If there was one thing that could convince Mariah her aunt was basically innocent, or at worst, a reluctant follower, it was that she couldn't lie any better than her son could.

But then, Mariah had to admit she'd been fooled by Erik,

even knowing how shallow he was. "Aunt Belle, my bed's just fine as it is. Whatever you were looking for, it's not in here. Come back to the living room and let's talk about what's going on."

"But Erik—"

"Forget Erik for the moment." With any luck, he was on his way to the Manteo jail by now. She didn't know which authorities Gray had called, but she had faith in his ability to get the job done. "Aunt Belle, are you sure you want to side with the others? I know Erik is your son, but Daddy was your brother. Would he have gone along with selling out our heritage? Think of all Maud went through—how hard she worked to hang on to this place just so she could hand it down to her children. Is that all her struggles mean to you?"

"It wasn't—I didn't—that is, we never—"

With her arm around the shaken woman, Mariah led her to the living room and sat her down, willing Gray to hurry back. She didn't really want to talk anymore, she just wanted to forget the whole ugly situation. Let someone else deal with the mess they'd got themselves into.

Seated in an orange chair that clashed wildly with her pink flowered slacks, Belle looked around for a tissue and finally pulled one from the breast pocket of her rose-colored blouse. "Nat's going to kill me. You have to tell him I didn't say anything. I really didn't, did I?" She blew again, then looked up with such a hopeless expression in her watery blue eyes that Mariah felt the urge to comfort her.

"It's the whole island, isn't it?" Mariah prompted. "Not just Maud's house. And don't bother to lie, we found the drawings."

Belle nodded and buried her face in her hands. "We knew they were here somewhere. Erik tried to find them."

"Tell me this much—was Daddy in on it?"

Without looking up, the older woman shook her head vigorously. "Eddie wouldn't. Nat tried to reason with him, we all did—the taxes and all the other expenses. Besides, it's not like you all even used your cottage anymore. But Eddie said Mama would just die.''

It was a figure of speech, Mariah decided, amused in spite of the grim circumstances. And then she heard someone coming up onto the deck. Don't let it be Uncle Nat, she thought. No matter what anyone said, she didn't trust Nat Detloff, not when he was fighting to keep his son out of prison. Or worse. It was bad enough that Erik was a user, but if he'd crossed someone higher up in the drug trade—God, no wonder he'd been terrified.

She heard the key in the front door then. Leaving Belle attempting to repair the ravages of tears, embarrassment and possibly guilt, Mariah hurried to the door to find Gray holding Orestes in his arms. Tracy, red-faced and breathing hard, stood a few feet behind them.

"Clear the junk off the bed," he said, angling through the doorway.

"Take him up to Maud's," Tracy said. She sounded petulant, as if they'd had this argument before and she'd lost.

Mariah hurried ahead to sweep off the stacks of notes and newspapers, some of them yellowed with age. There was a spread on the bed, but no sheets. She didn't even know if there was another set of linens in the cottage, but it was too late, anyway.

Gray carefully lowered the old man to the bed, high-top shoes and all. "No call to do this," Orestes mumbled. "Lef' m'windows open."

"I'll go back and close up before it rains, I promise."

"I'll go," said Tracy.

"Don't go near the place," Gray ordered quietly, and turned back to the man on the bed, unlacing his boots and easing them off his feet.

The two sisters huddled by the door, one looking angry, the other worried. Mariah heard them whispering, but couldn't catch more than the occasional word.

"...didn't say..."

"...not back yet."

"Oh, my poor baby!"

Gray backed away from the bed. "Okay, folks, let's clear out and give the gentleman some privacy." He removed three pill bottles from his shirt pocket and handed them to Mariah. "How about checking out the dosage, see if anything's needed right now. I'll call over to the medical center and see what I can find out. Meanwhile, ladies…" He gestured for the two older women to lead the way into the living room.

"I need to go home in case Nat calls," Belle said. "He went after—he went to the post office."

He'd gone after Erik. What father wouldn't? Mariah could almost find it in her heart to sympathize.

Tracy said, "I'm leaving. Come on, Belle."

Gray watched as Tracy, looking uncharacteristically flustered, shoved her younger sister out the front door. Turning to Mariah, he said, "Just as well. I need some breathing room before we tackle the next issue. Come on into the kitchen."

"Is he—?" Mariah glanced at the bedroom door, then turned back to Gray, who looked grim and exhausted, all but that rock-bound jaw of his.

"Orestes? He pushed himself way past his limit today, but maybe it's just as well."

"From my point of view I'd have to agree."

After a hesitation that lasted a beat or two too long, Gray said, "Me, too. Definitely." He unclipped his cell phone and placed it on the table, then sank down onto a chair, flexed his shoulder and stretched his legs out before him.

Mariah wanted to go to him and hold him in her arms the way he'd held her. Instead, she asked, "Where'd you find him?"

"Still in the boat. He'd grounded her about a hundred feet south of the dock. He was lying there on his back, waiting to die, I guess. Or waiting for the law to come claim him."

"The law? She's his boat, isn't she? Why would the law be involved?"

Gray levered himself up again and leaned forward, rubbing

his forehead. "I need a drink of water and then I need to make a few calls. Did you check out those pills yet?"

She was still holding the three bottles in her hand. Squinting at the labels, she read off what little information there was. "'PRN.' That means as required, doesn't it?"

"Required for what?" he prompted.

"Pain?"

"That's what I figured. I just wanted to be sure." He took a deep breath and looked at her, his eyes dark with more than exhaustion. "He's in bad shape, Riah. Pretty close to the edge, I'd say." Standing, Gray flexed his shoulders, then headed for the kitchen, poured himself a glass of water and downed half of it without stopping. "What happened today probably used up most of the little strength he had left."

"Oh, no," she said softly.

He finished the water and set the glass aside. "Don't do that to yourself, honey. If what I suspect is true, it was probably the best thing that could have happened to him."

"How can you say that? If what's true?"

Leaning over the sink again, he splashed his face and arms, spattering the sweat-stained shirt. Looping the towel around his neck, he urged her back to the living room.

At the door, she balked. "You're not going to tell me he was in on this land mess, because I refuse to believe it. Orestes loves this island. He's told me more than once how he came here as a boy, and when Maud married George, they let him stay to look after things while George was gone." She shook her head. "Orestes would never sell out. This is the only home he has." Her eyes pleaded with him to agree.

"Let me make some calls, then we'll talk."

She knew he still had contacts in the SBI. He'd told her that much. Chances were he had contacts and sources all over the country; it wouldn't surprise her at all. She read suspense novels. She used to love the old *Matlock* and *Columbo* reruns. Detectives always had sources.

Besides, there were public records. For the first time, she wondered just what kind of information could be gleaned from various county courthouses. Torn between listening in on his calls and checking on Orestes, she hurried back to the spare bedroom, leaving Gray his privacy.

At first she thought the old man was sleeping. He was so still she had to watch for several minutes just to make sure his chest was rising and falling. She was still watching when he opened his eyes and gazed up at her, his expression slightly unfocused, but surprisingly peaceful.

"He was a good man, your pappy."

"Daddy? I know he was. He thought the world of you, too. I think you took the place of his own father when he was growing up."

Orestes was silent for so long she thought he might have fallen asleep again. She didn't know whether to be glad or sorry. Now that it was too late, she wanted to hear more about her father as a little boy, going out with Maud and Orestes to fish a pound net, catching hard crabs and boiling them over a fire on the beach, steaming clams over a layer of seaweed in the same pot. Wading the shallows with a lantern at night, gigging flounders.

Once in a great while her father used to mention such things, but he'd never been much for reminiscing. Whenever he started talking about his boyhood on Henry Island, Roxie would usually break in with a suggestion that they eat out and maybe take in a show.

Mariah yawned. It was late. The day had been endless and it wasn't even dark yet. Her head no longer ached, but it was still sore to touch. She didn't even want to think about tackling the tangles.

Poor Orestes. She gazed down at the figure on the bed, so small, so still. Even his tremors were gone. Only a few days ago, according to Gray, he'd been clambering up on a scaffold, ready to repair his roof.

Crossing to the window, Mariah was reaching out to adjust the curtains so that the setting sun wouldn't disturb him when he spoke again. "Didn't need me. Had his own pappy. Kin on Momma's side, way back..."

Confused, Mariah sorted through the words in search of meaning, concluding that any meaning must be lost among some ninety-odd years of memories. He'd been kin to Maud, not her grandfather...hadn't he? Besides, George Henry had died back in the late forties, when her father was barely old enough to walk.

She waited but there was no more. Orestes was breathing evenly, but occasionally, a shudder would course down his frail body.

"When you shiver like that, you little ninny, it means a ghost just walked over your grave, doesn't it, Lynn?"

"It does not! You stop saying that! There's no such thing as ghosts, and 'sides, I don't have a grave, so there!"

After a moment Mariah slipped out, leaving the door ajar in case he roused and called out. Stories of her father's childhood could wait. There were still things she needed to know, and Gray was her best source. Her only reliable source.

She found him seated before his computer, cell phone in hand, staring at a screensaver that featured a baseball player making the same leaping catch over and over, to the barely audible sounds of a cheering crowd.

He turned, placed the cell phone on top of a stack of notes and waited, his eyes asking a silent question.

"He's sleeping now. He woke up and we talked some. I think he's confused, though. In fact I know he is. Is it the medicine, do you think? Or is he really that sick?"

"Both. He might not be quite as confused as he sounds, though. Depends on what you talked about."

"Not much of anything, really. I wanted to thank him for saving my life, but before I could say anything, he started talking about Daddy. He claimed my grandfather was still alive when Daddy was growing up." She sighed, shook her head and sat on the edge of the bed, staring down at her knees. Under the soft cotton knit, a few fresh bruises were beginning to show, but then, that was nothing new. At least these were a result of saving her life, not of trying to take it.

Not that Bruce had ever tried to kill her, but that wasn't to say things wouldn't have degenerated to that point if she'd been fool enough to stay. Pushing her down the stairs had been a pretty risky thing to do if he hadn't wanted her dead.

She didn't know which was worse—uncontrollable temper or cold, ruthless greed. "Tell me something," she said. "Am I wearing one of those signs that says Kick Me? Is there a bull's-eye painted on my backside where I can't see it?"

Gray leaned over and touched the hidden bruise as if he knew it was there. "I'm sorry I banged you up some getting you aboard. I was afraid we'd swing around broadside and the boat would slam down on you before I could lift you in over the side."

"If you hadn't come along when you did—"

"Someone else would have picked you up."

"Maybe. Maybe not." There'd been plenty of boats all around, only no one else had seen her. No one else had come to her rescue. "What did you find out about Erik? Has anyone caught up with him yet?"

"They're looking, checking out possibilities. Evidently he's not unknown in the area. There's a girlfriend up in Nags Head. I left word there that his family needs to get in touch with him."

"How'd you find out about the girlfriend?"

"Vicki, actually. She's scared."

"When did you talk to Vicki? I haven't even seen her today, not since…"

"Yesterday," he said, rising to move across to the window.

Mariah stared at his back, taking in the careless perfection of the man. Tousled hair, broad shoulders, long torso, narrow hips and long, muscular legs. Even sweaty and tired, wearing faded jeans and a plain old gray T-shirt, he looked infinitely better than the handsome man she'd once been married to—a man who wore three-thousand-dollar suits and five-hundred-dollar neckties.

And the parts that showed, as desirable as they were, weren't even the best part, she admitted. It was what was underneath all that tall, tanned perfection that had reeled her in before she'd even realized she'd been hooked. He was truly a good man, a strong man—a gentle man. Who else would have carried a smelly old hermit in his arms for nearly a mile, rather than leave him alone and ill in his own bed?

"You know something you're not telling me, don't you?" she asked quietly.

He turned then, the red glow of sunset behind him blinding her to his expression. He nodded.

"I already know about Henry Island Resort," she reminded him. "And the thing about the wills and all."

"What about the wills?" he asked. "No—first let's see what's left in the pantry. We need to be ready to get some food into Orestes next time he wakes up. I don't think he's eaten in days."

So they heated soup, and while she was setting a tray, she told him what she knew about her father's will and Maud's. "Actually, I don't know much at all about Maud's will. I wasn't here when she died, but I assume she left everything equally to her three children. And then Daddy left his share to me. North Carolina law says if women are married, their husbands are co-owners of any property they have."

Gray nodded, looking thoughtful. She waited, then gripped his arm and shook it. "Don't play games, please—not now. I've had about all I can take of survival games."

Turning with the cooking spoon in one hand, Gray took her in his arms and rocked her from side to side. "Sorry, I was just thinking."

"If you know something I don't, let me in on it. I'm still stumbling around in the dark." Her voice was muffled against his throat as she drew strength from his scent, his warmth. "I keep feeling like things are swirling all around me just under the surface. Every now and then something bobs up, but before I can grab hold it goes under again."

"Let's get some supper in our patient first. I sent for a practical nurse—she'll be out first thing tomorrow. It was the best I could do, short of ferrying him across the inlet and then having him flown to the nearest hospital." Gray shot her a smile that was purely a heartbreaker. "Which, incidentally, I considered doing to you."

"No way. We Henrys, whatever else we are, are made of sterner stuff. Takes more than a whack on the head and a dose of saltwater to do us in."

His eyes crinkled when he grinned. Never, she thought, had crows-feet looked so darned appealing.

Gray spoon-fed Orestes, who took only a few small tastes before he turned away, refusing to open his mouth. No amount of urging would change his mind.

"Did anyone ever tell you that you were too stubborn for your own good?" Mariah chided from the other side of the bed. "No, don't answer that. Here, let me wipe your chin."

He was helpless as a baby, she realized, feeling as if something precious were slipping away. He'd always been here, a part of her childhood—part of the good times. "All right, you just sleep awhile, hmm? We'll try some scrambled eggs later on. You'll like those. I'll put pepper sauce on them, all right?"

Gray took the dishes and nodded toward the living room. "Go sit down. Put your feet up. You ought to be in bed, too, you know, but you're going to keep on bugging me for answers, aren't you?"

"Yep. Am I going to get them?"

After a slight hesitation, he said, "Yep," and she left him to deal with the dishes.

Chapter 22

Gray sighed, exhausted, reluctant. "Where do you want to start?"

"At the beginning," Mariah said, looking grimly determined, but far more vulnerable than she would like to believe.

Crunch time. Gray relied on his analytical skills as much as he relied on instinct. When it came to a draw, he usually went with instinct. He paced a tight turn around the small room before sinking into a chair. "I'm going to give you my conclusions and you're going to have to accept them for the time being. It's too late for DNA, even if you wanted to go that route."

"DNA! I thought we were talking about selling Henry Island." She untwined herself and rose, her bony, elegant body bristling with restlessness.

"Yeah, well...we are. Believe it or not, there's a correlation. Let me offer you a premise. You can think about it and make up your mind." She shot him a dubious look, and he hurried on. "There's no real proof yet, just a theory and some papers that might or might not be legitimate."

Now she looked wary. He couldn't much blame her, the way things were spinning. If there was a chance in hell he could spare her, he'd cut off his right hand. But in the end, nothing would be changed. The facts were the facts.

He wondered at what point the need to get to the bottom of a convoluted case had been supplanted by the even stronger need to protect one of the principals. Trouble was, to protect her he had to figure out what was going on, and to do that, he had to scrape the bottom of the barrel.

"Let's start with the theory that Edgar wasn't your father," he said, and when she reacted predictably he held up a staying hand. "Hold on, just hear me out first, will you? Then if you want to pick holes in my reasoning, I'll shut up and take whatever you dish out."

Clearly unconvinced, Mariah subsided. He could tell by the way she sat that she was ready to launch herself at him, so he hurried to cover as much ground as possible before she blew up. "Your father—that is, Edgar—he was gone a lot, right?"

Reluctantly, she nodded. "But that doesn't mean—"

"No, it doesn't. But suppose—just suppose now, that one of those times before you were born, he sent your mother down here while he went abroad and she—look, there's no graceful way to say this. Suppose she had an affair with this guy Gallins?" Before she could fire the first shot in her arsenal, he overrode her. "It happens, Mariah—maybe more often than people realize."

Her eyes were narrowed, fists clenched in her lap. She was sitting upright, both feet planted firmly on the floor, ready to leap up again in defense of her parents. And he'd considered her a helpless victim?

In some ways she was, but not in the deepest sense.

"All right," he continued. "Now just suppose your mother got pregnant. Have you ever thought about where your dark coloring came from? Your mother was a redhead, right? And I've yet to see a Henry with anything resembling your coloring."

"Mama."

"Beg pardon?"

"Mama's hair was black. That's why she could stay out in the sun all day and never burn. Maud knew she dyed it."

"Ah…right. Okay, then, we don't have to go into the recessive gene thing, we'll just say your coloring came from your mother. Still, did you ever feel a close bond with your— that is, with Edgar?"

Mariah bit her lip, staring at a rope-framed print of Hatteras lighthouse. "He loved me. I know he did. He loved us both. The first time I ever saw a man cry was at Mama's funeral. Daddy kept breaking down and crying, and it scared me to death."

"I'm sure he loved you. He raised you, after all."

After a brief hesitation, she said, "Actually, it was mostly nannies. There was this older woman, Sara, who lived with us and kept house. She looked after me, took me shopping for school clothes and got me enrolled and all. Daddy was gone so much." Her shadowed eyes silently begged him to understand. "It was his job. He'd always traveled, but he always made sure I was taken care of. Sara stayed with us until I went off to boarding school."

Good Lord, no wonder she was digging around, trying to put down some roots. "What about your, uh—the rest of your family?"

"Aunt Tracy and Aunt Belle? I think Aunt Belle tried to do some matchmaking right after Mama died. Actually, Daddy didn't get along too well with either of them. All they really had in common was family. And the island, of course."

"Of course," he murmured, his mind racing ahead, trying to come up with a simple, logical way to convince her.

"I know Daddy and Uncle Nat used to argue a lot, but it didn't seem all that important. Poor Uncle Linwood…" She shrugged.

"Think back to the early years, before your mother died. How were things then?"

She frowned, her face looking thinner and paler than usual. "With the family, you mean? By the time we moved the last time, we hardly ever saw any of them unless it was here on the island. We usually got together down here for Thanksgiving, and then Mama and I used to come here, while Daddy was gone in the summertime.''

"Right," Gray said softly, and let it rest there for a moment. "And what was the big appeal for your mother? I understand she didn't particularly get along with her in-laws?''

Fire flashed in Mariah's eyes. "That doesn't prove anything. We had a summer place here. Where else would we have gone? Anyway, this is just some half-baked theory you dreamed up to justify Daddy's letting you have the cottage for practically the whole summer.''

She struck out in anger and he was the nearest target. Gray almost wished her big theory were true. "No, I can't prove anything," he said quietly. "But I believe Edgar knew, and for whatever reasons, he didn't hold it against your mother. Or maybe he did—that was between the two of them. I do know he loved you, though. I'm pretty sure he was worried about what might happen to you when…''

"When what?''

"Let's shift to chapter two," he said, but that was as far as he got.

She jumped up and stalked off toward the kitchen. "Don't let me stop you," she snapped. "You go right ahead and weave your sordid little fairy tale. Maybe you can even find a publisher.''

He followed her, just in case she planned to keep on going out the back door. He wouldn't put it past her to confront her aunts and demand the truth.

Instead, she was rummaging in the refrigerator, tears streaking her cheeks. "There's not one damned thing to eat around here. Don't you have any chocolate hidden out? Cookies or candy—or even chocolate syrup to go with the peanut butter?''

"Try peanut butter and sugar on toast.''

"Go to hell.''

"Not until you hear me out." Catching her by the arm, he pulled her around. Face-to-face at close range as they were, the stark misery in her eyes stabbed him painfully. He ached for her—for what she'd already endured and had yet to face. To accept. He was about to snatch away everything she had clung to her entire life.

He gathered her into his arms, ignoring her halfhearted struggles. "Ah, honey—listen, we can't change the past, but the past affects the future. And in this case, forewarned is forearmed."

She held herself stiffly at first. "I've already been warned, thank you. I don't think they're stupid enough to try anything else now that I know what they're up to. Besides, Erik's gone, the miserable, cowardly little worm."

"That's the spirit," Gray said, stroking her back—forcing his hand to stop at her waist. "You ready to hear me out?"

"No, but I suppose I have to. If I don't, you'll just follow me around until you get it out of your system."

"I probably will, but let's skip that. Let's back up a few years." He cupped her head, using his thumb to trace the outline of the swelling under thick layers of cloud-soft hair. He'd make sure the nurse checked her over in the morning. If necessary he would take her to Hatteras for X rays.

"You mean back before I became a bastard?" She tried to laugh, but couldn't quite pull it off.

"Listen to me, Riah, none of this is your fault, not one damned bit of it. Whatever problems your parents had—all three of them, if what I suspect is true—they evidently worked things out. You kept on coming down here, didn't you? You and your mother, with your father's approval?"

"Sometimes all three of us. Like I said, for Thanksgiving and Maud's birthday." A bitter smile showed briefly and disappeared as she let herself lean on him. "That was a hoot," she said, her voice muffled against his chest. "Mama and Maud sniping at each other and Daddy taking off to go fishing. Daddy hated fishing, but he hated unpleasantness even more."

"What about Gallins? Did your—that is, did Edgar know him?"

"Sure. Everybody knew everybody—that is, the old families. The Wallises, the Henrys and the Gallins have kinfolk all up and down the Banks, even over on the mainland. I've got cousins I've never even met. Distant ones.''

"Distant like Maud and Orestes?''

She nodded, then pulled away from his arms. Rummaging in the cabinets, she discovered a box of Fruit Loops and dug out a handful. Even stressed to the max and eating cereal from the palm of her hand, she was the most beautiful woman he'd ever seen. Beautiful in the classical sense, her features too strong for mere prettiness. They reflected a strength he was counting on to get her through this ugly business.

Because it wasn't over yet.

As they were still in the kitchen, he couldn't very well do what he wanted to do, not while she was gobbling down dry cereal. Not with Orestes just down the hall. Instead, Gray set about making hot tea. Hated the stuff, personally, but with enough canned milk and sugar, it was marginally palatable. The only coffee he had was high-test, and the last thing she needed now was a big dose of caffeine.

While he waited for the kettle to boil, he said, "Think back a few days to when you discovered your mama's grave marker damaged,'' he suggested once the tea was brewing. By then she'd finished off the last of his breakfast cereal.

"Hacked. Like someone wanted to—to kill it.''

"Where, exactly, did the blows land?'' He knew because he'd checked it out. What he didn't know was if she'd even considered the significance of it, other than as a spiteful act of vandalism.

"On the face of the stone. I told you.'' She eased into a chair and took the steaming mug he handed her.

"Narrow it down.''

She paused, looking thoughtful. "On the right side? Near the top?''

"The part that said Henry, right?'' He waited for the slow look of realization. "Can you think of anyone who resented your mother?'' Hell, that was easy. They'd all resented her, only maybe not for the same reasons. "Maud didn't like her,'' he prompted. "I think we've pretty well established that much, but what about the others?"

"They didn't—I mean, none of them really liked her, but Aunt Belle wouldn't... Neither would Aunt Tracy."

"And that leaves—?"

Her brow furrowed, a shallow Y forming between her silky dark eyebrows. Slowly, she shook her head. "I can't see either Uncle Nat or Uncle Linwood doing anything like that. They can be—well, grumpy—and I know they really want me to sign off on this sale thing. But that's now. I can't see either one of them doing something so spiteful back then. Besides, Aunt Tracy walks all over poor Uncle Linwood."

"How about Lynette? TA? What about Vicki or—"

"Erik?" Mariah picked up a bottle of liquid detergent, stared at the label, then set it down again. "I wouldn't have thought so before today, but—no, I don't think he'd have done it. If anything, he'd have taken more direct action. He did, in fact." She looked up then, her eyes so bleak it was all Gray could do not to drag her out of the house and get her the hell off the island if he had to steal a boat to do it.

But she had to know. Had to reach the same conclusion he had, and this way—moving step by step at her own speed—was the best way to get her there. If he'd tried to tell her, she'd have argued with him every step of the way.

"So we eliminate the Boxers and the Detloffs—for defacing a monument, at least. And that leaves...?"

"Not Orestes. I doubt if he's strong enough, and besides, he'd have no reason to do it. He loved Daddy. I can't remember ever hearing him say anything unpleasant to Mama, not that they ever spent much time together. He usually stayed on his side of the island when we were here, and Mama stayed on hers. Or out somewhere with—with Jack."

"Scratch Orestes, then."

Gray waited for the light to dawn. Saw Mariah's eyes widen as she counted down and realized who was left. Shook her head, closed her eyes, felt for a chair and sat down.

"Right," he murmured as her lips formed the name.

"But, why?" The eyes she lifted to his held stark pain. "I know they never liked each other—they were always bickering, but Mama didn't hate her. Mama never hated anyone—she didn't have a mean bone in her body."

He nodded. He'd heard it before, more than once, and had no reason to disbelieve it. "How about Maud? What was she like? I've heard a lot about her, and I can tell you now, the picture I've got is of a woman strong enough both physically and mentally to do almost anything to protect what she cherished most." And they all knew what that was.

"Protect? That was sheer vindictiveness, chopping at her tombstone. That was...sick!"

He nodded. "Warped. Obsessive."

"Same thing."

"Take your tea to the living room, I'm going to look in on our patient." He'd give her a few minutes to come to terms with that much before he told her the rest. As it was, he didn't have proof of any of it, but it all added up. It was the only logical conclusion.

Hearing his quiet footsteps moving toward the back of the house, Mariah huddled on the sofa, chilled to the bone despite the warm, humid air flowing in through the windows. Her father was not her father? How could that be? He'd been her father all her life.

Jack Gallins had never been a father to her. Had her mother told him? Could he have known? Not that Mariah was admitting there was anything to know, but even so...

Put your hat on, kiddo, you want to fry your brain?

That's your third candy bar, kiddo, you want to get the sugar diabetes?

Hey, them's the breaks, kiddo.

"Kiddo," she murmured. Was it possible—?

She had the pictures her mother had taken somewhere. Mostly of boats and birds and windswept live oak trees, many of them with Jack in the foreground.

And a few—maybe more than a few—of Jack and a little girl with crooked black braids, a childish potbelly under her striped bathing suit, who invariably squinted at the sun and refused to smile for the camera.

Her father—that is, Edgar—had given her the flat box of pictures the last time she'd seen him, telling her he was thinking of moving to a small apartment and wouldn't have room to store them.

Was that the only reason? Was he trying to tell her something else?

Oh, God, she was going to be sick.

"Still sleeping," Gray said, rousing her from the dark place she'd been in when he'd come into the room.

"Does he need something to drink? Maybe some tea or something stronger?"

"Like blackberry wine?" Gray laughed softly and dropped down beside her, taking her hand between both his. "I doubt it. Mariah, his systems are shutting down. I've seen it before. He might last a week—he might not wake up tomorrow."

She knew better than to ask if anything could be done. For three of the seven years she'd lived on the West Coast she'd been a hospice volunteer. It had been the only part of her life that had had real meaning. Bruce had hated it, but on that issue, she'd held out.

"I know," she murmured. "Otherwise he'd never have allowed you to take him away from the only home he's known for most of his life."

It was hard to imagine living so long in one place. As a child, she'd rarely lived in any house more than two or three years. That was one of the things she'd instinctively loved about the island, she realized now. The stability. The sense of permanence, of continuity. Maud and Orestes had always been here. Old, yet in some ways ageless.

"He's ready to go, Riah. I think he gave Mason some old pictures. There's a Brownie box camera in his bedroom. I guess he and your mother had something in common, after all." He smiled briefly, sobered and said, "He killed her, you know. Your mother."

* * *

It was nearly ten that evening when they heard the sound of a boat coming into the harbor. Both Nat and Linwood had returned earlier, then Nat had left again, ferrying the people from Merrick Realty over to Hatteras. Evidently he was back.

Orestes hadn't roused again, but he was breathing evenly, with no sign of discomfort.

He killed her, you know. Your mother.

Mariah stared at the old man now, hearing the sounds of Gray's voice from the next room. He'd been on the phone all evening, either that or on Gus.

What grown man in his right mind named his computer?

She wanted to go to him, to beg him to take back all he'd said. She wanted to return to yesterday—to last week, last month—even last year, as wretched as that had been. Dammit, it wasn't fair—she'd lost her mother. Now she had lost her father—two fathers. And she didn't even know which one to mourn.

Her relatives were over there trying to figure out how they could make her sign away the only thing she had left. She could never remember feeling so lost—so alone.

Gray came into the bedroom and lifted one of Orestes's gnarled hands in his, gazing down at the peaceful face. "Still hanging in there, hmm? Cast off, man—there's nothing you can do here now."

He turned to Mariah and held out a hand. "Come on, we still have some talking to do."

She went with him because there was nothing she could do for Orestes, and because there was more Gray had to tell her. She didn't want to hear it, but running away would change nothing.

He stood in the front door, looking out at the activity on the pier. The voices didn't carry, but the lights did. Now any activity at all was suspect, an indication of just how much things had changed.

Standing beside him, Mariah said, "This is going to be ugly, isn't it?"

"Depends on whether or not they're willing to concede defeat."

"I'm not even sure what that means."

"Just what it sounds like." And then he turned to her and took her in his arms. Unresisting, she leaned against him, knowing that he was right. That whatever was coming, she might as well get it over with now.

He whispered in her hair, "Hang in there, sweetheart, things are going to get interesting pretty soon now."

"Interesting?"

"One way to put it. Has it occurred to you that if you're not a Henry, then none of this has to involve you if you don't want it to?"

She was still for so long he wasn't sure she understood what he was getting at. Then she said wonderingly, "That's right, isn't it? If I don't want it to involve me, I can just walk away."

Renouncing an inheritance wasn't quite that simple, if that's what she decided to do. She would probably never know which man had fathered her, but her share of the island was still a legitimate inheritance. Either way she decided, she wasn't out of the woods yet. In fact, legally, things were more messed up than ever, but she didn't need to hear that now. Tomorrow would be soon enough.

Gray hooked the screen, closed and locked the front door, and led her down the hall. His arm was still around her, and neither of them questioned who was going where...or why. They'd been leading up to it almost since the beginning. Maybe even before he'd ever met her. He'd been intrigued by the image of a young girl on the verge of womanhood, glaring at the camera as if to say, "This is me, world. Like me or not, this is who I am. Deal with it."

If he were lucky, he'd be dealing with it for the rest of his life.

There was no false modesty, no pretense that either of them didn't know what was about to happen. The fact that he now had protection, thanks to a brief stop when they were in Hatteras, spoke volumes.

He stepped out of his jeans and tossed them aside, then watched as she nearly tripped over the rolled up legs of his sweats. Laughing, he sat her down on the bed and tugged them off while she leaned back on her elbows. "Knowing you," he teased, "you'd trip and get another knot on your noggin."

Not even teasing helped. He was so damned tense he felt as if he might explode. Arguments inside his head ran on the order of *It's too soon,* versus *It's now or never.*

Never wasn't even a faint possibility.

He uncovered at least two bruises he knew he was responsible for. "I'll be careful of your head," he promised.

"Don't. I don't want you to be careful, just make love to me," she said, and looked at him as if half expecting him to argue over the word *love.*

He wasn't about to argue. The word sounded just right, because if this wasn't love, he didn't know what the devil it was. It was different from anything he'd ever felt before—a different kind of love from what he'd felt for Sharon.

But then, Mariah was a different kind of woman.

Although it nearly ruined him, Gray allowed her to set the pace. Not until she held up her arms did he come down beside her, his excitement burning like a fever inside him. He kissed her first, trying to be gentle—to take it easy—missing the mark by a mile. The taste of her, the feel of her naked body pressed against his, heat against heat, softness against hardness, had him shaking with the effort to hold back.

She was wonderfully sensitive, everywhere.

He kissed her…everywhere. Lingering when she moaned and clutched at his shoulders. "I know, sweetheart—I know."

"Hurry," she urged, and lifted her hips to his touch, to his kisses. He'd been determined to go slow, not to rush her, because he had an idea she'd had a rough time with the bastard she'd married.

She stroked his back, then her hands moved over his shoulders, past the scar from his shoulder repair, trailing down over his nipples. Lightning raced through him and he caught his breath. He must have made some sound because she laughed, a gaspy, broken little giggle.

And then she said, "Gotcha."

"Oh, yeah," he breathed hoarsely. Rising up onto his knees, he ripped open the foil packet. While her fingertips trailed the crease of his thighs, flirting with danger, he spread her own thighs and moved between them. Like a starving man at a banquet, he was drunk with the sight of her, the scent of her, and his own ravening hunger.

Easy, easy, he cautioned himself, but easy wasn't even a faint possibility. She was hot and damp and ready. The moment he pressed himself against her welcoming flesh, she lifted her hips and grasped his buttocks, bringing him home.

There was no holding back. The pressure had been building too long. They rolled and panted, clutching and thrusting, timing all out of sync. It didn't matter. Nothing mattered but this obsessive, compulsive drive that had been building just under the surface until it reached critical mass.

Moments later she came apart in his arms, whimpering, a look of exquisite pain on her face. As her climax milked him dry he shuddered and died.

The waves of pleasure were slow to retreat, fading, echoing, whispering wordless affirmations as they drifted off into the night. He held her and thought she slept. God knows, she needed it. They both did, but sleep could wait, while he savored what had just happened.

Holding her, he listened to her quiet breathing, hoping—praying—she wasn't going to be hurt any more than she already had been. The worst might be over, but the wrap-up was going to be messy at best, painful at worst. They had yet to tackle the business of wills, of chain-of-ownership. A glitch or two there could hold up everything, regardless of whose wishes prevailed.

Chapter 23

She came awake suddenly, startling him when she spoke. "You know what? All this—everything that's happened, I mean, and what you said earlier—it's a great big, fat relief. After all this time, I don't have to feel guilty for not really liking them. My family, I mean."

That was one way to look at it, Gray thought, drowsily amused. "How do you feel about them?" he ventured.

She yawned. "I guess I still love Aunt Belle. She's always been flaky, but sweet. I don't care for Uncle Nat, and I've never liked Aunt Tracy, even though she's the most like Maud. But then, I didn't really like Maud, either, but as I grew older I had to admire her. Uncle Linwood's...sort of pathetic."

"Cousins?"

"If they really are my cousins," she said dryly, and yawned again. "Mostly okay, I guess. Lynn and TA...we'll never be close. Maud used to have a saying for people she disapproved of. 'They're not our kind of people.'" Mariah snuggled closer. "Not that I disapprove of them, we just don't have a whole lot in common."

Only the island, he thought, but soon that would be no longer a factor.

"Vicki will probably grow up all right if Erik doesn't influence her too much."

"I doubt if he'll be around for a while to influence anyone."

"And Mason. He's the only one I love," she said thoughtfully.

Holding her so close he could feel her heartbeat, Gray figured those were pretty generous sentiments on the whole. He felt her go limp in his arms, heard her breathing lapse into overdrive, and closed his eyes again. He'd wait until she was completely under, then he'd slip out and check on Orestes. Tomorrow would come soon enough.

It was still pitch dark when they heard the crash. Mariah bolted up, clutching his shoulder. "Did you hear that?" she whispered. "Gray! Wake up!"

He mumbled something, then came instantly awake.

"Did I dream that, or did you hear it, too?" Her fingers dug into his arm.

Hell of a watchdog he'd turned out to be. He'd lain awake for all of two minutes, holding her, planning for the next fifty-odd years of their life together. Next thing he knew she was shaking him awake.

He eased out from under her arm and the leg that had somehow hooked itself around his. "Stay here, I'll check it out."

She was right behind him. "Maybe the wind shifted," she whispered.

Right. And maybe someone was interested in finding out just how much the old guy knew, and whether or not he'd been able to talk.

Gray veered by the kitchen and collected his gun, just in case, before moving silently toward the back hall. A thin layer of moonlight fell through the bedroom window. The bed was clearly visible. Orestes was either sleeping or comatose.

"Stay back," he whispered. Waiting for his eyes to adjust, he checked out the shadows.

Mariah pointed silently to the closet, the only possible hiding place unless someone crawled under the bed. Gray eased into the room, gun in hand, flattened himself against the wall and fingered the knob on the closet door. In one smooth motion he flung it open, automatically assuming the position—feet spread, gun held in both hands, ready for whatever presented itself.

What presented itself was a row of plastic hangers, a yardstick, a sackful of old newspapers and the lingering smell of mothballs. By the time she nudged his side, he was feeling pretty foolish. "Better safe than sorry, right?" she whispered.

"Thanks," he said dryly. "I needed that."

"There's nobody under the bed. I looked. Orestes is sleeping. He must have knocked over the lamp, though, so watch your step."

They were both barefoot. Gray reached past her to switch on the dim overhead fixture and they both turned toward the sleeping man. One of his arms was hanging off the bed, as if he'd tried to get up. The bedside lamp had been left on the lowest setting with the shade tilted away, so that if he should wake in the night he wouldn't be completely disoriented. Gray's glance shifted to the screened window. There was no sign of any intrusion.

A sound from the bed drew their attention. Orestes's eyes were open, his hands clawing impotently at the bedspread.

"Easy there, old friend. You need something?" Gray moved closer, touching the old man's hand.

"...devil am I?" Orestes whispered.

"You're in Edgar's cottage. We brought you here last night, remember? You were having trouble getting out of the boat and we thought you'd be more comfortable here."

"Bed don't feel right."

Mariah moved closer. "Are you cold? I can get you another cover."

"Wanna tell ye 'bout it. Listen..." His voice trailed off and Gray knelt beside the bed and shifted his hand so that his two middle fingers rested lightly on the barely perceptible pulse.

He nodded toward the broken lamp and Mariah began collecting the shards and dropping them in the wastebasket.

"Just let me clean this up so you won't step on them when you get out of bed," she told the frail man lying there so still.

His eyes cracked open again and he cackled, but it was a weak parody of his former laughter. He started to speak, broke off in a fit of coughing, then waved them both closer with a weak flap of his free hand.

"You need something, just ask," Gray said, trying to ignore the odor. He figured Orestes must have been living in the same clothes for days.

He made up his mind to clean him up before the nurse arrived. "What's on your mind? Something you need, or something you want to tell us?"

"Boat—*Miss Maud.*"

"I'll see to having her pulled off and brought around to the wharf."

He shook his head. "Give 'er to the boy. Skiff, too."

"Mason?" Mariah edged closer, ignoring the foul odor. "You want us to give your boats to Mason?"

"Models, too. Great-grandson. Granddaughter's boy."

Mariah looked at Gray, puzzled, but he only nodded. She whispered, "Does he have a family? Shouldn't we be calling someone?"

"They're here—right, Orestes? You're talking about Tracy and Lynette. I'll see that the *Miss Maud* goes to Mason as soon as he's old enough. Linwood will see that she's taken care of."

"Nothing for that other one. Not worth penny's worth of snot." His eyes closed and Mariah placed her fingers at the side of his throat.

Gray said quietly, "Anything else you want us to do for you?"

Several minutes passed. No one moved. No one spoke. Outside the window the usual predawn chorus struck up. Tree frogs, an owl and the haunting cry of a loon from somewhere out on the reef.

"Got 'em both. C'gar box, bedroom. Papers."

"We'll sort it all out, don't worry."

Without moving his head, those cobalt eyes, dimmed now by cataracts, sought out Mariah. "Closer," he whispered. And when she leaned closer, he grasped her hand, his grip tremulous but surprisingly strong.

"Tell her I'm sorry. Edgar's girl. I'da not done it if I'd knowed she was crazy. Told 'er it weren't n'more than what we done, ourselves. Didn't kill the little girl, though. Waited...waited...."

No more was said. After a while, Gray nodded toward the door. "I'll bathe him while he's still asleep. It'll be less embarrassing that way."

"Do you think he's—aware?"

"Of what he's saying or of what's happening?"

"Both. Either. Most of it didn't make sense." They stood outside in the hallway. Mariah was holding the plastic wastebasket liner filled with broken pottery.

Gray pulled the door almost closed, leaving a crack for ventilation, and so they could hear if the old man roused. "I think he knows he's dying, and wants to unload his conscience. I have a feeling it's been eating on him for..."

"Twenty-seven years?"

"Longer. Try sixty-odd." Taking her arm, Gray steered her back to the front bedroom, where they both quickly dressed. He slid his gun under the rumpled bedclothes and Mariah hurried to the kitchen, deposited the shards in the trash and plugged in the coffeemaker.

"Wear shoes when you go back in there," she reminded him. "I haven't finished cleaning up."

"Yes, ma'am," he said, loving her, hurting for her—angry on her behalf. "I'll need a basin, soap, a washcloth and a large trash bag."

"I can help," she offered, but he shook his head.

"Go back to bed, see if you can catch a nap. If I need you, I'll call you."

Half an hour later, when he emerged from the back bedroom, Mariah was waiting, her eyes filled with questions. "Later," he said, setting the trash bag beside the back door and emptying the basin. "He's wearing my last clean pair of sweats. Don't fit him any better than they fit you, but I doubt if he'll complain. Coffee?"

"Fresh pot. Gray, you're going way above and beyond the call of duty. I just want you to know—"

"Shh." He poured two mugs of coffee, laced hers with sugar and canned milk and steered her out onto the front deck. A light breeze had sprung up out of the northeast, blowing the mosquitoes away for now. Seated side by side in dew-wet plastic chairs, with only a low table between them, they watched in silence as dawn spread across the sky.

Neither of them mentioned what had happened only a short time ago. It was still too fragile, too new, and Gray had a feeling Mariah still didn't get the significance.

"I've located just about everything we'll need to stake your claim—that is, if you still want to." He forced himself not to touch her because he knew that if he touched her again, all bets were off. They had a lot of ground to cover in a short time. Events weren't going to wait.

Apparently taking her cue from him, she sipped her coffee and kept her eyes on the horizon. "I thought my claim had already been staked by Daddy's will. But go on."

"Most of the missing pieces were in the cigar boxes, like Orestes said. Not all of it, unfortunately—at least, not the complete chain of events. From the scorch marks on some of the letters and other handwritten documents, I think someone—probably Maud—tried to burn a few things, but Orestes managed to rescue most of it. Enough, at any rate, to be able to piece things together." And he'd probably burned a few more himself.

Mariah took a deep breath, drawing his attention to the front of her shirt. It was one of those baggy knit things, no shape at all, but it managed to hit the high spots enough to distract him from what he was saying. "Mariah? Did you hear what I said?"

"I heard you. He has a family, right? A daughter?"

She still didn't get it. "Two daughters, three granddaughters, a grandson and a great-grandson, to be precise. Starting with Tracy and Belle."

Mariah's eyes widened. She plopped her mug dangerously close to the edge of the table. "Are you *serious?* I thought I must have misunderstood."

"Dead serious. Tracy and Belle are his."

"But how can you be sure? Did he tell you that? He's obviously confused. He mistook me for..." She shrugged, her hands lifted helplessly. "Don't tell me he had birth certificates in those old cigar boxes."

Gray drained his coffee mug and set it aside. "Everything else a parent might keep, but no—no birth certificates. Maud lied on those, anyway, like she lied about so many other things. Or rather, she didn't have to lie. The husband of record is always presumed to be the father of any children, unless otherwise stated."

Gray waited for Mariah to digest that much before he went on. At first he'd had trouble accepting it, too, even though parts of the puzzle had been staring him in the face all along.

"But what about Daddy? I mean Edgar?"

"I'm pretty sure he's the genuine article. I think he knew about the others—suspected, at least. But without proof, he couldn't say anything. It probably didn't matter to him before. Later on, though, once it started to matter—once they started trying to get him to sell out, if he'd even hinted at a problem..."

God knows what would have happened. They were basically decent people, but even decent people can get desperate enough to lose perspective.

"You said earlier that he—that Orestes..."

"Killed your mother?"

Wordlessly, she nodded. She was taking it better than he'd dared hope. Strong lady. Looks could be deceptive. "You want the short version or the long one, complete with whatever documentation I've managed to compile?"

"Both. Actually, neither, but I don't have a choice, do I?"

He reached across and took her hand, gripping it as if he could impart some of his strength. There was nothing sexual about it, but then, what he felt for her was far more than sexual. He was only beginning to realize just how deep it ran. For him, at least, and he had reason to hope it was the same for her. Some women were good at casual relationships. He'd bet his life that Mariah wasn't one of them.

"Okay, here goes. Linear story, timetable as exact as possible after more than sixty years. Maud and George had a son eleven months after they were married, then George left Maud and the baby here with his mother, while he went back to sea. There was a war on at the time. He was 4F, but he wanted to do his part. His mother died shortly after that, and the next time he came back, big surprise. He had two young daughters, one of them barely a month old."

"Tracy and Belle," Mariah whispered.

"Not all that hard to accept, once you catch on, is it?"

"But Maud…"

"Maud was a young woman, remember? George might've been patriotic, but he wouldn't have won many points as a husband, leaving a young mother and infant son here with a sickly mother-in-law."

"But Orestes was here…."

"Exactly. I suspect they all depended on him. I don't know why he wasn't drafted—might be he never registered, but at any rate, once the mother-in-law died, Orestes was left with Maud and baby Edgar. Things must have heated up pretty quickly after that. George was injured—I don't know how long he was away, but there was a brief write-up in a Manteo newspaper about George Henry, Dare County's latest hero. Anyway, once he came home, he had to know the girls weren't his. He chose to deal with it in his own way."

"But how? I mean, how could you know all this?"

"There's an amazing amount of information out there if you know where to look. George was killed overseas, his body was shipped home for burial along with his personal effects, including a handwritten will leaving everything he owned to his son, Edgar, with a dower right to Maud. No mention of either girl. The will was never recorded, by the way.''

''But that means…'' Mariah frowned, obviously trying to fit present-day reality into a distant and incompletely recorded past.

''Keep in mind, the first few events took place over a course of several years. Edgar's birth, George's sporadic visits home, the birth of the two daughters. Later on, Maud moved over to Hatteras every fall so that her three children could go to school there, leaving Orestes here to mind the store, so to speak. Either he found George's will or maybe Maud showed it to him. At any rate, she must have known Orestes resented seeing his daughters cut out of everything. They might not be Henrys, but this was his home, too. He figured they had as much right to a share as Maud did.''

The sun broke through the salt haze that had drifted in off the ocean. Mariah shaded her eyes against the glare and stood. ''I need more coffee. You need to check on Orestes. And it looks like we're about to have company.'' In the distance, a speck on the horizon announced the approach of Josh's launch bringing in the nurse and the supplies Gray had ordered.

He caught her as she reached for the door, held her a moment and said, breathing in the scent of her hair, her skin, ''It's a lot to take in, I know. Hang in there, we're on the home stretch.'' And then he kissed her, savoring the taste. ''There,'' he whispered long moments later. ''That's a down payment on tonight, or tomorrow, or however long it takes to secure a little privacy.''

Still tingling from the warm, sinewy feel of the man, Mariah grabbed a broom and dustpan and hurried to Orestes's room. Her mind was still struggling with all the revelations of the past few minutes. Gray wouldn't have said anything unless he was sure of the facts. It was what he did, after all—track down fragments of old evidence and link them together. What she couldn't seem to bring into focus was how the past affected what was happening now.

And Orestes, that poor old man. A murderer? Her whole world was beginning to feel like a B-grade psycho-thriller.

A few minutes later they met outside the kitchen door. Gray had put on yesterday's jeans and shirt. His jaw held a stubble that echoed the gray at his temples. He stepped out of his shoes and padded barefoot to the sink.

"You can take the boy out of the country, but you can't take the country out of the boy," she teased.

"Hey, this is the beach," he gibed softly. "I'm entitled. Is Orestes still sleeping?"

She nodded, emptying the dustpan in the trash. "We need to replace the lamp. How about getting the one from the other room?"

There was no more his and hers as far as bedrooms were concerned, only theirs. It seemed as if they'd been sharing forever. What was it about this man, she wondered, that made her feel as if he'd always been a part of her life, just waiting in the background for her to notice him?

They were on the pier when Josh arrived with a single passenger. Pearly Askin was sturdy, middle-aged and ready to take over. "Lordy, I'm surprised he's still living," she said, when introduced to her sleeping patient a few minutes later. "He's kin on my daddy's side way back. His granddaddy and my great-granddaddy were brothers."

Showing the woman where she could leave her bags, Mariah nodded. She was beginning to see the advantage of one of those rental machines. "We'll have to share the bathroom. Sorry."

"Honey, don't apologize, I've shared worse than that. One patient I had, he was still using an old pit toilet. Them things has been against the law since before I was born. Wonder the health department didn't catch him. You sure you don't want to see if we can get him over to the hospital?"

Gray hesitated, glanced at Mariah and then spoke for them both. "He's at home here, Ms. Askin. He's not going to get any better, so why not let him go out as easy as possible, here where he can hear the same sounds and smell the same things he's always known?''

Mariah thought about the mullet crock. Evidently, Gray did, too, because he caught her eye and grinned briefly. ''We'll leave you to—whatever,'' he said to the practical nurse. ''We'll be outside on the deck if you need anything.''

It was hot outside. Barely ten in the morning, but the sun glinted off the water, magnifying the effect. Mariah wandered over to the railing. ''Can you believe it's already June?'' she said, idly twining a tendril of Virginia creeper between her fingers.

Suddenly, she felt acutely self-conscious, wondering what Gray would do if they were alone together. Wondering if they would ever be alone together again, and feeling guilty for such selfish thoughts.

''Mariah, we need to get everything out in the open,'' he said.

If experience had taught her anything, it was to lower her expectations. If he said, ''Job's done, I'm outta here, been nice knowing you,'' she would break his leg.

''I have a feeling we're not going to be left alone much longer, so I'll have to talk fast,'' he continued.

''I'd rather not talk at all, but I suppose that's not an option. You want to pick up where Orestes is supposed to have murdered my mother?'' She turned away, stared out at the blackened remains of the boathouse, then shook her head and turned back. ''I'm sorry—it's not that I don't believe you, it's just that everything I've taken for granted all my whole life suddenly seems like—'' she shrugged ''—like it was all a mirage.''

Taking her arm, he led her down the steps and along the path, shaded now from the low-angled sun. ''I'll make it as quick as possible.'' He waited until they were out of sight of Layzy Dayz and said, ''Start with the fact that Maud had something to trade.''

''To trade who? Whom? Trade for what?''

''To trade Orestes for what she wanted. Honey, none of this

is going to make a lick of sense unless you accept the premise that your grandmother was—''

"Not." Coming to a halt, Mariah turned and held up a hand. "Maud was not my grandmother. I've accepted that much at least."

"Right. Then let's just say, Maud was, uh—not entirely rational where certain matters were concerned. Her husband's family, for instance."

Mariah nodded. That much she already knew. In a way, she'd always known, although she'd never thought of it in those terms. Henrys reigned supreme on Henry Island—always had, always would as far as Maud was concerned. It was one of those things that was taken for granted, like the sun's rising, the tide's ebbing and flowing.

"Start with the fact—and it is a fact—that George's will left the girls out entirely. Using that unrecorded handwritten will that had come home with his body, she made a bargain with Orestes. If he would arrange for an accident to happen to you and Roxie, she would destroy the will and replace it with one leaving the island in equal shares to all three children. A little matter like forgery didn't bother her in the least. Who would question a man's leaving his estate to his three kids?''

"But why? I mean, why did she hate Mama so much? Granted, they were as different as any two women could possibly be, but that's hardly cause for murder. Besides, Mama wasn't murdered, she died when the boat she was on exploded."

"As for why, I don't know. We have to assume Maud knew about your mother's affair with Gallins. Orestes hinted as much. Ironic, considering she'd done pretty much the same thing herself, but then, you know what they say about converted sinners."

Hearing voices coming from the other end of the path, he turned and led her back to the cottage. "As for why, I can only guess she thought that with Roxie out of the way, Edgar might remarry and produce some legitimate Henry heirs."

"I can't believe—but that's crazy!"

He simply nodded. "You called it. As for the other, it wasn't spontaneous combustion or static discharge. Definitely not a bomb—nothing at all like that. Near as I can figure, Orestes was hiding in the boathouse with his rifle. A well-placed bullet at the right time and—well, you know what happened next. He waited until you were out of range, though. As crazy as he was about Maud, he wasn't going to murder a child, not when he had grandchildren of his own by then."

They reached the steps and she still hadn't spoken. "Riah? You with me so far?"

"Are you sure? How can you possibly know after all this time?"

"I found parts of a metal fuel can with a bullet hole near the bottom in the rubble left behind after the boathouse burned. God knows why he didn't just haul everything farther offshore and sink it, but he netted everything he could find and kept it hidden in the boathouse. Scraps, mostly. Nothing that would ever have convicted him unless someone knew what to look for. It would never have occurred to me, but as it turned out, there was a witness who heard the shot."

When more moments passed in silence, he said, "He never wanted to hurt you, Riah. I'm sure he didn't want to do what he did, but Maud had him over a barrel. In his own way, I guess he loved her. I have a feeling he might have been in love with her when she married George, but he was a young man with nothing to offer her."

"Love would have been enough," Mariah whispered. She sank down onto one of the porch chairs and he took the other one.

"Sometimes it's not. As I said before, he had no way of providing for his daughters unless he could force her to write another will. Even though by that time they were both married and didn't need anything from him."

"Didn't need him," she whispered. "That's so sad."

"Near as I can figure, Maud withheld George's will and replaced it with the forgery. It was never questioned because, like I said, it left everything to his family. Things were a lot

more lax back in those days. Handwritten wills are still accepted as long as they're properly witnessed, but until a generation or so ago, people down here were allowed to survey
their own property, write deeds, have them notarized and recorded. Wills were probably even easier.''

She frowned, putting together various aspects of the story.
"But that means…'' She sent him a wondering look. "Gray,
that means there aren't any Henrys left at all.''

"Bingo,'' he said softly. "I think what finally blew Maud's
fuse was when the years passed and Edgar didn't produce any
more children. Maybe he couldn't. That might be why he
never— Look, we'll never know, and at this point it really
doesn't matter.''

Pearly Askin came out the door, shook her head and said,
"You want me to call Twiford's, or will you do it?''

Gray stood. Feeling suddenly chilled, Mariah rose and
moved to stand beside him, both of them facing the nurse.
"That's the funeral home. Is he—?''

"Yep. Went just like that. I was fixing to see if I could get
a specimen when he opened his eyes, looked up at the ceiling
and said, 'Papa?' I heard him say it, clear as a bell.''

"Papa?'' Gray and Mariah repeated.

Pearly nodded. "I seen it before. Don't know if it means
anything or not, but I like to think there's a big reunion going
on somewhere right about now.''

That evening the entire family gathered for a conference in
Maud's house. Mariah dreaded it, but it had to be done. Thank
goodness she had Gray with her, else she just might have left
everything dangling. Let them clean up their own messes.

Only this was Maud's mess. In a way, they were all victims.

"You know that storm Orestes kept talking about?'' Gray
murmured as he held the front door for her. "I think it's about
to hit.''

Mariah reached for his hand. The old house where she'd
played as a child, running in and out, tracking in sand, letting

in mosquitoes, felt oddly airless, as if all the life had leaked out of it.

Belle said, "We're in here. You all come on in."

Tracy said, "Wipe your feet first."

Vicki had left earlier, claiming she wasn't about to hang around for another funeral. The people from the funeral home had come and gone. Just before suppertime, Gray got a call saying that Erik had been picked up in Nags Head on a drug bust and was being held for possession of a controlled substance and attempted murder.

The company was unusually subdued. Linwood had aged ten years overnight and Nat's eyes were red, as if he'd been crying.

"Riah, you want to say something?" Gray offered her a chance to fire the first shot. God knows, she deserved it.

She stood as if making a formal announcement. "I'm considering not pressing charges against Erik. As for the gas leak, it could have been an accident. I could have someone come over and check it out if necessary."

Linwood mumbled something about it not being necessary.

Belle, predictably, burst into tears. "Thank you," she managed to say. Nat blew his nose noisily.

When Gray took center stage no one disputed his right to be there, a clear sign of how frightened they were. Methodically, he ran through the information he had collected concerning their lineage, Maud's role in Roxie's murder and the clouded title to Henry Island, offering to show proof if needed and referring them to certain records in the courthouse. One body blow right after another. He was relentless.

Mariah could almost feel sorry for them. When Gray sat down again, she said, "At this point, I don't think it would be possible for any one of us to claim a clear title. Any suggestions?"

They looked at one another. The dawn of hope?

Tracy said, "If we all agree to sell, I don't see what the problem is. I mean, the actual ownership's not in question, is it? Nobody else is claiming it."

Belle said, "We really do need the money. I'm sure Erik didn't mean any harm. You see, he owed these awful men a lot of money, and—"

"And my brilliant wife borrowed to the hilt on her credit cards," said Nat, not bothering to hide his disgust.

Belle predictably started crying again.

Mariah stood and looked around the familiar old room that no amount of redecorating could essentially change. It was as though she could smell the past—the fried mackerel and crackling corn bread, the pine-scented cleanser, the salty, mildewy mustiness that no amount of airing ever quite got rid of. Thoughtfully, she said, "There's one solution. We could offer the island to the Nature Conservancy. That way at least you'd all get a huge tax break." She looked from one to the other.

Nat said, "Now lookee here, young lady, my son's in a passel of trouble. What good's a damn tax break going to do him?"

They all turned to stare at him, and he quickly subsided.

Mariah continued as if there had been no interruption. "As I was saying, there might be a problem with the title, but they have enough lawyers to handle it. We don't. Who knows, with a property this unique, the attorney general will probably want in on the proceedings. Maybe the Park Service." She paused to let the idea sink in. "As for those people you all brought in, it could take years to clear up the title, and I seriously doubt if whoever drew up those fancy plans is going to be interested unless they can get a quick warranty deed."

She looked from one to the other. Belle continued to sob. Linwood looked as if he wanted to cry, too. Tracy's hair was a shambles and she had a run in her panty hose, but Nat looked as if he'd like to strangle someone.

Probably me, Mariah thought. "We might be able to stipulate that you all have lifetime rights to your cottages. I don't know about that. Aunt Tracy, you could check it out."

Tracy straightened her shoulders and glared at her. "What about your place?"

Mariah looked to Gray, who shrugged. "Your call," he told her.

"Let me think about it," she said. She might even want to deed it to Mason, but that could wait for now. "Are we all together on this?" She had more or less ridden roughshod over them all, but at the moment, no one was in any condition to argue.

"What about Orestes?" Belle asked, her voice tremulous.

He was her father, Mariah thought wonderingly. And while that might not affect their legal claim, the least bit of controversy and the whole scandal could come out, past and present. They didn't deserve that, but the potential was there with any property this valuable.

Twelve million dollars for the entire island?

There were plenty of estates on both coasts valued at that amount and more, but to the Detloffs and the Boxers, it had to be like a dream. People might speculate, but talk would eventually die down, and if they never came back...

"Orestes will be buried here on the island tomorrow," she said quietly. She'd made the decision herself—ironic, under the circumstances, as she was the only real outsider.

No one argued with her. "You'll all want to be there. But first we have some clearing to do in the cemetery." She looked from one to the other. "And that damned PVC fence had better disappear immediately, do I make myself clear?"

Linwood ducked his head. Nat glared at her. "Hollowell, I trust you'll do your share."

His share? Gray lifted a brow at Mariah, who smiled and nodded. "He'll do his share and I'll work right alongside him. Mama's getting a new stone, by the way. I ordered it when I ordered Orestes's monument. It won't be any bigger than Maud's and George's, but it won't be any smaller, either."

"Yes, but—"

"Is there a problem, Aunt Tracy?" Mariah asked sweetly. The older woman shook her head.

Mariah said, "Then we're all agreed. Today, rain or shine,

is cleanup day. You'll all be here for Orestes's funeral, and after that, you're free to leave.''

"Now just a damn minute here, who gave you the right to tell us what we can do?" Nat demanded.

"How long have you known about Erik's problem?" she asked softly. "Were you aware that the only reason he stayed here was because he thought no one could find him here? But then, maybe you even suggested it." Mariah looked from one to the other of the enablers. Fair or not, she blamed them almost as much as she did Erik.

Nat backed down at the subtly implied threat. They all did, figuratively, if not literally.

Hurrying along Cottage Row a few minutes later, Gray laughed and said, "Maud would've been proud of you, honey. You might not be a Henry, but you're definitely a chip off the old block."

"You don't want to go there," Mariah warned, but she was struggling to hide a smile. She felt light enough to fly.

He caught her hand and held her back, oblivious to any watching eyes. "There's only one place you're going," he told her, "and that's home with me as soon as we're done here."

"Really?" She gave him her patented haughty look.

"Hey, I'm asking, not telling. If you don't like city living, I happen to have a small farm out in the country. Place where I grew up, matter of fact. You could try it on for size and we can go from there."

Feeling as if an enormous weight had been lifted from her shoulders, Mariah reached up and used his ears to pull his face down to hers. She kissed him.

"Whatever," she whispered. "Wherever. The nice thing about us artistic types is that we're adaptable."

* * * * *

MONTANA MAVERICKS

The Kingsleys

A woman from the past. A death-defying accident. A moment in time that changes one man's life forever.

Nothing is as it seems beneath the big skies of Montana....

Return to Rumor, Montana, to meet the Kingsley family
in this exciting anthology featuring two brand-new stories!

First Love by Crystal Green
and
Second Chance by Judy Duarte

On sale July 2003 only from Silhouette Books!

Also available July 2003

Follow the Kingsleys' story in **MOON OVER MONTANA** by Jackie Merritt
Silhouette Special Edition #1550

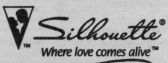

Where love comes alive™

If you enjoyed what you just read,
then we've got an offer you can't resist!

Take 2
bestselling novels FREE!
Plus get a FREE surprise gift!

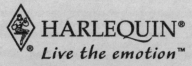